Praise for *Fluke*

"Readers new to the work of Christopher Moore will want to know two things immediately. First: Where has this guy been hiding? (Answer: In plain sight, since he has a devoted cult following.) . . . [H]e writes laid-back fables straight out of Margaritaville, on the cusp of humor and science fiction."
—Janet Maslin, *New York Times*

"Moore's career has plainly been one of scaling new peaks; with *Fluke*, he might just have outdone himself. . . . If the ghost of Jules Verne had conspired with Rudy Rucker and Tom Robbins to produce a novel, *Fluke* might very well make them hang their heads in defeat. . . . This novel is all ambergris, no blubber."
—*Washington Post Book World*

"Humor that seamlessly blends lunacy with larceny. . . . Habit-forming zaniness."
—*USA Today*

"[In his] outrageous new novel . . . Moore is endlessly inventive. . . . This cetacean picaresque is no fluke—it is a sure winner."
—*Publishers Weekly* (starred review)

"[O]ne of the finest pieces of imagination since Anatole France's *Penguin Island* or George Orwell's *Animal Farm*."
—*Denver Post*

"You're not likely to stumble across another book like [*Fluke*] . . . and it contains more than its fair share of goofy fun. . . . Definitely the perfect book for a day at the beach."
—*San Francisco Chronicle Book Review*

"*Fluke* is a lighthearted book that still manages to make some serious points about the human condition. . . . [Moore's] imagination is a gift to the reader."
—*Baltimore Sun*

D0181967

Charlee Rodgers

About the Author

CHRISTOPHER MOORE is the author of *Lamb, Practical Demonkeeping, Coyote Blue, Bloodsucking Fiends, Island of the Sequined Love Nun,* and *The Lust Lizard of Melancholy Cove.* He invites readers to e-mail him at BSFiends@aol.com.

FLUKE

Or,

I Know Why the Winged Whale Sings

CHRISTOPHER MOORE

HARPER

NEW YORK · LONDON · TORONTO · SYDNEY

Grateful acknowledgment is made for permission to reprint from the following:

The Log of the Sea of Cortez by John Steinbeck, copyright © 1941 by John Steinbeck and Edward F. Ricketts. Copyright renewed © 1969 by John Steinbeck and Edward F. Ricketts, Jr. Used by permission of Viking Penguin, a division of Penguin Putnam Inc.

The Selfish Gene by Richard Dawkins, copyright © 1976, 1989. Reprinted by permission of Oxford University Press.

With the Whales by Flip Nicklin, copyright © 1990. Reprinted by permission of NorthWord Press.

A hardcover edition of this book was published in 2003 by William Morrow, an imprint of HarperCollins Publishers.

HarperCollins books may be purchased for educational, business, or sales promotional use. For information please write: Special Markets Department, HarperCollins Publishers Inc., 10 East 53rd Street, New York, NY 10022.

First Perennial edition published 2004.

Designed by Adrian Leichter

The Library of Congress has catalogued the hardcover edition as follows:
Moore, Christopher.
Fluke, or, I know why the winged whale sings / Christopher Moore.
p. cm.
ISBN 0-380-97841-5
1. Human-animal relationships—Fiction. 2. Midlife crisis—Fiction.
3. Humpback whale—Fiction. 4. Whale sounds—Fiction. 5. Hawaii—Fiction.
I. Title: Fluke. II. Title: I know why the winged whale sings. III. Title.
PS3563.O594 F58 2003
813'.54—dc21
2002043231

ISBN 0-06-056668-X (pbk.)

09 ❖/RRD 20

For Jim Darling, Flip Nicklin,
and Meagan Jones:
extraordinary people who do
extraordinary work

Fluke (flook)1. A stroke of good luck

    2. A chance occurrence; an accident

    3. A barb or barbed head, as on a harpoon

    4. Either of the two horizontally flattened divisions of the tail of a whale

· CONTENTS ·

PART ONE

The Song

*An ocean without its
unnamed monsters would be like a
completely dreamless sleep.*
—JOHN STEINBECK

*The scientific method is nothing
more than a system of rules to keep us
from lying to each other.*
—KEN NORRIS

CHAPTER ONE

Big and Wet.
Next Question?

Amy called the whale punkin.

He was fifty feet long, wider than a city bus, and weighed eighty thousand pounds. One well-placed slap of his great tail would reduce the boat to fiberglass splinters and its occupants to red stains drifting in the blue Hawaiian waters. Amy leaned over the side of the boat and lowered the hydrophone down on the whale. "Good morning, punkin," she said.

Nathan Quinn shook his head and tried not to upchuck from the cuteness of it, of her, while surreptitiously sneaking a look at her bottom and feeling a little sleazy about it. Science can be complex. Nate was a scientist. Amy was a scientist, too, but she looked fantastic in a pair of khaki hiking shorts, scientifically speaking.

Below, the whale sang on, the boat vibrated with each note. The stainless rail at the bow began to buzz. Nate could feel the deeper notes resonate in his rib cage. The whale was into a section of the song they called the "green" themes, a long series of whoops that sounded like an ambulance driving through pudding. A less trained listener might have thought that the whale was rejoicing, celebrating, shouting howdy to the world to let everyone and everything know that he was alive and feeling good, but Nate was a trained listener, perhaps the most trained listener in the world, and to his expert ears the whale was saying— Well, he had no idea what in the hell the whale was saying, did he? That's why they were out there floating in that sapphire channel off Maui in a small speedboat, sloshing their breakfasts around at seven in the morning: No one knew why the humpbacks sang. Nate had been listening to them, observing them, photographing them, and poking them with sticks for twenty-five years, and he still had no idea why, exactly, they sang.

"He's into his ribbits," Amy said, identifying a section of the whale's song that usually came right before the animal was about to surface. The scientific term for this noise was "ribbits" because that's what they sounded like. Science can be simple.

Nate peeked over the side and looked at the whale that was suspended head down in the water about fifty feet below them. His flukes and pectoral fins were white and described a crystal-blue chevron in the deep blue water. So still was the great beast that he might have been floating in space, the last beacon of some long-dead space-traveling race—except that he was making croaky noises that would have sounded more appropriate coming out of a two-inch tree frog than the archaic remnant of a superrace. Nate smiled. He liked ribbits. The whale flicked his tail once and shot out of Nate's field of vision.

"He's coming up," Nate said.

Amy tore off her headphones and picked up the motorized Nikon with the three-hundred-millimeter lens. Nate quickly pulled up the hydrophone, allowing the wet cord to spool into a coil at his feet, then turned to the console and started the engine.

Then they waited.

There was a blast of air from behind them and they both spun around to see the column of water vapor hanging in the air, but it was far, perhaps three hundred meters behind them—too far away to be their whale. That was the problem with the channel between Maui and Lanai where they worked: There were so many whales that you often had a hard time distinguishing the one you were studying from the hundreds of others. The abundance of animals was both a blessing and a curse.

"That our guy?" Amy asked. All the singers were guys. As far as they knew anyway. The DNA tests had proven that.

"Nope."

There was another blow to their left, this one much closer. Nate could see the white flukes or blades of his tail under the water, even from a hundred meters away. Amy hit the stop button on her watch. Nate pushed the throttle forward and they were off. Amy braced a knee against the console to steady herself, keeping the camera pointed toward the whale as the boat bounced along. He would blow three, maybe four times, then fluke and dive. Amy had to be ready when the whale dove to get a clear shot of his flukes so he could be identified and cataloged. When they were within thirty yards of the whale, Nate backed the throttle down and held them in position. The whale blew again, and they were close enough to catch some of the mist. There was none of the dead fish and massive morning-mouth smell that they would have encountered in Alaska. Humpbacks didn't feed while they were in Hawaii.

The whale fluked and Amy fired off two quick frames with the Nikon.

"Good boy," Amy said to the whale. She hit the lap timer button on her watch.

Nate cut the engine and the speedboat settled into the gentle swell. He threw the hydrophone overboard, then hit the record button on the recorder that was bungee-corded to the console. Amy set the camera on the seat in front of the console, then snatched their notebook out of a waterproof pouch.

"He's right on sixteen minutes," Amy said, checking the time and recording it in the notebook. She wrote the time and the frame numbers of the film she had just shot. Nate read her the footage number off the recorder, then the longitude and latitude from the portable GPS (global positioning system) device. She put down the notebook, and they listened. They weren't right on top of the whale as they had been before, but they could hear him singing through the recorder's speaker. Nate put on the headphones and sat back to listen.

That's how field research was. Moments of frantic activity followed by long periods of waiting. (Nate's first ex-wife had once commented that their sex life could be described in exactly the same way, but that was after they had separated, and she was just being snotty.) Actually, the wait here in Maui wasn't bad—ten, fifteen minutes at a throw. When he'd been studying right whales in the North Atlantic, Nate had sometimes waited weeks before he found a whale to study. Usually he liked to use the downtime (literally, the time the whale was down) to think about how he should've gotten a real job, one where you made real money and had weekends off, or at least gotten into a branch of the field where the results of his work were more palpable, like sinking whaling ships—a pirate. You know, security.

Today Nate was actively trying not to watch Amy put on sunscreen. Amy was a snowflake in the land of the tanned. Most whale researchers spent a great deal of time outdoors, at sea. They were, for the most part, an intrepid, outdoorsy bunch who wore wind- and sunburn like battle scars, and there were few who didn't sport a semipermanent sunglasses raccoon tan and sun-bleached hair or a scaly bald spot. Amy, on the other hand, had milk-white skin and straight, short black hair so dark that the highlights appeared blue in the Hawaiian sun. She was wearing maroon lipstick, which was so wildly inappropriate and out of character for this setting that it approached the comical and made her seem like the goth geek of the Pacific, which was, in fact, one of the reasons her presence so disturbed Nate. (He reasoned: A well-formed bottom hanging in space is just a well-formed bottom, but you hook up a well-formed bottom to a whip-smart woman and apply a dash of the awkward and what you've got yourself is . . . well, trouble.)

Nate did not watch her rub the SPF50 on her legs, over her ankles and feet. He did not watch her strip to her bikini top and apply the sunscreen over her chest and shoulders. (Tropical sun can fry you even through a shirt.) Nate especially did not notice when she grabbed his hand, squirted lotion into it, then turned, indicating that he should apply it to her back, which he did—not noticing anything about her in the process. Professional courtesy. He was working. He was a scientist. He was listening to the song of *Megaptera novaeangliae* ("big wings of New England," a scientist had named the whale, thus proving that scientists drink), and he was not intrigued by her intriguing bottom because he had encountered and analyzed similar data in the past. According to Nate's analysis, research assistants with intriguing bottoms turned into wives 66.666 percent of the time, and wives turned into ex-wives exactly 100 percent of the time—plus or minus 5 percent factored for post-divorce comfort sex.)

"Want me to do you?" Amy asked, holding out her preferred sunscreen-slathering hand.

You just don't go there, thought Nate, not even in a joke. One incorrect response to a line like that and you could lose your university position, if you had one, which Nate didn't, but still. . . . You don't even think about it.

"No thanks, this shirt has UV protection woven in," he said, thinking about what it would be like to have Amy do him.

Amy looked suspiciously at his faded WE LIKE WHALES CONFERENCE '89 T-shirt and wiped the remaining sunscreen on her leg. " 'Kay," she said.

"You know, I sure wish I could figure out why these guys sing," Nate said, the hummingbird of his mind having tasted all the flowers in the garden to return to that one plastic daisy that would just not give up the nectar.

"No kidding?" Amy said, deadpan, smiling. "But if you figure it out, what would we do tomorrow?"

"Show off," Nate said, grinning.

"I'd be typing all day, analyzing research, matching photographs, filing song tapes—"

"Bringing us doughnuts," Nate added, trying to help.

Amy continued, counting down the list on her fingers, "—picking up blank tapes, washing down the trucks and the boats, running to the photo lab—"

"Not so fast," Nate interrupted.

"What, you're going to deprive me the joy of running to the photo lab while you bask in scientific glory?"

"No, you can still go to the photo lab, but Clay hired a guy to wash the trucks and boats."

A delicate hand went to her forehead as she swooned, the southern belle in hiking shorts, taken with the vapors. "If I faint and fall overboard, don't let me drown."

"You know, Amy," Nate said as he undressed the crossbow, "I don't know how it was at Boston doing survey, but in behavior, research assistants are only supposed to bitch about the humiliating grunt work and lowly status to other research assistants. It was that way when I was doing it, it was that way going back centuries, it has always been that way. Darwin himself had someone on the *Beagle* to file dead birds and sort index cards."

"He did not. I've never read anything about that."

"Of course you didn't. Nobody writes about research assistants." Nate grinned again, celebration for a small victory. He realized he wasn't working up to standards on managing this research assistant. His partner, Clay, had hired her almost two weeks ago, and by now he should have had her terrorized. Instead she was working him like a Starbucks froth slave.

"Ten minutes," Amy said, checking the timer on her watch. "You going to shoot him?"

"Unless you want to?" Nate notched the arrow into the crossbow. He tucked the windbreaker they used to "dress" the crossbow under the console. It was very politically incorrect to carry a weapon for shooting whales through the crowded Lahaina harbor, so they carried it inside the windbreaker, making it appear that they had a jacket on a hanger.

Amy shook her head violently. "I'll drive the boat."

"You should learn to do it."

"I'll drive the boat," Amy said.

"No one drives the boat." No one but Nate drove the boat. Granted, the *Constantly Baffled* was only a twenty-three-foot Mako speedboat, and an agile four-year-old could pilot it on a calm day like today. Still, no one else drove the boat. It was a man thing, being inherently uncomfortable with the thought of a woman operating a boat or a television remote control.

"Up sounds," Nate said. They had a recording of the full sixteen-minute cycle of the song now—all the way through twice, in fact. He stopped the recorder and pulled up the hydrophone, then started the engine.

"There," Amy said, pointing to the white fins and flukes moving under the water. The whale blew only twenty yards off the bow. Nate buried the throttle. Amy was wrenched off her feet and just caught herself on the railing next to the wheel console as the boat shot forward. Nate pulled up on the right side of the whale, no more than ten yards away as the whale came up for the second time. He steadied the wheel with his hip, pulled up the crossbow, and fired. The bolt bounced off the whale's rubbery back, the hollow surgical steel arrowhead taking out a cookie-cutter plug of skin and blubber the size of a pencil eraser before the wide plastic tip stopped the penetration.

The whale lifted his tail out of the water and snapped it in the air, making a sound like a giant knuckle cracking as the massive tail muscles contracted.

"He's pissed," Nate said. "Let's go for a measurement."

"Now?" Amy questioned. Normally they would wait for another dive cycle. Obviously Nate thought that because of their taking the skin sample the whale might start traveling. They could lose him before getting a measurement.

"Now. I'll shoot, you work the rangefinder."

Nate backed off the throttle a bit, so he would be able to catch the entire tail fluke in the camera frame when the whale dove. Amy grabbed the laser rangefinder, which looked very much like a pair of binoculars made for a cyclops. By taking a distance measurement from the animal's tail with the rangefinder and comparing the size of the tail in the frame of the picture, they could measure the relative size of the entire animal. Nate had come up with an algorithm that, so far, gave them the length of a whale with 98 percent accuracy. Just a few years ago they would've had to have been in an aircraft to measure the length of a whale.

"Ready," Amy said.

The whale blew and arched its back into a high hump as he readied for the dive (the reason whalers had named them humpbacks in the first place). Amy fixed the rangefinder on the whale's back; Nate trained the camera's telephoto on the same spot, and the autofocus motors made tiny adjustments with the movement of the boat.

The whale fluked, raising its tail high in the air, and there, instead of the distinct pattern of black-and-white markings by which all hump-backs were identified, were—spelled out in foot-high black letters across the white—the words BITE ME!

Nate hit the shutter button. Shocked, he fell into the captain's chair, pulling back the throttle as he slumped. He let the Nikon sag in his lap.

"Holy shit!" Nate said. "Did you see that?"

—◦◦◦—

"SEE WHAT? I GOT SEVENTY-THREE FEET," AMY SAID, PULLING DOWN the rangefinder. "Probably seventy-six from where you are. What were your frame numbers?" She was reaching for the notebook as she looked back at Nate. "Are you okay?"

"Fine. Frame twenty-six, but I missed it," he lied. His mind was shuffling though a huge stack of index cards, searching a million article abstracts he had read to find some explanation for what he'd just seen. It couldn't possibly have been real. The film would show it. "You didn't see any unusual markings when you did the ID photo?"

"No, did you?"

"No, never mind."

"Don't sweat it, Nate. We'll get it next time he comes up," Amy said. "Let's go in."

"You don't want to try again for a measurement?" To make the data sample complete, they needed an ID photo, a recording of at least a full cycle of the song, a skin sample for DNA and toxin figures, and a measurement. The morning was wasted without the measurement.

"Let's go back to Lahaina," Nate said, staring down at the camera in his lap. "You drive."

CHAPTER TWO

Maui No Ka Oi
(Maui Is the Best)

At first it was that old trickster Maui who cast his fishing line from his canoe and pulled the islands up from the bottom of the sea. When he was done fishing, he looked at those islands he had pulled up, and smack in the middle of the chain was one that was made up of two big volcanoes, sitting there together like the friendly, lopsided bosoms of the sea. Between them was a deep valley that Maui thought looked very much like cleavage, which he very much liked. And so, to that bumpy-bits island Maui gave his name, and its nickname became "The Cleavage Island," which it stayed until some missionaries came along and renamed it "The Valley Island" (because if there's anything missionaries do well, it's seek out and destroy fun). Then Maui landed his canoe at a calm little beach on the west coast of his new island and said to himself, "I could do with a few cocktails and some nookie. I shall go into Lahaina and get some."

Well, time passed and some whalers came to the island, bringing steel tools and syphilis and other wonders from the West, and before anyone knew what was happening, they, too, were thinking that they wouldn't mind a few cocktails and a measure of nookie. So rather than sail back around the Horn to Nantucket to hoist noggins of grog and the skirts of the odd Hester, Millicent, or Prudence (so fast the dear woman would think she'd fallen down a chimney and landed on a zucchini), they pulled into Lahaina, drawn by the drunken sex magic of old Maui. They didn't come to Maui for the whales, they came for the party.

And so Lahaina became a whaling town. The irony of it was that even though the humpbacks had starting coming to birth their calves and sing their songs only a few years earlier, and in those days the Hawaiian channels were teeming with the big-winged singers, it was not for the humpbacks that the whalers came. Humpbacks, like their other rorqual brothers—the streamlined blue, fin, sei, minke, and Bryde's whales—were just too fast to catch in sailing ships and man-powered whaling boats. No, the whalers came to Lahaina to rest and recreate along their way to Japanese waters where they hunted the great sperm whale, who would literally float there like a big, dumb log while you rowed up to it and stuck a harpoon in its head. It would take the advent of steamships and the decimation of the big, floaty-fat right whales (so named because they did float when dead and therefore were the "right" whales to kill) before the hunters would turn their harpoons on the humpbacks.

Following the whalers came the missionaries, the sugar farmers, the Chinese, Japanese, Filipinos, and Portuguese who all worked the sugar plantations, and Mark Twain. Mark Twain went home. Everyone else stayed. In the meantime, King Kamehameha I united the islands through the clever application of firearms against wooden spears and moved Hawaii's capital to Lahaina. Sometime after that Amy came cruising into the Lahaina harbor at the wheel of a twenty-three-foot Mako speedboat with a tall, stunned-looking Ph.D. sprawled across the bow seat.

The radio chirped. Amy picked it up and keyed the mike. "Go ahead, Clay."

"Something wrong?" Clay Demodocus was obviously in the harbor and could see them coming in. It wasn't even eight in the morning. He was probably still preparing his boat to go out.

"I'm not sure. Nate just decided to call it a day. I'll ask him why." To Nate she said, "Clay wants to know why."

"Anomalous data," Nate said.

"Anomalous data," Amy repeated into the radio.

There was a pause. Then Clay said, "Uh, right, understood. That stuff gets into everything."

The harbor at Lahaina is not large. Only a hundred or so vessels can dock behind her breakwater. Most are sizable, fifty- to seventy-foot cruisers and catamarans, boats full of sunscreen-basted tourists out on the water for anything from dinner cruises to sport fishing to snorkeling at the half-sunken crater of Molokini to, of course, whale watching. Jet-skiing, parasailing, and waterskiing were all banned from December until April, while the humpbacks were in these waters, so many of the smaller boats that would normally be used to terrorize marine life in the name of recreation were leased by whale researchers for the season. On any given winter morning down at the harbor at Lahaina, you couldn't throw a coconut without conking a Ph.D. in cetacean biology (and you stood a good chance of winging two Masters of Science working on dissertations with the rebound).

Clay Demodocus was engaged in a bit of research liars poker with a Ph.D. and a naval officer when Amy backed the Mako into the slip they shared with three tender zodiacs from sailing yachts anchored outside the breakwater, a thirty-two-foot motor-sailer, and the Maui Whale Research Foundation's other boat (Clay's boat), the *Always Confused,* a brand-new twenty-two-foot Grady White Fisherman, center console. (Slips were hard to come by in Lahaina, and circumstances this season had dictated that the Maui Whale Research Foundation—Nate and Clay—perform a nautical dog pile with six other small craft every day. You do what you have to do if you want to poke whales.)

"Shame," Clay said as Amy threw him the stern line. "Nice calm day, too."

"We got everything but a measurement on one singer," Amy said.

The scientist and the naval officer on the dock behind Clay nodded as if they understood completely. Clifford Hyland, a grizzled, gray-haired whale researcher from Iowa stood next to the young, razor-creased, snowy-white-uniformed Captain L. J. Tarwater, who was there to see that Hyland spent the navy's money appropriately. Hyland looked a little embarrassed at the whole thing and wouldn't make eye contact with Amy or Nate. Money was money, and a researcher took it where he could get it, but navy money, it was so . . . so nasty.

"Morning Amy," said Tarwater, dazzling a perfectly even, perfectly white smile. He was lean and dark and frighteningly efficient-looking. Next to him, Clay and the scientists looked as if they'd been run through the dryer with a bag of lava rock.

"Good morning, Captain. Morning Cliff."

"Hey, Amy," Cliff Hyland said. "Hey, Nate."

Nathan Quinn shook off his confusion like a retriever who had just heard his name uttered in context with food. "What? What? Oh, hi, Cliff. What?"

Hyland and Quinn had both been part of a group of thirteen scientists who had first come to Lahaina in the seventies ("The Killer Elite," Clay still called them, as they had all gone on to distinguish themselves as leaders in their fields). Actually, the original intention hadn't been for them to be a group, but they nevertheless became one early on when they all realized that the only way they could afford to stay on the island was if they pooled their resources and lived together. So for years thirteen of them—and sometimes more if they could afford assistants, wives, or girlfriends—lived every season in a two-bedroom house they rented in Lahaina. Hyland understood Quinn's tendency to submerge himself in his research to the point of oblivion, so he wasn't surprised that once again the rangy researcher had spaced out.

"Anomalous data, huh?" Cliff asked, figuring that was what had sent Nate into the ozone.

"Uh, nothing I can be sure of. I mean, actually, the recorder isn't working right. Something dragging. Probably just needs to be cleaned."

And everyone, including Amy, looked at Quinn for a moment as if to say, *Well, you lying satchel of walrus spit, that is the weakest story I've ever heard, and you're not fooling anyone.*

"Shame," Clay said. "Nice day to miss out on the water. Maybe you can get back with the other recorder and get out again before the wind comes up." Clay knew something was up with Nate, but he also trusted his judgment enough not to press it. Nate would tell him when he thought he should know.

"Speaking of that," Hyland said, "we'd better get going." He headed down the dock toward his own boat. Tarwater stared at Nate just long enough to convey disgust before turning on his heel and marching after Hyland.

When they were gone, Amy said, "Tarwater is a creep."

"He's all right. He's got a job to do is all," Clay said. "What's with the recorder?"

"The recorder is fine," Nate said.

"Then what gives? It's a perfect day." Clay liked to state the obvious when it was positive. It was sunny, calm, with no wind, and the underwater visibility was two hundred feet. It *was* a perfect day to research whales.

Nate started handing waterproof cases of equipment to Clay. "I don't know. I may have seen something out there, Clay. I have to think about it and see the pictures. I'm going to drop some film off at the lab, then go back to Papa Lani and write up some research until the film's ready."

Clay flinched, just a tad. It was Amy's job to drop off film and write up research. "Okay. How 'bout you, kiddo?" Clay said to Amy. "My new guy doesn't look like he's going to show, and I need someone topside while I'm under."

Amy looked to Nate for some kind of approval, but when he simply kept unloading cases without a reaction, she just shrugged. "Sure, I'd love to."

Clay suddenly became self-conscious and shuffled in his flip-flops, looking for a second more like a five-year-old kid than a barrel-chested, fifty-year-old man. "By calling you 'kiddo' I didn't mean to diminish you by age or anything, you know."

"I know," Amy said.

"And I wasn't making any sort of comment on your competency either."

"I understand, Clay."

Clay cleared his throat unnecessarily. "Okay," he said.

"Okay," Amy said. She grabbed two Pelican cases full of equipment, stepped up onto the dock, and started schlepping the stuff to the parking area so it could be loaded into Nate's pickup. Over her shoulder she said, "You guys both so need to get laid."

"I think that's reverse harassment," Clay said to Nate.

"I may be having hallucinations," said Nate.

"No, she really said that," Clay said.

⤙◦◦⤚

AFTER QUINN HAD LEFT, AMY CLIMBED INTO THE *ALWAYS CONFUSED* and began untying the stern line. She glanced over her shoulder to look at the forty-foot cabin cruiser where Captain Tarwater posed on the bow looking like an advertisement for a particularly rigid laundry detergent—Bumstick Go-Be-Bright, perhaps.

"Clay, you ever heard of a uniformed naval officer accompanying a researcher into the field before?"

Clay looked up from doing a battery check on the GPS. "Not unless the researcher was working from a navy vessel. Once I was along on a destroyer for a study on the effects of high explosives on resident populations of southern sea lions in the Falkland Islands. They wanted to see what would happen if you set off a ten-thousand-pound charge in proximity to a sea lion colony. There was a uniformed officer in charge of that."

Amy cast the line back to the dock and turned to face Clay. "What was the effect?"

"Well, it blew them the fuck up, didn't it? I mean, that's a lot of explosives."

"They let you film *that* for *National Science*?"

"Just stills," Clay said. "I don't think they anticipated it going the way it did. I got some great shots of it raining seal meat." Clay started the engine.

"Yuck." Amy untied the bumpers and pulled them into the boat. "But you've never seen a uniformed officer working here? Before now, I mean."

"Nowhere else," Clay said. He pulled down the gear lever. There was a thump, and the boat began to creep forward.

Amy pushed them away from the surrounding boats with a padded boat hook. "What do you think they're doing?"

"I was trying to find out this morning when you guys came in. They loaded an awfully big case before you got here. I asked what it was, and Tarwater got all sketchy. Cliff said it was some acoustics stuff."

"Directional array?" Amy asked. Researchers sometimes towed large arrays of hydrophones that could, unlike a single hydrophone, detect the direction from which sound was traveling.

"Could be," Clay said. "Except they don't have a winch on their boat."

"A wench? What are you trying to say, Clay?" Amy feigned being offended. "Are you calling me a wench?"

Clay grinned at her. "Amy, I am old and have a girlfriend, and therefore I am immune to your hotness. Please cease your useless attempts to make me uncomfortable."

"Let's follow them."

"They've been working on the lee side of Lanai. I don't want to take the *Confused* past the wind line."

"So you *were* trying to find out what they're up to?"

"I fished. No bites. Cliff's not going to say anything with Tarwater standing there."

"So let's follow them."

"We actually may get some work done today. It's a good day, after all, and we might not get a dozen windless days all season here. We can't afford to lose a day, Amy. Which reminds me, what's up with Nate? Not like him to blow off a good field day."

"You know, he's nuts," Amy said, as if it were understood. "Too much time thinking about whales."

"Oh, right. I forgot." As they motored out of the harbor, Clay waved to a group of researchers who had gathered at the fuel station to buy coffee. Twenty universities and a dozen foundations were represented in that group. Clay was single-handedly responsible for making the scientists who worked out of Lahaina into a social community. He knew them all, and he couldn't help it—he liked people who worked with whales— and he just liked it when people got along.

He'd started weekly meetings and presentations of papers at the Pacific Whale Sanctuary building in Kihei, which brought all the scientists together to socialize, trade information, and, for some, to try to weasel some useful data out of someone without the burden of field research.

Amy waved to the group, too, as she dug into one of the orange Pelican waterproof cases. "Come on, Clay, let's follow Tarwater and see what he's up to." She pulled a huge pair of twenty-power binoculars out of the case and showed them to Clay. "We can watch from a distance."

"You might want to go up in the bow and look for whales, Amy."

"Whales? They're big and wet. What else do you need to know?"

"You scientists never cease to amaze me," Clay said. "Come hold the wheel while I get a pencil to write that down."

"Let's follow Tarwater."

CHAPTER THREE

A Little Razor Wire
Around Heaven

The gate to the Papa Lani compound was hanging open when Nate drove up. Not good. Clay was adamant about their always replacing the big Masterlock on the gate when they left the compound.

Papa Lani was a group of wood-frame buildings on two acres northeast of Lahaina in the middle of a half dozen sugarcane fields that had been donated to Maui Whale by a wealthy woman Clay and Nate affectionately referred to as the "Old Broad." The property consisted of six small bungalows that had once been used to board plantation workers but had long since been converted to housing, laboratory, and office space for Clay, Nate, and any assistants, researchers, or film crews who might be working with them for the season. Getting the compound had been a godsend for Maui Whale, given the cost of housing and storage in Lahaina. Clay had named the compound Papa Lani (Hawaiian for "heaven") in honor of their good fortune, but someone had left the gate to heaven open, and from what Nate could tell as he drove in, the angel shit had hit the fan.

Before he even got out of the truck, Nate saw a beat-up green BMW parked in the compound and a trail of papers leading out of the building they used for an office. He snatched a few of them up as he ran across the sand driveway and up the steps into the little bungalow. Inside was chaos: drawers torn out of filing cabinets, toppled racks of cassette tape—the tapes strewn across the room in great streamers—computers overturned, the sides of their cases open, trailing wires. Nate stood among the mess, not really knowing what to do or even what to look at, feeling violated and on the verge of throwing up. Even if nothing was missing, a lifetime of research had been typhooned around the room.

"Oh, Jah's sweet mercy," came a voice from behind him. "This a bit of fuckery most heinous for sure, mon."

Nate spun and dropped into a martial-arts stance, notwithstanding the fact that he didn't know any martial arts and that he had loosed a little-girl shriek in the process. The serpent-haired figure of a gorgon was silhouetted in the doorway, and Nate would have screamed again if the figure hadn't stepped into the light, revealing a lean, bare-chested teenager in surfer shorts and flip-flops, sporting a giant tangle of blond dreadlocks and about six hundred nose rings.

"Cool head main ting, brah, cool head," the kid almost sang. There was pot and steel drums in his voice, bemusement and youth and two joints' worth of separation from the rest of reality.

Nate went from fear to confusion in an instant. "What the fuck are you talking about?"

"Relax, brah, no make li'dat. Kona and I come help out."

Nate thought he might feel better if he strangled this kid—just a little frustration strangle to vent some of the shock of the wrecked lab, not a full choke—but instead he said, "Who are you, and what are you doing here?"

"Kona," the kid said. "Dat boss name Clay hire me for the boats dat day before."

"You're the kid Clay hired to work with us on the boats?"

"Shoots, mon, I just said that? What, you a ninja, brah?"

The kid nodded, his dreads sweeping around his shoulders, and Nate was about to scream at him again when he realized that he was still crouched into his pseudo combat stance and probably looked like a total loon.

He stood up, shrugged, then pretended to stretch his neck and roll his head in a cocky way he'd seen boxers do, as if he had just disarmed a very dangerous enemy or something. "You were supposed to meet Clay down at the dock an hour ago."

"Some rippin' sets North Shore, they be callin' to me this morning." The kid shrugged. What could he do? Rippin' sets had called to him.

Nate squinted at the surfer, realizing that the kid was speaking some mix of Rasta talk, pidgin, surfspeak and . . . well, bullshit. "Stop talking that way, or you're fired right now."

"So you ichiban big whale kahuna, like Clay say, hey?"

"Yeah," Nate said. "I'm the number-one whale kahuna. You're fired."

"Bummah, mon," The kid said. He shrugged again, turned, and started out the door. "Jah's love to ye, brah. Cool runnings," he sang over his shoulder.

"Wait," Nate said.

The kid spun around, his dreads enveloping his face like a furry octopus attacking a crab. He sputtered a dreadlock out of his mouth and was about to speak.

Quinn held up a finger to signal silence. "Not a word of pidgin, Hawaiian, or Rasta talk, or you're done."

"Okay." The kid waited.

Quinn composed himself and looked around at the mess, then at the kid. "There are papers strewn around all over outside, hanging in the fences, in the bushes. I need you to gather them up and stack them as neatly as you can. Bring them here. Can you do that?"

The kid nodded.

"Excellent. I'm Nathan Quinn." Nate extended his hand to shake.

The kid moved across the room and caught Nate's hand in a powerful grip. The scientist almost winced but instead returned the pressure and tried to smile.

"Pelekekona," said the kid. "Call me Kona."

"Welcome aboard, Kona."

The kid looked around now, looking as if by giving his name he had relinquished some of his power and was suddenly weak, despite the muscles that rippled across his chest and abdomen. "Who did this?"

"No idea." Nate picked up a cassette tape that had been pulled out of the spools and wadded into a bird's nest of brown plastic. "You go get those papers. I'm going to call the police. That a problem?"

Kona shook his head. "Why would it be?"

"No reason. Grab those papers now. Nothing is trash until I look at it, eh?"

"Overstood, brah," Kona said, grinning back at Nate as he headed out into sun. Once outside, he turned and called, "Hey, Kahuna Quinn."

"What?"

"How come them humpies sing like dat?"

"What do you think?" Nate asked, and in the asking there was hope. Despite the fact that the kid was young and irritating and probably stoned, the biologist truly hoped that Kona—unburdened by too much knowledge—would give him the answer. He didn't care where it came from or how it came (and it would still have to be proved); he just wanted to know, which is what set him apart from the hacks, the wanna-bes, the backstabbers, and the ego jockeys in the field. Nate just wanted to know.

"I think they trying to shout down Babylon, maybe."

"You'll have to explain to me what that means."

"We fix this fuckery, then we fire up a spliff and think over it, brah."

❧

FIVE HOURS LATER CLAY CAME THROUGH THE DOOR TALKING. "WE got some amazing stuff today, Nate. Some of the best cow/calf stuff I've ever shot." Clay was still so excited he almost skipped into the room.

"Okay," Nate said with a zombielike lack of enthusiasm. He sat in front of his patched-together computer at one of the desks. The office was mostly put back in order, but the open computer case sitting on the desk with wires spread out to a diaspora of refugee drive units told a tale of data gone wild. "Someone broke in. Tore apart the office."

Clay didn't want to be concerned. He had great videotape to edit. Suddenly, looking at the fans and wires, it occurred to him that some-one might have broken his editing setup. He whirled around to see his forty-two-inch flat-panel monitor leaning against the wall, a long diagonal crack bisected the glass. "Oh," he said. "Oh, jeez."

Amy walked in smiling, "Nate you won't believe the—" She pulled up, saw Clay staring at his broken monitor, the computer scattered over Nate's desk, files stacked here and there where they shouldn't be. "Oh," she said.

"Someone broke in," Clay said forlornly.

She put her hand on Clay's shoulder. "Today? In broad daylight?"

Nate swiveled around in his chair. "They went through our living quarters, too. The police have already been here." He saw Clay staring at his monitor. "Oh, and that. Sorry, Clay."

"You guys have insurance, right?" Amy said.

Clay didn't look away from his broken monitor. "Dr. Quinn, did you pay the insurance?" Clay called Nate "doctor" only when he wanted to remind him of just how official and absolutely professional they really ought to be.

"Last week. Went out with the boat insurance."

"Well, then, we're okay," Amy said, jostling Clay, squeezing his shoulder, punching his arm, pinching his butt. "We can order a new monitor tonight, ya big palooka." she chirped, looking like a goth version of the bluebird of happiness.

"Hey!" Clay grinned, "Yeah, we're okay." He turned to Nate, smiling. "Anything else broken? Anything missing?"

Nate pointed to the wastebasket where a virtual haystack of audiotape was spilling over in tangles. "That was spread all over the compound along with all the files. We lost most of the tape, going back two years."

Amy stopped being cheerful and looked appropriately concerned. "What about the digitals?" She elbowed Clay, who was still grinning, and he joined her in gravity. They frowned. (Nate recorded all the audio on analog tape, then transferred it to the computer for analysis. Theoretically, there should be digital copies of everything.)

"These hard drives have been erased. I can't pull up anything from them." Nate took a deep breath, sighed, then spun back around in his chair and let his forehead fall against the desk with a thud that shook the whole bungalow.

Amy and Clay winced. There were a lot of screws on that desk. Clay said, "Well, it couldn't have been that bad, Nate. You got it all cleaned up pretty quickly."

"The guy you hired showed up late and helped me." Nate was speaking into the desk, his face right where it had landed.

"Kona? Where is he?"

"I sent him to the lab. I had some film I want to see right away."

"I knew he wouldn't stand us up on his first day."

"Clay, I need to talk to you. Amy, could you excuse us a minute, please?"

"Sure," Amy said. "I'll go see if anything's missing from my cabin." She left.

Clay said, "You going to look up? Or should I get down on the floor so I can see your face?"

"Could you grab the first-aid kit while we talk?"

"Screws embedded in your forehead?"

"Feels like four, maybe five."

"They're small, though, those little drive-mount screws."

"Clay, you're always trying to cheer me up."

"It's who I am," Clay said.

CHAPTER FOUR

Whale Men of Maui

Who Clay was, was a guy who liked things—liked people, liked animals, liked cars, liked boats—who had an almost supernatural ability to spot the likability in almost anyone or anything. When he walked down the streets of Lahaina, he would nod and say hello to sunburned tourist couples in matching aloha wear (people generally considered to be a waste of humanity by most locals), but by the same token he would trade a backhanded hang-loose shaka (thumb and fingers extended, three middle fingers tucked, always backhand if you're a local) with a crash of native bruddahs in the parking lot of the ABC Store and get no scowls or pidgin curses, as would most haoles. People could sense that Clay liked them, as could animals, which was probably why Clay was still alive. Twenty-five years in the water with hunters and giants, and the worst he'd come out of it was to get a close tail-wash from a southern right whale that tumbled him like a cartoon into the idling prop of a Zodiac. (Oh, there were the two times he was drowned and the hypothermia, but that stuff wasn't caused by the animals; that was the sea, and she'll kill you whether you liked her or not, which Clay did.) Doing what he wanted to do and his boundless affinity for everything made Clay Demodocus a happy guy, but he was also shrewd enough not to be too open about his happiness. Animals might put up with that smiley shit, but people will eventually kill you for it.

"How's the new kid?" Clay said, trying to distract from the iodine he was applying to Nate's forehead while simultaneously calculating the time to ship his new monitor over to Maui from the discount house in Seattle. Clay liked gadgets.

"He's a criminal," Nate said.

"He'll come around. He's a water guy." For Clay this said it all. You were a water guy or you weren't. If you weren't . . . well, you were pretty much useless, weren't you?

"He was an hour late, and he showed up in the wrong place."

"He's a native. He'll help us deal with the whale cops."

"He's not a native, he's blond, Clay. He's more of a haole than you are, for Christ's sake."

"He'll come around. I was right about Amy, wasn't I?" Clay said. He liked the new kid, Kona, despite the employment interview, which had gone like this:

Clay sat with the forty-two-inch monitor at his back, his world-famous photographs of whales and pinnipeds playing in a slide show behind him. Since he was conducting a job interview, he had put on his very best $5.99 ABC Store flip-flops. Kona stood in the middle of the office wearing sunglasses, his baggies, and, since he was applying for a job, a red-dirt-dyed shirt.

"Your application says that your name is Pelke—ah, Pelekekona Ke—" Clay threw his hands up in surrender.

"I be called Pelekekona Keohokalole—da warrior kine—Lion of Zion, brah."

"Can I call you Pele?"

"Kona," Kona said.

"It says on your driver's license that your name is Preston Apple-baum and you're from New Jersey."

"I be one hundred percent Hawaiian. Kona the best boat hand in the Island, yeah. I figga I be number-one good man for to keep track haole science boss's isms and skisms while he out oppressing the native bruddahs and stealing our land and the best wahines. Sovereignty now, but after a bruddah make his rent, don't you know?"

Clay grinned at the blond kid. "You're just a mess, aren't you?"

Kona lost his Rastafarian, laid-back-ness. "Look, I was born here when my parents were on vacation. I really am Hawaiian, kinda, and I really need this job. I'm going to lose my place to live if I don't make some money this week. I can't live on the beach in Paia again. All my shit got stolen last time."

"It says here that you last worked as a forensic calligrapher. What's that, handwriting analysis?"

"Uh, no, actually, it was a business I started where I would write people's suicide notes for them." Not a hint of pidgin in his speech, not a skankin' smidgen of reggae. "It didn't do that well. No one wants to kill himself in Hawaii. I think if I'd started it back in New Jersey, or maybe Portland, it would have gone over really well. You know business: location, location, location."

"I thought that was real estate." Clay actually felt a twinge of missed opportunity, here, for although he had spent his life having adventures, doing exactly what he wanted to do, and although he often felt like the dumbest guy in the room (because he'd surrounded himself with scientists), now, talking to Kona, he realized that he had never realized his full potential as a self-deluded blockhead. Ahhh . . . wistful regrets. Clay liked this kid.

"Look, I'm a water guy," Kona said. "I know boats, I know tides, I know waves, I love the ocean."

"You afraid of it?" Clay asked.

"Terrified."

"Good. Meet me at the dock tomorrow morning at eight-thirty."

⌘

NOW NATE RUBBED AT THE CRISSCROSSED BAND-AIDS ON HIS FORE-head as Clay went through the Pelican cases of camera equipment under the table across the room. The break-in and subsequent shit storm of activity had sidetracked him from what he'd seen this morning. It started to settle on him again like a black cloud of self-doubt, and he wondered whether he should even mention what he saw to Clay. In the world of behavioral biology, nothing existed until it was published. It didn't matter how much you knew—it wasn't real if it didn't appear in a scientific journal. But when it came to day-to-day life, publication was secondary. If he told Clay what he'd seen, it would suddenly become real. As with his attraction for Amy and the realization that years' worth of research was gone, he wasn't sure he wanted it to be real.

"So why did you need to send Amy out?" Clay asked.

"Clay, I don't see things I don't see, right? I mean, in all the time we've worked together, I haven't called something before the data backed it up, right?"

Clay looked up from his inventory to see the expression of consternation on his friend's face. "Look, Nate, if the kid bothers you that much, we can find someone else—"

"It's not the kid." Nate seemed to be weighing what he was going to say, not sure if he should say it, then blurted out, "Clay, I think I saw writing on the tail flukes of that singer this morning."

"What, like a pattern of scars that look like letters? I've seen that. I have a dolphin shot that shows tooth rakings on the animal's side that appear to spell out the word 'zap.' "

"No it was different. Not scars. It said, 'Bite me.' "

"Uh-huh," Clay said, trying not to make it sound as if he thought his friend was nuts. "Well, this break-in, Nate, it's shaken us all up."

"This was before that. Oh, I don't know. Look, I think it's on the film I shot. That's why I came in to take the film to the lab. Then I found this mess, so I sent the kid to the lab with my truck, even though I'm pretty sure he's a criminal. Let's table it until he gets back with the film, okay?" Nate turned and stared at the deskful of wires and parts, as if he'd quickly floated off into his own thoughts.

Clay nodded. He'd spent whole days in the same twenty-three-foot boat with the lanky scientist, and nothing more had passed between the two than the exchange of "Sandwich?" "Thanks."

When Nate was ready to tell him more, he would. In the meantime he would not press. You don't hurry a thinker, and you don't talk to him when he's thinking. It's just inconsiderate.

"What are you thinking?" Clay asked. Okay, he could be inconsiderate sometimes. His giant monitor was broken, and he was traumatized.

"I'm thinking that we're going to have to start over on a lot of these studies. Every piece of magnetic media in this place has been scrambled, but as far as I can tell, nothing is missing. Why would someone do that, Clay?"

"Kids," Clay said, inspecting a Nikon lens for damage. "None of my stuff is missing, and except for the monitor it seems okay."

"Right, your stuff."

"Yeah, my stuff."

"Your stuff is worth hundreds of thousands of dollars, Clay. Why wouldn't kids take your stuff? No one doesn't know that Nikon equipment is expensive, and no one on the island doesn't know that underwater housings are expensive, so who would just destroy the tapes and disks and leave everything?"

Clay put down the lens and stood up. "Wrong question."

"How is that the wrong question?"

"The question is, who could possibly care about our research other than us, the Old Broad, and a dozen or so biologists and whale huggers in the entire world? Face it, Nate, no one gives a damn about singing whales. There's no motive. The question is, who cares?"

Nate slumped in his chair. Clay was right. No one did care. People, the world, cared about the numbers of whales, so the survey guys, the whale counters, they actually collected data that people cared about. Why? Because if you knew how many whales you had, you knew how many you could or could not kill. People loved and understood and thought they could prove points and make money with the numbers. Behavior . . . well, behavior was squishy stuff used to entertain fourth-graders on Cable in the Classroom.

"We were really close, Clay," Nate said. "There's something in the song that we're missing. But without the tapes . . ."

Clay shrugged. "You heard one song, you heard 'em all." Which was also true. All the males sang the same song each season. The song might change from season to season, or even evolve through the season somewhat, but in any given population of humpbacks, they were all singing the same tune. No one had figured out exactly why.

"We'll get new samples."

"I'd already cleaned up the spectrographs, filtered them, analyzed them. It was all on the hard disks. That work was for specific samples."

"We'll do it again, Nate. We have time. No one is waiting. No one cares."

"You don't have to keep saying that."

"Well, it's starting to bother me, too, now," Clay said. "Who in the hell cares whether you figure out what's going on with humpback song?"

A kicked-off flip-flop flew into the room followed by the singsong Rastafarian-bruddah pomp of Kona returning, "Irie, Clay, me dready. I be bringing films and herb for the evening to welcome to Jah's mercy, mon. Peace."

Kona stood there, an envelope of negatives and contact sheet in one hand, a film can held high above his head in the other. He was looking up to it as if it held the elixir of life.

"You have any idea what he said?" Nate asked. He quickly crossed the room and snatched the negatives away from Kona.

"I think it's from the 'Jabberwocky,' " Clay replied. "You gave him cash to get the film processed? You can't give him cash."

"And this lonely stash can to fill with the sacred herb," Kona said. "I'll find me papers, and we can take the ship home to Zion, mon."

"You can't give him money and an empty film can, Nate. He sees it as a religious duty to fill it up."

Nate had pulled the contact sheet out of the envelope and was examining it with a loupe. He checked it twice, counting each frame, checking the registry numbers along the edge. Frame twenty-six wasn't there. He held the plastic page of negatives up to the light, looked through the images twice and the registry numbers on the edges three times before he threw them down, checked the earlier frames that Amy had shot of the whale tail, then crossed the room and grabbed Kona by the shoulders. "Where's frame twenty-six, goddamn it? What did you do with it?"

"This just like I get it, mon. I didn't do nothing."

"He's a criminal, Clay," Nate said. Then he grabbed the phone and called the lab.

All they could tell him was that the film had been processed normally and picked up from the bin in front. A machine cut the negatives before they went into the sleeves—perhaps it had snipped off the frame. They'd be happy to give Nate a fresh roll of film for his trouble.

≈

TWO HOURS LATER NATE SAT AT THE DESK, HOLDING A PEN AND LOOK-ing at a sheet of paper. Just looking at it. The room was dark except for the desk lamp, which reached out just far enough to leave darkness in all the corners where the unknown could hide. There was a nightstand, the desk, the chair, and a single bed with a trunk set at its end, a blanket on top as a cushion. Nathan Quinn was a tall man, and his feet hung off the end of the bed. He found that if he removed the supporting trunk, he dreamed of foundering in blue-water ocean and woke up gasping. The trunk was full of books, journals, and blankets, none of which had ever been removed since he'd shipped them to the island nine years ago. A centipede the size of a Pontiac had once lived in the bottom-right cor-ner of the trunk but had long since moved on once he realized that no one was ever going to bother him, so he could stand up on his hind hun-dred feet, hiss like a pissed cat, and deliver a deadly bite to a naked foot. There was a small television, a clock radio, a small kitchenette with two burners and a microwave, two full bookshelves under the window that looked out onto the compound, and a yellowed print of two of Gau-guin's Tahitian girls between the windows over the bed. At one time, be-fore the plantations had been automated, ten people probably slept in this room. In grad school at UC Santa Cruz, Nathan Quinn had lived in quarters about this same size. Progress.

The paper on Nate's desk was empty, the bottle of Myers's Dark Rum beside it half empty. The door and windows were open, and Nate could hear the warm trades rattling the fronds of two tall coconut palms out front. There was a tap on the door, and Nate looked up to see Amy silhouetted in the doorway. She stepped into the light.

"Nathan, can I come in?" She was wearing a T-shirt dress that hit her about midthigh.

Nate put his hand over the paper, embarrassed that there was nothing written on it. "I was just trying to put a plan together for—" He looked past the paper to the bottle, then back at Amy. "Do you want a drink?" He picked up the bottle, looked around for a glass, then just held the bottle out to her.

Amy shook her head. "Are you all right?"

"I started this work when I was your age. I don't know if I have the energy to start it all over again."

"It's a lot of work. I'm really sorry this happened."

"Why? You didn't do it. I was close, Amy. There's something that I've been missing, but I was close."

"It will still be there. You know, we have the field notes from the last couple of years. I'll help you put as much of it back together as I can."

"I know you will, but Clay's right. Nobody cares. I should have gone into biochemistry or become an ecowarrior or something."

"I care."

Nate looked at her feet to avoid looking her in the eye. "I know you do. But without the recordings . . . well—then . . ." He shrugged and took a sip from the rum bottle. "You can't drink, you know," he said, now the professor, now the Ph.D., now the head researcher. "You can't do anything or have anything in your life that gets in the way of re-searching whales."

"Okay," Amy said. "I just wanted to see if you were okay."

"Yeah, I'm okay."

"We'll get started putting it back together tomorrow. Good night, Nate." She backed out the door.

"Night, Amy." Nate noticed that she wasn't wearing anything under the T-shirt dress and felt sleazy for it. He turned his attention back to his blank piece of paper, and before he could figure out why, he wrote BITE ME in big block letters and underlined it so hard that he ripped the page.

CHAPTER FIVE

Hey, Buddy,
Why the Big Brain?

The next morning the four of them stood in a row on the front of the old Pioneer Hotel, looking across the Lahaina Harbor at the whitecaps in the channel. Wind was whipping the palm trees. Down by the breakwater two little girls were trying to surf waves whose faces were bumpy with wind chop and whose curls blew back over the crests like the hair of a sprinter.

"It could calm down," Amy said. She was standing next to Kona, thinking, *This guy's pecs are so cut you could stick business cards under them and they'd stay. And my, is he tan.* Where Amy came from, no one was tan, and she hadn't been in Hawaii long enough to realize that a good tan was just a function of showing up.

"Supposed to stay like this for the next three days," Nate said. As disappointed as he appeared to be, he was extraordinarily relieved that they wouldn't be going out this morning. He had a rogue hangover, and his eyes were bloodred behind his sunglasses. Self-loathing had set in, and he thought, *My life's work is shit, and if we went out there today and I didn't spend the morning retching over the side, I'd be tempted to drown myself.* He would rather have been thinking about whales, which is what he usually thought about. Then he noticed Amy sneaking glances at Kona's bare chest and felt even worse.

"Ya, mon. Kona can spark up a spliff and calm down that bumpy brine for all me new science dreadies. We can take the boat no matter what the wind be," Kona said. He was thinking, *I have no idea what the hell I'm talking about, but I really want to get out there with the whales.*

"Breakfast at Longi's, and then we'll see how it looks," Clay said. He was thinking, *We'll have breakfast at Longi's, and then we'll see how it looks.*

None of them moved. They just stood there, looking out at the blow-out channel. Occasionally a whale would blow, and the mist would run over the water like a frightened ghost.

"I'm buying," Clay said.

And they all headed up Front Street to Longi's restaurant, a two-story gray-and-white building, done in a New England architecture with shiplap siding and huge open windows that looked across Front Street, over the stone seawall, and out onto the Au' au Channel. By way of a shirt, Kona slipped on a tattered Nautica windbreaker he'd had knotted around his waist.

"You do a lot of sailing?" Amy asked, nodding to the Nautica logo. She intended the remark as dig, a return for Kona's saying, "And who be this snowy biscuit?" when they'd first met. At the time Amy had just introduced herself, but in retrospect she realized that she should probably have taken some offense to being called both snowy and a biscuit— *those things were objectifying, right?*

"Shark bait kit, me Snowy Biscuit," Kona answered, meaning that the windbreaker had come from a tourist. The Paia surfing community on the North Shore, from which Kona had recently come, had an economy based entirely on petty theft, mostly smash-and-grabs from rental cars.

As the host led them through the crowded dining room to a table by the windows, Clay leaned over Amy's shoulder and whispered, "A biscuit is a good thing."

"I knew that," Amy whispered back. "Like a tomato, right?"

"Heads up," Clay said, just as Amy plowed into a khaki package of balding ambition known as Jon Thomas Fuller, CEO of Hawaii Whale Inc., a nonprofit corporation with assets in the tens of millions that disguised itself as a research organization. Fuller had pushed his chair back to intercept Amy.

"Jon Thomas!" Clay smiled and reached around the flustered Amy to shake Fuller's hand. Fuller ignored Clay and took Amy by the waist, steadying her. "Hey, hey, there," Fuller said. "If you wanted to meet me, all you had to do was introduce yourself."

Amy grabbed his wrists and guided his hands to the table in front of him, then stepped back. "Hi, I'm Amy Earhart."

"I know who you are," said Fuller, standing now. He was only a little taller than Amy, very tan and very lean, with a hawk nose and a receding hairline like a knife. "What I don't know is why you haven't come to see me about a job."

Meanwhile, Nate, who had been thinking about whale song, had taken his seat, opened a menu, ordered coffee, and completely missed the fact that he was alone at the table. He looked up to see Jon Thomas Fuller holding his assistant by the waist. He dropped his menu and headed back to the site of the intercept.

"Well, partly"—Amy smiled at the three young women sitting at Fuller's table—"partly because I have some self-respect"—she curtsied—"and partly because you're a louse and a jamoke."

Fuller's dazzling grin dropped a level of magnitude. The women at his table, all dressed in khaki safari wear to approximate the Discovery Channel ideal of what a scientist should look like, made great shows of looking elsewhere, wiping their mouths, sipping water—not noticing their boss getting verbally bitch-slapped by a vicious research pixie.

"Nate," Fuller said, noticing that Nate had joined the group, "I heard about the break-in at your place. Nothing important missing, I hope."

"We're fine. Lost some recordings," Nate said.

"Ah, well, good. A lot of lowlifes on this island now." Fuller looked at Kona.

The surfer grinned. "Shoots, brah, you make me blush."

Fuller grinned. "How you doing, Kona?"

"All cool runnings, brah. Bwana Fuller got his evil on?"

There were neck-snapping double takes all around. Fuller nodded, then looked back at Quinn. "Anything we can do, Nate? There are a lot of our song recordings for sale in the shops, if those will help out. You guys get professional discount. We're all in this together."

"Thanks," Nate said just as Fuller sat down, then turned his back on all of them and resumed eating his breakfast, dismissing them. The women at the table looked embarrassed.

"Breakfast?" Clay said. He herded his team to their table.

They ordered and drank coffee in silence, each looking out across the street to the ocean, avoiding eye contact until Fuller and his group had left.

Nate turned to Amy. "A jamoke? What are you, living in a Cagney movie?"

"Who is that guy?" Amy asked. She snapped the corner off a piece of toast with more violence than was really necessary.

"What's a jamoke?" Kona asked.

"It's a flavor of ice cream, right?" Clay said.

Nate looked at Kona. "How do you know Fuller?" Nate held up his finger and shot a cautionary glare, the now understood signal for no Rasta/pidgin/bullshit.

"I worked the Jet Ski concession for him at Kaanapali."

Nate looked to Clay, as if to say, *You knew this?*

"Who is that guy?" Amy asked.

"He's the head of Hawaii Whale," Clay said. "Commerce masquerading as science. They use their permit to get three sixty-five-foot tourist boats right up next to the whales."

"That guy is a scientist?"

"He has a Ph.D. in biology, but I wouldn't call him a scientist. Those women he was with are his naturalists. I guess today was even too windy for them to go out. He's got shops all over the island—sells whale crap, nonprofit. Hawaii Whale was the only research group to oppose the Jet Ski ban during whale season."

"Because Fuller had money in the Jet Ski business," Nate added.

"I made six bucks an hour," Kona said.

"Nate's work was instrumental in getting the Jet Ski parasail ban done," Clay said. "Fuller doesn't like us."

"The sanctuary may take his research permit next," said Nate. "What science they do is bad science."

"And he blames you for that?" Amy asked.

"I—we have done the most behavioral stuff as it relates to sound in these waters. The sanctuary gave us some money to find out if the high-frequency noise from Jet Skis and parasail boats affected the behavior of the whales. We concluded that it did. Fuller didn't like it. It cost him."

"He's going to build a dolphin swim park, up La Perouse Bay way," Kona said.

"What?" Nate said.

"What?" said Clay.

"A swim-with-the-dolphins park?" said Amy.

"Ya, mon. Let you come from Ohio and get in the water with them bottlenose fellahs for two hundred dollar."

"You guys didn't know about this?" Amy was looking at Clay. He always seemed to know everything that was going on in the whale world.

"First I've heard of it, but they're not going to let him do it without some studies." He looked to Nate. "Are they?"

"It'll never happen if he loses his research permit," Nate said. "There'll be a review."

"And you'll be on the review board?" asked Amy.

"Nate's name would solidify it," Clay said. "They'll ask him."

"Not you?" Kona asked.

"I'm just the photographer." Clay looked out at the whitecaps in the channel. "Doesn't look like we'll be getting out today. Finish your breakfast, and then we'll go pay your rent."

Nate looked at Clay quizzically.

"I can't give him money," Clay said. "He'll just smoke it. I'm going to go pay his rent."

"Truth." Kona nodded.

"You don't still work for Fuller, do you, Kona?" Nate asked.

"Nate!" Amy admonished.

"Well, he was there when I found the office ransacked."

"Leave him alone," Amy said. "He's too cute to be bad."

"Truth," said Kona. "Sistah Biscuit speak nothin' but the truth. I be massive cute."

Clay set a stack of bills on the table. "By the way, Nate, you have a lecture at the sanctuary on Tuesday. Four days. You and Amy might want to use the downtime to put something together."

Nate felt as if he'd been smacked. "Four days? There's nothing there. It was all on those hard drives."

"Like I said, you might want to use the downtime."

CHAPTER SIX

Whale Wahine

As a biologist, Nate had a tendency to draw analogies between human behavior and animal behavior—probably a little more often than was strictly healthy. For instance, as he considered his attraction to Amy, he wondered why it had to be so complex. Why there had to be so many subtleties to the human mating ritual. *Why can't we be more like common squid?* he thought. The male squid simply swims up to the female squid, hands her a neat package of sperm, she tucks it under her mantle at her leisure, and they go on their separate ways, their duty to the species done. Simple, elegant, no nuance . . .

Nate held the paper cup out to Amy. "I poured some coffee for you."

"I'm all coffeed out, thanks," said Amy.

Nate set the cup down on the desk next to his own. He sat in front of the computer. Amy was perched on a high stool to his left going through the hardbound field journals covering the last four years. "Are you going to be able to put together a lecture out of this?" she asked.

Nate rubbed his temples. Despite a handful of aspirin and six cups of coffee, his head was still throbbing. "A lecture? About what?"

"Well, what were you planning to do a talk on before the office was ransacked? Maybe we can reconstruct it from the field notes and memory."

"I don't have that good a memory."

"Yes you do, you just need some mnemonics, which we have here in the field notes."

Her expression was as open and hopeful as a child's. She waited for something from him, just a word to set her searching for what he needed. The problem was, what he needed right now was not going to be found in biology field notes. He needed answers of another kind. It bothered him that Fuller had known about the break-in at the compound. It was too soon for him to have found out. It also bothered him that anyone could hold him in the sort of disdain that Fuller obviously did. Nate had been born and raised in British Columbia, and Canadians hate, above all things, to offend. It was part of the national consciousness. "Be polite" was an unwritten, unspoken rule, but ingrained into the psyche of an entire country. (Of course, as with any rule, there were exceptions: parts of Quebec, where people maintained the "dismissive to the point of confrontation, with subsequent surrender" mind-set of the French; and hockey, in which any Canadian may, with impunity, slam, pummel, elbow, smack, punch, body-check, and beat the shit out of, with sticks, any other human being, punctuated by profanities, name-calling, questioning parentage, and accusations of bestiality, usually—coincidentally—in French.) Nate was neither French-Canadian nor much of a hockey player, so the idea of having invoked enmity enough in someone to have that person ruin his research . . . He was mortified by it.

"Amy," he said, having spaced out and returned to the room in a matter of seconds, he hoped, "is there something that I'm missing about our work? Is there something in the data that I'm not seeing?"

Amy assumed the pose of Rodin's *The Thinker* on her stool, her chin teed up on her hand, her brow furrowed into moguls of earnest contemplation. "Well, Dr. Quinn, I would be able to answer that if you had shared the data with me, but since I only know what I've collected or what I've analyzed personally, I'd have to say, scientifically speaking, beats me."

"Thanks," Nate said. He smiled in spite of himself.

"You said there was something there that you were close to finding. In the song, I mean. What is it?"

"Well, if I knew that, it would be found, wouldn't it?"

"You must suspect. You have to have a theory. Tell me, and let's apply the data to the theory. I'm willing to do the work, reconstruct the data, but you've got to trust me."

"No theory ever benefited by the application of data, Amy. Data kills theories. A theory has no better time than when it's lying there naked, pure, unsullied by facts. Let's just keep it that way for a while."

"So you don't really have a theory?"

"Clueless."

"You lying bag of fish heads."

"I can fire you, you know. Even if Clay was the one that hired you, I'm not totally superfluous to this operation yet. I'm kind of in charge. I can fire you. Then how will you live?"

"I'm not getting paid."

"See, right there. Perfectly good concept ruined by the application of fact."

"So fire me." No longer *The Thinker*, Amy had taken on the aspect of a dark and evil elf.

"I think they're communicating," Nate said.

"Of course they're communicating, you maroon. You think they're singing because they like the sound of their own voices?"

"There's more to it than that."

"Well, tell me!"

"Who calls someone a maroon? What the hell is maroon?"

"It's a mook with a Ph.D. Don't change the subject."

"It doesn't matter. Without the acoustic data I can't even show you what I was thinking. Besides, I'm not sure that my cognitive powers aren't breaking down."

"Meaning what?"

Meaning that I'm starting to see things, he thought. *Meaning that despite the fact that you're yelling at me, I really want to grab you and kiss you,* he thought. *Oh, I am so fucked,* he thought. "Meaning I'm still a little hungover. I'm sorry. Let's see what we can put together from the notes."

Amy slipped off the stool and gathered the field journals in her arms.

"Where are you going?" Nate said. Had he somehow offended her?

"We have four days to put together a lecture. I'm going to go to my cabin and do it."

"How? On what?"

"I'm thinking, 'Humpbacks: Our Wet and Wondrous Pals of the Deep—' "

"There's going to be a lot of researchers there. Biologists—" Nate interrupted.

" '—and Why We Should Poke Them with Sticks.' "

"Better," Nate said.

"I got it covered," she said, and she walked out.

For some reason he felt hopeful. Excited. Just for a second. Then, after he'd watched her walk out, a wave of melancholy swept over him and for the thirtieth time that day he regretted that he hadn't just become a pharmacist, or a charter captain, or something that made you feel more alive, like a pirate.

THE OLD BROAD LIVED ON A VOLCANO AND BELIEVED THAT THE whales talked to her. She called about noon, and Nate knew it was her before he even answered. He knew, because she always called when it was too windy to go out.

"Nathan, why aren't you out in the channel?" the Old Broad said.

"Hello, Elizabeth, how are you today?"

"Don't change the subject. They told me that they want to talk to you. Today. Why aren't you out there?"

"You know why I'm not out there, Elizabeth. It's too windy. You can see the whitecaps as well as I can." From the slope of Haleakala, the Old Broad watched the activity in the channel with a two-hundred-power celestial telescope and a pair of "big eyes" binoculars that looked like stereo bazookas on precision mounts that were anchored into a ton of concrete.

"Well, they're upset that you're not out there. That's why I called."

"And I appreciate your calling, Elizabeth, but I'm in the middle of something."

Nate hoped he didn't sound too rude. The Old Broad meant well. And they, in a way, were all at the mercy of her generosity, for although she had "donated" the Papa Lani compound, she hadn't exactly signed it over to them. They were in a sort of permanent lease situation. Elizabeth Robinson was, however, very generous and very kindhearted indeed, even if she was a total loon.

"Nathan, I am not a total loon," she said.

Oh yes you are, he thought. "I know you're not," he said. "But I really have to get some work done today."

"What are you working on?" Elizabeth asked. Nate could hear her tapping a pencil on her desk. She took notes during their conversations. He didn't know what she did with the notes, but it bothered him.

"I have a lecture at the sanctuary in four days." Why, why had he told her? Why? Now she'd rattle down the mountain in her ancient Mercedes that looked like a Nazi staff car, sit in the audience, and ask all the questions that she knew in advance he couldn't answer.

"That shouldn't be hard. You've done that before, what, twenty times?"

"Yes, but someone broke in to the compound yesterday, Elizabeth. All my notes, the tapes, the analysis—it's all destroyed."

There was silence on the line for a moment. Nate could hear the Old Broad breathing. Finally, "I'm really sorry, Nathan. Is everyone all right?"

"Yes, it happened while we were out working."

"Is there anything I can do? I mean, I can't send much, but if—"

"No, we're all right. It's just a lot of work that I have to start over." The Old Broad might have been loaded at one time, and she certainly would be again if she sold the land where Papa Lani stood, but Nate didn't think that she had a lot of money to spare after the last bear market. Even if she did, this wasn't a problem that could be solved with cash.

"Well, then, you get back to work, but try to get out tomorrow. There's a big male out there who told me he wants you to bring him a hot pastrami on rye."

Nate grinned and almost snorted into the phone. "Elizabeth, you know they don't eat while they're in these waters."

"I'm just relaying the message, Nathan. Don't you snicker at me. He's a big male, broad, like he just came down from Alaska—frankly, I don't know why he'd be hungry, he's as big as a house. But anyway, Swiss and hot English mustard, he was very clear about that. He has very unusual markings on his flukes. I couldn't see them from here, but he says you'll know him."

Nate felt his face go numb with something approximating shock. "Elizabeth—"

"Call if you need anything, Nathan. My love to Clay. Aloha."

Nathan Quinn let the phone slip from his fingers, then zombie-stumbled out of the office and back to his own cabin, where he decided he was going to nap and keep napping until he woke up to a world that wasn't so irritatingly weird.

❧

RIGHT ON THE EDGE OF A DREAM WHERE HE WAS GLEEFULLY STEERING a sixty-foot cabin cruiser up Second Street in downtown Seattle, plowing aside slow-moving vehicles while Amy, clad in a silver bikini and looking uncharacteristically tan, stood in the bow and waved to people who had come to the windows of their second-story offices to marvel at the freedom and power of the Mighty Quinn—right on the edge of a perfect dream, Clay burst into the room. Talking.

"Kona's moving into cabin six."

"Get some lines in the water, Amy," Nate said from the drears of morpheum opus. "We're coming up on Pike's Place Market, and there's fish to be had."

Clay waited, not quite smiling, not quite not, while Nate sat up and rubbed sleep from his eyes. "Driving a boat on the street?" Clay said, nodding. All skippers had that dream.

"Seattle," said Nate. "The Zodiac lives in cabin six."

"We haven't used the Zodiac in ten years, it won't hold air." Clay went to the closet that acted as a divider between the living/sleeping area and the kitchen. He pulled down a stack of sheets, then towels. "You wouldn't believe how they had this kid living, Nate. It was a tin industrial building, out by the airport. Twenty, thirty of them, in little stalls with cots and not enough room to swing a dead cat. The wiring was extension cords draped over the tops of the stalls. Six hundred a month for that."

Nate shrugged. "So? We lived that way the first couple of years. It's what you do. We might need cabin six for something. Storage or something."

"Nope," said Clay. "That place was a sweat box and a fire hazard. He's not living there. He's our guy."

"But Clay, he's only been with us for a day. He's probably a criminal."

"He's our guy," said Clay, and that was that. Clay had very strong views on loyalty. If Clay had decided that Kona was their guy, he was their guy.

"Okay," said Nate, feeling as if he had just invited the Medusa in for a sandwich. "The Old Broad called."

"How is she?"

"Still nuts."

"How're you?"

"Getting there."

CHAPTER SEVEN

Sanctuary, Sanctuary, Cried the Humpback

When a visitor first drives into the Hawaiian Islands Humpback Whale Sanctuary—five baby blue shiplap buildings trimmed out in cobalt, crouching on the edge of the huge Maalaea Bay and overlooking the ruins of an ancient saltwater fish pond—his first reaction is usually "Hey, not much of a sanctuary. You could get maybe three whales in those buildings, tops." Soon, however, he realizes that these buildings are simply the offices and visitor centers. The sanctuary itself covers the channels that run from Molokai to the Big Island of Hawaii, between Maui, Lanai, and Kahoolawe, as well as the north shores of Oahu and Kauai, in which there is plenty of room for a whole bunch of whales, which is why they are kept there.

There were about a hundred people milling around outside the lecture hall when Nate and Amy pulled into the parking lot in the pickup.

"Looks like a good turnout?" Amy said. She'd attended only one of the sanctuary's weekly lectures, and that one had been given by Gilbert Box, an ill-tempered biologist doing survey work under a grant for the International Whaling Commission, who droned through numbers and graphs until the ten people in attendance would have killed a whale themselves just to shut him up.

"It's about average for us. Behavior always draws more than survey. We're the sexy ones," Nate said with a grin.

Amy snorted. "Oh, yeah, you guys are the Mae Wests of the nerd world."

"We're action nerds," Nate said. "Adventure nerds. Nerds of romance."

"Nerds," Amy said.

Nate could see the skeletal Gilbert Box standing off to the side of the crowd under a straw hat whose brim was so wide it could have afforded shade for three additional people and behind a pair of enormous wraparound sunglasses suitable for welding or as a shield from nuclear flash. His gaunt face was still smeared with residue of the white zinc oxide he used for sun protection when out on the water. He wore a long-sleeved khaki shirt and trousers and leaned on a white sun umbrella that he was never seen without. It was a half hour before sunset, a warm breeze was coming off Maalaea Bay, and Gilbert Box looked like Death out for his after-dinner stroll before a busy night of e-mailing heart attacks and tumors to a few million lucky winners.

Nate had given Box the nickname "the Count," after the *Sesame Street* vampire with the obsessive-compulsive need to count things. (Nate had been too old for *Sesame Street* as a preschooler, but he'd watched it through grade ten while baby-sitting his younger brother, Sam.) People agreed that the Count was the perfect name for a survey guy with an aversion to water and sunlight, and the name had caught on even outside Nate and Clay's immediate sphere of influence.

Panic rattled up Nate's spine. "They're going to know we're faking it. The Count will call us on it the first time I say something that we don't have the data to back up."

"How's he going to know? You had the data a week ago. Besides, what's this 'we'? I'm just running the projector."

"Thanks."

"There's Tarwater," Amy said. "Who are those women he's talking to?"

"Probably just some whale huggers," Nate said, pretending that all of his mental faculties were required for him to squeeze the pickup into the four adjacent empty parking spaces. The women Tarwater was talking to were Margaret Painborne, Ph.D., and Elizabeth "Libby" Quinn, Ph.D. They worked together with a couple of very butch young women studying cow/calf behavior and social vocalizations. They were doing good work, Nate thought, even if it appeared to have a gender-based agenda. Margaret was in her late forties, short and round, with long gray hair that she kept perpetually tied back in a braid. Libby was almost a decade younger, long-legged and lean, blond hair going gray, cut short, and she had once, not too long ago, been Nathan Quinn's third wife. A second and totally different wave of anxiety swept over Quinn. This was the first time he'd encountered Libby since Amy joined the team.

"They don't look like whale huggers," Amy said. "They look like re-searchers."

"How is that?"

"They look like action nerds." Amy snorted again and crawled out of the truck.

"That's not very professional," Nate said, "that snorting-laugh thing you do." But Amy had already walked off toward the lecture hall, a carousel of slides under her arm.

Nate counted more than thirty researchers in the crowd as he walked up. And those were just the ones he was acquainted with. New people would be coming back and forth from the mainland all season—grad students, film crews, reporters, National Fisheries people, patrons—all hitch-hiking on the very few research permits that were issued for the sanctuary.

For some reason Amy made a beeline for Cliff Hyland and his navy watchdog, Tarwater, who was out of uniform in Dockers and a Tommy Bahama shirt, but still out of place because his clothes were ironed to razor creases—his Topsiders had been spit-shined, and he stood as if there were a cold length of rebar wired to his spine.

"Hey, Amy," Cliff said. "Sorry to hear about the break-in. Bad?"

"We'll be all right," Amy said.

Nate strolled up behind Amy. "Hey, Cliff. Captain." He nodded to each.

"Sorry to hear about the break-in, Nate," Cliff said again. "Hope you guys didn't lose anything important."

"We're fucked," Nate said.

And Tarwater smiled—for the first time ever, Nate thought.

"We're fine." Amy grinned and brandished her carousel of slides like a talisman of power.

"I'm thinking about getting a job at Starbucks," Nate said.

"Hey, Cliff, what are you guys working on?" Amy asked, having somehow moved close enough into Cliff Hyland's personal space to have to look up at him with big, girly-blue eyes and the aspect of a fascinated child.

Nate cringed. It was . . . well, it was just not done. You didn't ask, not outright like that.

"Just some stuff for the navy," Cliff said, obviously wanting to back away from Amy, but knowing that if he did, somehow he'd lose face.

Nate watched while Amy grated his friend's middle-aged irrelevance against his male ego merely by stepping a foot closer. There, too, was a reaction from Tarwater, as the younger man seemed to be irritated by the fact that Amy was paying attention to Cliff. Or maybe he was just irritated with Amy because she was irritating. Sometimes Nate had to remind himself not to think like a biologist.

"You know, Cliff," Amy said, "I was looking at a map the other day—and I want you to brace yourself, because this may come as a shock—but there's no coastline in Iowa. I mean, doesn't that get in the way of studying marine mammals?"

"Sure, now you bring that up," Cliff said. "Where were you ten years ago when I accepted the position?"

"Middle school," Amy said. "What's in the big case on your boat? Sonar array? You guys doing another LFA study?"

Tarwater coughed.

"Amy," Nate interrupted, "we'd better get set up."

"Right," Amy said. "Nice seeing you guys."

She moved on. Nate grinned, just for a second. "Sorry, you know how it is?"

"Yeah." Cliff Hyland smiled. "We've got two grad students working with us this season."

"But *we* left our grommets at home, to analyze data," Tarwater added.

Nate and Cliff looked at each other like two old broken-toothed lions long driven from the pride—tired, but secure in the knowledge that if they teamed up, they could eat the younger male alive. Cliff shrugged, almost imperceptibly, that small gesture communicating, *Sorry, Nate, I know he's an asshole, but what am I going to do? It's funding.*

"I'd better go in," Nate said, patting the notes in his shirt pocket. He passed a couple more acquaintances, saying hello as he went by, then inside the door ran right into a minor nightmare: Amy talking to his ex-wife, Libby, and her partner, Margaret.

It had been like this: They'd met ten years ago, summer in Alaska, a remote lodge on Baranof Island on the Chatham Strait, where scientists were given access to a couple of rigid-hulled Zodiacs and all the canned beans, smoked salmon, and Russian vodka they could consume. Nate had come to observe the feeding behavior of his beloved humpbacks and record social sounds that might help him to interpret the song they sang when in Hawaii. Libby was doing biopsies on the population of resident (fish-eating) killer whales to prove that all the different pods were indeed part of one clan related by blood. He was two years divorced from his second wife. Libby, at thirty, was two months from finishing her doctoral dissertation in cetacean biology. Consequently, since high school she hadn't had time for anything but research—seasonal affairs with boat skippers, senior researchers, grad students, fishermen, and the occasional photographer or documentary filmmaker. She wasn't particularly promiscuous, but there was a sea of men you were set adrift in if you were going to study whales, and if you didn't want to spend your life alone, you pulled into a convenient, if scruffy, port from time to time. The transience of the work drove a lot of women out of the field. On the other hand, Nate tried to solve the male side of the equation by marrying other whale researchers, reasoning that only someone who was equally obsessed, distracted, and single-minded would be able to tolerate those qualities in a mate. That sort of reasoning, of course, was testament to the victory of romanticism over reason, irony over rationality, and pure foolishness over common sense. The only thing that being married to another scientist had gotten Nate was a reprieve from being asked what he was thinking about while lying in bed in a postcoital cuddle. They knew what he was thinking about, because they were thinking about the same thing: whales.

They were both lean and blond and weather-beaten, and one evening, as they were portaging gear from their respective Zodiacs, Libby unzipped her survival suit and tied the sleeves around her waist so she could move more freely. Nate said, "You look good in that."

No one, absolutely no one, looks good in a survival suit (unless a Day-Glo orange marshmallow man is your idea of a hot date), but Libby didn't even make the effort to roll her eyes. "I have vodka and a shower in my cabin," she said.

"I have a shower in my cabin, too," Nate said.

Libby just shook her head and trudged up the path to the lodge. Over her shoulder she called, "In five minutes there's going to be a naked woman in my shower. You got one of those?"

"Oh," said Nate.

THEY WERE BOTH STILL LEAN, BUT NO LONGER BLOND. NATE WAS completely gray, and Libby was getting there. She smiled when he approached. "We heard about the break-in, Nate. I meant to call you."

"That's okay," he said. "Not much you can do."

"That's what you think," Amy said. She was bouncing on the balls of her feet as if she were going to explode or Tigger off across the room any second.

"I think these might mitigate the loss a little," Libby said. She slung her day pack off her shoulder, reached in, and came out with a handful of CDs in paper sleeves. "You forgot about these, I'll bet? You loaned them to us last season so we could pull off any social noises in the background."

"It's all the singer recordings from the last ten years," Amy said. "Isn't that great!"

Nate felt as if he might faint. To lose ten years' work, then reconcile the loss, only to have it handed back to him. He put his hand on Libby's shoulder to steady himself. "I don't know what to say. I thought you gave those back."

"We made copies." Margaret stepped over to Quinn and in doing so got a foot between him and his ex-wife. "You said it would be okay. We were only using them for comparison to our own samples."

"No, it's okay," Nate said. He almost patted her shoulder, but as he moved in that direction she flinched and he let his hand drop. "Thank you, Margaret."

Margaret had interposed herself completely between Nate and Libby, making a barrier of her own body (behavior she'd obviously picked up from her cow/calf studies—a humpback mother did the same thing when boats or amorous males approached her calf).

Amy snatched the handful of CDs from Libby. "I'd better go through these. I can probably come up with a few relevant samples to play along with the slides if I hurry."

"I'll go with you," Margaret said, eyeing Amy. "My handwriting on the catalog numbers leaves something to be desired."

And off they went toward the projection station in the middle of the hall, leaving Nate standing with Libby, wondering exactly what had just transpired.

"She really does have an extraordinary ass, Nate," Libby said as she watched Amy walk away.

"Yep," Nate said, not wanting to have this conversation. "She's very bright, too."

Sometime in the last week a tiny voice in his head had started asking, *Could this get any weirder?* In two minutes he'd gone from anxiety to embarrassment to anxiety to relief to gratitude to scoping chicks with his ex-wife. *Oh, yes, little voice, it can always get weirder.*

"I think Margaret may be on a recruiting mission," Libby said. "I hope she checked our budget before she left."

"Amy's working for free," Nate said.

Libby leaned up on tiptoes and whispered, "I believe that a starting position on the all-girl team has just opened up." Then she kissed his cheek. "You knock 'em dead tonight, Nate." And she was off after Amy and Margaret.

Clay and Kona arrived just as Libby walked away, and, irritatingly, Kona was checking out Libby from behind.

"Irie, Boss Nate. Who's the biscuit auntie suckin' face with ya?" (Like many authentic Hawaiians, Kona called any woman a generation older "auntie," even if he was horning after her.)

"You brought him here," Nate said to Clay without turning to face him.

"He's got to learn," Clay said. "Libby seemed friendly."

"She's chasing Amy."

"Oh, she a blackheart thief that would take a man's Snowy Biscuit to have a punaani nosh. That Snowy Biscuit belong our tribe."

"Libby was Nate's third wife," Clay volunteered, as if that would somehow immediately illuminate why the blackheart Libby was trying to steal the Snowy Biscuit from their tribe.

"Truth?" Kona said, shaking his great gorgonation of dreadlocks in rag-doll confusion. "You married a lesbian?"

"Whale willies," said Clay, adding neither insight nor illumination.

"I should go over my notes," Nate said.

CHAPTER EIGHT

A Rippin' Talk

Biology," said the pseudo Hawaiian, "dat bitch make sex puppets of everyone." Clay had just told him the story. The story was this:

Five years into her marriage to Nathan Quinn, Libby had gone for the summer to the Bering Sea to put satellite-tracking tags on female right whales. She had already begun working with Margaret Painborne, who was at the time trying to find out more about the mating and gestation behavior of right whales. The best way to do that was to keep constant tabs on the females. Now, sexing whales can be an incredibly difficult task, as their genitalia, for hydrodynamic reasons, are all internal. Without a biopsy or without being in the water with the animal (which means death in three minutes in the Bering Sea), about the only way to determine sex is to catch a female when she is with her calf or while the animals are mating. Libby and Margaret had decided to tag the animals while they were mating. Their base ship was an eighty-foot schooner loaned to the project by Scripps, but to do the actually tagging they used a nimble twelve-foot Zodiac with a forty-horse engine.

They'd spotted a female trying to evade the advances of two giant males. The right whale is one of the few animals in the world that uses a washout strategy for mating. That is, the females mate with several males, but the one who can wash out the others' seed most efficiently will pass his genes on to the next generation. Consequently, the guy with the largest tackle often wins, and male right whales have the biggest tackle in the world, with testes that weigh up to a ton and ten-foot penises that are not only long but prehensile, able to reach around a female from the side and introduce themselves on the sly.

Libby took the front of the boat, where she braced herself with a fifteen-foot fiberglass pole tipped with a barbed stainless point attached to the satellite unit. Margaret steered the outboard, maneuvering over frigid seven-foot seas, into the position where Libby could set the tag. Right whales are not particularly fast (whalers caught them in rowboats, for Christ's sake), but they are big and broad, and in the frenzy of a mating chase, a small Zodiac provides about as much protection from their thrashing, sixty-ton bodies as would wearing aluminum-foil armor to a joust. And noble Libby, action-girl nerd that she was, did look somewhat like a gallant knight in Day-Glo orange, her lance ready to strike as her trusty warhorse, Evinrude, powered her over the waves.

And as they approached the big female, a male on either side of her, the two sandwiching her so she could not escape, she rolled over onto her back, presenting her genitals to the sky. At that she slowed, and Margaret steered between the two tails of the males so Libby could set the tag. The female stopped then and floated up under the Zodiac. Margaret powered down the motor so as not to rake the animal with the prop.

"Shit!" Libby screamed. "Get us off! Get us off!" A swipe from the flukes of any of the animals would put them in the water, minutes from hypothermia and death. Libby had rolled her survival suit down so she could maneuver the harpoon. She'd be pulled under in seconds.

Suddenly, out of the water on either side of them came two huge penises, the males searching for their mark, moving closer to the female, producing waves that knocked the two women into the floor of the boat. Above them the two pink towers curved around looking for their target, feeling the edges of the boat, running slime across the rubber, over the biologists, poking, beating about, and generally abusing the women. The female now had the Zodiac centered exactly over her genitals, using the rubber boat as an ad hoc diaphragm. Then the two giant whale willies encountered one another in the middle of the Zodiac, and each evidently thinking that the other had found his target and not wanting to be left out, they let loose with great gushing gouts of sticky whale semen, filling the boat, covering the equipment, the scientists, washing the gunwales, swamping the motor, generally leaving everything but the gal whale completely and disgustingly jizzed. Mission accomplished, off they swam to strain a little postcoital krill out of the fray. Margaret suffered a concussion and a partially detached retina, Libby a dislocated shoulder and various scrapes and bruises, but the real trauma could not be assuaged with snaps, slings, and Betadine.

Several weeks later Libby rejoined Nate, who was down at the Chatham Strait with Clay filming feeding behavior. She walked into his cabin, hugged him, then stepped back and said, "Nate, I don't think I want to be married anymore." But what she really meant was "I'm done with penises forever, Nate, and pleasant as you are, I know that you are still attached to one. I've had my fill, so to speak. I'm moving on."

"Okay," Nate said. He told Clay later that for hours he had been feeling hungry and kept telling himself that he should stop working and go eat, but after Libby showed up, then left, he realized that he hadn't been hungry at all. The emptiness inside was from feeling lonesome. And Nate had stayed relatively lonesome and mostly heartbroken since that day (although he didn't whine about it, he just wore it). Clay didn't tell Kona this part. Confessions made over whiskey and campfires were privileged communication. Loyalty.

"SO," SAID NATE, "SINCE THE SONG APPEARS, IN MOST CASES, TO ACTU-ally draw the attention of other males, who often join up with the singer, it would seem that the song cannot be directly connected to mating activity, other than it happens in the mating season. And since no one has actually observed humpbacks mating, even this assumption could be in error. If, indeed, the song is the male attempting to define his territory, it would seem ineffective, since other males tend to join singers, even those escorting cow/calf pairs. The study recommends that more studies be done to find out if there is, as previously thought, any direct correlation between humpback song and mating activity. Thank you. I'll take your questions."

Hands went up. Here it came: the crystal gazers, the whale huggers, the hippies, the hunters, the tourists, the developers, the wackos, the researchers (God help us, the researchers), and the idly curious. Nate didn't mind the curious. They were the only ones without an agenda. Everyone else was looking for confirmations, not answers. Should he go to a researcher first? Get it out of the way? Might as well go right to the dark side.

"Yes, Gilbert." He pointed to the Count. The tall researcher had taken off his sunglasses but had pulled down the brim of his hat as if to conceal the glowing red coals of his eyes. Or maybe Nate was just imagining that.

The Count said, "So with these small samplings—what was it, five instances of interactions among singers and others?—there's no real conclusion that you can reach about the relation to breeding or the robustness of the population? Correct?"

Nate sighed. *Fuckwad,* he thought. He spoke to the strange faces in the audience, the nonprofessionals. "As you know, Dr. Box, samples for whale-behavior studies are usually very small. It's understood that we have to extrapolate more from the data with whales than with other animals who are more easily observed. Small samples are an accepted limitation of the field."

"So what you are saying," Box continued, "is that you are trying to extrapolate the behavior of an animal that spends less than three percent of its time on the surface from observing its behavior on the surface. Isn't that akin to trying to extrapolate all of human civilization from looking at people's legs underwater at the beach? I mean, I don't see how you could possibly do it."

Nate looked around the room, hoping that one of the other behavior researchers might jump in, help him out, throw a bone to the podium, but apparently they were all finding the displays on the bulletin boards, the ceiling fans, or the wooden floor planks irresistibly interesting.

"Lately we've been spending more and more time observing the animals under the water. Clay Demodocus has over six hundred hours of videotape of humpback behavior underwater. But it's only recently, with digital videotape and rebreather technology, that underwater observation has become practical to do to any extent. And we still have the problem of propulsion. No diver can swim fast enough to keep up with the humpbacks when they're traveling. I think all the researchers in this room understand the value of observing the animals in the water, and it goes without saying that any research without consideration of underwater behavior is incomplete. You understand that, I'm sure, Dr. Box."

There were a few stifled snickers around the room. Nathan Quinn smiled. The Count would not go into the water, under any circumstances. He was either terrified of it or allergic to it, but it was obvious from watching him on his boat that he wanted no contact whatsoever with the water. Still, if he was going to get his funding from the International Whaling Commission, he had to get out there and count whales. *On* the water, never *in* it. Quinn believed that Box did bad science, and because of that he had gone into consulting, the "dark side." He performed studies and provided data for the highest bidder, and Nate had no doubt that the data was skewed to the agenda of the funding. Some nations in the IWC wanted to lift the moratorium on hunting whales, but first they had to prove that the populations had recovered enough to sustain hunting. Gilbert Box was getting them their numbers. Nate was happy to have embarrassed Box. He waited for the gaunt scientist to nod before he took the next question.

"Yes, Margaret."

"Your study seems to focus on the perspective of the male animals, without consideration for the female's role in the behavior. Could you speak to that?"

Jeez, what a surprise, thought Nate. "Well, I think there's good work being done on the cow/calf behavior, as well as on surface-active groups, which we assume is mating-related activity, but since my work concerns singers and as far as we know, all singers are males, I tend to observe more male behavior." There, that should do it.

"So you can't say definitively that the females are not the ones controlling the behavior?"

"Margaret, as my research assistant has repeatedly pointed out to me, the only thing I can say definitively about humpbacks is that they are big and wet."

Everyone laughed. Quinn looked at Amy and she winked at him, then, when he looked back to Margaret, he saw Libby beside her, winking at him as well. But at least the tension among the researchers was broken, and Quinn noticed that Captain Tarwater and Jon Thomas Fuller and his entourage were no longer raising their hands to ask questions. Perhaps they realized that they weren't going to learn anything, and they certainly didn't want to try to pursue their own agendas in front of a crowd and be slapped down the way Gilbert Box had. Quinn took the questions from the nonscientists.

"Could they just be saying hi?"

"Yes."

"If they don't eat here, and it's not for mating, then why do they sing?"

"That's a good question."

"Do you think they know that we've been contacted by aliens and are trying to contact the mother ship?"

Ah, always good to hear from the wacko fringe, Nate thought. "No, I don't think that."

"Maybe they're using their sonar to find other whales."

"As far as we know, baleen whales, toothless whales like the humpbacks who strain their food from the sea through sheets of baleen, don't echolocate the way toothed whales do."

"Why do they jump all the time? Other whales don't jump like that."

"Some think that they are sloughing skin or trying to knock off parasites, but after years of watching them, I think that they just like making a splash—the sensation of air on their skin. The way you might like to dangle your feet in a fountain. I think they're just goofing off."

"I heard that someone broke into your office and destroyed all of your research. Who do you think would want to do that?"

Nate paused. The woman who had asked the question was holding a reporter's steno pad. *Maui Times,* he guessed. She had stood to ask her question, as if she were attending a press conference rather than a casual lecture.

"What you have to ask yourself," said Nate, "is who could possibly care about research on singers?"

"And who would that be?"

"Me, a few people in this room, and perhaps a dozen or so researchers around the world. At least for now. Perhaps as we find out more, more people will be interested."

"So you're saying that someone in this room broke into your offices and destroyed all your research?"

"No. As a biologist, one of the things you have to guard against is applying motives where there are none and reading more into a behavior than the data actually support. Sort of like the answer to the 'why do they jump?' question. You could say that it's part of an incredibly complex system of communication, and you might be right, but the obvious answer, and probably the correct one, is that the whales are goofing off. I think the break-in was just a random act of vandalism that has the appearance of motive." *Bullshit,* Quinn thought.

"Thank you, Dr. Quinn," said the reporter. She sat down.

"Thank you all for coming," said Nate.

Applause. Nate arranged his notes as people gathered around the podium.

"That was bullshit," Amy said.

"Complete bullshit," said Libby Quinn.

"What a load of crap," said Cliff Hyland.

"Rippin' talk, Doc," Kona said, "Marley's ghost was in ye."

CHAPTER NINE

Relativity

Leathery bar girls worked the charter booths at the harbor, smoking Basic 100s and talking in voices that sounded like 151 rum poured into hot grease—a jigger of friendly to the liter of harsh. They were thirty-five or sixty-five, the color of mahogany, skinny and strong from living on boats, liquor, fish, and disappointment. They'd come here from a dozen coastal towns, some sailing from the mainland in small craft but forgetting to save enough courage for the trip home. Marooned. Man to man, boat to boat, year to year—salt and sun and drinking had left them dry enough to cough dust. If they lasted a hundred years—and some would—then one moonless night a great hooded wraith would swoop into the harbor and take them off to their own craggy island—uncharted and unseen more than once by any living man—and there they would keep the enchantment of the sea alive: lure lost sailors to the shore, suck out all of their fluids, and leave their desiccated husks crumbling on the rocks for the crabs and the black gulls. Thus were the sea hags born . . . but that's another story. Today they were just razzing Clay for leading two girls down the dock.

"Just like outboards, Clay, you gotta have two to make sure one's always running," called Margie, who had once, after ten mai-tais, tried to go down on the wooden sea captain who guarded the doorway of the Pioneer Inn.

Debbie, who had a secret source for little-boy pee that she put in the ears of the black-coral divers when they got ear infections, said, "You give that young one the first watch, Clay. Let her rest up a bit."

"Morning, ladies," Clay tossed over his shoulder. He was grinning and blushing, his ears showing red even where they weren't sunburned. Fifty years old, he'd dived every sea, been attacked by sharks, survived malaria and Malaysian pirates, ridden in a titanium ball with a window five miles down into the Tonga Trench, and still he blushed.

Clair, Clay's girlfriend of four years, a forty-year-old Japanese-Hawaiian schoolteacher who moved like she was doing the hula to a Sousa march (strange mix of regal order and island breeze), backhanded a hang-loose shaka at the cronettes and said, grinning, "She just along to pour buckets on his reels girls, keep him from burning up."

"Oh, you guys are so friggin' nautical," said Amy, who was wrestling with a huge Pelican case that held the rebreather. The case slipped out of her grip and barked her shin before she caught it. "Ouch. Damn it. Oh yeah, everyone loves your salty friggin' charm."

A chorus of cackles from the charter booths wheezed into coughing fits. Back to the cats, the cauldrons, the coconut oil, the sacred Jimmy Buffett songs sung at midnight into the ear of drunken, white-bearded Hemingway wanna-bes to make that rum-soaked member rise from the dead just this one last time. The leathery bar girls turned back to their business as Kona passed by.

"Irie, Sistah Amy. Give up ye burden," said Kona, bounding down the dock to sweep the heavy rebreather out of Amy's grip and up onto his shoulder.

Amy rubbed her arm. "Thanks. Where's Nate?"

"He go to the fuel dock to get coffee for the whole tribe. A lion, him."

"Yeah, he's a good guy. You'll be going out with him today. I have to go along with Clay and Clair as a safety diver."

"Slippers off in the boat," Clay said to Clair for the hundredth time. She rolled her eyes and kicked off her flip-flops before stepping down into the *Always Confused*. She offered Clay a hand, and he steadied her as if escorting a lady from the king's court to the ballroom floor.

Kona handed the rebreather down to Clay. "I can safety-dive."

"You'll never be able to clear your ears. You can't pinch your nostrils shut with those nose rings in."

"They come out. Look, out they come." He tossed the rings to Amy and she deftly sidestepped, letting them plop into the water.

"Oops."

"Amy's a certified diver, kid. Sorry. You're with Nate today."

"He know that?"

"Yeah, does he know that?" asked Clair.

"He will soon. Get those lines, would you, Amy."

"I can drive the boat." Kona was on the edge of pleading.

"No one but me drives the boat," said Clay.

"I'm driving the boat," corrected Clair.

"You have to sleep with Clay to drive the boat," said Amy.

"You just do what Nate tells you," Clay said. "You'll be fine."

"If I sleep with Amy can I drive the boat?"

"Nobody drives the boat," Clay said.

"I drive the boat," Clair said.

"Nobody sleeps with Amy," Amy said.

"I sleep with Amy," Clair said.

And everyone stopped and looked at Clair.

"Who wants cream?" asked Nate, arriving at that moment with a paper tray of coffee cups. "You can do your own sugar."

"That's what I'm saying," said Clair. "Sisters are doing it for themselves."

And Nate hung there in space, holding a cup and a sugar packet, a wooden stir stick, a baffled expression.

Clair grinned. "Kidding. Jeez, you guys."

Everyone breathed. Coffee was distributed, gear was loaded, Clay drove the *Always Confused* out of the harbor, pausing to wave to the Count and his crew, who were loading gear into a thirty-foot rigid-hull Zodiac normally used for parasailing. The Count pulled down the brim of his hat and stood in the bow of the Zodiac, his sun umbrella at port arms, looking like a skeletal statue of Washington crossing the Lethe. The crew waved, Gilbert Box scowled.

"I like him," Clay said. "He's predictable."

But Amy and Clair missed the comment. They were applying sunscreen and indulging in girl talk in the bow.

"You can talk like such a floozy sometimes," said Amy. "I wish I could be floozish."

Clair poked her in the leg with a long, red-lacquered fingernail. "Don't sell yourself short, pumpkin."

❧

THE ERSATZ HAWAIIAN STOOD ON THE BOW RAIL LIKE HE WAS HANGING ten off the twenty-two-foot Mako, waving to the Zodiac crew as they passed. "Irie, science dreadies! We be research jammin' now!" But when the Count ignored his greeting, Kona gave the traditional island response: "What, I owe you money?"

"Settle, Kona," Nate said. "And get down off of there."

Kona made his way back to the console. "Old white jacket givin' you the stink-eye. Why, he think you an agent of Babylon?"

"He does bad science. People come to me to ask me about him, I tell them he does bad science."

"And we do the good science?"

"We don't change our numbers to please the people who fund us. The Japanese want numbers that show recovery of the humpback population to levels where the IWC will let them start hunting them again. Gilbert tries to give them those numbers."

"Kill these humpies? No."

"Yes."

"No. Why?"

"To eat."

"No," said the blond Rastaman, shaking his head as if to clear the evil from his ears—his dreads fanning out into nappy spokes.

Quinn smiled to himself. The moratorium had been in effect since before Kona was born. As far as the kid knew, whales had been and always would be safe from hunters. Quinn knew better. "Eating whale is

very traditional in Japan. It sort of has the ritual of our Thanksgiving.
But it's dying out."

"Then it's all good."

"No. There are a lot of old men who want to bring back whale hunting as a tradition. The Japanese whaling industry is subsidized by the
government. It's not even a viable business. They serve whale meat in
the school-lunch program so kids will develop a taste for it."

"No. No one eats the whale."

"The IWC allows them to kill five hundred minke whales a year, but
they kill more. And biologists have found whale meat from half a dozen
endangered whale species in Japanese markets. They try to pass it off as
minke whale, but the DNA doesn't lie."

"Minke? That devil in the white war paint killing our minke?"

"We don't have any minkes here in Hawaii."

"Course not, the Count killing them. We going to chant down this
evil fuckery." Kona dug into his red, gold, and green fanny pack. Out
came an extraordinarily complex network of plastic, brass, and
stainless-steel tubing, which in seconds Kona had assembled into what
Quinn thought was either a very small and elegant linear particle accel-
erator or, more likely, the most complex bong ever constructed.

"Slow de boat, brah. I got to spark up for freedom. Chant down
Babylon, go into battle for Jah's glory, mon. Slow de boat."

"Put that away."

Kona paused, his Bic lighter poised over the bowl. "Take de ship
home to Zion, brah?"

"No, we have work to do." Nate slowed the boat and killed the
motor. They were about a mile off Lahaina.

"Chant down Babylon?" Kona raised the lighter.

"No. Put that away. I'll show you how to drop the hydrophone."
Quinn checked the tape in the recorder on the console.

"Save our minkes?" Kona waved the lighter, unlit, in circles over the
bowl.

"Did Clay show you how to take an ID photo?" Nate pulled the hydrophone and the coil of cord out of its case.

"Ride Jah's herb into the mystic?"

"No! Put that away and get the camera out of that cabinet in the bow."

Kona broke down the bong with a series of whirs and clicks and put it back in his fanny pack. "All right, brah, but when they have eated all your minkes, will not be Jah's fault."

An hour later, after listening, and moving, and listening again, they had found their singer. Kona stood balanced on the gunwale of the boat staring down in wonder at the big male, who was parked under the boat making a sound approximating that of a kidnap victim trying to scream through duct tape.

Kona would look from the whale to Nate, grin, then look back to the whale again, the whole time perched and balanced on the gunwale like a gargoyle on the parapet of a building. Nate guessed that he would be able to hold that position for about two minutes before his knees locked permanently and he'd be forced to finish life in a toadish squat. Still, he envied Kona the enthusiasm of discovery, the fascination and excitement of being around these great animals for the first time. He envied him his youth and his strength. And, listening to the song in the headphones, the song that seemed so clearly to be a statement of mating and yet refused to give up any direct evidence that it was, Nate felt a profound irrelevance. Sexually, socially, intellectually, fiscally, scientifically irrelevant—a sack of borrowed atoms lumpily arranged in a Nate shape. No effect, purpose, or stability.

He tried to listen more closely to what the whale was doing, to lose himself in analyzing what exactly was going on below, but that merely seemed to underscore the suspicion that not only was he getting old, he might be going crazy. This was the first time he'd been out since the "bite me" incident, and since then he had convinced himself that it must have been some sort of hallucination. Still, he cringed a bit every time the whale humped its tail to dive, expecting to see a message scrawled across the flukes.

"He's making them up noises, boss."

Nate nodded. The kid was learning fast. "Get your camera ready, Kona. He'll breathe three, maybe four times before he dives, so be ready."

Abruptly the singing in the headphones stopped. Nate pulled up the hydrophone and started the engine. They waited.

"He went that way, boss," Kona said, pointing off to the starboard side. Nate turned the boat slowly in place and waited.

They were looking in the direction in which Kona had seen the whale moving underwater when he surfaced behind them, not ten feet away from the boat, the blow making both of them jump, the spray wafting across them in a rainbow cloud.

"Ho! Dat buggah up, boss!"

"Thank you, Captain Obvious," Nate said under his breath. He pulled down the throttle and came in behind the whale. On its next breath the whale rolled and slapped a long pectoral fin on the surface, soaking Kona and throwing heavy spray over the console. At least the kid had had the sense to use his body to shield the camera from the splash.

"I love this whale!" Kona said, his Rastaspeak melting, leaving behind a middle-class Jersey accent. "I want to take this whale home and put him in a box with grass and rocks. Buy him squeaky toys."

"Get ready for your ID shot," Nate instructed.

"When we're done with him, can I keep him? Pleeeeeeeeeeeeeze!"

"Here he goes, Kona. Focus."

The whale humped, then fluked, and Kona fired off four quick frames with the motor drive.

"You get it?"

"Rippin' pics. Rippin'!" Kona put the camera down on the seat in front of the console and covered it with a towel.

Nate pointed the boat toward the last fluke print, a twenty-foot lens of smooth water formed on the surface by the turbulence of the whale's tail. These lenses would hold on the surface sometimes for as long as two minutes, serving as windows through which the researchers could watch the whales. In the old whaling days the hunters believed that fluke prints had been caused by oil excreted by the whale. Nate cut the engine and let the boat coast over the fluke print. They could hear the whale song coming up from below and could feel the boat vibrating under their feet.

Nate dropped the hydrophones, hit the "record" button, and put on the headphones. Kona was recording the frame numbers and GPS coordinates in the notebook as Nate had taught him. *A monkey can do my job,* Nate thought. *An hour's experience and this stoner is already doing it. This kid is younger, stronger, and faster than I am, and I'm not even sure that I'm smarter, as if that matters. I'm totally irrelevant.*

But maybe it did matter. Maybe it wasn't all about strength. Culture and language completely screwed up normal biological evolution. Why would we humans have developed such big brains if mating was always predicated on strength and size? Women must have chosen their mates based on intelligence as well. Perhaps early smart guys would say something like "There, right behind those rocks, there's a tasty sloth ripe for the spearing. Go get him, guys." Then, after he'd sent the stronger, dumber guys running off a cliff after the imaginary sloth, he'd settle down with the best of the Cro-Magnon cuties to mix some genes. "That's right, bite my brow ridge. Bite it!" Nate smiled.

Kona was looking over the side at the singer, whose tail was only twenty feet below the boat (although his head was forty feet deeper). He was only a couple of minutes into his song. He'd be down at least ten minutes more.

"Kona, we need to get a DNA sample."

"How we do that?"

Nate pulled a set of flippers out of the console and handed them and an empty coffee cup out to the surfer. "You're going to need to go get a semen sample."

The surfer gulped. Looked at the whale, looked at the cup, looked over the side at the whale again. "No lid?"

Safety

Clay Demodocus drifted silently down past the tail of the breath-holder, only the quiet hissing of his own breath in his ears. Breath-holders were called such because they hung there in the water for up to forty minutes, heads down like a singer, just holding their breath. Not swimming or singing or doing much of anything else. Just hanging there, sometimes three or four of them, tails spread out like the points of a compass. As if someone had just dropped a handful of sleeping whales and forgotten to pick them up. Except they weren't sleeping. Whales didn't really sleep, as far as they knew. Well, the theory was that they slept with only half of their brain at a time, while the other half took care of not drowning. For an air-breather, sleeping in the water and not drowning is a big problem. (Go ahead, try it. We'll wait.)

Falling asleep would be so easy with the rebreather, Clay thought. It was very quiet, which was why Clay was using it. Instead of using a tank of air that was exhaled through a regulator into the water as bubbles, the rebreather sent the diver's exhalation back through a scrubber that took out the carbon dioxide, past some sensors and a tank that added some oxygen, then back to the diver to be rebreathed. No bubbles, which made the rebreather perfect for studying whales (and for sneaking up on enemy ships, which is why the navy had developed it in the first place).

Humpbacks used bubble blowing as a means of communication, especially the males, who threatened one another with bubble displays. Consequently it was nearly impossible to get close to a whale with scuba gear, especially a static animal like a singer or a breath-holder. By blowing bubbles the diver was babbling away in whalespeak, without the slightest idea of what he was saying. In the past Clay had dropped on breath-holders with scuba gear, only to watch the animals swim off before he got within fifty feet of them. He imagined the whales saying, "Hey, it's the skinny, retarded kid talking nonsense again. Let's get out of here."

But this season they'd gotten the rebreather, and Clay was getting his first ever decent footage of a breath-holder. As he drifted by the tail, he checked his gauges, looked up to see Amy snorkeling at the surface, silhouetted in a sunbeam, a small tank strapped on her back ready to come to his rescue should something go wrong. The one big drawback to the rebreather (rather than a fairly simple hose on a tank as in a scuba setup) was that it was a very complex machine, and, should it break, there was a good chance it would kill the diver. (Clay's experience had taught him that the one thing you could depend on was that something would break.)

Around him, except for the whale, was a field of clear blue; below, nothing but blue. Even with great visibility he couldn't see the bottom, some five hundred feet down.

Just past the tail he was at a hundred feet. The navy had tested the rebreather to more than a thousand feet (and since he could theoretically stay down for sixteen hours if he needed to, decompression wasn't a problem), but Clay was still wary of going too deep. The rebreather wasn't set to mix gases for a deep dive, so there was still the danger of nitrogen narcosis—a sort of intoxication caused by pressurized nitrogen in the bloodstream. Clay had been narced a couple of times, once while under arctic ice filming beluga whales, and if he hadn't been tethered to the opening in the ice with a nylon line, he would have drowned.

Just a few more feet and he'd be able to sex the breath-holder, something that they hadn't done more than a few times before, and then it was by crossbow and DNA. The question so far was, are breath-holders all male like singers, and if so, does the breath-holding behavior have something to do with the singing behavior? Clay and Quinn had first come together over the question of sexing singers, some seventeen years before, when DNA testing was so rare as to be nearly nonexistent.

"Can you get under the tail?" Nate had asked. "Get photos of the genitals?"

"Kinky," Clay had said. "Sure, I'll give it a try."

Of course, except for a few occasions when he was able to hold his breath long enough to get under an animal, about a third of the time, Clay had failed at producing whale porn. Now, with this rebreather . . .

As he drifted below the tail, so close now that even the wide-angle lens could take in only a third of the flukes, Clay noticed some unusual markings on the tail. He looked up from the display just as the whale began to move, but it was too late. The whale twitched, and the massive tail came down on Clay's head, driving him some twenty feet deeper in an instant. The wash from the flukes tumbled him backward three times before he settled in a slow drift to the bottom, unconscious.

❧

AS HE WATCHED THE PSEUDO-HAWAIIAN TRY TO KICK DOWN TO THE singing whale for the eighth time, Nathan Quinn thought, *This is a rite of passage. Similar things were done to me when I was a grad student. Didn't Dr. Ryder send me out to get close-up blowhole pictures of a gray whale who had a hideous head cold? Wasn't I hit by a basketball-size gob of whale snot nearly every time the whale surfaced? And wasn't I, ultimately, grateful for the opportunity to get out in the field and do some real research? Of course I was. Therefore, I am being neither cruel nor unprofessional by sending this young man down again and again to perform a hand job on the singer.*

The radio chirped, signaling a call from the *Always Confused*. Nate keyed the mike button on the mobile phone/two-way radio they used to communicate between the two boats. "Go ahead, Clay."

"Nate, it's Clair. Clay went down about fifteen minutes ago, but Amy just dove after him with the rescue tank. I don't know what to do. They're too deep. I can't see them. The whale took off, and I can't see them."

"Where are you, Clair?"

"Straight out, about two miles off the dump."

Nate grabbed the binoculars and scanned the island, found the dump, looked out from there. He could make out two or three boats in the area. Six or eight minutes away at full throttle.

"Keep looking, Clair. Get ready to drop a hang tank if you have one set up, in case they need to decompress. I'll be there as soon as I get the kid out of the water."

"What's he doing in the water?"

"Just a bad decision on my part. Keep me apprised, Clair. Try to follow Amy's bubbles if you can find them. You'll want to be as close to them as you can when they come up."

Nate started the engine just as Kona broke the surface, spitting out the snorkel and taking in a great gasp of air. Kona shook his head, signifying that he hadn't accomplished the mission.

"Too deep, boss."

"Come, come, come. To the side." Nate waved him to the boat.

Quinn brought the boat broadside to Kona, then reached over with both hands. "Come on." Kona took his hands, and Quinn jerked the surfer over the gunwale. Kona landed in a heap in the bottom of the boat.

"Boss—"

"Hang on, Clay's in trouble."

"But, boss—"

Quinn buried the throttle, yanked the boat around, and cringed at the bunny-in-a-blender screech as the hydrophone cord wrapped around the prop, sheared the prop pin, and chopped itself into a whole package of expensive, waterproof licorice sticks.

"Fuck!" Nate snatched off his baseball cap and whipped it onto the console.

The hydrophone sank peacefully to the bottom, bopping the singer on the back as it went. Nate killed the engine and grabbed the radio. "Clair, are they up yet? I'm not going to be able to get there."

━━◦◉◦━━

AMY FELT AS IF SOMEONE WERE DRIVING ICE PICKS INTO HER EAR-drums. She pinched her nostrils closed and blew to equalize the pressure, even as she kicked to go deeper, but she was moving too fast to get equalized.

She was down fifty feet now. Clay was a hundred feet below her, the pressure would triple before she got there. She felt as if she were swimming through thick, blue honey. She'd seen the whale tail hit Clay and toss him back, but the good news was that she hadn't seen a cloud of bubbles come up. There was a chance that the regulator had stayed in Clay's mouth and he was still breathing. Of course, it could also mean that he was dead or that his neck had snapped and he was paralyzed. Whatever his condition, he certainly wasn't moving voluntarily, just sinking slowly, relentlessly toward the bottom.

Amy fought the pressure, the resistance of the water, and did math problems as she kicked deeper. The rescue tank held only a thousand pounds of air, a third of the capacity of a normal tank. She guessed that she'd be at around a hundred and seventy-five to two hundred feet before she caught Clay. That would give her just enough air to get him to the surface without stopping to decompress. Even if Clay was unhurt, there was a good chance he was going to get decompression sickness, the bends, and if he lived through that, he'd spend three or four days in the hyperbaric decompression chamber in Honolulu.

Ah, the big palooka is probably dead anyway, she thought, trying to cheer herself up.

━━◦◉◦━━

ALTHOUGH CLAY DEMODOCUS HAD LIVED A LIFE SPICED WITH ADVEN-tures, he was not an adventurer. Like Nate, he did not seek danger, risk, or fulfillment by testing his mettle against nature. He sought calm weather, gentle seas, comfortable accommodations, kind and loyal people, and safety, and it was only for the work that he compromised any of those goals. The last to go, the least compromised, was safety. The loss of his father, a hard-helmet sponge diver, had taught him that. The old man was just touching bottom at eight hundred feet when a drunken deck hand dragged his ass across the engine start button, causing the prop to cut his father's air line. The pressure immediately drove Papa Demodocus's entire body into the bronze helmet, leaving only his weighted shoes showing, and it was in his great helmet that he was lowered into the grave. Little Clay (Cleandros in those days in Greece) was only five at the time, and that last vision of his father haunted him for years. He never did see a Marvin the Martian cartoon—that great goofy helmet body riding cartoon shoes—when he did not have to fight a tear and sniffle for Papa.

As Clay drifted down into the briny blue, he saw a bright light and a dark shape waiting there on the other side. Out of the light came a short but familiar figure. The face was still dark, but Clay knew the voice, even after so many years. "Welcome, Earth Being," said the vacuum-packed Greek.

"Papa," said Clay.

~◦◦~

CLAIR DRAGGED THE HEAVY TANK OUT OF THE *ALWAYS CONFUSED*'S bait well and tried to attach the regulator in order to hang it off a line for Amy and Clay to breathe from so they could decompress before coming up. Clay had shown her how to do this a dozen times, but she had never paid attention. It was his job to put the technothingies together. She didn't need to know this stuff. It wasn't as if she was ever going to go diving without him. She'd let him drone on about safety this and life-threatening that while she applied her attention to putting on sunscreen or braiding her hair so it wouldn't tangle in the equipment. Now she was blinking back tears and cursing herself for not having listened. When she thought she finally might have the regulator screwed on correctly, she grabbed it and dragged the tank to the side of the boat. The regulator came off in her hands.

"Goddamn it!" She snatched the radio and keyed the mike. "Nate, I need some help here."

"Go ahead, sistah," came back. "He be in the briny blue, fixing the propeller."

"Kona, do you know how a regulator goes on a scuba tank?"

"Yah mon, you got to keep the bowl above the water or your herb get wet and won't take the fire."

Clair took a deep breath and fought back a sob. "See if you can put Nate on."

Back on the *Constantly Baffled*, Nate was in the water with snorkel and fins fighting the weight of half a dozen wrenches and sockets he'd put in the pockets of his cargo shorts. He almost had the propeller off the boat. With luck he could install the shear pin and be up and running in a couple of minutes. It wasn't a complex procedure. It had just been made a lot trickier when Nate found that he couldn't reach the prop to work on it from inside the boat. Then, suddenly, his air supply was cut off.

He kicked up, spit the snorkel out of his mouth, and found himself staring Kona right in the face. The fake Hawaiian hung over the back of the boat, his thumb covering the end of Nate's snorkel, his other hand holding the radio, which he'd let slip halfway underwater.

"Call for you, boss."

Nate gasped and snatched the receiver out of Kona's hand—held it up out of the water. "What in the hell are you doing? That's not water-proof." He tried to sling the water out of the cell phone and keyed the mike. "Clair! Can you hear me?" No sound, not even static.

"But it's yellow," said Kona, as if that explained everything.

"I can see it's yellow. What did Clair say? Is Clay all right?"

"She wanted to know how to put the regulator on the tank. You have to keep the bowl above the water, I tell her."

"It's not a bong, you idiot. It's a real scuba tank. Help me out."

Nate handed up his fins, then stepped on the trim planes on the stern and pulled himself into the boat. At the console he turned on the marine radio and started calling. "Clair, you listening? This is the *Constantly Baffled* calling the *Always Confused*. Clair, are you there?"

"*Constantly Baffled*," cut in a stern, official-sounding male voice, "this is the Department of Conservation and Resources Enforcement. Are you displaying your permit flag?"

"Conservation, we have an emergency situation, a diver in trouble off our other boat. I'm dead in the water with a broken shear pin. The other boat is roughly two miles off the dump."

"*Constantly Baffled,* why are you not displaying your permit flag?"

"Because I forgot to put the damn thing up. We have two divers in the water, both possibly in trouble, and the woman on board is unable to put together a hang tank." Nate looked around. He could see the whale cops' boat about a thousand yards to the west toward Lanai. They were alongside another boat. Nate could see the familiar figure of the Count standing in the bow, looming there like doom in an Easter bonnet. *Bastard!*

"*Constantly Baffled,* hold there, we are coming to you."

"Don't come to me. I'm not going anywhere. Go to the other boat. Repeat, they have an emergency situation and are not responding to marine radio."

The Conservation Enforcement boat lifted up in the water under the power of two 125-horse Honda outboards and beelined toward them.

"Fuck!"

Nate dropped the mike and started to shake, a shiver born not of temperature, as it was eighty degrees on the channel, but out of frustration and fear. What had happened to Clay to prompt Amy to go to his rescue? Maybe she had misjudged the situation and gone down needlessly. She didn't have much experience in the water, or at least he didn't think she had. But if things were okay, then why weren't they up . . . ?

"Kona, did Clair say whether she could see Amy and Clay?"

"No, boss, she just wanted to know about the regulator." Kona sat down in the bottom of the boat and hung his head between his knees. "I'm sorry, boss. I thought if it was yellow, it could go in the water. I didn't know. It slipped."

Nate wanted to tell the kid it was all right, but he didn't like lying to people. "Clay put you on the research permit, right, Kona? You remember signing a paper with a lot of names on it?"

"No, mon. That five-oh coming up now?"

"Yeah, whale cops. And if Clay didn't put you on the permit, you're going to be going home with them."

CHAPTER ELEVEN

The Mermaid
and the Martian

The depth gauge read two hundred feet by the time Amy finally snagged the top of Clay's rebreather and pulled herself down to where she was looking into his mask. If it weren't for a small trail of blood streaming from his scalp, making him look like he was leaking black motor oil into the blue, he might have been sleeping, and she smiled in spite of herself. *The sea dog survives.* Somehow—maybe through years of conditioning his reflexes to keep his mouth shut—Clay had bitten down on the mouthpiece of the rebreather. He was breathing steadily. She could hear the hiss of the apparatus.

She wasn't sure that Clay's mouthpiece would stay in all the way to the surface, and, if it came out, the photographer would surely drown, even if she replaced it quickly. Unlike a normal scuba regulator, which was frightfully easy to purge, you couldn't let water get into a rebreather or it could foul the carbon-dioxide scrubbers and render the device useless. And she'd need both her hands for the swim up. One to hold on to Clay and one to vent air from his buoyancy-control vest, which would fill with air as they rose, causing them both to shoot to the surface and get the bends. (Amy wasn't wearing a BC vest or a wet suit; she wasn't supposed to have needed them.) After wasting a precious thirty seconds of air to consider the problem, she took off her bikini top and wrapped it around Clay's head to secure his mouthpiece. Then she hooked her hand into his buoyancy vest and started the slow kick to the surface.

At a hundred and fifty feet she made the mistake of looking up. The surface might have been a mile away. Then she checked her watch and pulled up Clay's arm so she could see the dive computer on his wrist. Already the liquid-crystal readout was blinking, telling her that Clay needed two decompression stops on the way up. One at fifty feet and one at twenty, from ten to fifteen minutes each. With his rebreather he'd have plenty of air. Amy wasn't wearing a dive computer, but by ballparking it from her pressure gauge, she figured she had between five and ten minutes of air left. She was about half an hour short.

Well, this is going to be awkward, she thought.

❧

THE WHALE COPS WORE LIGHT BLUE UNIFORM SHIRTS WITH SHORTS and aviator-style mirrored sunglasses that looked as if they'd been surgically set into their faces. They were both in their thirties and had spent some time in the gym, although one was heavier and had rolled up his short sleeves to let his grapefruit biceps breathe. The other was thin and wiry. They brought their boat alongside Nate's and threw over a bumper to keep the boats from rubbing together in the waves.

"Howzit, bruddahs!" Kona said.

"Not now," Nate whispered.

"I need to see your permit," said the heavier cop.

Nate had pulled a plastic envelope out from under the console as they approached. They went through this several times a year. He handed it over to the cop, who took out the document and unfolded it.

"I'll need both of your IDs."

"Come on," Nate said, handing over his driver's license. "You guys know me. Look, we've sheared a pin and there's a diver emergency on our other boat."

"You want us to call the Coast Guard?"

"No, I want you to take us over there."

"That's not what we do, Dr. Quinn," said the thin cop, looking up from the permit. "The Coast Guard is equipped for emergencies. We are not."

"Dis haole, lolo pela, him," said Kona. (Meaning, he's just a dumb white guy.)

"Don't talk that shit to me," said the heavier cop. "You want to speak Hawaiian, I'll talk to you in Hawaiian, but don't talk that pidgin shit to me. Now, where's your ID?"

"Back at my cabin."

"Dr. Quinn, your people need to have ID at all times on a research vessel, you know that."

"He's new."

"What's your name, kid?"

"Pelekekona Keohokalole," said Kona.

The cop took off his sunglasses—for the first time ever, Nate thought. He looked at Kona.

"You're not on the permit."

"Try Preston Applebaum," said Kona.

"Are you trying to fuck with me?"

"He is," said Nate. "Just take him in, and on the way take me to our other boat."

"I think we'll tow both of you in and deal with the permit issues when we get into harbor."

Suddenly, amid the static of the marine radio on in the background, Clair's voice: "Nate, are you there? I lost Amy's bubbles. I can't see her bubbles. I need help here! Nate! Anyone!"

Nate looked at the whale cop, who looked at his partner, who looked away.

Kona jumped up on the gunwale of the police boat and leaned into the wiry cop's face. "Can we do the territorial macho power trip after we get our divers out of the water, or do you have to kill two people to show us how big your fucking dicks are?"

CLAIR RAN AROUND THE BOAT SEARCHING FOR AMY'S BUBBLE TRAIL, hoping she was just missing it, had lost it in the waves—hoping that it was still there. She looked at the hang tank sitting in the floor of the boat, still unattached to the regulator, then ran back to the radios, keying both the marine radio and the cell-phone radio and trying not to scream.

"SOS here. Please, I'm a couple of miles off the dump, I have divers down, in trouble."

The harbormaster at Lahaina came back, said he'd send someone, and then a dive boat who was out at the lava cathedrals at Lanai said they had to get their divers out of the water but could be there in thirty minutes. Then Nathan Quinn came back.

"Clair, this is Nate. I'm on the way. How long ago did the bubbles stop?"

"Clair checked her watch. Four, five minutes ago."

"Can you see them?"

"No, nothing. Amy went deep, Nate. I watched her go down until she disappeared."

"Do you have hang tanks in the water?"

"No, I can't get the damn regulators on. Clay always did it."

"Just tie off the tanks and tie the regulators to the tanks and get them over the side. Amy and Clay can hook them up if they get to them."

"How deep? I have three tanks."

"Ninety, sixty, and thirty. Just get them in the water, Clair. We'll worry about exact depth when I get there. Just hang them so they can find them. Tie glow sticks on them if you have any. Should be there in five minutes. We can see you."

Clair started tying the plastic line around the necks of the heavy scuba tanks. Every few seconds she scanned the waves for signs of Amy's bubbles, but there weren't any. Nate had said "*If* they get to them." She blinked away tears and concentrated on her knots. *If?* Well *if* Clay made it back—*when* he made it back—he could damn sure get himself a safer job. Her man wasn't going to drown hundreds of feet under the ocean, because from now on he was going to be taking pictures of weddings or bar mitzvahs or kids at JC Penney's or some goddamn thing on dry land.

ACROSS THE CHANNEL, NEAR THE SHORE OF KAHOOLAWE, THE TARGET
island, Libby Quinn had been following the exchange between Clair
and Nate over the marine radio. Without being asked, her partner, Margaret, said, "We don't have any diving equipment on board. That deep,
there's not much we could do."

"Clay's immortal anyway," said Libby, trying to sound more blasé
than she felt. "He'll come up yammering about what great footage he
got."

"Call them, offer our help," the older woman said. "If we deny our
instincts as caretakers, we deny ourselves as women."

"Oh, fuck off, Margaret! I'm calling to offer our help because it's the
right thing to do."

Meanwhile, on the ocean side of Kahoolawe, Cliff Hyland was sitting
in the makeshift lab belowdecks in the cabin cruiser, headphones on,
watching an oscilloscope readout, when one of his grad students came
into the cabin and grabbed him by the shoulder.

"Sounds like Nathan Quinn's group is in trouble," said the girl, a
sun-baked brunette wearing zinc-oxide war paint on her nose and
cheeks and a hat the size of a garbage-can lid.

Hyland pulled up the headphones. "What? Who? Fire? Sinking?
What?"

"They've lost two divers. That photographer guy Clay and that pale
girl."

"Where are they?"

"About two miles off the dump. They're not asking for help. I just
thought you should know."

"That's a ways. Start reeling in the array. We can be there in a half
hour maybe."

Just then Captain Tarwater came down the steps into the cabin.
"Stay that order, grommet. Stay on mission. We have a survey to finish
today—and a charge to record."

"Those guys are friends of mine," Hyland said.

"I've been monitoring the situation, Dr. Hyland. Our presence has
not been requested, and, frankly, there is nothing this vessel could do to
help. It sounds like they've lost some divers. It happens."

"This isn't war, Tarwater. We don't just *lose* people."

"Stay on mission. Any setback in Quinn's operation can only benefit this project."

"You asshole," Hyland said.

Back in the channel, the Count stood in the bow of the big Zodiac and watched as the Conservation and Resources Enforcement boat towed away the *Constantly Baffled*. He turned to his three researchers, who were trying to look busy in back of the boat. "Let that be a lesson to you all. The key to good science is making sure all the paperwork is in order. Now you can see why I'm such a stickler for you people having your IDs with you every morning."

"Yeah, in case some other researcher rats us out to the Conservation and Resources cops," one woman said.

"Science is a competitive sport, Ms. Wextler. If you're not willing to compete, you're welcome to take your undergrad degree and go baby-sit seasick tourists on a whale-watching boat. Nathan Quinn has attacked the credibility of this organization in the past. It's only fair play that I point out when he is not working within the rules of the sanctuary."

The ocean breeze carried the junior researchers' under-the-breath whispers of "asshole" away from the ears of Gilbert Box, over the channel to wash against the cliffs of Molokai.

～◈◈～

NATE WRAPPED HIS ARMS AROUND CLAIR AND HELD HER AS SHE sobbed. As the downtime passed the first half hour, Nate felt a ball of fear, dread, and nausea forming in his own stomach. Only by trying to stay busy looking for signs of Clay and Amy was he able to keep from being ill. When Amy's downtime passed forty-five minutes, Clair started to sob. Clay might have been able to stay down that long with the rebreather, but with only the tiny rescue tank, there was no way Amy could still be breathing. Two divemasters from a nearby tour boat had already used up a full tank each searching. The problem was, in blue water it was a three-dimensional search. Rescue searches were usually done on the bottom, but not when it was six hundred feet down. With the currents in the channel . . . well, the search was little more than a gesture anyway.

Being a scientist, Nate liked true things, so after an hour he stopped telling Clair that everything was going to be all right. He didn't believe it, and grief was already descending on him like a flight of black arrows. In the past, when he had experienced loss or trauma or heartbreak, some survival mechanism had kicked in and allowed him to function for months before he'd actually begin feeling the pain, but this time it was immediate and deep and devastating. His best friend was dead. The woman that he— Well, he wasn't exactly sure what he'd felt about Amy, but even when he looked past the sexuality, the differences in their ages and positions, he liked her. He liked her a lot, and he'd become used to her presence after only a few weeks.

One of the divers came up near the boat and spit out his regulator. "There's nowhere to look. It's just blue to fucking infinity."

"Yeah," Nate said. "I know."

～⊙✎～

CLAY SAW BLUE-GREEN BREASTS GENTLY BOBBING BEFORE HIS FACE and was convinced that he had, indeed, drowned. He felt himself being pulled upward and so closed his eyes and surrendered.

"No, no, no, son," said Papa. "You're not in heaven. The tits are not blue in heaven. You are still alive."

Papa's face was very much smashed against the glass of his helmet, wearing the sort of expression he might have had if he'd run full speed into a bulletproof window and someone had snapped a picture at maximum mash, yet Clay could see that his eyes were smiling.

"My little Cleandros, you know it is not time for you to join me?"

Clay nodded.

"And when it comes time for you to join me, it should be because you are old and tired and ready to go, not because the sea is wanting to crush you."

Clay nodded again, then opened his eyes. This time there was a stabbing pain in his head, but he squinted through it to see Amy's face through her dive mask. She held his regulator in his mouth and was gripping the back of his head to make him look at her. When she was sure that he was conscious and knew where he was, she gave him the okay signal and waited until he returned it. Amy then let go of Clay's regulator, and they swam slowly upward, to surface four hundred yards from where they'd first submerged.

Clay immediately looked around for the boat and found nothing where he expected it, the closest vessels being a group of boats too far away to be the *Always Confused*. He checked his dive computer. He'd been down for an hour and fifteen minutes. That couldn't be right.

"That's them," Amy said. She looked down into the water. "Oops. Let me get my top off of your face."

"Okay," Clay mumbled into the rebreather.

◦◦◦

KONA WAS IN TEARS, WAILING LIKE BOB MARLEY IN A BEAR TRAP— inconsolable. "Clay gone. The Snowy Biscuit gone. And I was going to poke squid with her, too."

"You were not," said Nate.

But the artificial Hawaiian didn't hear. "There!" Kona shouted as he leaped onto the shoulders of the stocky whale cop to get a better view. "It's the white wahine! Praise to Jah! Thanks be to His Imperial Majesty Haile Selassie. Go there, Sheriff. A saving be needed."

"Handcuff this kid," said the cop.

CHAPTER TWELVE

Here's My Coupon, He Said, Singing the Redemption Song

Normally, if the whale cops found an unauthorized person on a research vessel, they would simply record the violation, write a ticket, then remove the person from the boat and take him back to Lahaina Harbor. A fine was paid and violations were considered the following year when the permit came up for renewal. By contrast, Kona was delivered to the Maui county jail with both his wrists and ankles shackled and a swath of duct tape over his mouth.

Nate and Amy were waiting in the lobby of the Maui county jail in Wailuku, sitting in metal chairs designed to promote discomfort and waffled butt skin. "It's really okay if he has to stay in overnight," said Nate. "Or for a week or so if it would be easier."

Amy punched Nate in the shoulder. "You creep! I thought it was Kona that got them to let you come to us."

"Still, jail builds character. I've heard that. It might do him good to be off his herb for a few days." Kona had slipped his fanny pack full of pot and paraphernalia to Nate before he'd been taken away.

"Character? If he starts with his native-sovereignty speech stuff in there the real Hawaiians will pound him."

"He'll be okay. I'm worried about you. Don't you want to go get checked?" Clair had taken Clay to the hospital to get a CAT scan and have his scalp stitched up.

"I'm fine, Nate. I was only shaken up because I was worried about Clay."

"You were down a long time."

"Yes, and I went by Clay's dive computer. We decompressed completely. The worst part was I froze my ass off."

"I can't believe you had the presence of mind to decompress with Clay unconscious. I don't know if I would have. Hell, I couldn't have. I'd have run out of air in ten minutes. How did you manage—"

"I'm small, Nate. I don't use air like you. And I could tell that Clay was breathing okay. I could tell that the cut on his head wasn't that bad either. The biggest danger to both of us was decompression sickness, so I followed the computer, breathed off of Clay's rescue supply when I ran out, and nobody got hurt."

"I'm really impressed," said Nate.

"I just did what I was supposed to do. No big deal."

"I was really scared— I thought you— You had me worried." He patted her knee in a grandmotherly fashion, and she looked at his hand.

"Careful, I'll get all sniffly over here," Amy said.

⌘

THEY LED THE SURFER INTO THE HOLDING TANK, WHERE EVERYONE WAS WEARing the same orange jumpsuit that he was. "Irie, bruddahs," Kona said, "we all shoutin' down Sheriff John Brown in these Great Pumpkin suits, Jah."

They all looked up: a giant Samoan who had beaten an Oldsmobile to death with a softball bat when it stalled in the middle of the Kuihelani Freeway, an alcoholic white guy who had fallen asleep on the Four Seasons' private beach in Wailea and made the mistake of dropping his morning business in one of the cabanas, a bass player from Lahaina who had been brought in because at any given time a bass player is probably up to no good, an angry bruddah who had been caught doing a smash-and-grab from a rental car at La Perouse Bay, and two up-country pig hunters who had tried to back their four-wheeler full of pit bulls down a volcano after huffing two cans of spray paint. Kona could tell they were

huffers by the glazed look in their eyes and the large red rings that covered their mouths and noses from the bag.

"Hey, brah, Krylon?"

One of the pig hunters nodded and briefly lost control of the motion
of his head.

"Nothin' like a quality red."

"I hear dat," said the pig hunter. "I hear dat."

Then Kona made his way to the corner of the cell, the guard locked the
door, and everyone resumed looking at his shoes, except for the Samoan
guy, who was waiting for Kona to make eye contact so he could kill him.

"Ye know, brah," Kona said to him in a friendly, if seriously flawed
fake Jamaican accent, "I be learning from my science dreadies to look at
tings with the critical eye, don't ya know. And I think I know what the
problem with taking a stand against da man on Maui."

"Whad dat?" ask the Samoan.

"Well, it's an island, ain't it, mon? You got to be stone stupid going
outlaw here wid nowhere to escape."

"You callin' me stupid, haole?"

"No, mon, just speaking the truth."

"An' what you in for, haole girl?"

"Failing to give a humpback whale the proper scientific hand job, I tink."

"Goin' ta fuck ya and kill ya now."

"Could ya kill me first?"

"Whadeva," said the Samoan, climbing to his feet and expanding to
his full Godzilla proportions.

"Thanks, brah. Peace in Jah's mercy," said the doomed surfer.

~⊙⊙~

FORTY-FIVE MINUTES LATER, AFTER NATE HAD FILLED OUT THE REQUI-
site papers, the jailer, a compact Hawaiian with weightlifter shoulders,
led Kona through the double steel doors into the waiting room. The
surfer shuffled in, head down, looking ashamed and a little lopsided.
Amy put her arm around his shoulders and patted his head.

"Oh, Sistah Amy, 'twas heinous." He put his arm around Amy, then
let his hand slip to the curve of her bottom. "Heinous most true."

The jailer grinned. "Had a disagreement with a big Samoan guy. We stopped it before it got too far. The holding cells are monitored on closed-circuit video."

"Snatched half me dreads out." Kona pulled a handful of orphaned dreadlocks from the pocket of his surf shorts. "Going to cost some deep monies to hook these boys back up. I can feel my strength waning without them."

The jailer waived a finger under Kona's nose. "Just so you know, kid, if it had gone the other way—if the Samoan had decided to kill you second—I wouldn't have stepped in so early. You understand?"

"Yah, Sheriff."

"You stay out of my jail, or next time I tell him which end to start on, okay?" The jailer turned to Quinn. "They aren't filing any charges that merit incarceration. They just wanted to make a point." Then he leaned close to Nate and whispered, their height difference making it appear as if he were talking to the scientist's shirt pocket, "You need to get this kid some help. He thinks he's Hawaiian. I see these suburban Rasta boys all the time—hell, Paia's crawling with them—but this one, he's troubled. One of my boys goes that way, I'd pay for a shrink."

"He's not my kid."

"I know how you feel. His girlfriend is cute, though. Makes you wonder how they pick 'em, doesn't it?"

"Thanks, Officer," Nate said. Having shared all the paternal camaraderie he could handle, he turned and walked out into the blinding Maui sun.

To Kona, Amy said, "You better now, baby?"

Kona nodded into her shoulder, where he'd been pretending to seek comfort in a nuzzle.

"Good. Then move your hand."

The surfer played his fingers over her bottom like anemones in a tidal wash, anchored yet flowing.

"That's it," Amy said. She snatched a handful of his remaining dreads and quickstepped through the double glass doors, dragging the bent-over surfer behind her.

"Ouch, ouch, ouch," Kona chanted in perfect four/four reggae rhythm.

CHAPTER THIRTEEN

Spirits in the Night

Nate spent the whole afternoon and most of the evening trying to analyze spectrograms of whale-song recordings, correlate behavior patterns, and then chart the corresponding patterns of interaction. The problem was figuring out what actually defined interaction for an eighty-thousand-pound animal? Were animals interacting when they were five hundred yards away? A thousand? A mile, ten miles? The song was certainly audible for miles; the low, subsonic frequencies could travel literally thousands of miles in deep ocean basins.

Nate tried to put himself in their world—no boundaries, no obstacles. They lived, for the most part, in a world of sound, yet they had acute eyesight, both in and out of the water, and special muscles in the eye that allowed them to change focus for either medium. You interacted with animals you could both see and not see. When Nate and Clay used satellite tags, of which they could afford only a few, or rented a helicopter, from which they could observe animals from a wide perspective, it appeared that the whales were indeed responding to each other from miles apart. How do you study an animal that is socializing over a distance of miles? The key had to be in the song, in the signal somewhere. If for no other reason than that was the only way to approach the problem.

Midnight found him sitting alone in the office, lit only by the glow of his computer monitor, having forgotten to eat, drink, or relieve himself for four hours, when Kona came in.

"What's that?" asked the surfer, pointing to the spectrograph that was scrolling across the screen.

Nate nearly jumped out of the chair, then caught himself and pulled the headphones down. "The part that's scrolling is the spectrograph of the humpback song. The different colors are frequency, or pitch. The wiggly line in this box is an oscilloscope. It shows frequency, too, but I can use it to isolate each range by clicking on it."

Kona was eating a banana. He handed another one to Nate without taking his eyes off the screen. "So this is what it looks like? The song?" Kona had forgotten to affect any of his accents, so Nate forgot to be sarcastic in reply.

"It's a way of looking at it. Humans are visual animals. Our brains are better suited to process visual information rather than acoustic information, so it's easier for us to think about sound by looking at it. A whale or a dolphin's brain is structured to process acoustics more than visuals."

"What are you looking for?"

"I'm not sure. I'm looking for a signal. For some pattern of information in the structure of the song."

"Like a message?"

"Maybe a message."

"And it's not in the musical parts?" Kona asked. "The difference in notes? Like a song? You know the prophet Bob Marley gave us the wisdom of HIM in song."

Quinn swiveled in his chair and paused in midbite of his banana. "HIM? What's that?"

"His Imperial Majesty, Haile Selassie, emperor of Ethiopia, Lion of Judah, Jesus Christ on earth, son of God. His blessings upon us. Jah, mon."

"You mean Haile Selassie, the Ethiopian king who died in the 1970s? That Haile Selassie?"

"Yah mon. HIM, the direct descendant of David as foretold in Isaiah, through the divine consort Solomon and Makeda, the queen of Sheba, and from their sons all the emperors of Ethiopia have come. So we Rastas believe that Haile Selassie is Jesus Christ alive on earth."

"But he's dead, how's that work?"

"It helps to be stoned."

"I see," Nate said. Well, that did explain a lot. "Anyway, to answer your question, yes, we've looked at the musical transmission, but despite Bob Marley I think the answer is here, in this low register, but only because it travels the farthest."

"Can you freeze this?" said Kona, pointing to the oscilloscope, a green line dancing on a field of black.

Nate clicked it and froze a jagged line on the screen. "Why?"

"Those teeth? See, there are tall ones and not so tall ones."

"They're called microoscillations. You can only see them if you have the wave stopped like this."

"What if the tall one is a one and the short one is a zero? What's that?"

"Binary?"

"Yah, mon, what if it's computer talk, like that?"

Nate was stunned. Not because he thought Kona was right, but because the kid had actually had the cognitive powers to come up with the question. Nate wouldn't have been more surprised if he'd walked in on a team of squirrels building a toaster oven. Maybe the kid had run out of pot, and this spike in intelligence was just a withdrawal symptom.

"That's not a bad guess, Kona, but the only way the whales would know about this would be if they had oscilloscopes."

"And they don't?"

"No, they don't."

"Oh, and that acoustic brain? That couldn't see this?"

"No," said Nate, not entirely sure that he hadn't just lied. He'd never thought of it before.

"Okay. I go for to sleep now. You need more grinds?"

"No. Thanks for the banana."

"Jah's blessing, mon. Thanks for getting me out for jail this day. We going go out next morning?"

"Maybe not everyone. We'll have to see how Clay feels tomorrow. He went right to his cabin when Clair brought him home from the hospital."

"Oh, Boss Clay got cool runnings, brah. He having sweet agonies with Sistah Clair. I hear them love jams as I'm coming over."

"Well, good," Nate said, thinking from Kona's tone and his smile that whatever he said must have been good. "Good night, Kona."

"Good night, boss."

Before the surfer was out the door, Nate had turned to the monitor and started mapping out peaks in the wave pattern of the low end of the whale song. He'd need to look up some articles on blue-whale calls—the lowest, loudest, longest-traveling calls on the planet—and he'd have to see if anyone had done any numerical analysis on dolphin sonar clicks, and that was all he could think of right at the moment. In the meantime he had to have enough of a sample to see if there was any meaning there. It was ridiculous, of course. It would never be so simple, nor could it be so complex. Of course you could assign values of one or zero to parts of the song—that was easy. It didn't mean there would be any meaning to it. It wouldn't necessarily answer any of their questions, but it was a different way of looking at things. Whale-call binary, no.

Two hours later he was still assigning ones and zeroes to different microoscillations in wave patterns of different songs and felt as if he might actually, strangely, amazingly, be learning something, when Clay came through the door wearing a knee-length pink kimono emblazoned with huge white chrysanthemums. There was a small bandage on his forehead and what appeared to be a lipstick smear that ran from his mouth to his right ear.

"Any beer in there?" Clay nodded to the kitchen. The office cabin, like all the others at Papa Lani, had once been living quarters for a whole family, so it had a full kitchen in addition to the great room they used for a main office, two smaller rooms they used for storage, and a bathroom.

Clay padded past and threw open the refrigerator. "Nope. Water, I guess. I'm really dehydrated."

"You okay," Nate said. "How was the CAT scan?"

"I'm cat free." Clay came back to the office and fell into the chair in front of his broken monitor. "Thirteen stitches in my scalp, maybe a mild concussion. I'll be okay. Clair may kill me yet tonight, though—heart attack, stroke, affection. Nothing like a near-death experience to bring out the passion in a woman. You can't believe the stuff that woman is doing to me. And she's a schoolteacher. It's shameful." Clay grinned, and Nate noticed a little lipstick on his teeth.

"So that's shame?" Nate gestured for Clay to wipe his mouth.

The photographer took a swipe across his mug, came up with a handful of color, and examined it. "No, I think that's strawberry lip gloss. A woman her age wearing flavored lip gloss. The shame is in my heart."

"You really had her worried, Clay. Me, too. If Amy hadn't kept her head . . . well—"

"I fucked up. I know it. I started living in the viewfinder and forgot where I was. It was an amateurish mistake. But you can't believe the footage I was getting using the rebreather. It's going to be amazing for singers. I'm finally going to be able to get underneath them, beside them, whatever you need. I just need to remember where I am."

"You're unbelievably lucky." Nate knew that any lecture he might come up with, Clay had already put himself through a dozen times. Still, he had to say it. Regardless of the outcome, he had endured the loss of his friend, even if was for only forty minutes or so. "Unconscious, that deep, for that long—you used up a lot of lives on that one, Clay. The fact that your mouthpiece stayed in is a miracle."

"Well, that part wasn't an accident. I have the hoses tight because the rebreather is so temperamental about getting water in it. Over the years I've had mouthpieces knocked out of my mouth a hundred times, kicked out by another diver, camera caught on it, hit by a dolphin. Since you have to keep your head back to film most of the time anyway, with the hoses short so the thing stays in your mouth, it's just a matter of keeping the seal. Man's only instinct is to suck."

"And you suck, is that what you're saying?"

"Look, Nate, I know you're mad, but I'm okay. Something was going on with that animal. It distracted me. It won't happen again. I owe it to the kid, though."

"We thought we'd lost her, too."

"She's good, Nate. Really good. She kept her head, she did what needed to be done, and damned if I know how she did it, but she brought my ancient ass up alive and without the bends. Situation was reversed, I would have never done the decompression stops, but it turns out she did the right thing. You can't teach that kind of judgment."

"You're just trying to change the subject."

Clay was indeed trying to change the subject. "How'd Toronto do against Edmonton tonight?"

Oh, sure, thought Nate, try to appeal to his inherent Canadian weakness for hockey. Like playing the hockey card would distract him from—

"I don't know. Let's check the score."

From outside the screen door came Clair's voice. "Clay Demodocus, are you wearing my robe?"

"Why, yes, dear, I am," said Clay, shooting an embarrassed glance at Quinn, as if he'd only just noticed that he was wearing a woman's kimono.

"Well, that would mean that I'm wearing nothing, wouldn't it?" said Clair. She wasn't close enough to the door for him to actually see her through the screen, but Quinn had no doubt she was naked, had her hip cocked, and was tapping a foot in the sand.

"I guess," said Clay. "We were just going to check the hockey scores, sweetheart. Would you like to come in?"

"There's a skinny kid with a half order of dreadlocks and an erection out here staring at me, Clay, and it's making me feel a little self-conscious."

"I woke up with it, Bwana Clay," Kona said. "No disrespect."

"He's an employee, darling." Clay said reassuringly. Then to Quinn he whispered, "I had better go."

"You better had," said Quinn.

"See you in the morning."

"You should take the day off."

"Nah, I'll see you in the morning. What are you working on anyway?"

"Putting the subsonic part of the song in binary."

"Ah, interesting."

"Feeling vulnerable out here," Clair said. "Vulnerable and angry."

"I had better go," said Clay.

"Night, Clay."

⤙⦿⤚

AN HOUR LATER, JUST WHEN NATE WAS GETTING TO THE POINT WHERE he felt he had enough samples marked out in binary to start looking for some sort of pattern, the third spirit in the night came through the door: Amy, in a man's T-shirt that hung to midthigh, yawning and rubbing her eyes.

"The hell you doing up at this hour? It's three in the morning."

"Working?"

Amy padded barefoot across the floor and looked at the monitor where Quinn was working, trying to blink the bleariness out of her eyes. "That the low end of the song?"

"Yeah, that and some blue-whale calls I had, for comparison."

Quinn could smell some kind of berry shampoo smell coming off of Amy, and he became hyperaware of the warmth of her pressing against his shoulder. "I don't understand. You're digitizing it manually? That seems a little primitive. The signal is already digitized by virtue of being on the disk, isn't it?"

"I'm looking at it a different way. It will probably wash out, but I'm looking at the waveform of just the low end. There's no behavior for context, so it's probably a waste of time anyway."

"But still you're up at three in the morning anyway, making ones and zeroes on a screen. Mind if I ask why?"

Quinn waited a second before answering, trying to figure out what to do. He wanted to turn to look at her, but she was so close that he'd be right in her face if he did. This wasn't the time. Instead he dropped his hands into his lap and sighed heavily as if this were all too tedious. He looked at the monitor as he spoke. "Okay, Amy, here's why. Here it is. The whole payoff, the whole jazz of what we do, okay?"

"Okay." She sensed the unease in his voice and stepped back.

Nate turned and looked her in the eye. "It might be out on the boat, as you're coming in for the day—or it might be in the lab at four in the morning after working on the data for five years, but there comes a point where you'll find something out, where you'll see something, or where something will suddenly come together, and you'll realize that you know something that no one else in the world knows yet. Just you. No one else. You realize that all the value you have is in that one thing, and you're only going to have it for a short time until you tell someone else, but for that time you are more alive than you'll ever be. That's the jazz, Amy. That's why people do this, put up with low pay and high risk and crap conditions and fucked-up relationships. They do it for that singular moment."

Amy stood with her hands clenched in front of her, arms straight down, like a little girl trying to ignore a lecture. She looked at the floor. "So you're saying that you're about to have one of these moments and I'm bugging you?"

"No, no, that's not what I'm saying. I don't know what I'm doing. I'm just telling you why I'm doing it. And that's why you're doing it, too. You just don't know it yet."

"And what if someone told you that you'd never have one of those moments of knowing something again—would you keep doing it?"

"That won't happen."

"So you're close to something here? With this binary thing?"

"Maybe."

"Didn't Ryder analyze the song as far as how much information it could carry and come up with something really anemic like point six bits per second? That's not really enough to make it meaningful, is it?"

Growl Ryder had been Quinn's doctoral adviser at UC Santa Cruz. One of the first generation of greats in the field, along with Ken Norris and Roger Payne, a true kahuna. His first name was actually Gerard, but anyone who had known him called him Growl, because of his perpetually surly nature. Ten years ago, off the Aleutians, he'd gone out alone in a Zodiac to record blue-whale calls and had never come back. Quinn smiled at his memory. "True, but Ryder died before he finished that work, and he was looking at the musical notes and themes for information. I'm actually looking at waveform. Just from what I've done tonight, it looks like you can get up to fifty, sixty bits per second. That's a lot of information."

"That can't be right. That won't work," Amy said. She seemed to be taking this information a bit more emotionally than Nate would have expected. "If you could move that much information subsonically, the navy would be using it for submarines. Besides, how could the whales use waveform? They'd need oscilloscopes." She was up on her toes now, almost shouting.

"Calm down, I'm just looking into it. Dolphins and bats don't need oscilloscopes to image sonically. Maybe there's something there. Just because I'm using a computer to look at this data doesn't mean I think whales are digital. It's only a model, for Christ's sake." He was going to pat her shoulder to comfort her, but then remembered her attitude toward that at the jail.

"You're not looking at data, Nate, you're making it up. You're wasting your time, and I'm not sure you're not wasting my time. This whole job might have been a big mistake."

"Amy, I don't understand why—"

But she wouldn't give him a chance to defend himself. "Go to bed, Nate. You're delirious. We have real work to do tomorrow, and you'll be worthless if you don't get some sleep." She turned and stormed out into the night. Even as she moved across the courtyard to her cabin, Nate could hear her ranting to herself. The words "doofus," "deluded," and "pathetic loser" rang out above the tirade to settle on Nate's ego.

Strangely enough, a feeling of relief washed over him as he realized that the delusions of romantic grandeur that he'd been indulging—nay, fighting—about his research assistant had been just that: delusions. She thought he was a complete joke. At peace with himself for the first time since Amy had come on board, he saved his work, powered down the machine, and went off to bed.

CHAPTER FOURTEEN

Down to the Harbor

own to the harbor they went—past the condos, the cane fields, the golf course, the Burger King, the Buddhist cemetery with its great green Buddha blissed out by the sea, past the steak houses, the tourist traps, the old guy riding down Front Street on a girl's bike with a macaw perched on his head—down to the harbor they went. They waved to the researchers at the fuel dock, nodded to the haglets at the charter booths, shakaed the divemasters and the captains, and schlepped science stuff down the dock to start their day.

Tako Man stood in the back of his boat eating a breakfast of rice and octopus as the Maui Whale crew—Clay, Quinn, Kona, and Amy—passed by. He was a strong, compact Malaysian with long hair and a stringy soul-patch beard that, along with the bone fishhooks he wore in his ears, gave him the distinct aspect of a pirate. He was one of the black-coral divers who lived in the harbor, and this morning, as always, he wore his wet suit.

"Hey, Tako," Clay said. The diver glanced up from his bowl. His eyes looked as if someone had poured shots of blood into them. Kona noticed that the small octopus in the diver's bowl was still moving, and he scampered down the dock feeling a case of the creeps fluttering to life in his spinal cord.

"Nightwalkers, gray ones, on your boat last night. I seen them," said Tako Man. "Not the first time."

"Good to know," said Clay, patronizing the diver and moving down the dock. You had to keep peace with anyone who lived in the harbor, especially the black-coral divers, who lived far over the edge of what most people would consider normal life. They shot heroin, drank heavily, spent all day doing bounce dives to two hundred feet looking for the gemstone-valuable black coral, then spent their money on weeklong parties that had, more than once, ended with one of them dead on the dock. They lived on their boats and ate rice and whatever they could pull out of the sea. Tako Man had gotten his name because on any given afternoon, after the divers came in for the day, you'd see the grizzled Malaysian carrying a net bag full of tako (octopus) that he had speared on the reef for their supper.

"Hi," Amy said sheepishly to Tako Man as they passed. He glared at her through his bloody haze, and his head bobbed as he almost nodded out into his breakfast. Amy quickened her pace and ran a Pelican case she was carrying into the back of Quinn's thigh.

"Jeez, Amy," Quinn said, having almost lost his footing.

"Do those guys dive in that condition?" Amy whispered, still sticking to Quinn like a shadow.

"Worse than that. Would you back up a little?"

"He's scary. You're supposed to protect me, ya mook. How do they keep from getting into trouble?"

"They lose one or two a year. Ironically, it's usually an overdose that gets them."

"Tough job."

"They're tough guys."

Tako Man shouted, "Fuck you, whale people! You'll see. Fucking nightwalker fuckers. Fucking fuck you, haole motherfuckers!" He tossed the remains of his breakfast at them. It landed overboard, and tiny fish broke the water fighting for the scraps.

"Rum," said Kona. "Too much hostility in dat buzz. Rum come from da cane, and cane come from slavin' the people, and dat oppression all distilled in de bottle and come out a man mean as cat shit on a day."

"Yeah," said Clay to Quinn. "Didn't you know that about rum?"

"Where's your boat?" asked Quinn.

"My boat?"

"Your boat, Clay," said Amy.

"No," said Clay. He stopped and dropped two cases of camera equipment on the dock. The *Always Confused,* the spiffy and powerful twenty-two-foot Grady White center-console fisherman, Clay's pride and joy, was gone. A life jacket, a water bottle, and various other familiar flotsam bobbed gently in a rainbow slick of gasoline where the boat had once been.

Everyone thought someone else should say something, but for a full minute no one did. They just stood there, staring at what should have been Clay's boat but instead was a big, boatless gob of tropical air.

"Poop," Amy finally said, saying it for all of them.

"We should check with the harbormaster," said Nate.

"My boat," said Clay, who stood over the empty slip as if it were his recently run-over boyhood dog. He would have nuzzled it and stroked its little dead doggy ears if he could have, but instead he fished the oily life jacket out of the water and sat on the dock rocking it.

"He really liked that boat," Amy said.

"Can I get a duh for the sistah?" exclaimed the dreaded blond kid.

"I paid the insurance," Nate said as he moved away, headed for the harbormaster.

Tako Man had come down the dock from his own boat to stare at the empty water. Somber now. Amy backed up into Kona for protection, but Kona had backed up into the next person behind him, which turned out to be Captain Tarwater, resplendent in his navy whites and newly Kona-scuffed shoes.

"Irie, ice cream man."

"You're on my shoes."

"What happened?" asked Cliff Hyland, coming down the dock behind the captain.

"Clay's boat's gone," said Amy.

Cliff moved up and put his hand on Clay's shoulder. "Maybe someone just borrowed it." Clay nodded, acknowledging that Cliff was trying to comfort him, but comfort fell like sandwiches on the recently bombed.

By the time Quinn returned from the harbormaster's office with a Maui cop in tow, there were a half dozen biologists, three black-coral divers, and a couple from Minnesota who were taking pictures of the whole thing, thinking that this would be something they would want to remember if they ever found out what was happening. As the cop approached, the black-coral divers faded to the edges of the crowd and away.

Jon Thomas Fuller, the scientist/entrepreneur who was accompanied by three of his cute female naturalists, stepped up beside Quinn. "This is just horrible, Nate. Just horrible. That boat represented a major capital investment for you guys, I'm sure."

"Yeah, but mainly we liked to think of it as something that floated and moved us around on the water." Nate actually had a great capacity for sarcasm, but he usually reserved it for those things and people he found truly irritating. Jon Thomas Fuller was truly irritating.

"Going to be tough to replace it."

"We'll manage. It was insured."

"You might want to get something bigger this time. I know there's a measure of safety working off of these sixty-five-footers we have, but also with the cabin you can set up computers, bow cameras, a lot of things that aren't really possible on little speedboats. A good-size boat would add a lot of legitimacy to your operation."

"We sort of decided to go with the legitimacy we get from doing credible research, Jon Thomas."

"We didn't make those figures up." Fuller caught himself raising his voice. The cop interviewing Clay looked over his shoulder, and Fuller lowered his tone. "That was just professional jealousy on the part of our detractors."

"Your detractors were the facts. What did you expect when your paper concluded that humpbacks actually enjoyed being struck by Jet Skis?"

"Some do." Fuller pushed back his pith helmet and ventured a smile of sincerity, which collapsed under its own weight.

"What's your angle, Jon Thomas?"

"Nate, I can get you a boat like ours, with all the trimmings, and an operating budget, and you'd just have to do one little project for me. One season of work, maximum. And your operation can keep the boat, sell it, do whatever you want."

Unless Fuller was about to ask him to shove him off the dock into the oily water, Quinn pretty much knew he was going to turn down the offer, but he had to ask. Those were really nice boats. "Make your proposal."

"I need you to put your name on a study that says that human-dolphin interaction facilities are not harmful to the animals, and do a study that says that building one at La Perouse Bay wouldn't have a negative impact on the environment. Then I'd need you to stand up at the appropriate meetings and make the case."

"I'm not your guy, Jon Thomas. First, I'm not a dolphin guy, and you know that." Nate avoided adding what he wanted to say, which was *Second, you are a feckless weasel out to make a buck without any consideration for science or the animals you study.* Instead he said, "There are dozens of people doing studies on captive dolphins. Why don't you go to them?"

"I have the animal study. You don't have to do the study. I just want your name on it."

"Won't the people who actually did the study have some objection to that?"

"No. They'll be fine with it. I need your name and your presence, Nate."

"I don't think so. I can't see myself testifying before impact committees and county planning boards."

"Okay, fair enough. Clay or Amy can do the stand-ups. Just put your name on the paper and do the environmental impact study. I need the credibility of your name."

"Which I won't have as soon as I let you use me. I'm sorry, but my name is all I really have to show for twenty-five years of work. I can't sell it out, even for a really nice boat."

"Oh, right, the nobility of starvation. Fuck that, Nate, and fuck your high ideals. I'm doing more for these animals by exposing the public to them than you'll do in a lifetime of graphing out songs and recording behavior. And before you retire to your ivory tower on the ethical high ground, you'd better take a good look at your people. That kid is a common thief, and no one has ever heard of your precious new assistant." Fuller turned and signaled to his chorus line of whalettes that they were going to their boat.

Quinn looked for Amy, saw her on the other side of the cop who was talking to Clay, helping him fill in details. He ran up behind Fuller, grabbed the smaller man's arm, and spun him around. "What are you talking about? Amy studied at Woods Hole, with Tyack and Loughten."

"That right? Well, maybe you'd better give them a call and ask them. Because they've never heard of her. Despite what you think, I *do* my research, Nate. Do you? Now, get back to your one-boat operation, would you."

"If I find out you had anything to do with this . . ."

Fuller wrenched his arm out of Quinn's grip and grinned. "Right, you'll what? Become more irrelevant? Screw you, Nate."

"What did you say?"

But Fuller ignored him and boarded his million-dollar research vessel, while Quinn skulked back down the dock to his friends. Oily flotsam seemed to be losing its allure, however, and the crowd had dispersed somewhat, leaving only Amy, Clay, the cop, and the couple from Minnesota.

"You. You're somebody aren't you?" asked the woman as Nate walked up. "Honey, this guy is someone. I remember seeing him on the Discovery Channel. Get my picture with him."

"Who is he?" said "honey" as his wife took Nate by the arm and posed like he'd just handed her a check.

"I don't know, one of those ocean guys," she said through a grin, acting as if she were posing with one of the carved statues that decorated doorways around Lahaina. "Just take the picture."

"Are you one of those Cousteau fellas?"

"*Oui,*" said Nate. "Now I muss speak with my good fren' Sylvia Earle," he continued in his French-by-way-of-British-Columbia-and-Northern-California fake accent as he went over to Amy. "I need to talk to you."

"Sylvia Earle! She's a National Geographic person. Get their picture together, honey."

～◦ତ∽

"HE'S LYING, NATHAN," AMY SAID. "YOU CAN CHECK IF YOU WANT. IT was all on the résumé I gave to Clay." She didn't appear angry, just hurt, betrayed perhaps. Her eyes were huge and teary, and she was starting to look vaguely like one of those creepy Keane sad-eyed-kid pictures. Quinn felt like he'd just smacked a bag of kittens against a truck bumper.

"I know," he said. "I'm sorry. I just . . . well, Jon Thomas is an asshole. I let him get to me."

"It's okay," Amy sniffed. "It's just . . . just . . . I've worked so hard."

"I don't need to check, Amy. You do good work. My fault for doubting you. Let's get Clay squared away and get to work."

He tentatively put his arm around her and walked her back to where Clay was finishing up his interview with the cop. Clay saw the tear tracks down Amy's face and immediately took her in his arms and pressed her head to his shoulder. "I know, honey. I know. It was a great boat, but it was just a boat. We'll get another one."

"Where's Kona?" Nate asked.

"He was around here a second ago," said Clay.

Just then Nate's cell phone rang. He worked it out of his shirt pocket and answered it. "Nathan, it's me," said the Old Broad. Nate covered the mouthpiece. "It's the Old Broad," Nate said to Clay.

"Amy, you go round up Kona while I finish up with the officer, okay?" Clay said.

Amy nodded and was off down the dock. Clay turned back to the officer.

The Old Broad went on, "Nathan, I spoke to that big male again today, and he definitely wants you to take a hot pastrami on rye with you when you go out. He said it's very important."

"I'm sure it is, Elizabeth, but I'm not sure we're even going out today. Something's happened to Clay's boat. It's gone."

"Oh, my, he must be distraught. I'll come down and look after him, but *you* have to get out in the channel today. I just feel it's very important."

"I don't think you'll need to come down, Elizabeth. Clay will manage."

"Well, if you say so, but you have to promise me you'll go out today."

"I promise."

"And you'll take a pastrami on rye for that big male."

"I'll try, Elizabeth. I have to go now, Clay needs me for something."

"With Swiss cheese and hot mustard!" the Old Broad said as Nate disconnected.

Clay thanked the policeman, who nodded to Quinn as he walked off. Even the couple from Minnesota had moved on, and only Clay and Quinn were left on the dock. "Where are the kids?" asked Nate, cringing at the whole idea: he and Clay, the middle-aged couple being responsible and boring while the kids went off to play and have adventures.

"I asked Amy to find Kona. They could be anywhere."

"Clay, I need to ask you something before they get back."

"Shoot."

"Did you check any of Amy's references before you hired her? I mean, did you call anyone? Woods Hole? Her undergrad school—what was it?"

"Cornell. Nope. She was smart, she was cute, she seemed to know what she was talking about, and she said she'd work for free. The bona fides looked good on paper. Gift horse, Nate."

"Jon Thomas Fuller said that he checked and that no one at Woods Hole has heard of her."

"Fuller's an asshole. Look, I don't really care if she finished high school. The kid has proven herself. She's got balls."

"Still, maybe I should call Tyack. Just in case."

"If you need to. Call him this afternoon when you get back in."

"I'm sure Fuller was just yanking my chain. He tried to offer us a boat like his if we backed his dolphin-park project."

"And you turned him down?"

"Of course."

"But those are really nice boats. Our armada has been reduced by fifty percent. Our nautical resources have declined by more than one-half. Our boatage is deficient by point five."

"What's up?" Amy said. She'd come back down the dock and seemed to have shaken off her earlier melancholy.

"Clay's being scientific. Fuller offered us a sixty-foot research vessel like his, with operating budget, if we back his dolphin project."

"Do I have to sleep with him?"

"We haven't put that on the table," Clay said, "but I'll bet we could get a sonar array if you're enthusiastic."

"Hell, Nate, take it," Amy said.

"It would mean selling out my credibility," said Quinn, appalled at what total whores his colleagues had become. "We'd be going over to the dark side."

Amy shrugged. "Those are really nice boats." The corner of her mouth twitched as if she was trying not to grin, and Nate realized that she was probably goofing on him.

"Yeah," said Clay. "Nice." Clay was goofing, too. He'd be all right.

Nate shook his head, looking as if he were fighting disbelief, but actually he was trying to shake the memory of his dream of driving a big cabin cruiser through the streets of Seattle with Amy displayed as the bikinied figurehead. "If you're okay, Clay, we really should get out before the wind comes up."

"Go," Clay said. "I'll get the police report for the insurance company." To Amy he said, "You find Kona?"

"He's down there with that Tako guy."

"What's he doing down there?"

"It looked like he was building a saxophone. I didn't go close."

Quinn strode down the dock and looked to where Kona was talking with Tako Man. "No, that's his bong. It breaks down for easy portage."

"What's a bong?"

"Cute, Amy. Help me get the equipment in the boat."

Suddenly Kona started shouting and running down the dock toward them. "Bwanas! I found the boat!"

Clay perked up. "Where?"

"Right there. Tako Man says it's right there. He dove down there this morning."

Kona was pointing to a patch of murky jade green water in the center of the harbor. Jade green because of all the waste flushed from the live-aboards, as well as the bait, fish guts, seasickness, and bird poop that went into the water faster than the scavengers could clean it out, and so it caused a perpetual algae bloom.

"My boat," said Clay, looking forlornly at the empty water.

Amy stepped up and put her arm around Clay's shoulders to resume stage-two comfort. "He dove in that water?"

"The nightwalkers sank it, Bwana Clay. Tako Man saw them. Skinny blue-gray guys. He called them nightwalkers. I think aliens."

"Aliens are always gray, aren't they?" inquired Quinn.

"That's what I say to him," said Kona. "But he say no, not with the lightbulb head. He say they tall and froggy."

"You're high," said Clay.

"Tako Man got dank mystical buds, brah. Was a spiritual duty."

"He's not criticizing you, Kona," Quinn explained. "We just assume that you're high. Clay's just doubting the credibility of your story."

"You don't believe I? Give a man a mask, I'll dive down and get a ting off da boat for proof."

"Hepatitis, that's what you'll bring up," said Amy.

"I'm going to work," said Nate.

"My boat," said Clay.

Nate decided that perhaps he should offer a measure of solace. "Look at the bright side, Clay. At least whales are big."

"How is that the bright side?"

"We could be studying viruses. You have any idea what it costs to replace a scanning electron microscope?"

"My boat," said Clay.

CHAPTER FIFTEEN

A Song for Your Supper

Amy picked the whale. It had been a stressful morning for her, and Quinn wanted to convey his complete confidence in her, so he handed over the headphones and took directions as they narrowed down which of their whales was actually the singer.

"Wait a second," Amy said. "Shut down the engine."

And then she did something that Quinn had seen no one do for twenty-five years, and then it had been his mentor, Gerard Ryder, who most people agreed had been eccentric to the point of being full-blown bat shit. Amy hung over the side by her knees and put her head in the water. After about thirty seconds she swung up, spraying a great crest of seawater all over the boat, then pointed north.

"He's over there."

"That doesn't work, you know," said Quinn. It was pretty much accepted that humans didn't have directional hearing underwater. He was just gently trying to remind her.

"Go that way. That's where our whale is."

"Okay, there may indeed be a singer over there, but you didn't locate him by hearing him."

She just stood there next to him—dripping on his feet, the console, the field notes—looking at him.

"Okay, I'm going." He started the engine and pushed the throttle over. "Tell me when I get there."

A couple of minutes later Amy signaled for him to cut the engine, and she was hanging over the side with her head in the water while the boat was still coasting.

"Well, this is just stupid," Nate said while Amy was submerged.

Amy dedunked long enough to say, "I heard that."

"Looks like you're bobbing for whales, is what it looks like."

"Shut up," said Amy, up for a breath. "I'm trying to listen."

"You look like that cartoon character in 'B.C.' that used to watch fish all day."

"That way," said Amy, up again, pointing and dog-shaking the water out of her hair onto the Ph.D. "About six hundred yards."

"Six hundred yards? You're sure?"

"Give or take fifty."

"If we're within a half mile of a singer, I'll buy you dinner."

" 'Kay. What do you suppose the freight is to fly a lobster from Maine to my plate in Lahaina?"

"I'm not going to need to know that."

"Drive the boat, please. Over there." And she pointed again, not unlike Babe Ruth indicating the Wrigley Field fence over which he would hit the famous promised home run (except Amy was thin, a girl, and alive).

Quinn heard the singer even before they put the hydrophone in the water. The whole boat started resonating to the song as they coasted into a drift.

Amy hopped up on the bow and pointed to some white spots dancing below the surface—pectoral fins and a tail. "There he is!"

If there had been a crowd, they would have gone wild.

Quinn smiled. Amy looked back at him and grinned. "Steak *and* lobster," she said. "Something red and French and expensive for the wine, something on fire for dessert—don't care what it is, long as there's flames coming off it—then a backrub before I send you back to your cabin alone, disappointed and confused. Ha!"

"It's a date," said Quinn.

"No, it's not a date. It's a bet, which you have lost miserably because you had the audacity to doubt me, and for which you shall remain ever sorry. Ha!"

"Shall we work now? Or would you like to gloat a bit longer?"

"Hmmm, let me think about it. . . ."

She's so small, yet she contains so much evil, Quinn thought. He threw the field journal at her and read her the longitude and latitude off the GPS. "Film's in the camera. New roll. I loaded it this morning."

"I was thinking I'd gloat some more." Amy picked up the notebook, then paused as she opened it to begin writing. "Singing stopped."

"Sometimes I think they just stop singing to freak me out."

"He's moving," Amy said, pointing.

"Moving," Quinn repeated. He looked over the side and saw the white pec fins and flukes flash out of sight. "Hold on." He started the engine.

"They can hunt these kind, as far as I'm concerned," Quinn said after they'd been on the whale for two hours.

They'd recorded three full cycles of the song and gotten a crossbow biopsy, but the whale simply would not fluke, so they hadn't been able to get an ID photo. A lot of good it did to have a DNA sample when you couldn't identify the animal.

"Hunt them and make them into pet food," Nate continued. "Get their tainted, nonfluking genes out of the gene pool."

"Maybe you should have a doughnut or something, get your blood sugar up," Amy said.

"Use their pathetic, nonfluking baleen for corsets and umbrella stays. Use their vertebrae for footstools. Use their intestines to make giant, nonfluking whale sausages to serve at state fairs. Remove their putrid unfluking gonads and—"

"I thought you liked these animals."

"Yeah, but not when they won't cooperate."

The whale had led them five miles out toward Molokai and very close to the wind line, where the waves were too big and the current too fast to stay on a singer. If the whale continued in this direction, they would lose him within the next two dive cycles and the day would be wasted. What was even more frustrating was that this animal was hanging in the water and singing with his tail only a few feet below the surface. Typically, a singer in the channel would be thirty to fifty feet down—this guy was at about seven. Nate kept having to pull up the hydrophone to keep it from bopping the whale in the noggin as they drifted over it.

"He's coming up," Amy said. She grabbed the camera off the seat and aimed it at a spot twenty yards or so in front of the boat so the autofocus and exposure would already be set.

Nate pulled up the hydrophone with two yanks and started the engine. The whale was moving faster this time. Nate adjusted the throttle to put Amy at the right distance for a full-frame tail shot.

One breath and he was down for ten seconds, another breath twelve seconds, another breath and the great tail peduncle arched high into the air.

"Looks like he's going to do it," Nate said.

"Ready," Amy said.

The tail cleared the water by just a foot, presenting an edge view instead of a flat horizontal view that would give them all the markings, but Nate thought he saw something. Something that looked like black letters on the underside of the tail.

"You get that? You get that?"

"I got what there was. He didn't present very well." Amy had run the motor drive for the whole cycle of the dive, maybe eight frames.

"Did you see those markings? On the underside? The black . . . uh, stripes?" Quinn whipped off his sunglasses and wiped them with his T-shirt.

"Stripes? Nate, I didn't see anything but edge through the camera."

"Damn it!"

"Look, he fluked. Maybe he will again."

"That's not the point."

"It's not?"

"Get up on the bow, see if you can find him."

Amy stood on the bow and directed Quinn. When she dropped her arm, he killed the engine. And there was the whale, hanging there, singing, his tail not ten feet under the water. They weren't a hundred yards off the wind line, and the boat was drifting away from the whale faster than it had before. They'd be over it for only a minute or so. This close to the wind line, they'd probably lose him the next time he came up. Nate was not going to finish this day wondering if he was having hallucinations again.

"Amy, hand me my mask and flippers from the bow cabinet, would you?"

"You're going in the water?"

"Yes."

"But you never go in the water."

"I'm going in the water." Nate opened a plastic Pelican case and pulled out his Nikonos IV underwater camera, checked to make sure it was loaded.

"You're not a water guy."

"See if there's a weight belt in there, too."

"Clay says you're not a water guy. You're a boat guy."

"I'm going to get an ID photo from under his tail. If he's going to be accommodating enough to stay this close to the surface, I'm going to go get the photo."

"Can you do that?"

"Why not?"

She handed him a belt weighted with ten pounds of lead, and Nate buckled it around his hips. He pulled on the mask and fins, then sat on the gunwale with his back to the water. "You're going to drift off of me. I'm not going to try to swim to catch you, so come back and get me. Wait till I wave. I don't want you to start the engine until I'm sure I have the picture. Keep recording until you come get me."

" 'Kay." Amy's mouth was sort of hanging open as if she'd just been slapped.

"This is no big deal."

"Right. You want me to do it? It's my fault I didn't get the shot last time."

"Not your fault. The shot wasn't there. See ya."

Quinn put the snorkel in his mouth and rolled backward off the boat. At seventy-five degrees, the water was still cold enough to knock the breath out of him. He floated to the surface and tried to take controlled breaths until his system adjusted.

The whale was close, only a hundred or so feet away. The song reverberated in Nate's ribs as he kicked over to it. This had to be the "bite me" whale. Even if he'd somehow been wrong about there actually being letters, there were certainly some strange markings on this animal's tail. And there was more than that, too, if he could prove to himself that this was the same animal. It would mean that the whale had stayed in the general area of the Au'au Channel for over three weeks, which was fairly unusual. Of course, conclusions weren't reached from that lack of data. It could simply be that they hadn't computerized the catalog of Hawaiian ID photos the way they had in Alaska. And without the first picture there'd be no proof that this was the same animal, but Quinn would know. He would know. That had become the impetus of this silly mission, not just proving that he wasn't hallucinating. He was a man of science, of facts, of reason. He didn't need to prove he was sane.

I'm out of my mind, he thought. He'd never even heard of anyone trying to do an ID photo underwater.

The animal was perfectly motionless, a great swath of gray in a field of infinite blue. But Quinn thought he saw movement on the far side of the whale. He lifted his head out of the water and looked back at the boat. Amy gave him a thumbs-up. He took a deep breath and made his dive to take the photo.

If he'd been wearing tanks, he might have let the weight belt take him down slowly, but he knew he'd be able to stay down for only forty to sixty seconds, so he went headfirst, kicking hard until he was down twenty or so feet. Then he leveled off, holding the camera in front of him, and looked up at the underside of the whale's tail.

There it was, in big, sans-serif, spray-paint-like letters: BITE ME! He nearly forgot to take the picture. How could this possibly be? Had the animal somehow been caught in a net when it was younger and marked by a sardonic fisherman before being released? Was it one of those animals that had swum up a river and got stranded, then been rescued by an army of fish-and-game people?

He centered the tail in the viewfinder and hit the shutter. Advanced the film and shot again. Then he needed to breathe. He turned and kicked to the surface, but again he saw the dark shape moving near the whale. *Remora*, he thought. Although it looked too big to be one of the parasite fish that often attached themselves to whales.

At the surface he looked back down at the singer, near the left pec where he'd seen the movement. The animal was doing ribbits. Quinn smiled around his snorkel, took three deep breaths, held, then dove again.

This time, before he could get the camera up, he saw the movement of a dark fin on the far side of the whale, and he squinted to see deep into the blue distance. Blue-water willies, was how he'd always thought of it. The feeling you get when you realize that something big and carnivorous could come at you from any direction, then you start looking for gray missiles in the blue, like looking for a malevolent face to appear at a dark window.

Then the whale moved. The wash of the tail pushed Quinn back, but he maintained his bearings and started toward the surface, trying to keep his eye on the animal. The whale turned around in little more than its own length and shot toward Nate. He kicked laterally, trying to move to one side or another, then up, so he'd be tossed over the top of the animal rather than under it as it came up, because it was definitely going to bump him.

He looked back beyond his fins as he kicked and saw the whale adjust its direction to keep coming toward him. Nate kicked once for the surface, then looked back again to see the animal's enormous mouth opening beneath him. *No, this can't be happening,* he thought.

The panic rising in his chest demanded air, but it was as if the entire ocean had opened up a hole behind him, and he wasn't going to make it to the surface. The whale came halfway out of the water as it scooped him up, and Nate saw sky, and white water, and baleen fringing the upper jaw above—all of it framed by the huge trapezoid that was the whale's open mouth. Then he felt the whale sinking back, and he saw the baleen close over him. He rolled into a ball, hoping not to be crushed by the jaws, hoping to be spit out as a horrible dining mistake. But then the great tongue came forward, warm and rough, driving him against the baleen plates—it was like being smashed into a wrought-iron fence by a wet Nerf Volkswagen. He could feel the baleen ripping the skin on his back as the tongue covered him, pressing the seawater out around him as it would strain krill, then crushing him until the last of the air exploded from his body and he blacked out.

PART TWO

Jonah's People

Men really need sea monsters
in their personal oceans.

For the ocean, deep and black in the depths,
is like the low dark levels of our minds in which
the dream symbols incubate and sometimes rise
up to sight like the Old Man of the Sea.

—JOHN STEINBECK

CHAPTER SIXTEEN

Shoes Off in the Whale!

Shoes off in the whale!" a male voice said out of the dark.

Quinn could see nothing. His entire body ached like, well, like it had been chewed. He crawled to his hands and knees on what felt like wet latex. He reached down and felt for his feet. He still had his flippers on, and logic protested through his confusion. "I'm not wearing shoes. These are fins."

"Shoes off in the whale! And don't try and make a break for the anus."

Two things that, if asked about an hour earlier, Nate might have said with conviction he'd never hear in a lifetime of conversation.

"What?" Quinn said, squinting into the dark. He realized that he was still wearing his dive mask and reached up to push it back.

"I'll bet he didn't bring the pastrami on rye I asked for either, did he?" came the voice.

Shapes began to define themselves in the darkness, and Nate saw a face not a foot away from his. He gasped and pulled away from it, for although it seemed to be examining him with great interest, the face was not human.

CLAY DEMODOCUS WAS KNOWN THROUGHOUT THE WORLD AS ONE OF the calmest, most level-tempered, most generous and considerate individuals in the entire milieu of marine biology. His reputation preceded him when he went on assignment, and people took it for granted that he would remain amiable throughout a long voyage in cramped quarters, as well as efficient in his own work, respectful of the work of others, and cool-headed in an emergency. Because he often had to subjugate himself to the head researcher on any given assignment, Clay did not indulge in ego battles and testosterone-slinging contests with researchers or crew. None of these qualities were evident when he went over the desk of the Coast Guard commandant and stopped only inches from head-butting the tall, athletic-looking officer. "You call this search off now and I'll see to it that your name is remembered for all time in concert with Adolf Eichmann and Vlad the Impaler. Nathan Quinn is a legend in his field, and every time there's a documentary on whales on the Discovery Channel, or National Geographic, or Animal Planet, or PBS, or the fucking Cartoon Channel, I'll see to it that your name is mentioned right after Nate's as the man who left him out there. You'll be the official Coast Guard pariah for the next hundred years. This will be the Coast Guard's My Lai. Every time a kid drowns, your name will be mentioned— nay, every time someone gets a soaker, the name of Commodore What-everyournameis shall be brought forth and your effigy burned in the streets and your head stuck on a pole, lipsticked, and marched around school yards, forever. And all because you're too goddamned lame-brained to put a couple of helicopters into the air to find my friend. Is that what you want?"

Clay had strong views on loyalty.

The commodore had been in the Coast Guard for most of his adult life, spending the majority of his time and energy either rescuing people or training others to do so, and as a result he was taken aback more than somewhat by Clay's tirade. He looked across his office to where Kona and Amy stood by the door, looking nearly as haggard as he felt. The surfer looked at him and shook his head sadly.

"It's been three days, Mr. Demodocus. In open water with no life preserver? You're not a tourist—you know the odds. If he were alive, he'd have drifted far out of where we're able to patrol by now anyway. We're doing no fewer than ten rescues a day on Maui. I can't have our helicopters out to sea when there's just no chance."

"What about tide maps, currents?" Clay pleaded. "Can't we try to predict which way he might have drifted? Narrow the search area."

The commodore had to look away from Clay when he answered. The first thing the surfer kid with the uneven dreadlocks had said when they'd come into his office was "Sucks to be you." And right now the commodore couldn't have agreed more. He'd lost friends at sea; he understood. "I'm sorry," he said.

Clay sighed heavily, and his shoulders sagged. Amy came forward and took him by the arm. "Let's go home, Clay."

Clay nodded and allowed himself to be led out of the commodore's office.

As they made their way across the parking lot to Clay's truck Kona said, "That was amazing, Clay."

"Throwing a fit? Yeah, I'm proud of that, especially since it worked so well."

"Why didn't you say anything about the whale eating Nate?" In the three days since Quinn had disappeared, Kona had forgotten to speak brophonics and Rasta talk almost completely, and now he just sounded like a kid from New Jersey with a "whoa, dude" surfer accent.

"Whales don't eat people, Kona," Clay said. "You know better."

"I know what I saw," Amy said.

Clay stopped and stepped away from both of them. "Look, if you're going to do this stuff, you have to be practical. I believe that you saw what you say you saw, but nothing about it helps. First, a humpback's throat is only about a foot in diameter. They couldn't swallow a human if they wanted to. So if the whale did scoop up Nate, then there's a good chance he was spit out very quickly. Second, if I told that story to everyone else, either they'd think you were being hysterical or, if they believed you, they'd assume that Nate had been drowned immediately, and there wouldn't have been a search. I believe you, kid, but don't think anyone else will."

"So what now?" Kona asked.

Clay looked at the two of them, standing there like abandoned puppies, and he pushed aside his own grief. "We finish Nate's work. We do this work, we carry on. Right now I've got to go up the mountain and see the Old Broad. Nate was like a son to her."

"You haven't told her?" Amy asked.

Clay shook his head. "Why would I? I haven't given up on Nate. I've seen too much. Last year they thought they'd lost one of the black-coral divers. The boat came back to where they'd sent him down, and he was gone. A week later he called from Molokai for them to come get him. He'd swum over and had been so busy partying he'd forgotten to call."

"Doesn't sound like Nate," Kona said. "He told me that he hated fun."

"Still, it would be wrong not to let the Old Broad know what's happened," Amy said.

Clay patted them each on the back. "Intrepid," he said.

～◦◦～

AS HE DROVE UP THE VOLCANO, CLAY TRIED TO FORMULATE SOME GENtle way of breaking the news to the Old Broad. Since his mother had passed away, Clay had taken the bearing of bad news very seriously—so seriously, in fact, that he usually let someone else do the bearing. He'd been in Antarctica on assignment for *National Science*, snowed in at the naval weather station for six months when his mother, still in Greece, had gone missing. She was seventy-five, and the villagers knew she couldn't have gone far, yet, search as they might, they did not find her for three days. Finally her location was revealed by her ripening odor. They found her dead in an olive tree, where she had climbed to do some pruning. Clay's older brothers, Hektor and Sidor, would not hold the funeral without Clay, the baby, yet they knew their brother would be completely out of touch for months. "He is the rich American," came the ouzo-besotted lament. "He should take care of Mama. Perhaps he will even fly us to America for the funeral." And so the two brothers, having inherited their mother's weakness for alcohol and their father's bad judgment, packed the remains of Mother Demodocus in an olive barrel, filled the barrel with the preserving brine, and shipped it off to their rich younger brother's house in San Diego. The problem was, in their grief (or perhaps it was their stupor) they forgot to send a letter, leave a message, or, for that matter, put a packing label on the barrel, so months later, when Clay returned to find the barrel on his porch, he broke into it thinking he was about to enjoy a delicious snack of kalamata olives from home. It was not the way to find out about his mother's death, and it engendered in Clay very strong views about loyalty and the bearing of bad news.

I will do this right, he thought as he pulled into the Old Broad's driveway. *There's no reason for this to be a shock.*

❧

THERE WERE CATS AND CRYSTALS EVERYWHERE. THE OLD BROAD LED him through the house and had him sit in a wicker emperor's chair that looked out over the channel while she fetched some mango iced tea for them. The house could have been designed by Gauguin and landscaped by Rousseau. It was small, just five rooms and a carport, but it sat on twenty acres of fruit-salad jungle: banana trees, mango, lemon, tangerine, orange, papaya, and coconut palm, as well as a florist's dream of orchids and other tropical flowers. The Old Broad had cultivated a low, soft grass under all the trees that was like a golf-course green over sponge cake. The house was made almost entirely of dark koa wood, nut brown and with black grain running through it, polished to a smooth satin and as hard as ebony. There was a high-peaked galvanized-tin roof with a vented tower in the center to draw heat out the top and cool air in from under the wide eaves that surrounded the whole house. There were no windows, just open sliding walls. You could look through any part of the house to the other and see the tropical garden. The Old Broad's telescope and "big-eye" binoculars stood on steel and concrete mountings in front of where Clay sat, looking very much out of place: the artillery of science planted in paradise. At Clay's feet a skinny cat happily crunched the legs off a scorpion.

The Old Broad handed Clay a tall, icy glass and sat in another emperor's chair beside him. She was barefoot and wore a flowered caftan and a yellow-and-red hibiscus blossom in her hair that was half the size of her face. *She had probably been a dish back around the time of Lincoln,* Clay thought.

"It's so nice to see you, Clay. I don't get many visitors. Not that I'm lonely, you know. I have the cats and the whales to talk to. But that's not like having one of my boys to visit with."

Oh, jeez, Clay thought. *One of her boys. Oh, jeez.* He had to tell her. He knew he had to tell her. He had come up here to tell her, and he was going to tell her, and that was that. "This is excellent tea, Elizabeth. Mango, you say?"

"That's right. Just a little bit of mint. Now, what is it you needed to talk to me about?"

"And ice? I think the coldness makes it, gives it a fantastic, uh . . ."

"Temperature? Yes, ice is an essential ingredient in iced tea, Clay. Thus the name."

Sarcasm is so ugly on the aged, thought Clay. *No one likes a sarcastic oldster.* He said, "Iced tea, you mean?" *Oh, this is just going to kill her,* he thought.

"If this is about a new boat, Clay, don't be shy. I know how you loved that boat, and we'll get you another one. I'm just not sure we can go for one quite that nice. My investments haven't been doing well the last couple of years."

"No, no, it's not the boat. The boat was insured. It's Nate."

"And how is Nathan? I hope he's handling his little infatuation with your new researcher with a bit of dignity. He was wearing it on his sleeve that night at the sanctuary. You'd think a man as smart as Nathan would have better control over his impulses."

"Nate had a thing for Amy?" Clay was going to tell her, really. He was just working up to it.

"You said 'had,' " said the Old Broad. "You said Nate 'had' a thing for Amy."

"Elizabeth, there's been an accident. Three days ago Nate went into the water to get a better look at a singer, and . . . well, we haven't been able to find him." Clay put down his tea so he could catch the old woman should she faint. "I'm very sorry."

"Oh, that. Yes, I heard about that. Nate's fine, Clay. The whale told me."

And here Clay found himself balancing on another dilemma. Should he let her have her belief, no matter how crazy it might be, or should he dash her spirits to earth with the truth?

Although Nate had found Elizabeth's eccentricities irritating, Clay had always liked her insistence that the whales spoke to her. He wished it were true. He scooted to the edge of his chair and took her hand in his.

"Elizabeth, I don't think you understand what I'm saying—"

"He took the pastrami and rye, right? He said he would."

"Um, that's not exactly pertinent. He's been gone for three days, and they were right at the wind line toward Molokai when he was lost. Rough sea. He's probably gone, Elizabeth."

"Well, of course he's gone, Clay. You'll just have to carry on until he gets back." Now *she* patted *his* hand. "He did take the sandwich, right? The whale was very specific."

"Elizabeth! You're not listening to me. This is not about the whales singing to you through the trees. Nate is gone!"

"Don't you shout at me, Clay Demodocus. I'm trying to comfort you. And it wasn't a song through the trees. What do you think? I'm some crazy old woman? The whale called on the phone."

"Oh, Jesus, Joseph, and Mary, I don't know how to do this."

"More tea?" asked the Old Broad.

⤙◈⤚

AS CLAY MADE THE LONG DRIVE DOWN THE VOLCANO AND BACK TO Papa Lani, he tried to fight letting his spirits rise. The Old Broad was completely convinced that Nathan Quinn was just fine and dandy, although she could give no reason other than to say that the whale, after ordering a pastrami on rye, had told her that everything would be all right.

"And how did you know it was the whale on the phone?" asked Clay.

"Well, he told me that's who he was."

"And it was a male voice?"

"Well, it would be. He's a singer, isn't he?"

She'd gone on like that, reassuring him, encouraging him to go back to work, dismissing any guilt or grief, until he was almost to the gates of the compound before he remembered.

"She's a total loony!" he said to himself, as if he just needed to hear the words, to feel their truth. *Nothing is all right. Nate's dead.*

Clair would be sleeping at her house tonight, and although it was late, Clay could not make himself go to sleep. Instead he went to the office, knowing that nothing in the world could eat up time like editing video. He attached a digital video camera to his computer and turned on the recently replaced giant monitor. Blue filled the screen, and then he could sense the motion of descent, but there was only a faint hiss of his breathing, not the usual fusillade of bubbles from a regulator. This was the rebreather footage, from the day he had almost drowned. He'd completely forgotten about it. The breath-holder's tail came into frame.

Clay's first instincts had been right. This was great footage of a breath-holder—the best they'd ever recorded. As he passed the tail, the genital slit came into view, and he could tell that they were dealing with a male. There were black marks on the underside of the tail, but the view was still edge on, and he couldn't make out their shape. He heard a faint kazoo sound in the background and ran back the tape, with the sound turned up.

This time his breath sounded like a bull snorting before a charge, the kazoo sound, louder now, like a voice through wax paper. He ran back the tape again and cranked the sound all the way up, bringing down the high frequency to kill some of the hiss. Definitely voices.

"There's someone outside, Captain."

"Does he have my sandwich with him?"

"He's close, Captain, really close. Too close."

Then the tail came down, and there was a deafening thud. The picture jerked in a half dozen directions, then settled as tiny bubbles passed by the lens in a field of blue. The lens caught a shot of Clay's fin as he sank, and then it was just blue and the occasional shot of the lanyard that secured the camera to his wrist.

Clay ran the tape back again, confirmed the voices, then set it to dub onto the computer hard drive so he could manipulate the audio in a waveform, the way they did with sound recordings. Even though he was sure what was on the tape, he couldn't figure out how it could possibly have gotten there. Only five minutes of watching little progress bars move across the monitor, and he could stand the suspense no longer. He smiled to himself, because now was the time he would have gone to Nate, as he had so many times before, to help him figure out exactly what it was they were hearing or looking at, but Nate was gone. He checked his watch, and, deciding that it wasn't too insanely late, he headed across the compound to get Amy.

CHAPTER SEVENTEEN

Jonathan Livingston Reaper

Amy wore an oversized, tattered "I'M WITH STUPID" nightshirt and Local Motion flip-flops. Her hair was completely flat on one side and splayed out into an improbable sunburst of spikes on the other, making it appear that she was getting hit in the side of the head by a tiny hurricane, which she wasn't. She was, however, performing the longest sustained yawn Clay had ever seen.

"Ooo ahe-e, I aya oa a," she said in yawnspeak, a language—not unlike Hawaiian—known for its paucity of consonants. (*You go ahead, I'm okay*, she was saying.) She gestured for Clay to continue.

Clay cued the tape and fiddled with the audio. A whale tail in a field of blue passed by on the monitor.

"There's someone outside, Captain."

"Does he have my sandwich with him?"

Amy stopped yawning and scooted forward on the stool she was perched upon behind Clay. When the whale tail came down, Clay stopped the tape and looked back at her.

"Well?"

"Play it again."

He did. "Can we get a feeling for direction?" Amy asked. "That housing has stereo microphones, right? What if we move the speakers far apart—can we get a sense where it's coming from?"

Clay shook his head. "The mikes are right next to each other. You have to separate them by at least a meter to get any spatial information. All I can tell you is that it's in the water and it's not particularly loud. In fact, if I hadn't been using the rebreather, I'd never have heard it. You're the audio person. What can you tell me?"

He ran it back and played it again.

"It's human speech."

Clay looked at her as if to say, *Uh-huh, I woke you up because I needed the obvious pointed out.*

"And it's military."

"Why do you think it's military?"

Now Amy gave Clay the same look that he had just finished giving her. " 'Captain'?"

"Oh, right," said Clay. "Speaker in the water? Divers with underwater communications? What do you think?"

"Didn't sound like it. Did it sound like it was coming from small speakers to you?"

"Nope." Clay played it again. "Sandwich?" he said.

"Sandwich?"

"The Old Broad said that someone called her claiming to be a whale and asked her to tell Nate to bring him a sandwich."

Amy squeezed Clay's shoulder. "He's gone, Clay. I know you don't believe what I saw happened, but it certainly wasn't about a sandwich conspiracy."

"I'm not saying that, Amy. Damn it. I'm not saying this had anything to do with Nate's"—he was going to say drowning and stopped himself—"accident. But it might have to do with the lab getting wrecked, the tapes getting stolen, and someone trying to mess with the Old Broad. Someone is fucking with us, Amy, and it might be whoever is recorded on this tape."

"And there's no way the camera could have pulled a signal out of the air, something on the same frequency or something? A mobile phone or something?"

"Through a half-inch of powder-coated aluminum housing and a hundred feet of water? No, that signal came in through the mike. That I'm sure of."

Amy nodded and looked at the paused picture on the screen. "So you're looking for two things: someone military and someone who has an interest in Nate's work."

"No one—" Clay stopped himself again, remembering what he'd said to Nate when the lab had been wrecked. That no one cared about their work. But obviously someone did. "Tarwater?"

Amy shrugged. "He's military. Maybe. Leave the tape out. I'll run a spectrograph on the audio in the morning, see if I can tell if it's coming through some kind of amplifier. I've got nothing left tonight—I'm beat."

"Thanks," Clay said. "You get some rest, kiddo. I'm going to hit it, too. I'll be heading down to the harbor first thing."

" 'Kay."

"Oh, and hey, the 'kiddo' thing, I didn't mean—"

Amy threw her arms around him and kissed the top of his head. "You big mook. Don't worry, we'll get through this." She turned and started out the door.

"Amy?"

She paused in the doorway. "Yeah?"

"Can I ask you a . . . personal question, kinda?"

"Shoot."

"The shirt—who's stupid?"

She looked down at her shirt, then back at him and grinned. "Always seems to apply, Clay. No matter where I am or who I'm with, the smoke clears and the shirt is true. You gotta hang on to truth when you find it."

"I like truth," Clay said.

"Night, Clay."

"Night, kiddo."

THE NEXT DAY THE WEATHER WAS BLOWN OUT, WITH WHITECAPS frosting the entire channel across to Lanai and the coconut palms whipping overhead like epileptic dust mops. Clay drove by the harbor in his truck, noting that the cabin cruiser that Cliff Hyland's group had been using was parked in its slip. Then he turned around and caught a flash of white out of the corner of his eye as he drove past the hundred-year-old Pioneer Inn—Captain Tarwater's navy whites standing out against the green shiplap. He parked his truck by the giant banyan tree next door and humped it over to the restaurant.

When Clay came up to the table, the hostess was just seating Cliff Hyland, Tarwater, and one of their grad students, a young blond woman with a raccoon sunburn and straw-dry hair.

"Hey, Cliff," Clay said. "You got a minute?"

"Clay, how you doing?" Hyland took off his sunglasses and stood to shake hands. "Please, join us."

Clay looked at Tarwater, and the naval officer nodded. "Sorry to hear about your partner," he said. Then he looked back down at his menu. The young woman sitting with them was watching the dynamic between the three men as if she might write a paper on it.

"Just a second," Clay said. "If I could talk to you outside."

Now Tarwater glanced up and gave Cliff Hyland an almost imperceptible shake of the head.

"Sure, Clay," Cliff said, "let's walk." He looked to the junior researcher. "When she comes, coffee, Portuguese sausage, eggs over easy, whole wheat."

The girl nodded. Hyland followed Clay out to the front of the hotel, which overlooked the harbor fueling station and the *Carthaginian,* a steel-hulled replica of a whaling brig, now used as a floating museum. They stood side by side, watching the harbor, each with a foot propped on the seawall.

"What's up, Clay?"

"What are you guys working on, Cliff?"

"You know I can't talk about that. I signed a nondisclosure thing."

"You got divers in the water, people with underwater coms?"

"Don't be silly, Clay. You've seen my crew. Except for Tarwater, they're just kids. What's this about?"

"Somebody's fucking with us, Cliff. They sank my boat, tore up the office, took Nate's papers and tapes. They're even messing with one of our benefactors. I'm not even sure they don't have something to do with Nate's—"

"And you think it's me?" Hyland took his foot off the seawall and turned to Clay. "Nate was my friend, too. I've known you guys, what? Twenty-two, twenty-three years? You can't think I'd do anything like that."

"I'm not saying you personally. What are you and Tarwater working on, Cliff? What would Nate know that would interfere with what you're doing?"

Hyland stared at his feet. Scratched his beard. "I don't know."

"You don't know? You know what we're doing—figure it out. Listen, I know you guys are using a big towable sonar rig, right? What's Tarwater looking at? Some new kind of active sonar? If it didn't have a hinky element, he wouldn't be here on site. Mines?"

"Damn it, Clay, I can't tell you! I can tell you that if I thought it was going to hurt the animals, or anyone in the field for that matter, I wouldn't be doing the work."

"Remember the navy's Pacific Biological Ocean Science Program? Were you in on that?"

"No. Birds, wasn't it?"

"Yeah, seabirds. The navy came to a bunch of field biologists with a ton of money—wanted seabirds tagged and tracked, behavior recorded, population information, habitat, everything. Everyone thought the heavens had opened up and started raining money. Thought the navy was doing some sort of secret impact study to preserve the birds. Do you know what the study was actually for?"

"No, that was before my time, Clay."

"They wanted to use the birds as delivery systems for biological weapons. Wanted to make sure they could predict that they'd fly to the enemy. Probably fifty scientists helped in that study."

"But it didn't happen, Clay, did it? I mean, the data was valuable scientifically, but the weapons project didn't pan out."

"As far as we know. That's the point. How would we know, until a seagull drops fucking anthrax on us?"

Cliff Hyland had aged a couple of years in the few minutes they'd been standing there. "I promise, Clay, if there's any indication that Tarwater or the navy or any of the spooky guys that come around from time to time are involved with trying to sabotage you guys, I'll call you in an instant. I promise you. But I can't tell you what I'm working on, or why. I don't exactly have funding coming out my ears. If I lose this, I'm teaching freshmen about dolphin jaws. I'm not ready for that. I need to be in the field."

Clay looked at him sideways and saw that there was real concern, maybe even a spark of desperation in Hyland's eyes. "You know, your funding might be a little easier to come by if you weren't based in Iowa. I don't know if you've noticed, but there's no ocean in Iowa."

Hyland smiled at the old dig. "Thanks for pointing that out, Clay."

Clay extended his hand. "You promise you'll let me know?"

"Absolutely."

Clay left feeling totally spent. The great head of steam he'd built up through a night of fitful sleep had wilted into exhaustion and confusion. He got in his truck and sat while sweat rolled down his neck. He watched tourists in aloha wear mill around under the great banyan tree like gift-wrapped zombies.

❧

CLIFF HYLAND'S EGGS WERE STILL STEAMING WHEN HE RETURNED TO the table.

Tarwater looked up from his own breakfast and moved his snow-white hat away from Hyland's plate, as if the rumpled scientist might splash yolk over the gold anchors in a fit of disorganized eating. "Everything all right?"

The young woman at the table fidgeted and tried to look invisible.

"Clay's still a little shaken up. Understandably. He and Nathan Quinn have been working together a long time."

"Lucky they made it this long without self-destructing," Tarwater said. "Slipshod as they run that operation. You see that kid that works for them? Not worth grinding up for chum."

Cliff Hyland dropped his fork in his plate. "Nathan Quinn was one of the most intuitively brilliant biologists in the field. And Clay

Demodocus may very well be the best underwater photographer in the world, certainly when it comes to cetaceans. You have no right."

"The world turns, Doc. Yesterday's alphas are today's betas. Losers lose. Isn't that what you biologists teach?"

Cliff Hyland came very close to burying a fork in Tarwater's tanned forehead, but instead he slowly climbed to his feet. "I need to use the restroom. Excuse me."

As he walked away, Hyland could hear Tarwater lecturing the junior researcher on how the strong survive. Cliff dug his mobile phone out of the pocket of his safari shirt and began scrolling through the numbers.

CLAY WAS JUST DOZING OFF IN THE DRIVER'S SEAT WHEN HIS MOBILE trilled. Without looking at the display, he figured it was Clair checking up on him. "Go, baby."

"Clay, it's Cliff Hyland."

"Cliff? What's up?"

"You've got to keep this under your hat, Clay. It's my ass."

"I got you. What is it, Cliff?"

"It's a torpedo range. We're doing site studies for a torpedo test range."

"Not in the sanctuary?"

"Right in the middle of the sanctuary."

"Jeepers, Cliff, that's terrible. I don't know if my hat is big enough to hold that."

"You gave me your word, Clay. What's with 'jeepers'? Who says 'jeepers'?"

"Amy does. She's a little eccentric. Tell me more. Does the navy have divers in the water?"

CHAPTER EIGHTEEN

Heinous Fuckery Most Foul

"Jeepers," said Amy. She was at Quinn's computer. Streamers of digital videotape were festooned across her lap and over the desk.

"Oh, that's heinous fuckery most foul," said Kona. He was perched on the high stool behind Amy and actually appeared to be trying to learn something when Clay came in.

"They've been simulating explosions on the lee of Kahoolawe with a big towable array of underwater speakers, measuring the levels. The speaker array is what's in that big case we've seen on their boat."

"We have a couple of explosions on the singer tapes, but distant," Amy said. "Nate thought it might be naval exercises out at sea."

"Speaking of tapes?" Clay picked up a strand of tape. "This isn't my rebreather footage, is it?"

"I'm sorry, Clay. I didn't get the video, but I pulled the audio off before this happened. Want to see the spectrograph?"

Kona asked, "You think those voices in the water be navy divers?"

Clay looked at Amy, raised an eyebrow.

"He wanted to learn."

"Cliff says there're no divers in the water, that his operation is it, militarily, in the sanctuary anyway. But he might not even know."

Amy wadded up the videotape and chucked the resulting bird's nest into the wastebasket. "How can they do that, Clay? How can they put a torpedo range in the middle of the humpback sanctuary? It's not like people won't notice."

"Yeah, she's a big ocean. Why here?" Kona said.

"I have no idea. Maybe they don't want there to be any mistake about whose waters they're blowing up ordnance in. If they blow them up in between a bunch of American islands, maybe there can't be any misinterpretation about what they're doing."

"Lost now," Kona said. "Does not compute. Danger. Danger. Control room needs herb." The Rastafarian had affected an accent that seemed an excellent approximation of how a stoned robot might sound.

"Submarine warfare is all about hide and seek with other submarines," Clay said. "The crews are autonomous when they're underwater. They make decisions on whether they're being attacked and whether to defend. Maybe if the navy just shot torpedoes off in the middle of the open sea, someone might misinterpret the action as an attack. It's damn unlikely that a Russian sub is going to be cruising up to Wailea for brunch and misinterpret an attack."

"They can't do that," Amy said. "They can't let them set off high explosives around the mothers and calves. It's just insane."

"They'll go deep and say it doesn't bother them. The navy will guarantee they won't blow up anything shallower than, say, four hundred feet. The humpbacks don't dive that deep in this channel."

"Yes they do," Amy said.

"No they don't," Clay said.

"Yes they do."

"There's no data on that, Amy. That's specifically what Cliff Hyland asked me about. He wanted to know if we were doing any research on the depth of humpback dives. Said that it would be the only thing the navy would care about."

Amy stood up and shoved the wheeled desk chair away. It bounced off Kona's shins, causing him to wince. "Ease on up, sistah."

"Amy, this wasn't my idea," Clay said. "I'm just telling you what Hyland told me."

"Fine," Amy said. She pushed her way past Clay and headed for the door.

"Where are you going?"

"Somewhere else." She let the screen door slam behind her.

Clay turned to Kona, who appeared to be studying the ceiling with great concentration. "What?"

"You makin' up that submarine war story?"

"Kind of. I read a Tom Clancy book once. Look, Kona, I'm not supposed to know stuff. Nate knew stuff. I just take the pictures."

"You think the navy sink your boat? Maybe make something bad happen to Nate?"

"The boat, maybe. I don't think they could have had anything to do with Nate. That was just bad luck."

"The Snowy Biscuit—all this getting under her skin."

"Mine, too."

"I'll go put the calm on her."

"Thanks," Clay said. He walked to the other side of the office, slumped in his chair, and pulled his editing tools up on the giant monitor.

⤙◦⤚

A HALF HOUR LATER HE HEARD A TINY VOICE COMING THROUGH THE screen door. "Sorry," Amy said.

"It's okay."

She stepped into the room and stood there, not looking as glazed as he would have expected if Kona had put the calm on her in an herbal way. "Sorry about your tape, too. The camera was making crunching noises on playback, so I sort of rushed taking it out."

"Not a problem. It was your big rescue scene. It just made me look like an amateur. I got most of it on the hard drive, I think."

"You did?" She stepped over to the monitor. "That it?" Frame stopped, the whale tail from the edge, black marks barely visible.

"Just going through it to see if there's anything else the audio picked up. The camera was running the whole time you were saving my bacon."

"Why don't you let it rest and let me take you out to lunch."

"It's ten-thirty."

"What, you're Mr. Rigid Schedule all of a sudden? Come out to lunch with me. I feel bad."

"Don't feel bad, Amy. It's a huge loss. I . . . I'm not dealing well myself. You know, to keep this work going, we'll be needing some academic juice."

Amy just stared at the frozen image of the whale tail, and then she caught herself. "What? Oh, you'll get someone. You put the word out, you'll have Ph.D.'s knocking the door down to work with you."

"I was thinking about you."

"Me? I'm crap. I don' t even have a bona fide hair color. Ink on my master's isn't even dry. You read my résumé."

"Actually, I didn't."

"You didn't?"

"You seemed intelligent. You were willing to work for nothing."

"Nate read it, though, right?"

"I told him you were good. And if it's any consolation, he thought the world of you."

"That's how you hire? I'm smart and I'm cheap—that's it? What kind of standards do you guys have?"

"Have you met Kona?"

She looked back at the monitor, then at Clay again. "I feel so used. Honored, but used. Look, I'm thrilled you want to keep me on, but I'm not going to bring you funding or legitimacy."

"I'll worry about that."

"Worry about it after lunch. Come on, I'll buy."

"You're poor. Besides, I'm meeting Clair for lunch at one."

"Okay. Can I borrow Nate's—uh, the green truck?"

"Keys are on the counter." Clay waved over his shoulder toward the kitchen.

Amy took the keys, then started out the door, caught herself, then ran back, and threw her arms around the photographer. "I really appreciate your asking me to stay."

"Go. Take Kona with you. Feed him. Hose him off."

"Nope, if you're not coming, I'm going solo. Tell Clair hi for me."

"Go."

He looked back at the computer, looked past the window at the brilliant Maui sun, then shut the computer down, feeling very much as if nothing he did mattered or would ever matter again.

CHAPTER NINETEEN

Scooter Don't Meep

The whale tossed like a roller coaster moving through tomato soup—great gut-flopping waves of muscular motion. Quinn rolled to his hands and knees and urped his breakfast into a splatter pattern across the rubbery gray floor, then heaved in time with the rhythm of the whale's swimming until he was empty and exhausted.

"Hurl patrol," came a voice out of the dark.

"Flush and gush, boys, the doc blew ballast back here," came another voice.

Quinn rolled onto his bottom and scooted away from the voices until he came against a bulkhead, which was warm and moist and gave at his touch. He felt huge muscles moving behind the skin and nearly jumped. He scooted away, then sat balled up near where he'd been sick. Cold seawater rolled down from the front of the whale and over his feet, taking his recently vacated breakfast with it. His ears popped with a pressure increase, and in a second the water was gone.

The interior of the whale looked like a bad van conversion done by a latex freak: damp, rubbery skin over everything, lit by a light blue haze coming from the eyes up front, the rest dimly lit by bioluminescent strips of green that ran over the top of the teardrop-shaped chamber. At the front of the chamber, on either side by the eyes, two things sat in seats that wrapped around their bodies. Quinn didn't know what they were, and his mind felt as if it were ripping open trying to grasp the whole of the situation. Details like nonhuman humanoids decked out in gray skin couldn't register enough space in his consciousness to be examined or analyzed. In fact, he could keep his eyes open for only a few seconds before the nausea returned.

Inside the whale smelled like fish.

Standing, or sort of standing—riding was a more appropriate term, as everything inside the whale was moving—behind the seated creatures were two men, one about forty, the other twenty-five, both barefoot but wearing military khakis without insignias or any badges of rank, but the older man was obviously in command. Quinn had tried for five minutes to ask them the questions coming into his mind, but each time he opened his mouth, he had to stop himself from throwing up. He'd always considered himself pretty seaworthy until now.

"What . . . ?" he managed to get out before his gorge rose again.

"It really helps with the incredulity if you accept that you're dead," said the older man.

"I'm dead?"

"I didn't say that, but if you accept that you are, it sort of quells the anxiety."

"Yeah, if you're already dead, what bad can really happen?" said the younger guy.

"Then I *am* dead?"

"Nope. Breathe and go with the motion," said the older guy. "It's not going to stop, so if you fight it, you'll lose."

"Your lunch," added the young guy, and then he let loose a giggle at his own joke.

"There's less motion toward the front. The head tracks close to level. But you knew that."

Quinn hadn't been able to apply any of his analytical powers to the situation because he flat couldn't accept it. Yes, in another world he realized that he knew that the whale's head would have less motion than the tail, but he'd never even considered that he might be thinking about it from the perspective of an internal organ.

"I'm inside a whale?"

"Ding, ding, ding, he's gotten the bonus answer." The young guy leaned back against the back of the seat where one of the gray creatures was sitting, and a chairlike protrusion rose out of the floor to catch him. "Tell him what he's won, Captain."

"Hospitality, Poe. Help the doctor up to the front so we can talk without him tossing his cookies."

The younger guy helped Quinn to his feet and across the undulating floor to the chair thing that had risen behind one of the gray creatures facing the back of the ship. Once close to the creatures, Quinn couldn't take his eyes off them. They were humanoid, in that they had two arms, two legs, a torso, and a head, but their heads were like that of a pilot whale, with a large melon in the front—for transmitting and receiving sound underwater, Quinn guessed—and their eyes were set wide to the side, so the creatures would see with binocular vision. Their hands were inserted into consoles that rose out of the floor and appeared to have no instrumentation whatsoever except for some bioluminescent nodules that looked like cloudy eyeballs and emitted different colors of light. The creatures appeared as if they had become part of the whale.

"We call them the whaley boys," the older man said. "They pilot the whale."

"The one directly behind you is Scooter, the other one is Skippy. Say hi, guys."

The creatures turned as far as the chairs would allow and made clicking and squeaking noises, then seemed to smile at Quinn. While smiling they showed mouthfuls of sharp, peglike teeth. With the teeth set against their dark gray skins and the melon above, the whaley boys put Quinn in mind of more cheerful versions of the creature from the *Alien* movies. Scooter saluted Nate with a hand consisting of four very long webbed fingers and only the suggestion of a thumb.

"They say hi," said Poe. "I'm Poe. This is Captain Poynter."

Poynter, the older man, tipped his hat and offered a hand to shake. Quinn took it and waggled it limply.

"The whaley boys don't speak English as we know it," Poe said, "although they have a few squeaks that come out like words. They're tapped directly in to the whale's nervous system. They steer it, control all the processes at any given time. We can't do much on the whales without them. Certainly could never drive one. The whales and the whaley boys are made for each other."

Poe pushed against the back of Skippy's seat, and another seat formed out of the floor to cradle him as he leaned back into it. "I love that," Poe said.

Poynter backed up to a rubbery bulkhead, and a seat formed out of the wall to catch him as well.

"If they're paying attention, they'll never let you fall." Poe grinned. "Of course, almost everything in here is soft—child safe, don't you know—except the spine, which runs over the top, so you wouldn't be hurt if you did fall. But just the same, we're secured when they're doing maneuvers. You think you're sick now—wait until we go for a breach. Don't freak out." Poe turned to the whaley boys. "Secure the doc, boys."

The arms of the seat shape wrapped over Quinn's lap. Parts came over his shoulders and fused across his chest, then around his hips and over his lap. Quinn freaked out.

"Get it off me! Get it off me! I can't breathe!"

"Prepare for breach," said Poynter.

Scooter chirped. Skippy grinned. Similar restraints extruded from all their seats, securing them.

The attitude of the whale changed, going up at a nearly sixty-degree angle—and then the angle went sharper as they moved. Quinn was looking backward at the tail section of the teardrop interior. The lurching movement of the luminescent strips was starting to nauseate him. He could feel his internal organs shifting with the acceleration, and then the whale ship went vertical and airborne. At the apex of the motion, Quinn's stomach tried to escape through his diaphragm, then shifted as they fell sideways. There was an enormous concussion as the ship hit the water. Slowly the whale came back around, and they were horizontal again.

The whaley boys chirped and clicked gleefully, grinning back at

Quinn, then at each other, then back at Quinn, nodding as if to say, *Was that cool, or what?* Their necks were nearly as wide as their shoulders, and Quinn could see heavy muscles moving under the skin.

"They love that," said Poynter.

"I kind of like it, too," said Poe. "Except when they go overboard and do twenty or thirty breaches in a row. Even I get sick when they do that. And the noise . . . well, you heard it."

Quinn shook his head, closed his eyes, then opened them again. The only way to deal with this experience was to accept it at face value: He was in a whale, one that was somehow being used as a submarine by human and nonhuman sentient creatures. Everything he knew no longer applied, but then again, maybe it did. What put him on the less loopy side of sanity was noticing the whaley boys' thick necks.

"They're amphibious, right?" Quinn asked Poynter. "Their necks are thick to take the stress of swimming at high speeds?" Quinn rose in his chair as far as the restraints would allow and saw that Scooter did indeed have a blowhole just behind his melon. He was a humanoid whale, or a dolphin creature. Scooter was impossible. All of this was impossible. *The details, not the big picture,* Quinn reminded himself. *In the big picture there be madness.* "They're like a whale/human hybrid, aren't they?"

"Which would be why we call them the whaley boys," said Poynter.

"Wait, are you accusing us of something?" asked Poe. "Because these guys are not the love children of us and some whales. We don't do that kind of thing."

"Well, there was that one time," said Poynter.

"Okay, yeah, just that one time," said Poe.

But Quinn was studying Scooter, and Scooter was eyeing him right back. "Although they appear to be able to turn their heads, like beluga whales. Their neck vertebrae probably aren't fused like most whales'." The scientist rising, Quinn was comfortable now, his fear taken away by curiosity. He was focused on finding out things, which was his home turf, even in this completely unreal situation. If he focused on the details, the big picture wouldn't throw him over the edge into drooling lunacy.

"Let's ask them," said Poe. "Scooter, are your vertebrae fused together, or are you just a big, no-necked gray thug?"

Scooter turned his head to Poe and made a loud raspberry sound, spraying whaley spit all down the front of Poe's khakis and increasing the odor of decaying fish in the cabin by a factor of ten.

"We don't know what they are, Dr. Quinn," said Captain Poynter. "They were here when we got here, and we got here just like you did. We've all been on this ride."

"Meep," said Skippy.

"I taught him that," said Poe.

"That's from a Warner Brothers' cartoon," Quinn said. "Road Runner."

"No, that would be two meeps. Skippy only does one. Therefore, it's original. Isn't that right, Skippy?"

"Meep."

For some reason the meep did it. Some minds, particularly those with a scientific bent, a love of truth and certainty, have limits to how much absurdity they can handle. And here Quinn found himself well over the limit.

"Skippy and Scooter and Poynter and Poe—I can't handle it!" he screamed.

He felt as if his mind were a rubber band being stretched to breaking, and the meep had tweaked it. He screamed until he could feel veins pulsing in his forehead.

"You let it out now," said Captain Poynter. "Just go with it." Then, to Poe, "You know, I wouldn't have thought the alliteration would have done it. You ever hear of that?"

"Nope, I had an uncle who used to get nauseated at *Reader's Digest* article titles—you know, 'Terrible Truths of Toxic Toe Jam'—but I thought it was more because he read them in the doctor's office than the alliteration. You sure it wasn't the meep that did it?"

"This can't be happening. This can't be happening," Quinn chanted. He was hyperventilating, and his vision had gone to a blur, his heart pounding like he'd been running a sprint across an electrified floor.

"Anxiety attack," said Poynter. He put his hand on Quinn's forehead and spoke softly. "Okay, Doc, here's the skinny. You are in a living ship that resembles a whale but is not a whale. There are two other guys aboard who have lived through this, so you can live through this. In addition, there are two guys who are not strictly human, but they won't hurt you. You are going to live and deal with this. This is real. You are not insane. Now, calm the fuck down."

And it was then that Poynter stepped back and Poe threw the bucket of cold seawater in Quinn's face.

"Hey," Quinn said. He sputtered and blinked seawater out of his eyes.

"I told you to go with the dead thing, but you didn't listen," Poe said.

Nothing had changed, but things, his heart, slowed down, and Quinn looked around. "Where did that bucket come from? There was no bucket in here. There was nothing but us. And where did you get the water?"

Poe held the bucket at ready. "You're sure you're okay? I don't want to freak you out again."

"Yeah. I'm okay," said Quinn. And actually, he was. He'd decided to go with the idea that he was already dead, and that seemed to make everything fall into perspective. "I'm dead."

"That's the spirit," said Poe. He held the bucket against a wall, and a small portal opened and sucked the bucket in. Quinn would have sworn there hadn't been any seams in the wall to indicate there'd been an opening there.

"Hey," said Poynter, taking on the tone of the deeply offended, "now that you're dead, I've got a bone to pick with you about not bringing me my sandwich."

Quinn looked at the sharp features and narrowed eyes of the captain—who now seemed genuinely angry—and a shiver ran through his body that had nothing to do with the cold seawater running out of his hair. "Sorry," he said, shrugging as much as he could in the restraints.

"Damn it, how hard could that have been? You've got a Ph.D. for Christ's sake—you can't get a fucking pastrami on rye? I've got a good mind to chuck you out the anus."

"Shhhhhhhh, Cap," Poe said. "That was gonna be a surprise."

"Meep," said Skippy.

CHAPTER TWENTY

Missing Biscuit,
Flopping Tuna

"Bwana Clay, you seen the Snowy Biscuit?"

Clay and Clair sat on the lanai of Clay's bungalow drinking mai-tais and watching smoke roll out the vents of a Weber kettle barbecue. Kona had his long board tucked underneath his arm and was heading for his Maui cruiser, a lime Krylon-over-rust 1975 BMW 2002, with no windows and seats that were covered in ratty blankets.

Clay was two mai-tais south of lucid, but he could still talk, "She took Nate's truck into town this morning. Haven't seen her since."

"Sistah wanted me to teach her some surfing. Got some easy sets rolling on West Shore, good for that."

"Sorry," said Clay. "We're smoking a big hunk of ahi tuna if you 'd like to join us."

"No," said Clair.

"Tanks, but I'm going down to Lahaina town and see if I can find that Snowy Biscuit. We going to work tomorrow?"

"Maybe," said Clay, trying to think through a rum cloud. They'd pulled the *Always Confused* up out of the bottom of the harbor, and the boatyard had said it would be a week or so before it was ready to float again, although even then it would need some major cleaning. Still, they had Nate's boat. He looked at Clair.

"You're not sitting home tomorrow whining to me about your hangover," Clair said. "You get out there on the water and be sick like a proper man." She'd revised her thoughts on Clay's staying off the water. He was who he was.

"Yeah, plan on going out if it's not too windy," Clay said. "Hey, we supposed to have wind?" It occurred to Clay that he hadn't checked the weather since Nate had disappeared.

"Calm morning, trades in the afternoon," Kona said. "We can work."

"Tell Amy when you see her, okay. Take my cell phone with you. Call me when you find her. You sure you won't have dinner with us?"

"No," said Clair.

"No," said Kona, grinning at Clair. "Auntie, you embarrassed that Kona seen you naked? You look fine, yeah."

Clair stood up. "You go ahead, call me 'Auntie' again, see if I don't snatch out the rest of those dreads and use them to make cat toys."

"Ease up, I'm going to find the Biscuit." And he loped to the Beemer, slid the long board in through the back window, hooked the skeg over the passenger seat to secure it, and then drove off to Lahaina to look for Amy.

◦◦◦

IT WAS TWO IN THE MORNING WHEN THE PHONE IN CLAY'S BUNGALOW rang. "Tell me you're not in jail," Clay said.

"Not in jail, Bwana Clay, but maybe you need to sit down."

"I'm in bed sleeping, Kona. What?"

"The truck, Bwana Nate's truck. It's here at the kayak rental in Lahaina. They say Amy rent a kayak this morning, about eleven."

"They're still there?"

"I waked the guy up."

"They don't know where she went? They let her go alone? He didn't call us when it got dark?"

"She said she was just using it to tow behind the boat, for research. He know she a whale researcher, so he didn't think nothing of it. Sometime they take kayaks two, three days."

"You checked? She's not on the boat?"

"You mean the not sunk one?"

"Yes, that would be the one."

"Yeah, I check. The boat in the slip. No kayak."

"Stay there. I'll be down in a few minutes. I have to get dressed and call the Coast Guard."

"This kayak guy says it not on him—she signed a wafer. That some kind of religious thing?"

"Waiver, Kona, she signed a waiver. Are you high?"

"Yes."

"Of course. Sorry. Okay, I'll be right there."

NATE WAS THREE DAYS INSIDE THE WHALE BEFORE HE ASKED, "YOUR names aren't really Poynter and Poe, are they?"

"What?" said Poynter. "You're eaten by a giant whale ship and you're worried that we might be traveling under assumed names? Go for it, Poe."

"Give us a flush, boys!" Poe said.

Water came gushing down the floor of the whale from the front. Pantsless, Ensign Poe took three steps and went into a slide toward the tail like he was sliding into third base on a wet rain tarp. As he reached the end of the chamber, he spread his arms out to his sides at right angles. There was a sucking sound, and he sank up to his armpits into an orifice that only a second ago had appeared as just an impression in solid skin.

"Wow, that's cold," said Poe. "How deep are we?"

Scooter clicked and whistled a couple of times.

"Ninety feet," said Poynter. "Can't be that bad."

"Feels colder. I think my 'nads have crawled up inside my body."

Nate simply stared, gape-jawed, at the arms and head of the ensign, just above floor level.

"You see, Doc," said Poynter, "most of the time we call it the 'back orifice' instead of the anus, you know, because otherwise, with us moving in and out of it, there's implications. His lower body is in the sea right now, at three atmospheres, yet the back orifice is sealed around him and it's not crushing his chest. It's not crushing your chest, is it, Poe?"

"No, sir. It's snug for sure, but I can breathe."

"How is that possible?" asked Nate.

"You're a diver. You've been down, what, a hundred and twenty, hundred and thirty feet?"

"A hundred and fifty, by accident, but what does that have to do with this?"

"You never had sphincter failure at that depth, did you? Blow up like a puffer fish?"

"No."

"Well, there you go, Nate. This here is just advanced poop-chute technology. We don't even understand it ourselves, but it's the key to sanitation on these small ships, and it's how we get in and out. Normally the mouth on these humpback ships doesn't even open, which gives us a lot more room, but this one was made specially to retrieve 'Dirts.' That's you people."

"Made? By whom?" Of course they were made. Nothing like this could have evolved.

"Later," said Poynter. "Poe, you done?"

"Aye, aye, Captain."

"Get back in here."

"Mighty cold out here, sir. I'm telling you, my tackle's going to look like I'm posing for a baby picture."

"I'm sure the doc will take that into account, Poe."

Nate could feel a slight change in pressure in his ears, and Poe oozed back into the whale. The orifice sealed behind him, leaving almost no water on the floor. The ensign sidled, crablike, to the front of the ship, shielding his privates with his hands. He retrieved his pants from a storage nook that opened with a flap of skin like the blowhole on a killer whale. The whale's interior was lined with the storage nooks, but you couldn't even see the seams by the dim bioluminescence when they were closed.

"You're going to learn how to do that, Nate. It's just the civilized thing to do until we transfer you to the blue. Can't have you doing your business in the ship."

When he'd had to go to the bathroom, they'd sent Nate to the back of the whale, where he'd gone on the floor. Seconds later the whaley boys had let a bit of water in through a crack in the mouth, which washed across the floor and effectively flushed the mess out the back orifice.

"The blue?" Nate asked.

"Yeah, we can't take you where they want you in this little thing. We'll transfer you to a blue and send you on. You'll have to go through the poop chutes."

"So there's a blue-whale ship as well?"

"Ships," Poynter corrected. "Yeah, and other species, too."

"Right whales are my favorites," Poe said. "Slower than hell, but really wide. Plenty of room. You'll see."

"So they—the whaley boys—can regulate the pressure that precisely? They can let in water, expel it, keep the pressure in here from giving us the bends? Allow us to transfer from one of these ships to another?"

"Yep, they're tapped in to the whale directly. They're like his cerebral cortex, I guess. The whale ships have a brain, but that only takes care of autonomic functions. Allows it to act like a whale for hours on end—diving, breathing, stuff like that. But without one of the whaley boys tapped in, they're just dumb machines, limited function. The pilots control higher functions—navigation and such. They really show off their stuff in these humpbacks—the breaching, the singing, you know."

"This thing sings?" Nate couldn't help himself. He wanted to hear a whale sing from the inside.

"Of course it sings. You heard it sing."

Since Nate had been on, the only sound the whale ship had made was the beating of its enormous flukes and the explosive blow every ten minutes or so."

"I hate it when they sing," said Poe.

"What's the purpose of the song?" Nate asked. He didn't care who these guys were or what they were doing. He now had the opportunity to get the answer to a question he'd pursued for most of his adult life. "Why do they sing?"

"Because we tell them to," said Poynter. "Why'd you think?"

"No. It's not right." Nate buried his face in his hands. "Kidnapped by morons."

Scooter let loose with a series of frantic chirps. The whaley boy was staring out the eye into the blue Pacific.

"School of tuna outside," said Poe.

"Go, Scooter," said Poynter. "Go get some."

The restraints retracted from around Scooter's waist, and the creature stood up for the first time since Nate had come on board. He was taller than Nate, maybe six-six, with lean gray legs that looked like those of a giant bullfrog crossbred with a fullback and terminated in long, webbed feet that resembled the rear flippers of a walrus. Scooter took three quick steps and dove at the floor in the back of the whale. There was a whooshing sound, and he disappeared, headfirst, through the back orifice, which sealed behind him with a distinct pop.

Poe stepped into the seat that Scooter had vacated and looked out through the eye. "Nate, check this out. Watch how these guys hunt."

Nate looked out the whale's eye and saw Scooter's lithe form swim by at incredible speed, darting back and forth with astounding agility in pursuit of a twenty-pound tuna.

In the water the whaley boy's eyes no longer bugged out as they did inside the whale. Like whales and dolphins, Nate realized, whaley boys possessed muscles that could actually change the shape of the eye for focusing in either air or water. Scooter did a rapid turn and snatched the tuna in his jaws not ten feet from the eye of the whale. Nate could hear the snap and saw blood in the water around Scooter's mouth.

"Yes!" said Poe. "It's sashimi tonight."

Nate had eaten nothing but raw fish since he'd been on board the whale ship, but this was the first time he'd seen it caught. Still, he couldn't quite share Poe's enthusiasm. "Is this all you eat? Raw fish?"

"It beats the alternatives," said Poe. "The whale carries a nutrient paste that's like krill puree."

"Oh, my God," said Nate.

Poynter leaned in close to Nate, so he was only inches from the scientist's ear. "Thus the somewhat substantial demand for culinary variety, as in—oh, I don't know—a pastrami on rye!"

"I said I was sorry," Nate muttered.

"Yeah, right."

"Drop me off anywhere. I'll go get you one."

"We don't land these things on shore."

"You don't?"

"Except to paint 'bite me' on the flukes," said Poe.

"Yeah, except for that," said Poynter.

Skippy meeped as Scooter scooted in through the poop chute with tuna in hand. Upon seeing the pilot's entrance, Nate started thinking, for the first time since he'd been eaten, about how to escape.

THIS IS JUST STUPID, AMY THOUGHT. SHE'D BEEN PADDLING LIKE A madwoman for four hours and was still barely halfway to Molokai. She'd been past the channel wind line for two of those four hours and so battled four-foot swells and a crosswind that threatened to take her out to sea.

"Who gives GPS coordinates for a meeting? Who does business like that?" She'd been shouting into the wind on and off for an hour, then checking the little liquid-crystal map on the display of the GPS receiver. The "you are here" dot never seemed to move. Well, that wasn't true. If she paused from paddling to take a drink of water or apply some sunscreen, the dot seemed to jump off course a mile at a time.

"Are you guys on drugs?" she screamed into the wind.

Her shoulders ached, and she'd drunk nearly all of the two-liter bottle of water she'd brought with her. She started to regret not having brought along some kind of snack. "An easy paddle. 'Just rent a kayak. You won't need a power boat.' I'm adrift on a piece of Tupperware, you nitwits!"

She leaned back on the kayak to catch her breath and watched the direction and speed indicators change on the GPS. She could rest maybe five minutes without drifting too far. She closed her eyes and let the swells rock her into a light doze. It was quiet, just the white noise of wind and water, not even a slap of waves on the kayak—she was so light that it rode high in the water and over the tops of the waves without a sound. She thought about Nate, about how frightened he must have been in those last moments, about how much she'd started to enjoy working with him. *Action nerd.* She smiled to herself, a melancholy smile as she dozed off, but then the sound of a fusillade of bubbles breaking the surface near the kayak jolted her to alertness. It was a huge expulsion of air, as if someone had set off an explosion deep under the water.

She started paddling away from the eruptions of bubbles, but even as she moved, the sea began to darken around her, the crystal blue turning to shadow in a huge pool under the kayak. Then something hit the little boat, tossing Amy into the air twenty feet before she hit the water and the darkness surrounded her.

CHAPTER TWENTY-ONE

I Lick the Body Electric

The Maui sunset had set the sky on fire and everything in the bungalow had taken on the glowing pink tone of paradise—or hell, depending on where you were standing. Clay dismembered the bird and put the severed pieces on a platter to transport them to the grill.

"You'll need something to bring those in on," Clair said. Her dress was a purple hibiscus-flower print, and the orchid she wore in her hair looked like lavender dragonflies humping. She was dicing pickles into the macaroni salad.

"What's wrong with this?" Clay held up the plate with the raw chicken.

"You can't use the same plate. You'll get salmonella."

"Fine, fuck it," Clay said, tossing the plate into the yard. The chicken parts bounced nicely, breading themselves with a light coating of sand, ants, and dried grass. "When did chicken become like plutonium anyway, for Christ's sake? You can't let it touch you or it's certain fucking death. And eggs and hamburgers kill you unless you cook them to the consistency of limestone! And if you turn on your fucking cell phone, the plane is going to plunge out of the sky in a ball of flames? And kids can't take a dump anymore but they have to have a helmet and pads on make them look like the Road Warrior. Right? Right? What the fuck happened to the world? When did everything get so goddamn deadly? Huh? I've been going to sea for thirty damned years, and nothing's killed me. I've swum with everything that can bite, sting, or eat you, and I've done every stupid thing at depth that any human can—and *I'm* still alive. Fuck, Clair, I was unconscious for an hour underwater less than a week ago, and it didn't kill me. Now you're going to tell me that I'm going to get whacked by a fucking chicken leg? Well, just fuck it then!"

He didn't know where to go, so he came back in and slammed the screen door behind him, then opened it and slammed it again. "Goddamn it!" And he stood there, breathing hard. Not really looking at anything.

Clair put down her knife and pickle, then wiped her hands. As she came toward Clay she pulled a large bobby pin from the back of her hair, and her long, thick locks cascaded down her back. She took Clay's right hand and kissed each of his fingertips, licked his thumb, then took his index finger in her mouth and made a show of removing it slowly and with maximum moisture. Clay looked at the floor, shaking.

"Baby," she said as she placed the bobby pin firmly between Clay's wet thumb and index finger, "I need you to go over to that wall and take this bobby pin and insert it ever so firmly into that electrical outlet over there."

Clay looked up at her at last.

"Because," she continued, "I know that you aren't mad at me and that you're just grieving for your friends, but I think you need to be reminded that you aren't invulnerable and that you can hurt even more than you do now. And I think it would be better if you did it yourself, because otherwise I'll have to brain you with your own iron skillet."

"That would be wrong," Clay said.

"It is a cruel world, baby."

Clay took her in his arms and buried his face in her hair and just stood there in the doorway for a long time.

Amy had been missing for thirty-two hours. That morning a fisherman had found her kayak washing against some rocks on Molokai and had called the rental company in Maui. A life jacket was still strapped on the front of the boat, he said. The Coast Guard had stopped looking already.

"Now, let me go," Clair said. "I have to get that chicken out of the yard and rinse it off."

"I don't think we should eat that."

"Please. I'm going to cook it up for Kona. You're taking me out."

"I am?"

"Of course."

"After I stick this in the outlet, right?"

"You can grieve, Clay—that's as it should be—but you can't feel guilty for being alive."

"So, I don't have to stick this in the outlet?"

"You used foul language at me, baby. I don't see any way around it."

"Oh, well, that's true. You go get Kona's chicken out of the yard. I'll do this."

❦

ON THE SECOND MORNING AFTER AMY WAS LOST AT SEA, CLAY WALKED to the seaside, a rocky beach between some condos north of Lahaina— too short for morning runners, too shallow for a bathing crowd. He stood on an outcropping of rocks with the waves crashing around him and tried to let pure hatred run out of his heart. Clay Demodocus was a guy who liked things, and among the things he had liked the most was the sea, but this morning he held nothing but disdain for his old friend. The sapphire blue was indifferent, the waves elitist. She'd kill you without even learning your name. "You bitch," Clay said, loud enough for the sea to hear. He spit into her face and walked back home.

That old trickster Maui had been sitting on a rock nearby watching, and he laughed at Clay's hubris. Maui admired a man with more balls than brains, even a haole. He cast a small blessing at the photographer— just a trinket for the laugh, a trifling little mango of magic—and then he headed off to the great banyan tree to fog the film of Japanese tourists.

❦

BACK IN WHAT WAS NOW ONLY *HIS* OFFICE, CLAY DUG AMY'S RÉSUMÉ out of his files and made the call. He braced himself, trying to figure out how, exactly, he was going to tell these strangers that their daughter was missing and assumed to have drowned. He felt sad and alone, and his elbow hurt from the jolt of electricity he'd taken the night before. He didn't want to do this. He reached for the phone, then stopped and closed his eyes, as if he could make the whole thing go away, but on the back of his eyelids he saw the face of his mother as he had last seen her, looking up at him out of her barrel of brine, "Make the call, you pussy. If anyone knows how not to get bad news, it's you. Part of loyalty is following up, you sniveling coward. Don't be like your brothers."

Ah, sweet Mama, Clay thought. He dialed the phone—a number with a 716 area code, Tonawanda, New York. It rang three times, and the recorded operator came on, saying that the number he'd reached was not in service at this time. He checked it, then dialed the next number down, which also turned out not to be working. He called Tonawanda information for Amy's parents, and the operator told him there was no such listing. At a loss, he called Woods Hole Oceanographic Center, where Amy had gotten her master's. Clay knew one of her advisers, Marcus Loughten, an irascible Brit who had worked at Woods Hole for twenty years and was famous in the field for his work in underwater acoustics. Loughten answered on the third ring.

"Loughten," Loughten said.

"Marcus, this is Clay Demodocus. We worked together on—"

"Yes, Clay, I bloody know who you are. Calling from Hawaii, are you?"

"Well, yes, I—"

"Probably, what, seventy-eight degrees with a breeze? It's seven below zero Fahrenheit here. I'm out installing bloody sound buoys in a monthlong blizzard to keep right whales from getting run over by supertankers."

"Right, the sound buoys. How are those working out?"

"They're not."

"No? Why not?"

"Well, right whales are stupid as shit, aren't they? It's not like a supertanker is quiet. If sound was going to deter them, then they'd be bloody well deterred by the engine noise, wouldn't they? They don't make the connection. Stupid shits."

"Oh, sorry to hear that. Uh, why keep doing it then?"

"We have funding."

"Right. Look, Marcus, I need some information on one of your students who came out here to work with us. Amy Earhart? Would have been with you guys until fall of last year."

"No, I don't know that name."

"Sure you do, five-five, thin, pale, dark hair with kind of unnatural blue highlights, smart as a whip."

"Sorry, Clay. That doesn't fit any of my students."

Clay took a deep breath and trudged on. Biologists were notorious for treating their grad students as subhuman, but Clay was surprised that Loughten didn't remember Amy. She was cute, and if Clay could judge from a night of drinking he'd done with Loughten at a marine mammal conference in France, the Brit was more than a bit of a horndog.

"Great ass, Marcus. You'd remember."

"I'm sure I would, but I don't."

Clay studied the résumé. "What about Peter? Would he—"

"No, Clay, I know all of Peter's grad students as well. Did you call to confirm her references when you took her on?"

"Well, no."

"Good work, then. Abscond with your Nikons, did she?"

"No, she's missing at sea. I'm trying to contact her family."

"Sorry. Wish I could be of help. I'll check the records, just to be sure—in case I've had a ministroke that killed the part of the brain that remembers fine bottoms."

"Thanks."

"Good luck, Clay. My best to Quinn."

Clay cringed. It turned out he really wasn't up for bearing bad news. "Will do, Marcus. Good-bye." Clay hung up and resumed staring at the phone. *Well,* he thought, *I knew absolutely nothing about this woman that I thought I knew.* Libby Quinn had already called (sobbing) to say that they should have some kind of joint service at the sanctuary for Nate and Amy, and that Clay should speak. What was he going to say about Amy? *Dearly beloved, I think we all knew Amy as scientist, a colleague, a friend, a woman who showed up out of nowhere with a com-*

pletely manufactured history, but I think, because she saved my life, that I came to know her better than anyone here, and I can tell you unequivo- cally, she was a smart aleck with a cute butt.

Yeah, he'd need to work on that. Damn it, he missed them both.

～◦◦～

CLAY DECIDED TO KILL THE DAY BY EDITING VIDEO: TIME-EATING busywork that supplied at least an imaginary escape from the real world. The afternoon found him going through the rebreather footage he'd taken on the day the whale had conked him, for the first time going past the point where he was unconscious, just to see if the camera picked up anything usable. Clay let the video run: minutes of blue water, the cam- era tossing around at the end of the wrist lanyard, then Amy's leg as she comes down to stop his descent. He cranked the audio. Hiss of ambient noise, then the bubbles from Amy's regulator, the slow hiss of his own breathing through the rebreather. As Amy starts to swim to the surface, the camera catches his fins hanging limply against a field of blue, then Amy's fins kicking in and out of the frame. Both their breathing is steady on the audio track.

Clay looked at the time signature of the video. Fifteen minutes when the motion stops. Amy making her first decompression stop. On the audio he hears the chorus of distant singing humpbacks, a boat motor not too far off, and Amy's steady bubbles. Then the bubbles stop.

The camera settles against his thigh and drifts, the lens up, catches light from the surface, then Amy's hand holding on to his buoyancy vest, reading the data off his dive computer. Her regulator is out of her mouth. On the audio there's only his breathing. The camera swings away.

Ten minutes more pass. Clay listens for Amy's breathing to resume. The motion from her hooking into the rescue tank on the rebreather should move the camera, but there's just the same gentle drift. They move up. Clay guesses maybe to seventy-five feet. Amy is doing another decompression stop, doing it by the book, despite the emergency. Ex- cept he still can hear only one person breathing.

She pulls him to more shallow depth. The frame lightens up, and the camera swings around, the wide angle showing Clay's unconscious form and Amy kicking, the regulator out of her mouth, looking at the surface. She hasn't used the bail-out tank on Clay's rebreather, and she hasn't taken a breath for, as far as Clay can tell, forty minutes. This can't be right.

He listens, watching until the time signature shows sixty and the tape ends—the entire thing having been dubbed to the hard drive. He rewinds it on-screen, slowing down when the camera shows anything but blue, listening again.

"No fucking way."

Clay backed away from the monitor, watching as the video ran out again and froze on the image of Amy holding him steady at twenty or so feet down, no regulator in her mouth.

He ran out the door, calling, "Kona! Kona!"

The surfer came shuffling out of his bungalow in a cloud of smoke. "Just tracking down navy spies, boss."

"Where did you guys put the rebreather? The day they took me to the hospital?"

"She's in the storage shed."

Clay made a beeline for the bungalow they used to store dive and boat equipment. He waved Kona after him. "Come."

"What?"

"Did you guys refill the oxygen or the bail-out tanks?"

"We just rinsed it and put it in the case."

Clay pulled the big Pelican case off a stack of scuba tanks and popped the latches. The rebreather was snug in the foam padding. Clay wrenched it out onto the wooden floor and turned on the computer that was an integral part of it. He hit buttons on the display console and watched the gray liquid-crystal display cycle through the numbers. The last dive: Downtime had been seventy-five minutes, forty-three seconds. The oxygen cylinder was nearly full. The bail-out air supply was full. Full. It hadn't been touched. Somehow Amy had stayed underwater for an hour without an air supply.

Clay turned to the surfer. "Do you remember anything that Nate showed you about what he was working on? I need details—I know in general." Clay wasn't sure what he was looking for, but this had to mean something, and all he had to fall back on was Nate's research.

The surfer scratched the dreadless side of his head. "Something about the whales singing binary."

"Come show me." Clay stormed through the door and back to the office.

"What you looking for?"

"I don't know. Clues. Mysteries. Meaning."

"You gone lolo, you know?"

CHAPTER TWENTY-TWO

Deep Below, Bernard Stirs

About the time that Nathan Quinn had started to master his nausea in the whale ship's constant motion (four days on board), another force started working on his body. He felt an uneasiness come over him in waves, and for twenty or so seconds he would feel as if he needed to crawl out of his skin. Then it would pass and leave him feeling a little numb for a few seconds, only to start up again.

Poynter and Poe were moving around the small cabin looking at different gobs and bumps of bioluminescence as if they were gleaning some meaning from them, but, try as he might, Nate couldn't figure out what they were monitoring. It would have helped to be able to get out of the seat and take a closer look, but Poynter had ordered him strapped in after he made his first break for the back orifice. He'd nearly made it, too. Had dived at it just like he'd seen the whaley boys do, except that only one arm had gone through, and he ended up stuck to the floor of the whale, his face against the rubbery skin, his hand trailing out in the cold ocean.

"Well, that was phenomenally stupid," said Poynter.

"I think I've dislocated my shoulder," Nate said.

"I should leave you there. Maybe a remora or two will latch on to your hand and teach you a lesson."

"Or a cookie-cutter shark," said Poe. "Nasty bastards."

The whaley boys turned in their seats and snickered, bobbing their heads and blowing the occasional raspberry, which could inflict considerable moisture off a four-inch-wide tongue. Evidently Quinn was a cetacean laugh riot. He'd always suspected that, actually.

Poynter got down on his hands and knees and looked Nate in the eye. "While you're down there, I'd like you to think on what might have happened if you'd been successful at launching yourself through that orifice. First, we're at— Skippy, what's the depth?"

Skippy chirped and clicked a number of times.

"A hundred and fifty feet. Beyond the fact that you'd probably have blown out your eardrums almost immediately, you might think on how you were going to get to the surface on one breath of air. And should you have gotten to the surface, what were you going to do then? We're five hundred miles from the nearest land."

"I hadn't worked out the whole plan," Nate said.

"So, actually, I might be looking at success, right? You just wanted to test the outside water temperature?"

"Sure," said Nate, thinking it might be best to stay agreeable.

"Can you feel your hand?"

"It's a little chilly, but, yes."

"Oh, good."

And so they'd left him there a couple of hours, his hand and about six inches of his arm hanging out in the open sea as the whale ship swam along, and when they finally pulled him up, they put him in his seat and kept him restrained except to eat and go to the bathroom. He'd tried to relax and observe—learn what he could—but then a few minutes ago these waves of uneasiness had started hitting him.

"He's got the sonic willies," said Poe.

Poynter looked away from Skippy's console. "It's the subsonics, Doc. You're feeling the sound waves even though you can't hear them. We've been communicating with the blue for about ten minutes now."

"You might have said something."

"I just did."

"Couple of hours you'll be in the blue, Doc. You can stand up again, walk around a little. Have some privacy."

"So you're communicating with it in low-frequency sound?"

"Yep. Just like you thought, Doc, there was meaning in the call."

"Yeah, but I didn't think this, that there were guys, and guylike things, riding about inside whales. How in the hell can this be happening? How can I not know about this?"

"So you're giving up on the being-dead strategy?" asked Poe.

"What is it? Space aliens?"

Poynter unbuttoned his shirt and showed some chest hair. "Do I look like a space alien?"

"Well, no, but them." Nate nodded toward the whaley boys. They looked at each other and snickered, a sort of wheezing laughter coming from their blowholes, paused, looked back at Nate, then snickered some more.

"Maybe on their planet sentient life evolved from whales rather than apes," Quinn continued. "I can see how they might have landed here, deployed these whale ships, and kept under the radar of human detection while they looked around. I mean, man obviously isn't the most peaceful of creatures."

"That work for you, Doc?" asked Poynter.

"On their planet they developed an organically based technology, rather than one based on combustion and manipulation of minerals like ours."

"Oh, that *is* good," said Poe.

"He's on a roll," said Poynter. "Unraveling the mystery, he is."

Skippy and Scooter nodded to each other and grinned.

"So that's it? This ship is extraterrestrial?" Quinn felt the small victory rush that one gets from proving a hypothesis—even one as bizarre as space aliens riding in whale ships.

"Sure," said Poe, "that works for me. You, Cap?"

"Yeah, moon men, that's what you guys are," Poynter said to the whaley boys.

"Meep," said Scooter.

And in a high, squeaky, little-girl voice, Skippy croaked, "Phone home."

The whaley boys gave each other a high four and collapsed into fits of hysterical wheezing.

"What did he say?" Nate nearly snapped his neck trying to turn around against the restraints. "They can talk?"

"Well, I guess, if you call that talking," Poe said. He exchanged high fives with Poynter at the expense of the whaley boys, who paused in their own laughter to roll the whale ship in three quick spirals, which tossed the unsecured Poe and Poynter around the soft cabin like a couple of rag dolls.

Poynter came up with a bloody lip from connecting with his own knee. Poe had barked his shin on one of the whaley boys' heads as he went over. Strapped in, Nate concentrated on not watching a rerun of his lunch of raw tuna and water.

"Bastards!" said Poe.

"That what you expected in your race of superintelligent, space-faring extraterrestrials, Nate?" Poynter wiped blood from his lower lip and flung it at Scooter.

~❦~

CARL LINNAEUS, AN EIGHTEENTH-CENTURY SWEDISH DOCTOR WHO specialized in the treatment of syphilis, is credited with inventing the modern system that is used for classifying plants and animals. Linnaeus is responsible for naming the humpback whale *Megaptera novaeangliae,* or "big wings of New England," and later naming the blue whale *Balaenoptera musculus,* or "little mouse": at 110 feet long, over a hundred tons, an animal whose tongue alone is larger than a full-grown African elephant—the largest animal to ever live on the planet. "Little mouse"? Some speculated that this ironic misnomer was perpetrated entirely to confuse Linnaeus's lab assistants, as in *Run out and bring me back a "little mouse," Sven.* Others think that the pox had gone to Carl's head.

~❦~

QUINN WAS CROUCHED OVER THE BACK ORIFICE, SKIPPY AND SCOOTER holding him by either arm, Poynter and Poe crouched before him, saluting. He could feel the texture of the opening under his bare feet, like wet tire tread.

"It's been a pleasure, Doc," Poynter said. "Have a great trip."

"We'll see you back at base," said Poe. "Now, just relax. You're barely going to contact water. Hold your nose and blow."

Quinn did.

Poynter counted, "One, two—"

"Meep."

Nate was sucked out the orifice, felt a brief chill and some pressure pushing back against his ears, and found himself in a chamber only a little taller than that in the humpback, with a fairly amused woman.

"You can stop blowing now," she said.

"Yet another phrase I didn't think I'd be hearing in this lifetime," Nate said. He let go of his nostrils and took a deep breath. The air seemed fresher than in the humpback.

"Welcome to my blue, Dr. Quinn, I'm Cielle Nuñez. How do you feel?"

"Pooped." Quinn grinned. She was about his age, Hispanic with short dark hair peppered gray and wide brown eyes that caught the bioluminescence off the walls and reflected what looked like laughter. She was barefoot and wearing generic khakis like Poynter and Poe. He shook her hand.

"Cute," she said. "Come forward with me, Doctor. I'm sure it's been a while since you were able to stand up straight." She led him down the corridor, which reminded Nate of when, as kids, he and his buddies had explored storm drains in Vancouver. It was tall enough to walk in, but not tall enough to stand in comfortably.

"Actually, Cielle, I'm not a doctor. I have a Ph.D., but the doctor thing—"

"I understand. I'm captain of this rig, but if you call me 'Captain,' I'll ignore you."

"I wanted to hear the humpback sing before I left. You know, from the inside."

"You will. There'll be time."

The corridor started to widen as they moved forward, and Nate was actually able to walk normally, or as normally as one can walk when barefoot on whaleskin. This skin had a mottled appearance, whereas on the humpback it had been nearly solid gray. He noticed that on this ship there were wide veins of bioluminescence on the floor, casting a yellow light up upward that gave everything a sinister green glow. Nuñez paused by what appeared to be portals on either side of them.

"This is as good a place as any," she said. "Now, turn sideways and take my hand."

Quinn did as he was asked. Her hand felt warm but dry. She was a small woman, but powerfully built, he could feel the strength in her grip. "Now, we're just going to walk as the ship moves. Don't stop until I say, or you'll fall on your ass."

❧

"WHAT?"

"Okay, Scooter, roll it."

"Scooter?"

"All pilots are called Scooter or Skippy. They didn't tell you?"

"They weren't very forthcoming with information."

"Humpback crews are a bunch of yahoos." Nuñez smiled. "You know the type, like navy fighter pilots topside? All ego and testosterone."

"I got more cretin than yahoo," Nate said.

"Well, with that particular bunch, yes."

The whole corridor started to move.

"Here we go, step, step, step, that's good." They were walking across the walls as the ship rolled. When they were standing on the ceiling, the roll stopped. "Nice, Scooter," Nuñez said, obviously communicating through some sort of hidden intercom. Then, to Nate, "He's so good."

"We were upside down to make the transfer?"

"Exactly. You're a smart guy. Look, these are cabins." She touched a lighted node on the wall, and a skin portal folded back on itself. Again Nate was put in mind of the blowhole of a toothed whale, but it was so big, nearly four feet across, it was just . . . unnatural. Lines of light pumped to life past the portal to reveal a small cabin, a bed—apparently made of the same skin as the rest of the interior—but also a table and a chair. Nate couldn't make out what material they might be made of, but it looked like plastic.

"Bone," Nuñez said, noticing him noticing. "They're as much a part of the ship as the walls. All living tissue. There are shelves and cubbyholes for your stuff in the bulkheads, closed now. Obviously everything has to be stowed for little maneuvers like the one we just performed. The motion isn't as bad as on the humpbacks. You'll find you'll get used to it, and then you can move about just as if you were on land."

"You're right. I didn't even notice we were moving."

"That would be because we're not," said Nuñez.

The sound of whaley-boy snickering wheezed down the corridor toward them.

"You guys are supposed to be working," Nuñez said to the air. "Prepare to get under way." She turned to Quinn. "Can I buy you a cup of joe? Maybe answer some of your questions?"

"You're offering?" Quinn felt his heart jump with excitement. Information, without Poynter and Poe's goofing obfuscation? He was thrilled. "That would be fantastic."

"Don't pee all over yourself, Quinn. It's just coffee."

❧

THE CORRIDOR OPENED UP INTO A LARGE BRIDGE. THE HEAD OF THE blue was huge compared to the humpback's. On either side of the entry a whaley boy stood grinning at them as they passed. They were both taller than Quinn, and unlike the Scooter and Skippy of the humpback, their skin was mottled and lighter in color.

Nate paused and grinned back at them. "Let me guess—Skippy and Scooter?"

"Actually, Bernard and Emily 7," said Nuñez.

"You said they all were—"

"I said all pilots were named Skippy and Scooter." She gestured to the front of the bridge, where two whaley boys sitting at control consoles were turning in their seats and grinning. Maybe, thought Nate, they always appeared to be grinning, much like dolphins. He'd made an amateur mistake, assuming that their facial expressions were the analog of human expressions. People often did that with dolphins, even though the animals had no facial muscles to facilitate expression. Even sad dolphins appeared to be smiling.

"What are you two grinning at?" asked Nuñez. "Let's get on the way."

The pilots frowned and turned back to their consoles.

"Well, crap," Nate said.

"What?"

"Nothing, just another theory shot in the ass."

"Yeah, this operation does that, doesn't it?"

Nate felt something stirring in his back pocket and spun around to see a thin, fourteen-inch-long pink penis that was protruding from Bernard's genital slit. It waved at him.

"Holy moly!"

"Bernard!" Nuñez snapped. "Put that away. That is not procedure."

Bernard's unit drooped noticeably from the scolding. He looked at it and chirped contritely.

"Away!" Nuñez barked.

Bernard's willy snapped back up into his genital slit. "Sorry about that," Nuñez said to Nate. "I've never gotten used to that. It's really disconcerting when you're working with one of them and you ask them to hand you a screwdriver or something and his hands are already full. Coffee?"

She led him to a small white table around which four bone chairs protruded from the floor. They looked like old-style Greek saddle chairs—no backs, organic curves, and the high gloss of living bone—but more Gaudi than Flintstone. Quinn sat while Nuñez touched a node on the wall that opened a meter-wide portal that had concealed a sink, several canisters, and what looked like a percolator. Nate wondered about the electricity but forced himself to wait before asking.

While Nuñez prepared the coffee, Quinn looked around. The bridge was easily four times the size of the entire cabin in the humpback. Instead of riding in a minivan, it was like being in a good-size motor home—a very curvy, dimly lit motor home, but about that size. Blue light filtered in through the eyes, illuminating the pilots' faces, which shone like patent leather. Nate was starting to realize that even though everything was organic, living, the whale ship had the same sort of efficiency found on any nautical vessel: every spaced used, everything stowed against movement, everything functional.

"If you need to use the head, it's back down the corridor, fourth hatch on the right."

Emily 7 clicked and squealed, and Nuñez laughed. She had a warm laugh, not forced; it just rolled out of her smooth and easy. "Emily says it seems as if it would be more logical for the head to be in the head, but there goes logic."

"I gave up logic a few days ago."

"You don't have to give it up, just adjust. Anyway, facilities in the head are like everything on the ship—living—but I think you'll figure out the analogs pretty quickly. It's less complicated than an airliner bathroom."

Scooter chirped, and the great ship started to move, first in a fairly radical wave of motion, then smoothing out to a gentle roll. It was like being on a large sailing ship in medium seas.

"Hey, a little more warning, Scooter, huh?" said Nuñez. "I nearly dumped Nathan's coffee. Okay if I call you Nathan?"

"Nate's good."

Moving with the roll of the ship, she made it back to the table and put down the two steaming mugs of coffee, then went back for a sugar bowl, spoons, and a can of condensed milk. Nate picked up the can and studied it.

"This is the first thing from the outside that I've seen."

"Yeah, well, that's special request. You don't want to try whale milk in your coffee. It's like krill-flavored spray cheese."

"Yuck."

"That's what I'm saying."

"Cielle, if you don't mind my saying, you don't seem very military."

"Me? No, I wasn't. My husband and I had a sixty-foot sailboat. We got caught in a hurricane off of Costa Rica and sank. That's when they took me. My husband didn't make it."

"I'm sorry."

"It's okay. It was a long time ago. But, no, I've never been in the military."

"But the way you order the whaley boys around—"

"First, we need to clear up a misconception that you are obviously forming, Nate. I—we, the human beings on these ships—are not in charge. We're just—I don't know, like ambassadors or something. We sound like commanders because these guys would just goof off all day without someone telling them what to do, but we have no real authority. The Colonel gives the orders, and the whaley boys run the show."

Scooter and Skippy snickered like their counterparts on the humpback ship, Bernard and Emily 7 joined them—Bernard extending his prehensile willy like a party horn.

"And whaley girls?" Nate nodded toward Emily 7, who grinned—it was a very big, very toothy grin, but a little coquettish in the way one might expect from, say, an ingenue with a bite that could sever an arm.

"Just whaley boys. It's like the term 'mankind,' you know—alienate the female part of the race at all costs. It's the same here. Old-timers gave them the name."

"Who's the Colonel?"

"He's in charge. We don't see him."

"Human, though?"

"I'm told."

"You said you'd been here a long time. How long?"

"Let me get you another cup, and I'll tell you what I can." She turned. "Bernard, get that thing out of the coffeepot!"

Clair Stirs a Brainstorm

For all his admiration for the field biologists he'd worked with over the years, secretly Clay harbored one tiny bit of ego-preserving superiority over them: At the end of the day, they were going to have only nicked the surface of the knowledge they were trying to attain, but if Clay got the pictures, he went home a satisfied man. Even around Nathan Quinn he'd exercised an attitude of rascally smugness, teasing about his friend's ongoing frustration. For Clay it was get the pictures and what's for dinner? Until now. Now he had his own mysteries to contend with, and he couldn't help but think that the powers of irony were flexing their muscles to get back at him for his having lived carefree for so long.

Kona, on the other hand, had long paid homage to his fear of irony by, like many surfers, never eating shark meat. "I don't eat them, they don't eat me. That's just how it work." But now he, too, was feeling the sawtoothed edge of irony's bite, for, having spent most of his time from the age of thirteen knocking the edge off his mental acuity by the concerted application of the most epic smokage that Jah could provide (thanks be unto Him), he was now being called upon to think and remember with a sharpness that was clearly painful.

"Think," said Clair, rapping the surfer in the forehead with the spoon she had only seconds earlier used to stir honey into a cup of calming herbal tea.

"Ouch," said Kona.

"Hey, that's uncalled for" said Clay, coming to Kona's aid. Loyalty being important to him.

"Shut up. You're next."

"Okay."

They were gathered around Clay's giant monitor, which, for all the good it was doing them, could have been a giant monitor lizard. A spectrogram of whale song from Quinn's computer was splashed across the screen, and for the information they were getting from it, it might have been the aftermath of a paint-ball war, which is what it looked like.

"What were they doing, Kona?" Clair asked, spoon—steaming with herbal calmness—poised to strike. As a teacher of fourth-graders in a public school, where corporal punishment was not allowed, she had years of violence stored up and was, truth be told, sort of enjoying letting it out on Kona, who she felt could have been the poster child for the failure of public education. "Nate and Amy both went through this with you. Now you have to remember what they said."

"It's not these things, it's the oscilloscope," Kona said. "Nate pulled out just the submarine stuff and put it on the spectrum."

"It's all sub*marine*," Clay said. "You mean sub*sonic*."

"Yeah. He said there was something in there. I said like computer language. Ones and ohs."

"That doesn't help."

"He was marking them out by hand," Kona said. "By freezing the green line, then measuring the peaks and troughs. He said that the signal could carry a lot more information that way, but the whales would have to have oscilloscopes and computers to do it."

Clay and Clair both turned to the surfer in amazement.

"And they don't," Kona said. "Duh."

It was as if a storm of coherence had come over him. They just stared.

Kona shrugged. "Just don't hit me with the spoon again."

Clay pushed his chair back to let the surfer at the keyboard. "Show me."

Late into the night the three of them worked, making little marks on printouts of the oscilloscope and recording them on yellow legal pads. Ones and ohs. Clair went to bed at 2:00 A.M. At 3:00 A.M. they had fifty handwritten legal-pad pages of ones and ohs. In another time this might have felt to Clay like a job well done. He'd helped analyze data on shipboard before. It killed some time and ingratiated him to whatever scientist was leading the project he was there to photograph, but he'd always been able to hand off the work for someone else to finish. It was slowly dawning on him: Being a scientist sucked.

"This sucks," said Kona.

"No it doesn't. Look at all we have," said Clay, gesturing to all they had.

"What is it?"

"It's a lot, that's what it is. Look at all of it."

"What's it mean?"

"No idea."

"What does this have to do with Nate and the Snowy Biscuit?"

"Just look at all of this," said Clay, looking at all of it.

Kona got up from his chair and rolled his shoulders. "Mon, Bwana Clay, Jah has given you a big heart. I'm goin' to bed."

"What are you saying?" Clay said.

"We got all the heart we need, brah. We need head."

" 'Scuse me?"

And so, in the morning, with the promise of a colossal piece of information for barter (the torpedo range) but without a true indication of what he really needed to know in return (everything else), Clay talked Libby Quinn into coming to Papa Lani.

"So let me get this straight," said Libby Quinn as she paced from Clay's computer to the kitchen and back. Kona and Clay were standing to the side, following her movement like dogs watching meatball tennis. "You've got an old woman who claims that a whale called her and instructed her to have Nate take him a pastrami sandwich?"

"On rye, with Swiss and hot mustard," Kona added, not wanting her to miss any pertinent scientific details.

"And you have a recording of voices, underwater, presumably military, asking if someone brought them a sandwich."

"Correct," said Kona, "No bread, or meat, or cheese, specified."

Libby glared at him. "And you have the navy setting off simulated explosions in preparation to put a torpedo range in the middle of the Humpback Whale Sanctuary." She paused meaningfully and pivoted thoughtfully—like Hercule Poirot in flip-flops. "You have a tape of Amy doing a breath-hold dive for what appears to be an hour, with no ill effects."

"Topless," Kona added. Science.

"You have Amy claiming that Nate was eaten by a whale, which we all know is simply not possible, given the diameter of the humpback's throat, even if one were inclined to bite him, which we know they wouldn't." (She was just a deerstalker, a calabash, and a cocaine habit short of being Sherlock Holmes here.) "Then you have Amy taking a kayak out for no apparent reason and disappearing, presumed drowned. And you say that Nate was working on finding binary in the lower registers of the whale song, and you think that means something? Have I got that right?"

"Yeah," said Clay. "But you have the break-in to our offices to get the sound tapes, and you have my boat being sunk, too. Okay, it sounded more connected when we were talking about it last night."

Libby Quinn stopped pacing and turned to look at both of them. She wore cargo shorts, tech sandals, and a running bra and appeared ready at any moment to just take off and do something outdoorsy and strenuous. They both looked down, subdued, as if they were still under the threat of Clair's deadly spoon of calm. Clay had always had a secret attraction to Libby, even while she'd been married to Quinn, and it was only within the last year or so he'd been able to make eye contact with her at all. Kona, on the other hand, had studied dozens of videotapes on the lesbian lifestyle, especially as it pertained to having a third party show up in the middle of an intimate moment (usually with a pizza), so he had long ago assigned a "hot" rating to Libby, despite the fact that she was twice his age.

"Help us," Kona said, trying to sound pathetic, staring at the floor.

"This is what you guys have, and you think because I know a little biology I can make something of all this?"

"And that," said Clay, pointing at the now arranged and collated pages of ones and ohs on his desk.

Libby walked over and flipped through the pages. "Clay, this is nothing. I can't do anything with this. Even if Nate *was* on to something, what do you think? That even if we recognize a pattern, it's going to mean something to us? Look, Clay, I loved Nate, too, you know I did, but—"

"Just tell us where to start," Kona said.

"And tell me if you see anything in this." Clay went to his computer and hit a key. A still of the edge view of the whale tail from his rebreather dive was on the screen. "Nate said that he had seen some markings on a whale tail, Libby. Some writing. Well, I thought there was something on this whale, too, before it knocked me out. But this is the best shot of the tail we have. It could mean something."

"Like what?" Her voice was kind.

"I don't know what, Libby. If I knew what, I wouldn't have called you. But there's too much weird stuff going on that almost fits together, and we don't know what to do."

Libby studied the tail still. "There *is* something there. You don't have a better shot?"

"No, this is something I *do* know about. This is the best I have."

"You know, Margaret and I were helping a guy from Texas A&M who was designing a software program that would shift perspective of tail shots, so edge and bad-angle views could be shifted and extrapolated into usable ID photos. You know how many get tossed because of bad angles?"

"You have this program?"

"Yes, it's still in beta tests, but it works. I think we can shift this shot, and if there's something meaningful there, we'll see it."

"Cool runnings," Kona said.

"As far as this binary thing, I think it's a shot in the dark, but if it's going to mean anything, you're going to have to get your ones and ohs in the computer. Kona, can you type?"

"Well, on ones and ohs? I shred most masterful, mon."

"Right. I'll set you up with a simple text file—just ones and ohs—and we'll figure out if we can do anything with it later. No mistakes, okay?"

Kona nodded.

Clay finally looked up and smiled. "Thanks, Libby."

"I'm not saying it's anything, Clay, but I wasn't exactly fair to Nate when he was around. Maybe I owe him one now that he's gone. Besides, it's windy. Fieldwork would have sucked today. I'm going to call Margaret, have her bring the program over. I'll help you if you promise that you'll put all your weight into stopping this torpedo range and you'll sign Maui Whale on to the petition against low-frequency active sonar. You guys have a problem with that?"

She was giving them the "spoon of death" look, and it occurred to both of them that this might be something that was innate to all women, not just Clair, and that they should be very, very afraid.

"Nope," said Kona.

"Sounds good to me. I'll put on a pot of coffee," said Clay.

"Margaret is absolutely going to shit when she hears about the torpedo range," said Libby Quinn as she reached for Clay's phone.

CHAPTER TWENTY-FOUR

Orientation to the Blues

A small explosion went off over his head, and Nate dove under the table. When he looked up, Emily 7 was bent over staring at him with her watery whale eyes and a mild expression of distress, and Nuñez was crouched at the other end of the table smiling.

"That was the blow, Nate," Nuñez said. "A little more intense than the humpback's, huh? These ships act like real whales, remember. The blowhole is right above our heads. Vented to the rest of the ship, but, you know, every twenty minutes or so it's going to go. You get used to it."

"Sure, I knew that," said Nate, crawling out from under the table. He'd been out off of Santa Cruz searching for the blues. You usually found them by the sound of their blows, which you could hear up to a mile and a half away. He looked up, expecting to see sky through the blowhole, but instead he saw just more smooth whaleskin.

"They behave like whales, but the physiology is completely different to allow for the living quarters. I don't really understand it, but for instance the blowhole is vented down the sides somewhere to some axillary lungs that do the oxygen exchange with the blood. I don't know how they got us electricity at all. I mean, I said I wanted a coffeepot, and they put in an outlet. There are circuits all over the bridge for our machinery. The other bodily functions seem to be handled by smaller versions of liver, kidneys, and so forth around the outside of the cabins. The main spine runs over the top of the ship. There's no digestive system. The ship's digestive system is at the base; it hooks up and pumps nutrient-rich blood into the ship, which stores enough energy in blubber to run it for six months at sea, or around the world at least once. We can cruise at twenty knots as long as no one is watching."

"What do you mean, 'no one is watching'?"

"I mean you guys. Biologists. If one of you guys is watching us, we have to slow it down after a couple of hours. Especially if we're tagged."

"This ship has been satellite-tagged? What do you do?"

"We go to silent running for a while. Then we dive, and one of the whaley boys goes outside and pulls the tag off. We've been tagged twice by that Bruce Mate guy from Oregon State. That guy's a menace. Probably has a satellite tag on his wife to track her trips to the can. If they'd asked me, *he'd* be the one riding with us now."

"You know who he is?" Nate was aghast. As a scientist, you were always fighting being overwhelmed by what you don't know, but the magnitude of this whole operation—it was too much.

"Of course. Since commercial whaling backed off, cetacean biologists have been the main focus of our intelligence program. Why do you think you're here?"

"Okay, why am I here?"

"I don't know the whole story, but it's something to do with the song. Evidently you were a little too close to finding our signal in the song, so they yanked you."

"The aliens were that interested in what I was doing?"

"What aliens?"

"These aliens," Nate said, nodding toward the pilots and Bernard and Emily 7, who had moved to another table on the other side of the corridor.

"The whaley boys aren't aliens. Who told you that?"

"Well, Poynter and Poe implied that they were."

"Those jerks. No, they're not aliens. They're a little weird, but not from-another-planet weird."

Bernard looked up from what appeared to be a chart of some sort and gave a half-assed signature raspberry.

"They do that a lot," Nate said.

"If you had a tongue four inches wide, you'd do that a lot, too. It's sort of a display move with them, like the penis waving that Bernard was doing."

"Like male killer whales do."

"Bingo. See, a guy with your background, this is easy to explain. I didn't understand squat at first."

"I'm sorry, but I can't believe that this ship, the whaley boys, the whole perfection of the way they work, could possibly be products of natural selection. There had to be a design. Someone made all this."

Cielle nodded, smiling. "I've known a number of scientists in my life-time, Nate, but I'm sure this is the first time I've heard one arguing in favor of a grand designer. What's that called, the 'watchmaker argument'?"

She was right, of course. It was an accepted premise that intelligent design in nature was not necessarily a product of intelligence, but merely the mechanism of natural selection of traits for survival and really, really long periods of time for the selections to assert themselves. Nate's life's work had been built on that assumption, but now he was giving Darwin the old heave-ho simply because his—Nate's—mind was too small to adapt to the idea of this craft. Well, yes, damn it. Screw Darwin. This was too strange.

"I'm sorry, I'm just having a little trouble getting my head around this. I don't know how you take to being a prisoner, but I don't care for it. On top of that, I could barely sleep on the humpback with the blow going off every few minutes, and I haven't eaten anything but raw fish and water for about five days. I'd be addled even if this didn't seem im-possible."

Bernard made a whimpering noise, and Skippy and Scooter fol-lowed along in a moment until they sounded like a basketful of hungry puppies, and then they all broke out into wheezing snickers. Emily 7 frowned at them.

"Of course, I understand, Nate," Nuñez said. " Maybe you should finish up your coffee and go to your quarters. I have a few sports shakes in my cabin that will get some carbohydrates to your brain, and I can get you something to help you sleep—the ship's doctor has a full stock of pharmaceuticals." She patted his hand maternally. Nate felt a little ashamed for having complained.

"You're not the only human on this ship, then?"

"No, there are four humans and six whaley boys on board. The others are in their quarters. But they're all excited to meet you. Everyone's been talking about it for weeks."

"You've known for weeks you were going to take me?"

"Well, sort of. We were on standby. We just got the go-ahead the day before we took you."

"And you, and the rest of the crew, you're prisoners, too?"

"Nate, every person on this ship, on any whale ship, has been pulled out of a sinking or sunken ship, a plane crash at sea, or some other disaster that would have killed them. This is a gift of time, and frankly, once you accept where you are and what you're doing, I'm going to ask you where you'd rather be. Okay?"

Nate searched her face for any sign of sarcasm or malice. All he found was a gentle smile. "Okay."

"You go to your quarters now. I'll send around your supplies in a bit. Bernard, would you show Dr. Quinn to his quarters?"

"I'm not really a doctor," Nate whispered.

"Take whatever respect you can get from them, Nate."

Bernard waited at the entry to the corridor, rubbing his shiny-smooth stomach and grinning. A white coffee mug stood out in contrast against Bernard's abdomen, suspended as it was in the grasp of his penis.

"I've always wanted to do that," said Nate, deciding that he wasn't going to let the whaley boy get the satisfaction of intimidating him. "Would be really handy for driving." Nate bowed toward the corridor. "Lead on, Bernard."

Bernard skulked down the hall in what would have been a full pout posture, had he any lips to do the actual pouting. He spilled a trail of coffee along the way.

CHAPTER TWENTY-FIVE

The Inner Secrets
of Cetacean Sluts

Nate was just settling into the idea of the organic bunk he was going to be sleeping on before actually settling into the bed. He was not a God kind of guy, but he found himself thanking one nonetheless for the crisp cotton sheets and pillowcase on a feather pillow. He didn't think he really wanted to sleep with his face against whaleskin. There was a soft whistle outside the portal, and the great flap of skin retracted to open to the corridor. Emily 7 stood there with a tray that held two cans of protein shake, a glass of water, and a single small pill. She grinned but did not try to step into the cabin. The small portal required a bit of a crouching and climbing action for Nate to enter, so he guessed she'd dump the tray trying to get through. Then again, she might just be trying to be polite. She waited while Nate took the cans from the tray and set them on the low table, then swung around to take the pill and water from her.

Emily 7 whistled and gave him a sidelong glance, causing her right eye to bulge out at him, as he'd actually seen humpbacks do when checking out a boat at the surface. She gestured for him to take the pill.

"You're not leaving until you see me take my medicine?"

Emily 7 nodded.

"Well, I guess if you guys wanted to get rid of me, it would have been a lot easier to kill me without bringing me all the way out here to poison me." Nate took the pill, downed the water, and opened his mouth to show that the pill was gone. "That okay, nurse?"

Emily whistled and nodded, then gently took the empty glass from Nate's hand. She reached up to hit the node, and the portal closed between them. Nate heard her whistle the first few bars of a lullaby.

She's sweet, Nate thought, in a tall, malevolent rubber-puppet sort of way.

⤛◉⤜

FOR ALMOST A WEEK THE ONLY SLEEP NATE HAD BEEN ABLE TO GET was while he was restrained in the chair in the humpback, and even then it was restless—with the ship blowing every few minutes and the whaley boys whistling communications—so, despite the blow of the blue-whale ship, he fell into a deep sleep filled with vivid dreams. He dreamed of himself and Amy, their naked bodies entwined, slick with sweat under soft candlelight. Strangely, even as he dreamed, he had the semilucid thought that before, whenever he'd taken a sleeping pill, he didn't remember ever dreaming. But that thought was pushed away by the feel of Amy's smooth skin, his fingers softly caressing her muscular legs, her four long, webbed fingers wrapped lovingly around his—

"Hey!" Nate opened his eyes. A softly lit fence of spiky teeth smiled over at him, steamy fish breath washed over his face.

"Uh-oh," said Emily 7, her voice high and rasping, verging on duck-speak.

Nate leaped out of bed and bounced off the wall on the other side of the cabin.

Emily 7 pulled the sheet up over her head and burrowed against the wall, digging her melon under the pillow. Then she lay still.

Nate stood trying to catch his breath. As soon as he'd hit the floor, the biolighting had come up to high. He pushed back against the flexible wall, then suddenly became self-conscious and pulled his T-shirt off the back of the chair to cover his erection, which was rapidly losing its will to live.

She was just lying there.

"Hello? I can see you."

Curled up. Not moving. There under the sheets. All whaley.

"You aren't fooling anyone. You're bigger than I am. You're not hidden."

Just the soft sound of her blowhole opening and closing. Nate realized that it might be easier to hide under the covers if one had a blowhole, as one could cover one's mouth and face and still breathe. Addled by sleep deprivation, residual sleep medication, two cups of coffee, and now a few endorphins, he started to speculate on how a creature might adapt for hiding under the covers, then shook off the biologist rising up in him.

"Come on, we're different species and stuff. That's creepy."

Now a bit of a squeak, more like a whimper, followed by a tiny "Uh-oh," like a small elf had been mashed under the covers with a heavy book and had uh-ohed its last pathetic gasp.

"Well, you can't stay here."

He remembered how he'd felt when Libby had left him and by way of explanation she'd said, "Nate, I don't know, I don't even feel like we're the same species." At the time he'd felt as if his stomach were being turned inside out. It had ruined him socially for more than a year. Longer than that if he counted the fiasco attraction to Amy.

He stepped over to the bunk. Emily 7 scrunched into the corner between the wall and the bed. Nate worked the edge of the sheet loose and cautiously slid one leg under the covers. The lump that was Emily 7's head moved as if she was listening.

"You have to stay on your side, okay?"

"Okay," wheezed Emily 7 in the mashed-elf voice.

⸻◦◦⸻

NATE AWOKE TO THE EXULTATIONS OF KILLER WHALES—HIGH-PITCHED hunting calls. The pod seemed to be gleefully celebrating a hunt, or at least calling another pod to come along and help. It occurred to him that he was actually riding in a craft that qualified as food for the orcas, and the ship might be in danger of attack. He'd have to ask Nuñez about that. He swung his feet off the bunk, and the lights came up. He realized that he was alone and sighed with relief.

There was a fresh set of khakis hung over the chair and a bottle of water on the table. There was a small basin on the wall opposite the bunk, no bigger than a cereal bowl and made out of the same skin as the rest of the ship. He hadn't even noticed it the night before. There were three lit nodules above the basin, like those used to activate the portals, but Nate could see nowhere for the water to come out. He pushed one of the nodules, and the basin started filling from a sphincter in the bottom. He pushed another, and the water was sucked out the same orifice. He tried to foster scientific detachment toward the whole thing but failed miserably: He was creeped out. Nate desperately needed a shave and a shower, but he didn't want to try to wash his whole six-foot-two-inch body in an eight-inch bowl with a . . . well, a butt hole at the bottom. He'd had just about enough of advanced poop-chute technology, thank you. He splashed some water on his face and dressed in the khakis, wondering as he did if the whale ship could actually grow a mirror for him to shave in if he needed it.

The whole crew appeared to be up and milling about the bridge when Nate came in. There were four whaley boys at the table with the charts to the right of the hatch, the two pilots at their consoles. Nuñez stood by the table to the left of the hatch, where there were seated a blond woman in her thirties and two men, one dark, perhaps in his early twenties, and one bald and gray-bearded, a healthy fifty, maybe. Not a very military-looking bunch. Everyone turned when Nate came in. All conversations—words or whistles—stopped abruptly. The echo of killer-whale calls bounced around the bridge. Emily 7 turned away from Nate's gaze. Nuñez was leaning against the wall near the nook that housed the coffeepot, actively trying not to look at him.

"Hi," Nate said, catching eye contact with the bald guy, who smiled.

"Have a seat," said the bald guy, gesturing toward the empty seat at the table. "We'll get you something to eat. I'm Cal Burdick." He shook Nate's hand. "This is Jane Palovsky and Tim Milam."

"Jane, Tim," Nate said, shaking hands. Nuñez smiled at him, then looked away quickly as if the coffeepot needed some immediate attention or she was going to crack up—or both.

Everyone at the table nodded, sort of staring at the spot in front of them, like *So here we are on a giant blue-whale ship, hundreds of feet below the surface of the ocean, with killer whales calling about us, and Nate fucked an alien, so . . .*

"Nothing happened," Nate said to the whole bridge.

"What?" said Jane.

"Your quarters satisfactory, then?" asked Tim, an eyebrow raised.

"Nothing happened," Nate repeated, and even though nothing *had* happened, from the tone of his voice he wouldn't have believed it either. "Really."

"Of course," said Tim.

All of the whaley boys except Emily 7 were snickering. When he looked around, all the males were waving their willies back and forth in time in the air, as if swaying to a pornographic Christmas carol. Emily 7 put her big whaley head down on the table and covered it with her arms.

"Nothing happened!" Nate shouted at them. Silence again on the bridge, just the echo of killer-whale calls. "Are we in danger?" Nate asked Nuñez, trying desperately to change the subject. "Are they going to attack the ship? Those are feeding calls, right?" Often, when killer whales found a whale that was too big to be taken by their family pod, or when they happened on to an especially rich school of fish, they would call to other pods for help. Nate recognized the calls from some work he'd done with a biologist friend in Vancouver.

"No, these are residents," Nuñez said. "They're just excited about a bait ball they've found. Probably sardines." *Resident* killer whales ate only fish; *transients* ate mammals, whales and seals. Over the last few years scientists tended to refer to them as completely different species, even though they appeared the same to the layman.

"You know what they are by their call?"

"More than that," Cal said, "we know what they're saying. The whaley boys can translate."

"All killer whales are named Kevin. You knew that, right?" said Jane. She had a slight Eastern European accent, Russian maybe. She looked a little amused, her blue eyes dark under the yellow cast of the bioluminescence, but she didn't appear to be joking. She patted the seat next to her, indicating that Nate should sit down.

"Like all the pilots are named Scooter and Skippy?" Nate said.

"Actually, they have numbers like Emily—their choice, by the way—but since there are never more than one pair of them on a ship, we don't bother with the numbers."

Nate suddenly realized that in all his time on both of the whale ships, except when one of the pilots had gone outside to catch fish, the pilots always seemed to be at the controls. "Don't they ever sleep?"

"Sure," said Jane. "We're pretty sure they sleep with half their brain at a time, like whales, so between two of them the ship always has a full pilot. Without one of them at the controls, it's basically a big lump of meat."

"You said that you're pretty sure. You don't know?"

"Well, *they* don't know for sure," said Jane, "and they're not very excited about our doing experiments on them. Now that you've joined us, though, maybe you'll be able to figure out what's going on with them. We sort of play it all by ear. The whaley boys and the Colonel run things. Cielle, you didn't tell him all this?"

"He was pretty beat," Nuñez said. "I tried to get him settled in as soon as I could."

Nate wanted to protest the "settled in" comment. After all, he was a prisoner here, but these people didn't behave at all like captors. They immediately impressed him as having the same dynamic that he'd seen in research teams, a "we're all in this together, let's make the best of it" attitude. He didn't want to yell at these people. Still, it made him a little uncomfortable that she was so forthcoming with information. When your kidnappers showed you their faces, they were giving you the message that you weren't going home.

Nuñez set a plate down in front of him. It had a salad of mixed seaweeds, carrots, and mushrooms, a piece of cooked fish, which looked like halibut, and what appeared to be rice.

"Eat up," she said. "A couple of nutrition drinks aren't going to get you back up to speed. We do eat a lot of raw fish, even on the blue, but you need some carbs until you adjust to this diet. There's plenty of rice when you finish that."

"Thanks." Nate dug in while the others, all but Cal, excused themselves to work in other parts of the ship. The older man had obviously been charged with Nate's second orientation lecture.

Cal scratched his beard, looked around at the pilots, then leaned over to Nate and spoke in a lowered voice. "They're very promiscuous. You know how dolphin females will mate with all the males in the pod so no one can be assured of who the father of her calf is? They think it keeps the males from murdering her calf when it's born."

"That's the theory," Nate said.

"They're sort of like that, and back at base you have a big pod to deal with. You start down that path . . . well, you've got a lot of whaley boys to sex up."

"I didn't sex her up," Nate hissed, spraying rice out over the table. "I'm not sexing up any whaley boys . . . er, girls—"

"Whatever. Look, they're very close. Here on the ship they don't have separate quarters—they share one big cabin. Sex is very casual with them, but they understand that we're a little more hung up about it. Some of them seem to affect human shyness. We generally don't mix sexually with them. It's not forbidden, but it's . . . you know, frowned upon. It's only natural for a guy to be curious—"

Nate put down his fork. "Cal, I did not have sex with anyone—I mean, any*thing*."

"Right. And be careful around the males. Especially if you're in the water with them. They'll bung-hole you just to watch you twitch."

"Jeez."

"I'm just telling you for your own good."

"Thanks, but I'm not going to be around long enough to worry about it." *Might as well throw it in their faces,* Nate thought.

The older man laughed, almost shooting coffee out his nose. When he recovered, he said, "Well, I hope you mean you plan on dying soon, because no one ever leaves."

Nate leaned into Cal's face. "Doesn't it bother you, that you're a prisoner?"

"There's not one of us here who wouldn't be dead if the whaley boys hadn't picked us up."

"Not me."

"Especially you. You were always twelve hours from dead since we started watching you. Certainly it had to occur to you how much easier it would have been just to kill you?"

Nate just stared for a second. Actually, it *had* occurred to him, and he didn't see the logic in keeping him alive if all they wanted to do was stop his research. He wasn't going to make that argument verbally, but still . . .

"Don't overthink it, Nate. If you ever doubted that life was an adventure, it definitely is now."

"Right," Nate said. "But before you ask me where I'd rather be, let me remind you that there's a sphincter in the bottom of my sink."

"You haven't seen the shower, then? Just you wait."

After he ate, Cal loaned him a copy of *Treasure Island* to read, but when Nate returned to his cabin, he could barely concentrate on the book at all. Funny what you learn about yourself in a short conversation. One, that he would rather have been accused of having sex with another species than with another male (even of another species). Interesting prejudice. Two, that he actually was grateful, not only to be alive, but grateful to be having completely new experiences every moment, even as a prisoner. Three, that learning was still a high, but he burned to share it with someone. And finally, that he was feeling a little jealous, a little less special, now that he knew that Emily 7 was having sex with all the male whaley boys on board. That fickle little slut.

He dozed off with Robert Louis Stevenson on his chest and the sound of killer whales calling in the distance.

~~⌒⦿⌒~~

OUTSIDE, THE POD OF TWENTY KILLER WHALES, MOST THE SONS OR daughters of the matriarch female, were calling frantically to each other as they worried away at a huge bait ball of herring. Biologists had long speculated on the incredibly complex vocabulary of the killer whale, identifying specific linguistic groups that even "spoke" the same dialect, but they had never been able to put meaning to the calls other than to identify them as "feeding," "distress," or "social" noises. However, had they had the benefit of translation, this is what they would have heard:

"Hey, Kevin, fish!"

"Fish! I love fish!"

"Look, Kevin, fish!"

"Mmmm, fish."

"You, Kevin, take a run down that trench, fake left, go right, hit the bait ball, nothing but fish!"

"Did someone say 'fish'?"

"Yeah, fish. Over here, Kevin."

"Mmmmm, fish."

And it went on like that. Actually, orcas aren't quite as complex as scientists imagine. Most killer whales are just four tons of doofus dressed up like a police car.

CHAPTER TWENTY-SIX

Picking the Lock to Davy Jones's Locker

"Bite me'?" Libby Quinn said, reading the tail.

The whale tail slowly twisted in space, pixel by pixel, as the computer extrapolated the new angle. Margaret Painborne sat at the computer. Clay and Libby stood behind her. Kona was working across the room on Quinn's reassembled machine.

" 'Bite me'?" Clay repeated. "That can't be right." He thought about what Nate had said about seeing a tail just like this and shivered.

Margaret hit a few keys on the keyboard, then swiveled in Clay's chair. "This some kind of joke, Clay?"

"Not mine. That was raw footage, Margaret." As attractive as Clay found Libby, he found Margaret equally scary. Maybe the latter because of the former. It was complex. "The tail image before you shifted it is exactly what I saw when I was down there."

"You've all been saying how sophisticated their communication ability was," said Kona, trying to sound scientific but essentially just pissing everyone off.

"How?" said Libby. "Even if you wanted to, how would you paint a whale's flukes like that?"

Margaret and Clay just shook their heads.

"Rust-Oleum," suggested Kona, and they all turned and glared at him. "Don't give me the stink-eye. You'd need the waterproof, huh?"

"Did you finish inputting those pages?" Clay said.

"Yah, mon."

"Well, save them and go rake something or mow something or something."

"Save as a binary," Margaret added quickly, but Kona had already saved the file, and the screen was clear.

Margaret wheeled her chair across the office, her gray hair trailing out behind her like the Flying Sorceress of Clerical Island. She pushed Kona aside. "Crap," she said.

"What?" asked Clay.

"What?" asked Libby.

"You said save it," Kona said.

"He saved it as an ASCII file, a text file, not a binary. Crap. I'll see if it's okay." She opened the file, and text appeared on the screen. Her hand went to her mouth, and she sat back slowly in Clay's chair. "Oh, my God."

"What?" came the chorus.

"Are you sure you put this in, just as it came off the graphs?" she asked Kona without looking at him.

"Truth," said Kona.

"What?" said Libby and Clay.

"This has got to be some sort of joke," said Margaret.

Clay and Libby ran across the room to look at the screen. "What!"

"It's English," Margaret said, pointing to the text. "How is that possible?"

"That's not possible," Libby said. "Kona, what did you do?"

"Not me, I just typed ones and ohs."

Margaret grabbed one of the legal pages with the ones and ohs and began typing the numbers into a new file. When she had three lines, she saved it, then reopened the file as text. It read, WILL SCUTTLE SECOND BOAT TO—

"It can't be."

"It is." Clay jumped into Margaret's lap and started scrolling through the text from Kona's transcription. "Look, it goes on for a while, then it's just gobbledygook, then it goes on some more."

Margaret looked back at Libby with *Save me* in her eyes. "There is no way that the song is carrying a message in English. Binary was a stretch, but I refuse to believe that humpbacks are using ASCII and English to communicate."

Libby looked over to Kona. "You guys took these off of Nate's tapes, exactly the way you showed me?"

Kona nodded.

"Kids, look at this," Clay said. "These are all progress reports. Longitude and latitude, times, dates. There are instructions here to sink my boat. These fuckers sank my boat?"

"What fuckers?" Margaret said. "A humpback with 'Bite me' on his flukes?" She was trying to look around Clay's broad back. "If this were possible, then the navy would have been using it a long time ago."

Now Clay jumped up to face Kona. "What tape is this last part from?"

"The last one Nate and Amy made, the day Nate drown. Why?"

Clay sat back on Margaret's lap, looking stunned. He pointed to a line of text on the screen. They all leaned in to read: QUINN ON BOARD— WILL RENDEZVOUS WITH BLUE-6__AGREED COORDINATES__1600 TUESDAY__ NO PASTRAMI

"The sandwich," Clay said ominously.

Just then Clair, home from school, stepped into the office to discover an impromptu dog pile of action nerds in front of Quinn's computer. "All you bastards want to be part of a sandwich, and you don't even know what to do with one woman."

"Not the spoon!" squealed Kona, his hand going to the goose egg on his forehead.

❧❧❧

NATHAN QUINN AWOKE FEELING AS IF HE NEEDED TO CRAWL OUT OF his skin. If he hadn't felt it before, he would have thought he had the generic heebie-jeebies (scientifically speaking), but he recognized the feeling as being hit with heavy subsonic sound waves. The blue-whale ship was calling. Just because it was below the frequency of his hearing didn't mean it wasn't loud. Blue-whale calls could travel ten thousand miles, he assumed that the ship was putting out similar sounds.

Nate slipped out of his bunk and nearly fell reaching for his shirt. Another thing he hadn't noticed immediately—the ship wasn't moving, and he still had his sea legs on.

He dressed quickly and headed down the corridor to the bridge. There was a large console that spanned the area between the two whaley-boy pilots that hadn't been there before. Unlike the rest of the ship, it appeared to be man-made, metal and plastic. Sonar scopes, computers, equipment that Quinn didn't even recognize. Nuñez and the blond woman, Jane, were standing at the sonar screens wearing headphones. Tim was seated beside one of the whaley boys at the center of the console in front of two monitors. Tim was wearing headphones and typing. The whaley boy appeared to be just watching.

Nuñez saw Nate come in, smiled, and motioned for him to come forward. These people were completely incompetent as captors, Nate thought. Not a measure of terror among them, the humans anyway. If not for the subsonic heebie-jeebies, he would have felt right at home.

"Where did this come from?"

The electronics looked incredibly crude next to the elegant organic design of the whale ship, the whaley boys, and, for that matter, the human crew. The idea of comparing designs between human-built devices and biological systems hadn't really occurred to Nate before because he'd been conditioned never to think of animals as designed. The whale ship was putting a deep dent in his Darwin.

"These are our toys," Nuñez said. "The console stays below the floor unless we need to see it. Totally unnecessary for the whaley boys, since they have direct interface with the ship, but it makes us feel like we know what's going on."

"And they can't type for shit," said Tim, tucking his thumbs under and making a slamming-the-keys gesture. "Tiny thumbs."

The whaley boy next to him trumpeted a raspberry all over Tim's monitor, leaving large dots of color magnified in the whaley spit. He chirped twice, and Tim nodded and typed into the computer.

"Can they read?" Nate asked.

"Read, kind of write, and most of them understand at least two human languages, although, as you probably noticed, they're not big talkers."

"No vocal cords," said Nuñez. "They have air chambers in their heads that produce the sounds they make, but they have a hard time forming the words."

"But they *can* talk. I've heard Em— I mean, them."

"Best that you just learn whaleyspeak. It's basically what they use to talk to each other, except they keep it in the range of our hearing. It's easier to learn if you've learned other tonal-sensitive languages like Navajo or Chinese."

"I'm afraid not," Nate said. "So the ship is calling?"

Tim pulled off his headphones and handed them to Nate. "The pitch is raised into our range. You'll be able to hear it through there."

Nate held a headphone to one ear. Now that he could hear the signal, he could also feel it start and stop more acutely in his chest. If anything, it relieved the discomfort, because he could hear it coming. "Is this a message?"

"Yep," said Jane, pulling up a headphone. "Just as you suspected. We type it in, the computer puts the message into peaks and troughs on the waveform, we play the waveform for the whaley boys, and they make the whale sing that waveform. We've calibrated it over the years."

Nate noticed that the whaley boy at the metal console had one hand in an organic socket fitted into the front of the console—like a flesh cable that ran to the whale ship through the console's base, similar to the ones on the flesh consoles the pilots used.

"Why the computers and stuff at all if the whaley boys do it all by . . . what? Instinct?"

The whaley boy at the console grinned up at Nate, squeaked, then performed the international signal for a hand job.

"It's the only way we can be in the loop," Jane said. "Believe me, for a long time we were just along for the ride. The whaley boys have the same navigational sense that the whales themselves do. We don't understand it at all. It's some sort of magnetic vocabulary. It wasn't until the

Dirts—that's you—developed computers and we got some people who could run them that we became part of the process. Now we can surface and pull a GPS coordinate, transmit it, communicate with the other crews. We have *some* idea of what we're doing."

"You said for a long time? How long?"

Jane looked nervously at Nuñez, who looked nervously back. Nate thought for a moment that they might have to dash off to the bathroom together, which in his experience was what women did right before they made any major decisions, like about which shoes to buy or whether or not they were ever going to sleep with him again.

"A long time, Nate. We're not sure how long. Before computers, okay?"

By which she meant she wasn't going to tell him and if he pressed it, she'd just lie to him. Nate suddenly felt more like a prisoner, and, as a prisoner, he felt as though his first obligation was to escape. He was sure that was your first obligation as a prisoner. He'd seen it in a movie. Although his earlier plan of leaping out the back orifice into the deep ocean now seemed a tad hasty, with some perspective.

He said, "So how deep are we?"

"We usually send at about two thousand feet. That puts us pretty squarely in the SOFAR channel, no matter where we are geographically."

The SOFAR channel (sound fixing and ranging) was a natural combination of pressure and temperature at certain depths that cause a path of least resistance in which sound could travel many thousands of miles. The theory had been that blues and humpbacks used it to communicate with each other over long distances for navigational purposes. Evidently whaley boys and the people who worked their ships did, too.

"So does this signal replicate a natural blue-whale call?"

"Yes," said Tim. "That's one of the advantages of communicating in English within the waveform. When the whaley boys were doing the direct communication, there was a lot more variation in the call, but our signal is hidden, more or less. Except for a few busybodies who may run across it."

"Like me?"

"Yes, like you. We're a little worried about some of the acoustic people at Woods Hole and Hatfield Marine Center in Oregon. People who spend way too much time looking at spectrograms of underwater sound."

"You realize," said Nate, "that I might never have found out about your ships. I didn't make any sort of intuitive leap to look at a binary signal in the call. It was a stoned kid who came up with that."

"Yeah," said Jane. "If it makes you feel any better, you can blame him for your being here. We were on hold until you started to look in the signal for binary. That's when they called you in, so to speak."

Nate sincerely wished he could blame Kona, but since it appeared that he might never see civilization again, having someone to blame didn't seem particularly pertinent right now. Besides, the kid had been right. "How'd you know? I didn't exactly put out a press release."

"We have ways," said Nuñez, trying not to sound spooky but failing. This evidently amused the whaley boy at the console and the two pilots no end, and they nearly wheezed themselves out of their seats.

"Oh, fuck you guys," said Nuñez. "It's not like you guys are a bunch of geniuses."

"And you guys were the nightwalkers that Tako Man was talking about," Nate said to the pilots. "You guys sank Clay's boat."

The pilots raised their arms over their heads in a menacing scary-monster pose, then bared their teeth and made some fake growling noises, then collapsed into what Nate was starting to think of as whale giggles. The whaley boy at the console started clapping and laughing as well.

"Franklin! We're not done here. Can we get the interface back?"

Franklin, obviously the whaley boy who had been working the console, slumped and put his hand back in the socket. "Sorry," came a tiny voice from his blowhole.

"Bitch," came another tiny voice from one of the pilots, followed by whaley snickering.

"Let's send one more time. I want base to know we'll be there in the morning," Nuñez said.

"Morale's not a problem, then?" asked Nate, grinning at Nuñez's loss of temper.

"Oh, they're like fucking children," Nuñez said. "They're like dolphins: You dump them in the middle of the ocean with a red ball and they'll just play all day long, stopping only long enough to eat and screw. I'm telling you, it's like baby-sitting a bunch of horny toddlers."

Franklin squeaked and clicked a response, and this time Tim and Jane joined in the laughter with the whaley boys.

"What? What?" asked Nate.

"I do *not* just need to get laid!" shouted Nuñez. "Jane, you got this?"

"Sure," said the blonde.

"I'm going to quarters." She left the bridge to the snickering of the whaley boys.

Tim looked back at Nate and nodded toward the sonar screen and headset that Nuñez had vacated. "Want to stand in?"

"I'm a prisoner," said Nate.

"Yeah, but in a nice way," said Jane.

That was true. Everyone since he'd come on board had been very kind to him, seeing to his every need, even some he didn't want seen to. He didn't feel like a prisoner. Nate wasn't sure that he wasn't experiencing the Helsinki syndrome, where you sympathized with your captors—or was that the Stockholm syndrome? Yeah, the Helsinki syndrome had something to do with hair loss. It was definitely the Stockholm syndrome.

He stepped up to the sonar screen and put on the headset. Immediately he heard the distant song of a humpback. He looked at Tim, who raised his eyebrows as if to say, *See.*

"So tell me," Nate said, "what's the singing mean?" It was worth a shot.

"We were just going to ask you," said Jane.

"Swell," said Nate. Suddenly he didn't feel so well. After all this, even people who traveled inside whales didn't know what the song meant?

"Are you all right, Nate?" Jane asked. "You don't look so good."

"I think I have Stockholm syndrome."

"Don't be silly," said Tim. "You've got plenty of hair."

"You want some Pepto?" asked Jane, the ship's doctor.

Yes, he thought, escape would seem a priority. He was pretty sure that if he didn't get away, he was going to snap and kill some folks, or at least be incredibly stern with them.

Funny, he thought, how your priorities could change with circumstances. You go along for the greater part of your life thinking you want something—to understand the humpback song, for instance. So you pursue that with dogged single-mindedness at the expense of everything else in your life, only to be distracted into thinking maybe you want something in addition to that—Amy, for instance. And that becomes a diversion up until the time when circumstances make you realize what it is you really want, and that is—strangely enough—to get the fuck out of a whale. Funny, Nate thought.

<hr/>

"SETTLE DOWN, KONA," CLAIR SAID, DROPPING HER PURSE BY THE door, "I don't have a spoon."

Clay jumped off Margaret's lap. He and Kona watched as Clair crossed the room and exchanged hugs with Margaret and Libby, lingering a bit while hugging Libby and winking over her shoulder at Clay.

"So nice to see you guys," Clair said.

"I'm not going out to get the pizza, mon. No way," said Kona, still looking a bit terrified.

"What are you guys doing?" Clair asked.

And so Margaret took it upon herself to explain what they had discovered over the last few hours, with Kona filling in the pertinent and personal details. Meanwhile, Clay sat down in the kitchen and pondered the facts. Pondering, he felt, was called for.

Pondering is a little like considering and a little like thinking, but looser. To ponder, one must let the facts roll around the rim of the mind's roulette wheel, coming to settle in whichever slot they feel pulled to. Margaret and Libby were scientists, used to jamming their facts into the appropriate slots as quickly as possible, and Kona . . . well, a thought rolling around in his mind was rather like a tennis ball in a coffee can— it was just a little too fuzzy to make any impact—and Clair was just catching up. No, the pondering fell to Clay, and he sipped a dark beer from a sweating bottle on a high stool in the kitchen and waited for the roulette ball to fall. Which it did, right about the time that Margaret Painborne was reaching a conclusion to her story.

"This obviously has something to do with defense," Margaret said. "No one else would have a reason—hell, *they* can't even have a *good* reason. But I say we write our senators tonight and confront Captain Tarwater in the morning. He's got to know something about it."

"And that's where you're completely wrong," Clay said. And they all turned. "I've been pondering this"—here he paused for impact—"and it occurs to me that two of our friends disappeared right about the time they found out about this stuff. And that everything from the break-in to the sinking of my boat"—and here he paused for a moment of silence— "has had something to do with someone not wanting us to know this stuff. So I think it would be reckless of us to run around trying to tell everybody what we know before we know what we know is."

"That can't be right," said Libby.

" 'Before we know what we know is'?" quoted Margaret. "No, that's not right."

"Is making perfect sense to me," said Kona.

"No, Clay," said Clair, "I'm fine with you and the girl-on-girl action, and I'm fine with a haole Rasta boy preaching sovereignty, but I'm telling you I won't stand for that kind of grammatical abuse. I *am* a schoolteacher, after all."

"We can't tell anyone!" Clay screamed.

"Better," said Clair.

"No need to shout," Libby said. "Margaret was just being a radical hippie reactionist feminist lesbian communist cetacean biologist, weren't you, dear?" Libby Quinn grinned at her partner.

"I'll have an acronym for that in a second," mumbled Clair, counting off words on her fingers. "Jeez, your business card must be the size of a throw rug."

Margaret glared at Libby, then turned to Clay. "You really think we could be in danger?"

"Seems that way. Look, I know we wouldn't know this without your help, but I just don't want anyone hurt. We may already be in trouble."

"We can keep it quiet if you feel that's the way to go," said Libby, making the decision for the pair, "but I think in the meantime we need to look at a lot more audio files—see how far back this goes. Figure out why sometimes it's just noise and sometimes it's a message."

Margaret was furiously braiding and unbraiding her hair and staring blankly into the air in front of her as she thought. "They must use the whale song as camouflage so enemy submarines don't detect the communication. We need more data. Recordings from other populations of humpbacks, out of American waters. Just to see how far they've gone with this thing."

"And we need to look at blue-, fin-, and sei-whale calls," said Libby. "If they're using subsonic, then it only makes sense that they'll imitate the big whales. I'll call Chris Wolf at Oregon State tomorrow. He monitors the navy's old sonar matrix that they set up to catch Russian submarines. He'll have recordings of everything we need."

"No," said Clay. "No one outside this room."

"Come on, Clay. You're being paranoid."

"Say that again, Libby. He monitors *whose* old sonar matrix? The military still keeps a hand in on that SOSUS array."

"So you think it is military?"

Clay shook his head. "I don't know. I'm damned if I can think of a reason the navy would paint 'Bite me' on the tail of a whale. I just know that people who find out about this stuff disappear, and someone sent a message saying that Nate was safe after we all thought he was dead."

"So what are you going to do?"

"Find him," Clay said.

"Well, that's going to totally screw up the funeral," said Clair.

PART THREE

The Source

*We are built as gene machines and
cultured as meme machines, but we have
the power to turn against our creators.
We, alone on earth, can rebel against
the tyranny of selfish replicators.*

—RICHARD DAWKINS

The Selfish Gene

*Ninety-five percent of all the species
that have ever existed are now extinct,
so don't look so goddamn smug.*

—GERARD RYDER

The Found World

The whale ship opened its mouth, and Nate and the crew spilled out onto the shore like sentient drool, which was some coincidence, since that's exactly what lay beneath the hard shell of the landing. They were met by a group of whaley boys, one of whom handed Nate a pair of Nikes, then went off to trade clicks and squeals and greeting rubs with the returning crew. It was so bright after nearly ten days in the whale ship that Nate couldn't immediately tell what was happening. The rest of the human crew were wearing sunglasses as they sat down on the ground to put on their shoes, only a few feet from the ship's mouth. From the rigid feel of the ground, Nate thought they might be on a dock of some kind, but then Cal Burdick took off his own sunglasses and handed them to Nate.

"Go ahead. I've been looking at all of this for a lot of years, but I think you'll find it interesting."

With the dark glasses, Nate was able to see. His eyes were fine, but his mind was having a hard time processing what they were telling him. It was as light as daylight (on an overcast day, at least), but they were not outdoors. They were inside a grotto so immense that Nate could not even make out the edges of it. A dozen stadiums could have fit inside the space and still left room for a state fair, a casino, and the Vatican if you snipped off a basilica or two. The entire ceiling was a source of light, cold light, it appeared—some sections yellow, some blue—great blotches of light in irregular shapes, as if Jackson Pollock had painted a solar storm across the ceiling. Half of the grotto was water, flat and reflective as a mirror, the smoothness broken by small whaley boys porpoising here and there in groups of five and six, their blowholes sending up synchronized blasts of steam every few yards. Whaley kids, he thought. Fifty or so whale ships of different species pulled up to the shore, their crews coming and going. Huge segmented pipes that looked like giant earthworms were attached to each of the ships, one on each side of the head, and ran off to connections on shore. The ground—the ground was red, and as hard as linoleum, polished, yet not quite shiny. It ran out for hundreds of yards, perhaps over a mile, and appeared to continue halfway up the walls of the immense grotto. Nate could see openings in the walls, oval passages or doorways or tunnels or something. From the size of the people and whaley boys passing in and out, he could tell that some of the openings were perhaps thirty feet around, while others seemed only the size of normal doors. There were windows next to some of the smaller ones—or what he guessed were windows—their shapes all curves and slopes. There wasn't a right angle in the grotto. Hundreds of people moved about amid as many whaley boys, maintaining the ships, moving supplies and equipment on what seemed very normal hand trucks and carts.

"Where in the hell are we?" Nate said, nearly wrenching his neck trying to look at all of it at once. "I mean, what in the hell is this?"

"Pretty amazing," Cal said. "I like to watch people when they see Gooville for the first time."

Nate ran his hand over the ground, or floor, or whatever this surface was they were sitting on. "What is this stuff?" It appeared smooth, but it had texture, pores, a hidden roughness, like stoneware or—

"It's living carapace. Like a lobster shell. This whole place is living, Nate. Everything—the ceiling, the floor, the walls, the passageway in from the sea, our homes—it's all one huge organism. We call it the Goo."

"The Goo. Then this is Gooville?"

"Yes," Cal said, with a big smile that revealed perfect teeth.

"And that would make you?"

"That's right. The Goos. There's a wonderful Seussian logic to it, don't you think?"

"I *can't* think, Cal. You know how all your life you hear people talk about things that are mind-boggling? It's just a meaningless cliché—a hyperbole—like saying that you're wasted or that something is blood-curdling?'

"Yep."

"Well, I'm boggled. I'm totally boggled."

"You thought the ships were impressive, huh?"

"Yeah, but this? One living organism shaped itself into this complex . . . what? System? I'm boggled."

"Imagine how the bacteria who live in your intestinal tract feel about you."

"Well, right now I think they're pissed off at me."

A group of whaley boys was gathering about ten yards away from them, pointing at Nate and snickering.

"They're coming down to check out the newcomer. Don't be surprised if you get rubbed up against in the streets. They're just saying hi."

"Streets?"

"We call them streets. They're sort of streets."

Now, out of the dim yellow light of the whale ships, Nate realized that there was a wide variety in the whaley boys' coloring. Some were actually mottled blue, like the skin of a blue whale, while others were black like a pilot whale, or light gray like a minke whale. Some even had the black-on-white coloring of killers and Pacific white-sided dolphins, while a few here and there were stark white like a beluga. The body shapes of all were very similar, differing only in size, with the killer whaley boys, who were taller by a foot and heavier by perhaps a hundred pounds, having jaws twice the width of the others'. He also noticed in the brighter light that he was the only human who had a tan. The people, even Cal and the crew, looked healthy; it just appeared that none of them had ever seen the sun. Like the British.

Nuñez came over and helped Cal, and then Nate, to his feet.

"How're the shoes?" she asked Nate.

"They're strange after not wearing any for so long."

"You'll be wobbly for a few hours, too. You'll feel the motion when you stand still for a day or so. No different from having been at sea in a normal ship. I'll take you to your new quarters, show you around a little, get you settled in. The Colonel will probably send for you before too long. People will help you out, humans and whaley boys. They'll all know you're new."

"How many, Cielle?"

"Humans? Almost five thousand live here. Whaley boys, maybe half that many."

"Where is here? Where are we?"

"I told him about Gooville," said Cal.

Nuñez looked up at Nate and then pulled her sunglasses down on her nose so he could see her eyes. "Don't freak out on me, huh?"

Nate shook his head. What did she think, that whatever she was going to tell him was going to be weirder, grander, or scarier than what he'd seen already?

"The roof above this ceiling—which is thick rock, although we're not exactly sure how thick—anyway, it's around six hundred feet below the surface of the Pacific Ocean. We're about two hundred miles off the coast of Chile, under the continental shelf. In fact, we came in through a cliff in the continental rise, a cliff face.

"We're six hundred feet underwater right now. The pressure?"

"We came in through a very long tunnel, a series of pressure locks that pass the ships along until we're at surface pressure. I would have shown you as we came through, but I didn't want to wake you."

"Yeah, thanks for that."

"Let's get you to your new house. We've got a long walk ahead of us." She headed away from the water, motioning for him to follow.

Nate nearly stumbled trying to look back at the whale ships lining the harbor. Tim caught him by the arm. "It's a lot to take in. People really have freaked out. You just have to accept that the Goo won't let anything bad happen to you. The rest is simply a series of surprises. Like life."

Nate looked into the younger man's dark eyes to see if there was any irony showing there, but he was as open and sincere as a bowl of milk. "The Goo will take care of me?"

"That's right," said Tim, helping him along toward the grotto wall, toward the actual village of Gooville, with its organically shaped doorways and windows, its knobs and nodules, its lobster-shell pathways, its whaley-boy pods working together or playing in the water, where was housed an entire village of what Nate assumed were all happy human wack jobs.

❧

AFTER TWO DAYS OF LOOKING FOR MEANING IN HASH MARKS ON WAVEforms and ones and ohs on legal pads that were hastily typed into the machine, Kona found a surfer/hacker on the North Shore named Lolo who agreed to write it all into a Linux routine in exchange for Kona's old long board and a half ounce of the dankest nugs.*

"Won't he just take cash?" asked Clay.

"He's an artist," explained Kona. "Everyone has cash."

"I don't know what I'm going to put that under for the accountant."

"Nugs, dank?"

Clay looked forlornly at the legal-pad pages piling up on the desk next to where Margaret Painborne was typing. He handed a roll of bills over to Kona. "Go. Buy nugs. Bring him back. Bring back my change."

"I'm throwing in my board for the cause," said Kona. "I could use some time in the mystic myself."

"Do you want me to tell Auntie Clair that you tried to extort me?" Clay had taken to using Clair as a sort of sword of Damocles/assistant principal/evil dominatrix threat over Kona, and it seemed to work swimmingly.

"Must blaze, brah. Cool runnings."

Suddenly something sparked in Clay's head, a déjà vu trigger snapping electric with connections. "Wait, Kona."

The surfer paused in the doorway, turned.

---

*Marijuana buds of the finest quality.

"The first day you came here, the day that Nate sent you to the lab to get the film—did you actually do it?"

Kona shook his head, "Nah, boss, the Snowy Biscuit see me going. She say keep the money and she go to the lab. When I come back with my ganja, she give me the pictures to give to Nate."

"I was sort of afraid of that," Clay said. "Go, blaze, be gone. Get what we need."

SO THREE DAYS LATER THEY ALL STOOD WATCHING AS LOLO HIT THE return key and the subsonic waveform from a blue-whale call began scrolling across the bottom of the screen, while above it letters were transcribed from the data. Lolo was a year older than Kona, a Japanese-American burned nut brown by the sun with ducky-yellow minidreads and a tapestry of Maori tattoos across his back and shoulders.

Lolo spun in the chair to face them. "I mixed down a fifty-minute trance track with sixty percussion loops that was way harder than this." Lolo's prior forays into sound processing had been as a computer DJ at a dance club in Honolulu.

"It's not saying anything," said Libby Quinn. "It's just random, Clay."

"Well, that's the way it's gone so far, right?"

"But there's been nothing since that first day."

"We knew that might happen, that there couldn't be messages on all of them. We just have to find the right ones."

Libby's eyes were pleading. "Clay, it's a short season. We have to get out in the field. Now that you have this program, you don't need the manpower. Margaret and I will bring back more tapes—we have them coming in from people we trust—but we can't afford to blow off the season."

"And we need to go public with the torpedo range," Margaret added, less sympathetic than Libby had been.

Clay nodded and looked at his bare feet against the hardwood floor. He took a deep breath, and when he looked up, he smiled. "You're right. But don't just blow a whistle and hope someone will notice. Cliff Hyland told me that the diving data was the only thing they were worried about.

You're going to need proof that humpbacks dive close to the bottom of the channel, or the navy will claim that you're just being whale huggers and there's no danger to the animals. Even with the range."

"You're okay if we go public, then?" asked Libby.

"People are going to know about the torpedo range soon enough. I don't think that's dangerous for you. Just don't say anything about the rest of this, okay?"

The two women looked at each other, then nodded. "We have to go," Libby said. "We'll call you, Clay. We're not running out on you."

"I know," Clay said.

After they left, Clay turned to the two surfers. Thirty years working with the best scientists and divers in the world, and this was what it came down to: two stoner kids. "If you guys need to go do things, I understand."

"Outta here," said Lolo, on his feet and bounding toward the door.

Clay looked at the screen where Lolo had been sitting. Scrolling across it: WILL ARRIVE GV APPRX 1300 MONDAY__HAVE__SIZE 11 SNEAKERS WAITING FOR QUINN__END MSS__AAAA__BAXYXABUDAB

"Get him back," Clay said to Kona. "We need to know which tape this was."

"Libby gave them all to him."

"I know that. I need to know where she got it. Where and when it was recorded. Call Libby's cell phone. See if you can get hold of her." Clay was trying to make the screen print before the message scrolled away. "How the hell does this thing work?"

"How you know I'm not leaving?"

"You woke up this morning, Kona. Did you have a reason to get out of bed other than waves or pot?"

"Yah, mon, need to find Nate."

"How'd that feel?"

"I'm calling Libby, boss."

"Loyalty is important, son. I'll go catch Lolo. Confirm which tape it was."

"Shut up, boss. I'm trying to dial."

Behind them the cryptic message scrolled out of the printer.

CHAPTER TWENTY-EIGHT

Single-Celled Animal

Stockholm syndrome or not, Nate was starting to get tired of the whole hippie-commune, everything-is-wonderful-and-the-Goo-will-provide attitude. Nuñez had come by for three days running to take him out on the town, and every person he met was just a little too damn satisfied with the whole idea that they were living inside a giant organism six hundred feet under the ocean. Like this was a normal thing. Like he just wasn't getting with the program because he continued to ask questions. At least the whaley boys would blow wet raspberries at him and snicker as he walked by. At least they had some sense of the absurdity of all this, despite the fact that they shouldn't even have existed in the first place, which did seem to be a large point of denial on their part.

They'd installed him in what he guessed was a premier apartment, or what you'd call an apartment, on the second floor, looking out over the grotto. The windows were oval, and the glass in them, although perfectly clear, was flexible. It was like looking out on the world through a condom, and that was just the beginning of the things that creeped him out about this place. He had a kitchen sink, a bathroom sink, and a shower—all of which had big honking sphincters in the bottom of them—and the seal on the door around his refrigerator, if that's what you called it, appeared to be made out of slugs, or at least something that left an iridescent slime on you if you brushed up against it. There was also a toothed garbage disposal in the kitchen, which he wouldn't even go near. The worst of it was that the apartment didn't make any attempt to conceal that it was alive. His first day there, when the human crew from the whale ship had come by for a drink—a housewarming—there had been a scaly knob on the wall by the front door that when pushed would cause the door to open. After the crew left and Nate returned from his shower, the doorknob had healed over. There was a scar there in the shell, but that was all. Nate was locked in.

There was a tom-tom thrumming of stones hitting his front picture window. Nate went to the window, looked out on the vast grotto and harbor, then down on the source of his torment. A pod of whaley-boy kids was winging stones at his window. Thump, thump-a, thump. The stones bounced off, leaving no mark. When Nate appeared at the window, the thumping became more furious, as the whaley kids picked up the pace and aimed right at him, as if a well-placed shot might drop him in a dunking tank.

"There's a reason cetaceans don't have hands in the real world!" Nate screamed at them. "You are that reason! You little freaks!"

Thump, thump-a, thump, thump, clack. Occasionally a missed throw hit the shell-like frame of the window, sounding like a marble hitting tile.

I sound like Old Man Spangler yelling at my brother and me for raiding his apple trees, Nate thought. *When did I turn into that guy? I don't want to be that guy.*

There was a soft knock on the shell of his front door. As he turned, the door flipped open like shutters, two pieces of shell retracting on muscles hidden in the wall. Nate felt like a surprised box turtle. Cielle Nuñez stood in the doorway with canvas shopping bags folded under her arm. She was a pleasant woman, attractive, competent, and non-threatening; Nate was sure that's why she'd been chosen to be his guide.

"You ready to do some shopping, Nate? I called to tell you I was coming, but you didn't answer."

The apartment had a speaking apparatus, a sort of ornate tube thing that whistled and buzzed green metallic beetle wings when there was a call. Nate was afraid of it.

"Cielle, can we drop any pretense that we are just buddies out for the day? You lock me in here when you leave."

"For your own safety."

"Somehow that always seems to be the argument the jailer uses."

"You want to go get some food and clothes or not?"

Nate shrugged and followed her out the door. They walked along the perimeter of the grotto, which seemed a cross between an old English village and an Art Nouveau hobbit housing project: irregularly shaped doors and windows looking into shops that displayed baked goods and other prepared foods. Evidently the Goo wasn't big on having fire around for home cooking. All the cooked foods were prepared somewhere else in the complex. There was a warming cabinet in Nate's apartment that looked like a breadbox made out of a giant armadillo shell. It worked great. You rolled the top open, put the food in, then promptly lost your appetite.

"Let's get you something to wear today," Cielle said. "Those khakis are on loan. Only the whale-ship crews are supposed to wear them."

As they walked, a half dozen whaley kids followed them, chirping and giggling all the way.

"So I'd get in trouble if I started kicking whaley kids down the street?"

"Of course," Cielle laughed. "We have laws here, just like anywhere else."

"Evidently not ones that forbid kidnapping and unjustified imprisonment."

Nuñez stopped and grabbed his arm. "Look, what are you complaining about? This is a good place to be. You're not being mistreated. Everyone's been kind to you. What's the problem?"

"What's the problem? The problem is that all you people were yanked out of your lives, taken away from your families and friends, taken from everything that you knew, and you all act like it doesn't bother you in the least. Well, it bothers me, Cielle. It fucking bothers me a lot. And I don't understand this whole colony, or city, or whatever this thing is. How does it even exist without anyone knowing about it? In all these years, why has no one gotten out and spoiled the secret of this place?"

"I told you, we were all going to drown—"

"Bullshit. I don't buy that for a second. That gratitude toward your rescuer only lasts for a short while. I've seen it. It doesn't take over your life. Everyone I've met is blissed out. You people worship the Goo, don't you?"

"Nate, you don't want to be locked in, you won't be locked in. You can have the run of Gooville—go anywhere you want. There's hundreds of miles of passages. Some of them even I haven't seen. Go. Leave the grotto and go down any one of those passages. But you know what? You'll be back looking for your apartment tonight. You are not a prisoner, you're just living in a different place and a different way."

"You didn't answer my question."

"The Goo is the source, Nate. You'll see. The Colonel—"

"Fuck the Colonel. The Colonel is a fucking myth."

"Should we get some coffee? You seem grumpy."

"Damn it, Cielle, my caffeine headache is not relevant." Actually it was, sort of. He hadn't had any coffee today. "Besides, how do I know it's coffee we're drinking? It's probably some mutant sea otter/coffee bean hybrid beverage."

"Is that what you want?"

"No, that's not what I want. What I want is a doorknob. And not an organic nodule thing—I want a dead doorknob. One that always *has* been dead, too. Not something that you used to be friends with."

Cielle Nuñez had backed away from him several feet, and the whaley kids who'd been following them had quieted down and gone into a defensive pod formation, the big kids on the outside. People who were out walking, and who normally made a point of nodding and smiling as they passed, took a wide detour around Nate. There was an inordinate amount of whistling among the milling whaley boys.

"That going to do it for you?" Nuñez asked. "A doorknob. I get you a doorknob, you're a happy man?"

Why should he be embarrassed? Because he'd scared the kids? Because he'd made his captors uncomfortable? Nevertheless, he was embarrassed.

"I could use some earplugs, too, if you have them. For sleeping."

For ten hours out of twenty-four, the grotto went dark. Cielle explained that this was for the comfort of the humans, to help them keep some semblance of their normal circadian rhythms. People needed day and night—without the change many people couldn't sleep. The problem was, the whaley boys didn't sleep. They rested, but they didn't sleep. So when the grotto went dark, they went on about their business. In the dark, however, they were all constantly emitting sonar clicks. At night the grotto sounded like it was being marched upon by an army of tap dancers. Consequently, so did Nate's apartment.

Nuñez nodded. "We can probably do that. You want to go get a steaming hot cup of sea otter now?"

"What?"

"I'm just kidding. Lighten up, Nate."

"I want to go home." He'd said it before he even realized it.

"That's not going to happen. But I'll send word. I think it's time you met with the Colonel."

They spent the day going to shops. Nate found some cotton slacks that fitted him, some socks and underwear, and a pile of T-shirts from one tiny shop. There was no currency exchanged. Nuñez would just nod to the shopkeeper, and Nate would take what he needed. There was little variety in any of the shops, and most of what they carried was goods from the real world: clothes, fabric, books, razor blades, shoes, and small electronics. But a few shops carried items that appeared to have been grown or made right there in Gooville: toothbrushes, soaps, lotions. All the packaging seemed to come out of the seventeenth century—the shopkeepers wrapped parcels in a ubiquitous oilcloth that Nate thought smelled vaguely of seaweed and indeed had the same olive color as giant kelp. Patrons brought their own jars to carry oils, pickles, and other soft goods. Nate had seen everything from a modern mayonnaise jar to hand-thrown crockery that had to have been made a hundred years ago.

"How long, Cielle?" he asked as he watched a shopkeeper count sugared dates into a hand-blown glass jar and seal it with wax. "How long have people been down here?"

She followed his gaze to the jar. "We get a lot of the surface goods from shipwrecks, so don't be impressed if you see antiques; the sea is a good preserver. We may have salvaged it only a week ago. A friend of mine keeps potatoes in a Grecian wine amphora that's two thousand years old."

"Yeah, and I'm using the Holy Grail to catch my spare change. How long?"

"You are so hostile today. I don't know how long, Nate. A long time."

He had dozens, hundreds more questions, like where the hell did they get potatoes when they didn't have sunlight to grow anything? They weren't bringing potatoes up from a shipwreck. But Cielle was letting him get only so far before claiming ignorance.

They had lunch at a four-stool lunch counter where the proprietor was a striking Irishwoman with stunning green eyes and a massive spill of red hair and who, like everyone, it seemed, knew Cielle and knew who Nate was.

"Got you a Walkman then, Dr. Quinn? Whaley boys will drive you to drink with that sonar at night."

"We're going to get him some earplugs today, Brennan," Cielle said.

"Music, that's the way to wash the whaley-boy whistles," the woman said. Then she was off to her kitchen. The walls of the café were decorated with a collection of antique beer trays, glued in place, as Nate had learned, with an adhesive that was similar to what barnacles secreted to fasten themselves to ships. Nailing things up was frowned upon, as the walls would bleed for a while if injured.

Nate took a bite of his sandwich, meatballs and mozzarella on good crusty French bread.

"How?" he asked Cielle, blowing crumbs on the counter. "How does any of this stuff get made if there's no flame?"

Cielle shrugged. "No idea. A bakery, I'd guess. They make all the prepared food outside the grotto. I've never been there."

"You don't know how? How can that be?"

Cielle Nuñez put down her own sandwich and leaned on one elbow, smiling at Nate. She had remarkably kind eyes, and Nate had to remind himself that she had been ordered to be his friend. Interesting, he thought, that they'd choose a woman. Was she bait?

"You ever read *A Connecticut Yankee in King Arthur's Court,* Nate?"

"Of course, everybody does."

"And that guy goes back to Camelot from the late nineteenth century and dazzles everyone with his scientific knowledge, mainly because he can make gunpowder, right?"

"Yes, so?"

"You're a scientist, so you might do better than most, but take your average citizen, a guy who works at a discount store, say. Drop him in the twelfth century, you know what he'll achieve?"

"Make your point?"

"Death by bacterial infection, more than likely. And the last words on his lips will probably be, 'There's such a thing as an antibiotic, really.' My point is, I don't know how this stuff is made because I haven't needed to know. Nobody knows how to make the things they use. I suppose I could find out and get back to you, but I promise you I'm not holding out on you just to be mysterious. We do a lot of salvage on the whale ships, and we have a trade network into the real world that gets us a lot of our goods. When a freighter leaves pallets of goods for the people on remote islands in the Pacific, all they know is that they've been paid and they've delivered to shore. They don't stay to see who takes the goods away. The old-timers say that it used to be that the Goo provided everything. Nothing came in from the outside that wasn't on their backs when they got here."

Nate took a bite of his sandwich and nodded as if considering what she'd just said. Since he'd arrived in Gooville, he had spent every waking moment thinking about two things: one, how this whole place could possibly function; and two, how to get out of it. The Goo had to get energy from somewhere. The energy to light the huge grotto alone would require tens of millions of calories. If it got energy from outside, maybe you could use that same pathway to get out.

"So do you guys feed it? The Goo?"

"No."

"Well, then—"

"Don't know, Nate. I just don't know. How does dry-cleaning work?"

"Well, I assume that they use solvents, that, uh— Look, biologists don't have a lot of stuff that needs to be dry-cleaned. I'm sure it's not that complicated a process."

"Yeah, well, right back at you on all of your questions about the Goo."

Cielle stood and gathered up her parcels. "Let's go, Nate. I'm taking you back to your apartment. Then I'm going right to the whaley-boy den and find out if they can get the Colonel to see you. Today."

Nate still had a couple bites of his sandwich left. "Hey, I've still got a couple of bites of my sandwich left," he said.

"Really? Well, did you ask yourself where in Gooville we got meat-balls? What sort of meat might be in them?"

Nate dropped his sandwich.

"Bit of the whining wussy boy, aren't we?" said Brennan as she came out of the kitchen to take away their plates.

❧

NATE WAS READING A CHEESY LAWYER NOVEL THAT HE'D FOUND IN THE small library in his apartment when the whaley boys came for him. There were three of them, two large males with killer-whale coloring and a smaller female blue. Only when the blue squeaked "Hi Nate" in a mashed-elf voice did he recognize it as Emily 7.

"Wow, hi, Emily. Is just Emily okay, or should I always say the Seven?" Nate always felt awkward with someone afterward, even if there wasn't anything for the ward to be after.

She crossed her arms over her chest and bugged out her left eye at him.

"Okay," Nate said, moving on, "I guess we'll be going, then. Did you see my new doorknob? Brand-new. Stainless steel. I realize it doesn't go with everything else, but, you know, it feels a little like freedom." *Right, Nate. It's a doorknob,* he thought.

They led him around the perimeter of the grotto, beyond the village, and into one of the huge passageways that led away from the grotto.

They walked for half an hour, tracing a labyrinth of passageways that got narrower and narrower the farther off they went, the bright red lobster-shell surface fading into something that looked like mother-of-pearl the deeper in they went. It glowed faintly, just enough so they could see where they were going.

Finally the passageway started to broaden again and open into a large room that looked like some sort of oval amphitheater, all of it pearlescent and providing its own light. Benches lined the walls around the room, all in view of a wide ramp that led to a round portal the size of a garage door, closed now with an iris of black shell.

"Ooooh, the great and powerful Oz will see you now," Nate said.

The whaley boys, who normally found practically anything funny, just looked away. One of the black-and-whites started whistling a soft tune from his blowhole. "In the Hall of the Mountain King" or a Streisand tune—*something* creepy, Nate thought.

Emily 7 backhanded the whistler in the chest, and he stopped abruptly. Then she put her hand on Nate's shoulder and gestured for him to go up the steps to the round portal.

"Okay, I guess this is it." Nate started backing up the ramp as the whaley boys started backing away from him. "You guys better not leave me, because I'll never find my way back."

Emily 7 grinned, that lovely hack-a-salmon-in-half smile of hers, and waved him on.

"Thanks, Em. You look good, you know. Did I mention? Shiny." He hoped shiny was good.

The iris opened behind him, and the whaley boys fell to their knees and touched their lower jaws to the floor. Nate turned to see that the pearlescent ramp led into a vibrant red chamber that was pulsing with light and glistening with moisture as the walls appeared to breathe. Now, *this* looked like a living thing—the inside of a living thing. Really much more what he'd expected to see when the whale had eaten him. He made his way forward. A few steps in, the ramp melded into the red-dish flesh, which Nate could now see was shot through with blood vessels and what might be nerves. He couldn't get the size of the space he was in. It just seemed to expand to receive him and contract behind him, as if a bubble were moving along with him inside it. When the iris disappeared into the pink Goo, Nate felt a wave of panic go through him. He took a deep breath—damp, fecund air—and strangely enough he remembered what Poynter and Poe had told him back on the humpback ship: It's easier if you just accept that you're already dead. He took another deep breath and ventured forward a few more feet, then stopped.

"I feel like a friggin' sperm in here!" he yelled. What the hell, he was dead anyway. "I'm supposed to have a meeting with the Colonel."

On cue, the Goo began to open in front of him, like the view of a flower opening from the inside. A brighter light illuminated the newly opened chamber, now just large enough to house Nate, another person, and about ten feet of conversational distance. Reclining in a great pink mass of goo, dressed in tropical safari wear and a San Francisco Giants baseball hat, was the Colonel.

"Nathan Quinn, good to see you. It's been a long time," he said.

• CHAPTER TWENTY-NINE •

Talking Up the Dead

Nate hadn't seen his old teacher, Gerard "Growl" Ryder, in fourteen years, but except for the fact that he was very pale, the biologist looked exactly the same as Nate remembered him: short and powerful, a jaw like a knife, and a long swoop of gray hair that was always threatening to fall into his pale green eyes.

"*You're* the Colonel?" Nate asked. Ryder had disappeared twelve years ago. Lost at sea in the Aleutians.

"I toyed with the title for a while. For a week or so I was Man-Meat the Magnificent, but I thought that sounded like I might be compensating for something, so I decided to go with something military-sounding. It was a toss-up between Captain Nemo from *Twenty Thousand Leagues* and Colonel Kurtz from *Heart of Darkness*. I finally decided to go with just 'the Colonel.' It's more ominous."

"That it is." Once again reality was taking a contextual tilt for Nate, and he was trying to keep from falling. This once brilliant, brilliant man was sitting in a mass of goo talking about choosing his megalomaniacal pseudonym.

"Sorry to keep you waiting for so long before I brought you down here. But now that you're here, how's it feel to stand in the presence of God?"

"Respectfully, sir, you're a fucking squirrel."

～◇～

"THIS DOESN'T FEEL RIGHT," CLAY WHISPERED TO LIBBY QUINN. "WE shouldn't be having a funeral when Nate's still alive."

"It's not a funeral," said Libby. "It's a service."

They were all there at the Whale Sanctuary. In the front row: Clay, Libby, Margaret, Kona, Clair, and the Old Broad. Moving back: Cliff Hyland and Tarwater with their team, the Count and his research grommets, Jon Thomas Fuller and all of the Hawaii Whale Inc. boat crews, which constituted about thirty people. On back: whale cops, bartenders, and a couple of waitresses from Longi's. From the harbor: liveaboards and charter captains, the harbormaster, booth girls and dive guides, boat hands and a guy who worked the coffee counter at the fuel dock. Also, researchers from the University of Hawaii and, strangely enough, two black-coral divers—all crowded into the lecture hall, the ceiling fans stirring their smells together into the evening breeze. Clay had scheduled the service in the evening so the researchers wouldn't miss a day of the research season.

"Still," said Clay.

"He was a lion," said Kona, a tear glistening in his eye. "A great lion." This was the highest compliment a Rastafarian can bestow upon a man.

"He's not dead," said Clay. "You know that, you doof."

"Still," said Kona

It was a Hawaiian funeral in that everyone was in flip-flops and shorts, but the men had put on their best aloha shirts, the women their crispest flowered dresses, and many had brought leis and head garlands, which they draped over the wreaths at the front of the room that represented Nathan Quinn and Amy Earhart. A Unity Church minister spoke for ten minutes about God and the sea and science and dedication, and then he opened up the floor to anyone who had something to say. There was a very long pause before the Old Broad, wearing a smiling-whale-print muumuu and a dozen white orchids in her hair, tottered to the podium.

"Nathan Quinn lives on," she said.

"Can I get an amen!" shouted Kona. Clair yanked his remaining dreadlocks.

All the biologists and grad students looked at each other, eyes wide, confused, wondering if any of them had actually brought an amen that they could give up. No one had told them they were going to need an amen, or they would have packed one. All the harbor people and Lahaina citizens were intimidated by the science people, and they were not about to give up an amen in front of all of these eggheads, no way. The whale cops didn't like the fact that Kona was not in jail, and they weren't giving him shit, let alone an amen. Finally one of the black-coral divers who had that night found the perfect cocktail for grieving in a hit of ecstasy, a joint, and a forty of malt liquor, sighed a feeble "Amen" over the mourners like a sleepy, stinky, morning-breath kiss.

"And I know," continued the Old Broad, "that if it were not for his stubbornness in procuring a pastrami on rye for that singer in the channel, he would be here with us today."

"But if he were here with us—" whispered Clair.

"Shhhhhh," shushed Margaret Painborne.

"Don't you shush me, or you'll be munching carpet through a straw."

"Please, honey," said Clay.

The Old Broad rambled on about talking to the whales every day for the last twenty-five years, about how she'd known Nate and Clay and Cliff when they first came to the island and how young and stupid they were then, and how that had changed, as now they weren't that young anymore. She talked about what a thoughtful and considerate man Nate was, but how, if he hadn't been so absentminded, he might have found a decent woman to love him, and how she didn't know where he was, but if he didn't get his bottom back to Maui soon, she would twist his ear off when she saw him. And then she sat down to resounding silence and tittering pity, and everyone looked at Clay, who looked at a ceiling fan.

After a long, awkward minute, when the Unity minister had to head-

fake to the podium a couple of times, as if he would have to call a conclusion to the service, Gilbert Box—the Count—got up. He wasn't
wearing his hat for once, but he still wore his giant wraparound sunglasses, and without the balance of the giant hat, the glasses atop his an-
gular frame made him appear insectlike, a particularly pale praying
mantis in khakis. He adjusted the microphone, cleared his throat with
great pomp, and said, "I never liked Nathan Quinn. . . ." And everyone
waited for the "but," but it never came. Gilbert Box nodded to the
crowd and sat back down. Gilbert's grommets applauded.

Cliff Hyland spoke next, talking for ten minutes about what a great
guy and fine researcher Nate was. Then Libby actually went forward
and spoke at length about Nate's Canadianness and how he had once
defended the Great Seal of British Columbia as being superior to all
the other provincial seals in that it depicted a moose and a ram smoking
a hookah, showing a spirit of cooperation and tolerance, while On-
tario's seal depicted a moose and an elk trying to eat a bear, and
Saskatchewan's showed a moose and a lion setting fire to a fondue pot—
both of which clearly exploited the innate Canadian fear of moose—and
the seal of Quebec depicted a woman in a toga flashing one of her boobs
at a lion, which was just fucking French. He'd named all the provinces
and their seals, but those were the ones Libby could remember. Then
Libby sniffled and sat down.

"That's what you could come up with?" hissed Clay. "What, five
years of marriage?"

Libby whispered in his ear, "I had to go with something that
wouldn't threaten Margaret. I don't see *you* storming the podium."

"I'm not going to talk about my dead friend when I don't think he's
dead."

And before they knew it, Jon Thomas Fuller was at the podium being
thankful for Nate's support for his new project, then going on about how
much he appreciated how the whale-research community had gotten behind his new "dolphin interaction center," all of which was big news to
the whale-research community who was listening. During the short
speech, Clair had caught Clay's neck in what appeared to be an embrace
of consolation but was in fact a choke hold she'd learned from watching

cops on the news. "Baby, if you try to go after him, I'll have you unconscious on the floor in three seconds. That would be disrespectful to Nate's memory." But her effort left Kona unattended on the other side, and he managed to cough "Bullshit" as Jon Thomas took his seat.

Next a grad student who worked for Cliff Hyland stood and talked about how Nate's work had inspired her to go into the field. Then someone from the Hawaiian Department of Conservation and Resources talked about how Nate had always been at the forefront of conservation and protection of the humpbacks. Then the harbormaster talked about Nate's being a competent and conscientious boat pilot. All told, an hour had passed, and when it seemed obvious that no one else was going to stand up, the minister moved toward the podium but was beaten to it by Kona, who had slipped from Clair's steely grip and high-stepped his way to the front.

"Like old Auntie say, Nathan is living on. But no one here today say a thing about the Snowy Biscuit, who—Jah's mercy be on her—is feeding fishes in the briny blue about now." (Sniff.) "I know her only short time, but I think I can say for all of us, that I always want to see her naked. Truth, mon. And when I think upon the round, firm—"

"—she will be missed," Clay said, finishing for the faux Hawaiian. He had clamped a hand over Kona's mouth and was dragging him out the door. "She was a bright kid." With that, the minister jumped to the podium, thanked everyone for coming, and declared, with a prayer, all respects paid in full. Amen.

~◦~

"WELL, YES, MENTAL HEALTH CAN BE A PROBLEM," SAID GROWL RYDER. "Being God's conscience is a tough job."

Nate looked around, and, as if following his gaze, the Goo receded around them until they were in a chamber about fifteen feet in diameter—a bubble. *It was like camping in someone's bladder*, Nate thought.

"That better?" Ryder asked.

Nate realized that the Colonel was the one controlling the shape of the chamber they were in.

"Someplace to sit would be good."

The Goo behind Nate shaped itself into a chaise longue. Nate touched it tentatively, expecting to pull his hand back trailing strings of slime, but although the Goo glistened as if it were wet, on the chair it felt dry. Warm and icky, but dry. He sat down on the chaise.

"Everyone thinks you're dead," Nate said.

"You, too."

Nate hadn't thought about it much, but, of course, the Colonel had to be right. They would have thought him long dead.

"You've been here since you disappeared, what, twelve years ago?"

"Yes, they took me with a modified right whale, ate my whole Zodiac, my equipment—everything. They brought me here in a blue whale. I went mad during the trip. Couldn't handle the whole idea of it. They kept me restrained most of the way here. I'm sure that didn't help." Ryder shrugged. "I got better, once I accepted the way things are down here. I understood why they took me."

"And that would be . . . ?"

"The same reason they took you. I was about to figure out their existence from what was hidden in the signal of different whale calls. They took both of us to protect the whale ships and, ultimately, the Goo. We should be grateful they didn't just kill us."

Nate had wondered about that before. Why the trouble? "Okay, why didn't they?"

"Well, they took me alive because the Goo and the people here wanted to know what I knew, and by what path I came to suspect the content in the whale calls. They took you alive because I ordered it so."

"Why?"

"What do you mean, 'why'? Because we were colleagues, because I taught you, because you're bright and intuitive and I liked you and I'm a decent guy. 'Why?' Fuck you, 'why?' "

"Growl, you live in a slime lair and maintain an identity as the mysterious overlord of an undersea city, you command a fleet of meat dreadnaughts with crews of humanoid whale people, and you're currently reclining in a pulsating mass of gelatinous goo that looks like it escaped from hell's own Jell-O mold—so excuse the fuck out of me if I question your motives."

"Okay, good point. Can I get you something to drink?"

Like many scientists Nate had known, Ryder had plodded on only to realize midcourse that he'd forgotten certain social niceties practiced by other civilized humans, but in this case he was completely missing the point. "No, I don't need anything to drink. I need to know how this happened. What is this stuff? You're a biologist, Growl, you have to have been curious about this."

"I'm still curious. But what I do know is that this stuff makes up everything in Gooville, everything you've seen here, the buildings, the corridors, most of the machinery—although I guess you'd call it biomachinery—all of it is the Goo. One giant, all-encompassing organism. It can form itself into nearly any organism on earth, and it can design new organisms as the need arises. The Goo made the whale ships and the whaley boys. And here's the kicker, Nate: It didn't make them over thirty million years. The entire species isn't more than three hundred years old."

"That's not possible," Nate said. There were certain things that you accepted if you were going to be a biologist, and one of them was that complex life was a process of evolution by natural selection, that you got a new species because the genes that favored survival in a certain environment were replicated in that species, selected by being passed on, often a process that took millions of years. You didn't put in your order and pick up a new species at the window. There was no cosmic fry cook, there was no watchmaker, there was no designer. There was only process and time. "How could you possibly know that anyway?"

"I just know things by being in contact with the Goo, but I'm not far off. It might be less time—two hundred years."

"Two hundred years? The whaley boys are definitely sentient by any definition, and I don't even know what the whale ships are, but they're definitely alive, too. That kind of complexity doesn't happen in that short a time."

"No, I'd say the Goo has probably been here as long as three and a half billion years. The rocks around these caves are some of the oldest in the world. I'm just saying the whaley boys and the ships are new. They're only a few hundred years old because that's how long ago the Goo needed them."

"The Goo needed them, so it made them to serve it? Like it has will?"

"It does have will. It's self-aware, and it knows a lot. In fact, I'd venture to say that the Goo is a repository for every bit of biological knowledge on the planet. This, Nate, this Goo is as close to God as we are ever going to see. It's the perfect soup."

"As in primordial soup?"

"Precisely. Four billion years ago some big organic molecules grouped up, probably around some deep-sea source of geothermal heat, and they learned how to divide, how to replicate. Since replication is the name of life's game, it very quickly—probably in the span of less than a hundred million years—covered the entire planet. Big organic molecules that couldn't exist now because there are millions of bacteria that would eat them, but back then there were no bacteria. At one time the entire oceanic surface of the earth was populated by one single living thing that had learned to replicate itself. Sure, as the replicators were exposed to different conditions they mutated, they developed into new species, they fed on each other, some colonized each other and turned into complex animals, and then more complex animals, but part of that original living animal pulled back into its original niche. By this time chemical information was being exchanged—first by RNA, then by DNA—and as each new species evolved, it carried on all the information for making the next species, and that information came back to the original animal. But it had its safe niche, pulling energy from the earth's heat, sheltered in the deep ocean and by rock. It took in all the information from the animals that it came in contact with, but it changed only enough to protect itself, replicate itself. While a million million species lived and died in the sea, this original animal evolved very slowly, learning, always learning. Think of it, Nate: Within the cells of your body is not only the blueprint for every living thing on earth but everything that has ever lived. Ninety-eight percent of your DNA is just hitching a ride, just lucky little genes that were smart enough to align themselves to other successful genes, like marrying into money, if you will. But the Goo, not only does it have all of those genes, it has the diagram to turn them on and off. That seat you're sitting on may well be three billion years old."

Nate suddenly felt something he'd felt before only when waking up in a hotel with the bedspread pulled up around his face: a deep and earnest hope, motivated by disgust, that in all the time it had been there, someone had cleaned the cast-off genetic material from it. He stood up, just for safety. "How could you possibly know this, Growl? It goes against everything we know about evolution."

"No it doesn't. It completely fits. Yes, a complex process like life can develop, given enough time, but we also know that an animal that fits perfectly into its niche isn't pressured to change. Sharks have remained basically the same for a hundred million years, the chambered nautilus for five hundred million. Well, you're just looking at the animal that found its niche first. The first animal, the source."

Nate shook his head at the magnitude of it. "You might be able to explain the evolutionary path being preserved, but you can't explain consciousness, analytical thought, processes that require a very complex mechanism to perform. You can't pull off that sort of complexity of function with big, fluffy organic molecules."

"The molecules have evolved, but they remembered. The Goo is a complex, if amorphous, life form; there are no analogs for it. Everything is a model of it, and nothing is a model of it."

Nate stepped back from the Colonel, and the Goo flexed to make room for him. The movement gave him a brief moment of vertigo, and he lost his balance. The Goo caught him, the surface moving forward against his shoulder blades just enough to steady him on his feet. Nate whipped around quickly and the Goo pulled back.

"God, that's creepy!"

"There you go, Nate. Aware. You'd be amazed at what the Goo knows—at what it can tell us. You can have a life here, Nate. You'll see things here you would never see, you'll do things you could never do. And in the process you can help me unravel the greatest biological riddle in the history of the world."

"I think you're supposed to laugh manically after saying something like that, Colonel."

"If you help me, I'll give you what you've always wanted."

"Despite what you think, what I want is to go home."

"That's not going to happen, Nate. Not ever. You're a bright man, so I won't insult you by pretending the circumstances are any different than they are: You are not ever going to leave these caverns alive, so now you have to make the decision of how you want to spend your life. You can have everything here that you could have on the surface—much more, in fact—but you're not leaving."

"Well, in that case, Colonel, see if you can get your giant booger to duplicate you so you can go fuck yourself."

"I know what the whale song means, Nate. I know what it's for."

Nate felt as if he'd been sucker-punched by his own obsession, but he tried not to show the impact. "Doesn't really matter now, does it?"

"I understand. You take a little time to work into the idea, Nate, but there is some urgency. This isn't just standing back and collecting data—we need to do something. I want your help. We'll talk soon."

The Goo came down and seemed to envelop the Colonel. There was a sound like ripping paper, and a long, pink tunnel opened behind Nate, leading all the way to the iris door through which he'd entered. He took one last look over his shoulder, but there was nothing except Goo, Ryder was gone.

Nate was met in the hall by the two big killer whaley boys, who took one look at his face, then looked at each other, then snickered, with big toothy grins. Emily 7 was nowhere to be seen.

"He's a fucking squirrel," Nate said.

The whaley boys went into wheezing fits of laughter, doubling over as they led Nate down the corridor and back to the grotto. *Say what you want,* Nate thought. *The Goo designed these guys to enjoy themselves.*

～◦◦～

AS SOON AS NATE ENTERED THE APARTMENT, HE KNEW HE WASN'T alone. There was a smell there, and not just the ubiquitous ocean smell that permeated the whole grotto, but a sweeter, artificial smell. He quickly checked the main living rooms and the bathroom. When the portal to the bedroom opened, he could see a shape under the covers in his double bed. The biolighting hadn't come on in the bedroom as usual. Nate sighed. The shape under the covers nuzzled into the corner of the bed exactly the way she had on the whale ship.

"Emily 7, you are a lovely—ah—person, really, but I'm—" He was what? He had no idea what he was going to say. He was just trying to get to know himself better? He needed some space? But then he realized that whatever, whoever was under the sheets was too small to be the enamored whaley boy. Nuñez, he thought. This was going to be worse than Emily 7. Nuñez was really his only human contact in Gooville, even if she was working for the cause. He didn't want to alienate her. He couldn't afford to. He moved into the room, trying to think of a way that this could possibly not make things worse.

"Look, I know that we've spent a lot of time together, and I like you, I really do—"

"Good," said Amy, throwing back the covers. "I like you, too. You coming in?"

CHAPTER THIRTY

Motherfluker

Clay and Kona had spent the day cleaning the muck out of the raised-from-the-deep *Always Confused*. Now Clay stood on the breakwater at the Lahaina Harbor, watching the sun bubble red into the Pacific and throw purple fire over the island. He was feeling that particular mix of melancholy and agitation that usually comes with drinking coffee and Irish whiskey at the wake of someone you never knew, and it usually ends in a fight. He felt as if he should do something, but he didn't know what. He needed to move, but he didn't know where. Libby had confirmed that the last message about Nate had been recorded more than a week after he'd disappeared, and it seemed to be more evidence that Nate had survived his ordeal in the channel, but where was he? How do you rush in to save someone when you don't know where he is? All their analysis of the tapes since then had yielded nothing but whale calls. Clay was lost.

"What you doing?" Kona, barefoot and smelling of bleach, came up behind him.

"I'm waiting for the green flash." He wasn't, really, but sometimes, just as the sun dipped below the horizon, it happened. He needed something to happen.

"Yeah, I seen that. What cause that?"

"Uh, well"—and that was another thing, he didn't have enough of a handle on the natural sciences to keep this whole project going—"I believe as the sun disappears under the horizon, the residual spectrum bounces off the mucusphere, thus causing the green flash."

"Yah, mon. The mucusphere."

"It's science," said Clay, knowing that it wasn't science.

"When the boat clean, then we going out, record whales and like dat?"

Good question, Clay thought. He could collect the data, but he didn't have the knowledge necessary to analyze it. He had hoped that Amy would do that.

"I don't know. If we find Nate, maybe."

"You think he still living, then? Even after all this time?"

"Yeah. I hope. I guess we should keep up the work until we can find him."

"Yeah. Nate say them Japanese going to kill our minkes if you don't work hard."

"Minke whales, yeah. I've been on one of their ships. Norwegians, too."

"That's some evil fuckery."

"Maybe. The minke herd is large. They're not endangered. The Japanese and the Norwegians aren't really taking enough of them to hurt the population, so why shouldn't we let them hunt them? I mean, what's the argument for stopping them? Because whales are cute? The Chinese fry kitties—we don't protest them."

"The Chinese fry kitties?"

"I'm not saying I agree with killing them, but we really don't have a good argument."

"The Chinese fry kitties?" Kona's voice was getting higher each time he spoke.

"Maybe some of the work we do here can prove that these animals have culture, that they're closer to us than they perceive. *Then* we'll have an argument."

"Kitties? Like, little meow kitties? They just fry them?"

Clay was musing, watching the sunset and feeling sad and frustrated, and words came out of him like a long, rambling sigh: "Of course, when I was on the whaling ship, I saw how the Japanese whalers looked at the animals. They see them as fish. No more or less than a tuna. But I was photographing a sperm-whale mother and her calf, and the calf got separated from the pod. The mother came back to get the calf and pushed it away from our Zodiac. The whalers were visibly moved. They recognized that mother/child behavior. It wasn't fish behavior. So it's not a lost cause."

"Kitties?" Kona sighed, taking on the same tone of resignation that Clay had used.

"Yeah," said Clay.

"So how we going to find Nate so we can do good work and save them humpies and minkes?"

"Is that what we're doing?"

"No. Not now. Now we just watching for a green flash."

"I don't know any science, Kona. I made that up, about the green flash."

"Ah, I didn't know. Science you don't know just looks like magic."

"I don't believe in magic."

"Oh, brah, don't say dat. Magic come bite you in the ass for sure. You going to need my help for sure now."

Clay felt some of the weight of his melancholy lift by sharing a moment with the surfer, but his need to act was worrying at him like a flea in the ear. "Let's take a drive up-country, Kona."

"They really fry kitties in China?" Kona said, his voice so high now that dogs living around the harbor winced.

"AMY, WHAT, HOW—WHAT?" THE LIGHTS HAD COME UP, AND NATE could see that it was Amy in his bed. It was a lot of Amy that he hadn't seen before.

"They took me, Nate. Just like you. A few days later. It was horrible. Quick, hold me."

"A whale ship ate you, too?"

"Yes, just like you. Hold me, I'm so afraid."

"And they brought you all the way here?"

"Yes, just like you, only it's worse for a dame. I feel . . . so . . . so naked. Hold me."

" 'Dame'? No one says 'dame' anymore."

"Well, African-American, then."

"You are *not* African-American."

"I can't remember all the politically correct terms. Christ, Nate, what do you need, a diagram? Crawl in." Amy flapped the covers, threw them back, then struck a cheesecake pose, grinning.

But Nate backed away. "You put your head in the water to listen for the whale. The only other person I ever saw do that was Ryder."

"Look at my tan line, Nate." She danced her fingertips over her tan line, which to Nate looked more like a beige line. Nevertheless, she had his attention. "I've never had a tan line before."

"Amy!"

"What!"

"You set me up!"

"I'm naked over here. Haven't you thought about that?"

"Yes, but—"

"Ha! You admit it. I was your research assistant. You had firing power over me. Yet there you are, thinking about me naked."

"You *are* naked."

"Ha! I think I've made my point."

"That 'ha' thing is unprofessional, Amy."

"Don't care. I no longer work for you, and you are not the boss of me anymore, and furthermore, look at this butt." She rolled over. He did. She looked back over her shoulder and grinned. "Ha!"

"Stop that." He looked at the wall. "You spied on me. You caused all this to happen."

"Don't be ridiculous. I was just part of it, but all that is forgiven. Look how luscious I am." Amy did a presentation wave over herself, as if Nate had just won her in a game show.

"Would you stop that?" Nate reached over and pulled the covers up to her chin.

"Lus-cious," she said, pulling the covers down, revealing a breast with each syllable.

Nate walked out of the room. "Put on some clothes and come out here. I'm not going to try to talk to you like that."

"Fine, don't talk," she called after him. "Just crawl in."

"You're just bait," he called from the kitchen.

"Hey, buster, I'm not that young."

"This conversation is over until you come out here fully dressed." Nate sat down at his little dining table and tried to will away his erection.

"What are you, some kind of fruitcake, some kind of sissy boy, some kind of fairy, huh?"

"Yes, that's it," Nate said.

For a moment nothing but quiet from the bedroom. Then: "Oh, my God, I feel like such a maroon." Her voice was softer now. She came stumbling out of the bedroom, the sheet wrapped around her. "I'm really sorry, Nate. I had no idea. You seemed so interested. I wouldn't have—"

"Ha!" Nate said. "See how it feels."

THE OLD BROAD HAD GIVEN THEM ICED GINGER TEA AND SET KONA UP at one of her telescopes to look at the moon. She sat down next to Clay on the lanai and they listened to the night for a while.

"It's nice up here," Clay said. "I don't think I've been up here at night before."

"Clay, I'm usually in bed by now, so I hope you don't think me dense if I get things clear in my mind."

"Of course not, Elizabeth."

"Thank you. As I see it, for years you and Nate have been telling everyone that I'm a nut job because I said I could communicate with whales. Now you drive up here in a froth—in the middle of the night— to deliver the earth-shattering news that what I've been telling you all along is possible?" She leaned her chin on her fist and looked wide-eyed at Clay. "That about right?"

"We never called you a nut job, Elizabeth," Clay said. "That's an overstatement."

"Doesn't matter, Clay. I'm not mad." She sipped her tea. "And I'm not angry either. I've been in these islands a very long time, Clay, and I've lived on the side of this volcano for most of it. I've spent more time looking down on that channel than most people have spent on the planet, but not once did you or Nate ask me why. Didn't want to look a gift horse in the mouth, I guess. Easier to think I was just a few bananas short of a bunch than to ask me why I was interested."

Clay felt sweat running down the small of his back. He'd been uncomfortable around the Old Broad before, but in a totally different way—the way one feels when a matron aunt pinches your cheek and starts to ramble inanely about the old days, not like this. This was like getting sandbagged by a prosecutor. "I don't think that Nate or I could answer that question, Elizabeth, so it's not out of order that we didn't ask you."

"That's a load a shark balls, old Auntie," Kona said, not looking away from the eyepiece of the eight-inch mirror telescope.

"He's a sweet boy," the Old Broad said. "Clay, you know that Mr. Robinson was in the navy. Did I ever tell you what it was that he did?"

"No, ma'am, I just assumed he was an officer."

"I can understand how you might think that, but all the money came from my family. No, sweetheart, he was a noncom, a chief petty officer, a sonar man. In fact, I'm told he was the best sonar man in the navy at the time."

"I'm sure he was, Elizabeth, but—"

"Shut up, Clay. You came here for help, I'm helping you."

"Yes, ma'am." Clay shut up.

"James—that was Mr. Robinson's first name—he loved to listen to the humpbacks. He said they made his job a damn sight harder, but he loved them. We were stationed in Honolulu then, but submarine crews were on and off on hundred-day duty shifts, so when he would have time in port, we would come over to Maui, rent a boat, and go out in the channel. He wanted me to be part of the world he lived in all the time—the world of sound under the sea. You can understand that, can't you, Clay?"

"Of course." But Clay was getting a not-so-good feeling about this trip down memory lane. He had things he needed to know, but he wasn't sure that this was part of them.

"That's when I bought Papa Lani with some of my father's money. We thought we'd live there full-time eventually, maybe turn it into a hotel. Anyway, one day James and I decided to rent a little powerboat and camp on the ocean side of Lanai. It was a calm day and an easy trip. On our way over, a big humpback came up beside the boat. It even seemed to change course when we did. James slowed down so we could stay with our new friend. There were no rules then about getting close to the whales like there are now. We didn't even know we were supposed to save them back then, but James loved the humpbacks, and I had come to as well.

"There was no one but the pineapple-company workers on Lanai at that time, so we found a deserted beach where we thought we'd build a fire, cook some dinner, drink highballs from tin cups, swim naked, and . . . you know, make love on the beach. See there, I've shocked you."

"No you haven't," said Clay.

"Yes I have. I'm sorry."

"No you haven't. Really, I'm fine, tell the story." *Old ladies,* he thought.

"When the trade winds came up that evening, we pitched the tent a little ways off the beach in a small canyon sheltered from the wind. Well, I gave James my best hummer, and he fell asleep right away."

Clay choked on his iced tea.

"Oh, my dear, did an ice cube go down the wrong pipe? Kona, come here and Heimlich Clay, dear."

"No, I'm fine." Clay waved the surfer away. "Really, I'm okay." Tears streamed down his cheeks, and he wiped his nose on his shirttail. He was suddenly incredibly grateful he hadn't brought Clair. "Just need to catch my breath."

Kona sat down cross-legged at their feet, having suddenly found that he was interested in history. "Go ahead, old Auntie."

"Well, I got a little bit of a headache. So I decided to go back to the boat to get an aspirin from the first-aid kit. Come to think of it, it must have been from the tension in my neck. I always got a crick in my neck when I did that, but James loved it so."

"Jesus, Elizabeth, would you get on with the story," Clay said.

"I'm sorry, dear, I've shocked you, haven't I?"

"No, I'm fine. I'm just curious to find out what happened."

"Well, as long as I didn't shock you. I suppose I should be more discreet in front of the boy, but it *is* part of the story."

"No, please. What happened on the beach?"

"You know, we could fuck like mad monkeys, all night long, and it never gave me a headache, but one—"

"The beach, please."

"When I got to the beach, there were two men near the boat. It looked like they were doing something to the engine. I ducked behind a rock before they saw me. I watched them in the moonlight, a short one and the tall one. The tall one seemed to be wearing some sort of helmet or diving suit. But then the short one said something, and the tall one started laughing—snickering, really—and I saw his face in the moonlight. It wasn't a helmet, Clay. It was a face—a smooth, shiny face, with a jaw full of teeth. I could see the teeth even from where I was. It wasn't human, Clay.

"Well, I went back and woke James, told him he had to come see. I took him back to my hiding place. The two men, or the man and that thing were still there, but behind them, right there almost on the beach, was also a humpback, a big one. The water couldn't have been ten feet deep where he was, yet he was sitting there calm as could be.

"Well, all James saw was the two men messing with our boat. We had drunk quite a few cocktails, I guess, and James had his big, strong man act to do. He told me to stay where I was and not to move for anything. Then he went after them—shouting at the top of his lungs for them to get away. The tall one, the nonhuman thing, dove under the water right away, but the man looked around like he'd been trapped. He started wading out toward the whale, and James went right in after him. Then, at last, James saw the whale. He just stopped there in the surf and looked. That's when the thing came up out of the water behind him. Suddenly it was just there, looming behind James. I wanted to yell, but

I was so afraid. The thing, it hit James with something, maybe a rock, and he fell forward into the water. Then I screamed for all I was worth, but I'm not sure they even heard me over the noise of the wind and the surf.

"The man took one of James's arms, the thing the other, and they swam to the whale with James in tow. Then, Clay, as crazy as this sounds, this is what happened: That whale rolled over, and they stuffed James into it, back by the genital slit, I think. Then they both crawled into it as well. Then the whale kicked its tail until it was in deeper water and swam away. I never saw my husband again." The Old Broad took Clay's hand and squeezed it. "I swear to you, that's how it happened, Clay."

Clay didn't know what to say. Over the years she'd said a lot of crazy-sounding stuff, but this was the mother of all crazy stuff. Yet she was more serious than he'd ever seen her. It didn't matter what he believed—there was only one thing to say to her. "I believe you, Elizabeth."

"That's why, Clay. That's why I've helped finance you over the years, it's why I've watched the channel all these years, it's why I own two acres right near the water, yet I've lived up-country for all these years."

"I don't understand, Elizabeth."

"They came back, Clay. That night the whale came back, and the thing came back to the beach, but I hid. They came back for me. The next day I didn't even go back to the boat. I hiked my way to the pineapple plantation and got help there. They brought me back to Lahaina on one of their big freighters. I haven't been on the water since. The closest I ever go near the water is when there's an event at the sanctuary, and then there are a lot of people around."

Clay thought about the Japanese soldier they'd found on a Pacific island who'd been hiding from the Americans for twenty years after the war was over. Elizabeth Robinson had obviously been hiding from something that wasn't looking for her. "Didn't you tell anyone? Surely the navy would have wanted to find out what happened to one of their best sonar men."

"They asked. I told them. They dismissed it. They said James went swimming at night, he drowned, and I was drunk. They sent some men over there, and so did the Maui police. They found the boat, still on the beach, with everything in working order. They found our camp, and they found an empty bottle of rum. That was the end of it."

"Why didn't you ever tell me? Or Nate?"

"I wanted you to keep doing the work that you do. Meanwhile, I kept watching. I read all the scientific journals, too, you know. I look for anything that might make sense of it. Come with me."

She got up and went into her house, Clay and Kona following without a word. In the bedroom she opened a cedar chest and took out a large scrapbook. She laid it on the bed and flipped it open to the last page. It was Nate's obituary.

"Nathan was one of the best in the field, and that little girl said that a whale ate him. Then *she* disappeared at sea." She flipped a page. "Twelve years ago this Dr. Gerard Ryder disappeared at sea, also studying whale calls at the time, although blue whales." She flipped another page. "This fellow, a Russian sonar expert who defected to England, disappeared off Cornwall in 1973. They said it was probably KGB."

"Well, it probably was KGB. I'm sorry, Elizabeth, but each of these incidents seems to have a perfectly normal explanation, and they happen over such a long period of time in different places. I don't see what the connection is."

"It's underwater sound, Clay. And they're *not* normal. All these men, including my James, were experts at listening to the ocean."

"Even so, are you saying that someone has trained whales? That creatures have been abducting sonar guys and shoving them up whales' bums?"

"Don't be crude, Clay. You came to me because you wanted help, I'm trying to give it to you. I don't know who they are, but what you've told me about there being language hidden in the whale song—it just confirms in my mind that they took Nate, and James, and all these other people. That's all I know. I'm telling you that I'm sure that Nate is alive, too. It's another piece to the puzzle."

Clay sat down on the bed next to the scrapbook. There were articles from scientific journals on cetacean biology, on underwater acoustics, news items about whale strandings, some that didn't seem connected at all. It was the search path of someone who didn't know what she was looking for. He'd gone so long thinking of her as crazy that he'd never given her credit for how knowledgeable she really was. He was realizing only now what had been driving her. He felt like a shit.

"Elizabeth, what about the call about the sandwich? What about the crystals and the whales talking to you—all of that? I don't understand."

"I did get the call, Clay. And as for the other, I have dreams of the whales talking to me, and I pay attention to them. Fifty years of searching, I take clues where I can get them. Given what I was looking for, I thought magic and divination as valid a method as any tool in the search."

"See," Kona said, "I told you. Science you don't know? Magic."

"I guess I was casting my faith around carelessly, I just hope I didn't do something awful."

"Nah, old Auntie, Jah's love on ye anyway, even if you're trampin' around your faith like a ho."

"Kona, shut up," Clay said. "What do you mean, you might have done something awful, Elizabeth?"

She picked up the scrapbook, closed it, then sat down on the bed next to Clay and hung her head. A tear dripped down onto the black pasteboard cover of the book.

"When the call came, and the whale said that he wanted a pastrami on rye, I recognized the voice, Clay. I recognized the voice, and I insisted Nathan go out there and take the sandwich with him."

"It was probably a prank, Elizabeth, someone you've met. Nate was going out that day anyway. You didn't cause this."

"No, you don't understand, Clay. Pastrami on rye was my James's favorite. I always had one waiting for him when he came in from submarine duty. The voice on the phone was my James."

CHAPTER THIRTY-ONE

Booty and the Beasts

The second time Amy came out of the bedroom, she was dressed in her familiar hiking shorts, flip-flops, and a WHALES ARE OUR PALS T-shirt. "Better?"

"I don't feel any better, if that's what you're asking." Nate sat at the table with a can of grapefruit juice and a pint of vodka in front of him.

"I mean, are you more comfortable now that I'm dressed? Because I can be naked again in a flash—"

"You want a drink?" Nate needed to forget the whole naked encounter as quickly as possible. Applying alcohol seemed like the most efficient method at this point.

"Sure," she said. She pulled a glass out of one of the kitchen cubbies, the clear door folding back like the protective cover of a frog's eye. "You want a glass?"

Nate had been sipping alternately from the juice can and the vodka bottle until he had enough room in the can to pour in some vodka. "Yeah. I don't like reaching into the cupboards."

"You're kind of squeamish for a biologist, but I guess it does take some getting used to." Amy set the glasses in front of him and let him mix the drinks. There was no ice. "You adjust."

"You seem to have adjusted. When did they take you? You must have been really young."

"Me? No, I was born here. I've always been here. That's why I was perfect to work for you guys. The Colonel has been teaching me cetacean biology for years."

It occurred to Nate that he had seen a few human children around and hadn't really thought about growing up in Gooville. Someone had to teach them. Why not the infamous Colonel? "I should have known. When you were trying to locate the whale by listening for it that last day. I should have known."

"Correction, when I *did* locate the whale by listening for it, for which you still owe me dinner."

"I think this is one of those all-bets-are-off situations, Amy. You were a spy."

"Nate, before you get too angry, you need to remember the alternative to my spying and finding out what you were working on in detail. That would have been to just kill you. It would have been much easier."

"You and Ryder act like you did me a favor. Like you saved me from some great danger. The only danger I was in was from you in the first place. So stop trying to impress me with the quality of your mercy. You did it all—tore up the lab, sank Clay's boat, all of it—didn't you?"

"No, not directly. Poynter and Poe tore up the lab. The whaley boys sank Clay's boat. I took the negatives out of the packet at the photo lab. I kept them informed, and I made sure you were where they needed you to be, that's all. I never wanted to hurt you, Nate. Never."

"I wish I could believe that. Then you show up here like that, trying to convince me that this is a great place to live right after Ryder has given me the speech." He drained his glass, poured himself another drink, this one with just a splash of grapefruit juice over the top.

"What are you talking about? I haven't seen Ryder since I've been back. I just got in a few hours ago."

"Well, then it's always been a part of the plan: Let Amy lure the biologist into staying."

"Nate, look at me." She took his chin in her hand and looked him right in the eye. "I came here of my own free will, without any instructions from Ryder or anyone else. In fact, no one knows where I am, except maybe the Goo—you can never be sure about that. I came here to see you, with all the masks and the role-playing out of the way."

Nate pulled away from her. "And you didn't think I'd be mad? And what was with the whole 'Look how luscious I am' act?"

She looked down. *Hurt,* Nate thought. Or acting hurt. If she cried, it wouldn't matter. He'd be useless.

"I knew you'd be mad, but I thought you might be able to get over it. I was just trying to be floozish. I'm sorry if I'm not very good at it. It's not a skill you get to use a lot in an undersea city. Truth be told, the dating pool is sort of shallow here in Gooville. I was just trying to be sexy. I never said I was a good floozy."

Nate reached over and patted her hand. "No, you're a fine floozy. That's not what I was saying. I wasn't questioning your . . . uh, floozishness. I was just questioning its sincerity."

"Well, it's sincere. I really do like you. I really did come here to see you, to be with you."

"Really?" What was the biological analog for this? A black widow spider male falling for one of her lines, knowing innately where it was going. Knowing right down to his very DNA that she was going to kill and eat him right after they mated, but he would worry about that after. So time and again Mr. Black Widow passed his dumb-ass, sex-enslaved genes on to the next generation of dumb-ass, sex-enslaved males who would fall for the same trick. Spinning a little conversation: *Interesting name, Black Widow. How'd you come about that? Tell me all about yourself. Me? Nah, I'm a simple guy. I'm doomed by my male nature to follow my little spider libido into oblivion. Let's talk about you. Love the red hourglass on your butt.*

"Really," Amy said. There were tears welling in her eyes, and she lifted his hand to her lips and kissed it gently.

"Amy, I don't want to stay here. I'm not— I want— I'm too old for you, even if you weren't a lying, destructive, evil—"

"Okay." She held his hand to her cheek.

"What do you mean, 'okay'?"

"You don't have to stay. But can I stay with you tonight?"

He pulled his hand back from her, but she held his gaze. "I need to be way more drunk for this," he said.

"Me, too." She went over to the scary fridge thing. "Do you have more vodka?"

"There's another bottle over there in that thing—that other thing that I'm afraid of." He caught himself watching her bottom while she found the bottle. "You said 'okay.' You mean you know a way out?"

"Shut up and drink. You gonna drink or you gonna talk?"

"This isn't healthy," Nate observed.

"Thank you, Dr. Insight," Amy said. "Pour me one."

"Nice red hourglass."

"What?"

～◦⊙◦～

BACK AT HIS BUNGALOW AT PAPA LANI, CLAY SAT ON THE BED WITH HIS head in his hands while Clair rubbed the knots out of his shoulders. He'd told her the Old Broad's story, and she'd listened quietly, asking a few questions as he went along.

"So do you believe her?" Clair asked.

"I don't even know what I'm admitting to believing. But I believe she thinks she's telling the truth. She offered us a boat, Clair. A ship. She offered to buy us a research vessel, hire a crew, pay them."

"What for?"

"To find Nate and her husband, James."

"I thought she was broke."

"She's not broke. She's loaded. I mean, the ship will be a used one, but it's a ship. It will still run in the millions. She wants me to find one— and a crew."

"And could you find Nate if you had a ship?"

"Where do I look? She thinks he's on an island somewhere, some secret place where these things live. Hell, if she's telling the truth, they could be from outer space. If she's not . . . well, I can't just run a ship around the world stopping at islands and asking them if they happen to have seen people crawling out of a whale's butt."

"Technically, baby, whales don't have butts. You have to walk upright to have booty. This is why we are the dominant species on the planet, because we have booty."

"You know what I mean."

"It's an important point." She slid into his lap, her arms around his neck.

Clay smiled despite his anxiety. "Technically, man is not the dominant species. There's at least a thousand pounds of termites for every person on earth."

"Well, you can have my termites, thanks."

"So man isn't really dominant, whether it's brains or booty."

"Baby, I wasn't saying that *man* was the dominant species, I was saying that *we* are the dominant species. *Wo-man.*"

"Because you have booty?"

She wiggled on his lap by way of an answer, then leaned her forehead against his, looked in his eyes.

"Good point," Clay said.

"What about this ship? You going to let the Old Broad buy it for you? You going to go look for Nate?"

"Where do I start?"

"Follow one of these signals. Find whatever is making it and follow them."

"We'd need location for that."

"How do you do that?"

"We'd need to have someone working the old sonar grid the navy put down all over the oceans during the Cold War to track submarines. I know people at Newport who do it, but we'd have to tell them what we're doing."

"You couldn't just say you were trying to find a certain whale?"

"I suppose we could."

"And if you have your ship and that information, you can follow the whale, or the ship, or whatever it is to its source."

"My ship?"

"Roll over, I'll rub your back."

But Clay wasn't moving. He was thinking. "I still don't know where to start."

"Who has the booty? Turn over, Captain."

Clay slipped off his aloha shirt and rolled over onto his stomach. "My ship," he said.

❧

NATE WAS SUDDENLY COLD, AND WHEN HE OPENED HIS EYES, HE WAS pretty sure that his head was going to explode. "I'm pretty sure my head is going to explode," he said. And someone rudely jostled his bed.

"Come on, party animal, the Colonel sent for you. We need to go."

He peeked between the fingers he was using to hold the pieces of his head together and saw the menacing but amused face of Cielle Nuñez. It wasn't what—who—he expected, and he did a quick sweep of the bed with one leg to confirm that he was alone. "I drank," Nate said.

"I saw the bottles on the table. You drank a lot."

"I didn't get a knob so just anyone could use it anytime they want."

"I noticed your knob. It looks out of place."

About that time Nate realized that he was naked, and Nuñez was standing over his naked body, and he was going to have to let the pieces of his head go where they may if he was going to cover himself. He felt for a sheet, pulled it up as he sat up and threw his legs off the bed.

"I'm going to need a moment."

"Hurry."

"I have to pee."

"That will be fine."

"And throw up."

"Also fine."

"Okay. You go away now."

"Brush your teeth." And she left the room.

Nate looked around the room for signs of Amy, but there were none. He didn't remember where her clothes were, but the last time he'd seen them, he was pretty sure they weren't on her. He stumbled into the bathroom and looked into the basin, mother of pearl with its little siphon fixtures and the green sphincter drain. Seeing that pretty much did it for him, and he heaved into the sink.

"Hi," Amy said, poking her head out of the retracting shower door.

Nate tried to say something—something about trapdoor spiders, in keeping with an arachnid theme he was developing with regard to Amy—but it came out more bubbly and moist than he intended.

"You go ahead," Amy said. "I'll be in here." And the door clicked shut like a frightened clam.

When Nate had finished reviewing the contents of his stomach, he rinsed his face and the sink, emptied his bladder into the thing on which he would not sit, then leaned against the sink and moaned for a second while he gathered his thoughts.

A head popped out of the shower. "So, that went well."

"The water's not running."

"I'm not showering, I'm hiding. I didn't want Nuñez to see me. The Colonel shouldn't know I've been here. I'll leave after you go. Brush your teeth." And then she was back in her shell.

He brushed, rinsed, repeated, then said, "Okay."

Out she came, grabbed him by the hair, kissed him hard. "Nice night," she said. The shower clicked shut, Amy inside.

"I'm too old for this."

"Yeah, I was going to talk to you about that. Not now, later. Go. She's waiting."

CHAPTER THIRTY-TWO

The Replicator Versus
the Imitator

Nuñez bought him a large cup of coffee at a café where whaley boys stood around pouring down lattes the size of fire extinguishers and exchanging clicks and whistles at an irritating volume.

"If ever there was a creature that didn't need caffeine," Nate said.

Nuñez kept him moving, while he kept trying to stop to lean on things. "Don't ever drink with them," Nuñez said. "Especially the males. You know their sense of humor. You're as likely as not to get a wet willy in the ear, and it's a real wet willy."

"I may have to hurl again."

"Don't destroy yourself out of spite, Nate. Just accept things how they are."

He wasn't trying to destroy himself, and he wasn't spiteful. He was just confused, hungover, and kind of in love, or something remotely like love, except that the pain was more localized in his temples rather than being the overall, life-ruining pain it usually caused him. "Can we stop in at the Lollipop Guild and get a couple aspirins?"

"You're late already."

In the corridors she handed him off to a pair of killer whaley boys.

"You should be honored, you know?" Nuñez said. "He doesn't meet with many people."

"You can take my appointment if you want."

❧◦❧

THE COLONEL HAD A GOO RECLINER WAITING FOR HIM WHEN HE walked through the iris door. Nate sat in it and held his coffee cup like a security blanket against his chest.

"Well, can you see now that life wouldn't be so bad here?"

Nate's mind raced. Amy said the Colonel didn't know, but maybe the Goo knew, but the Colonel was tapped in to the Goo, so did he know? Or had he sent her in the first place and this was all a scam, just like when he'd sent her to Hawaii to spy on him? She'd fooled him for a month there, why couldn't she be fooling him now? He wanted to trust her. But what was Ryder getting at?

"What's different, Growl? When I saw you nine hours ago, I was a prisoner, and I'm a prisoner now."

Ryder seemed surprised. He wiped the lock of gray hair out of his eyes furiously, as if it had caused him to make some sort of mistake. "Right, nine hours. So you've had some time to think." He didn't sound sure.

"I got drunk and passed out. In the clear, lightning-bug light of day, Colonel, I still want to go home."

"You know, time"—Ryder patted the living chair he was sitting in as if he were petting a dog, sending waves of blush through the pink Goo outward from where he touched. Nate shivered at the sight of it—"time is different down here, it's . . ."

"Relative?" Nate offered.

"It's on a different scale."

"What do you want from me, Colonel? What can I possibly offer you that I get the special treatment of being spared and granted multiple audiences with the . . . the grand pooh-bah?" Nate was going to say "with the alpha whacko," but he thought of Amy and realized that something had changed. He no longer felt like he had nothing to lose.

Rider swiped at his hair and clutched at the flesh of his chair with the other hand. He began rocking slightly. "I want someone to tell me I'm thinking clearly, I guess. I dream things that the Goo knows, and I think it knows things that I dream, but I'm not sure. I'm overwhelmed."

"You might have thought about that before you declared yourself wizard."

"You think I chose this? I didn't choose this, Nate. The Goo chose me. I don't know how many people have been brought down here over the years, but I was the first biologist. I was the first one who had some idea how the Goo worked. It had the whaley boys bring me to a place like this, where there was raw, unformed animal, and it never let me leave. I've tried to make things better for people in Gooville, but—" Ryder's eyes rolled up in his head as if he were starting to have a seizure, but then he was back again. "Did you see the electricity on the whale ships? I did that. But it's not— It's different now than it has been."

Nate suddenly felt bad for the older man. Ryder was behaving like an early Alzheimer's patient who is realizing that he's losing recognition of his grandchildren's faces.

"Tell me," Nate said.

Ryder nodded, swallowed hard, pressed on—hardly the picture of the powerful leader he'd appeared the night before.

"I think that after the Goo found its safe haven here under the sea, it needed to have more information, more DNA sequences to make sure it could protect itself. It produced a minute bacterium that could spread throughout the oceans, be part of the great world ecosystem but could pass genetic information back to the source. We call the bacteria SAR-11. It's a thousand times smaller than normal bacteria, but it's in every liter of seawater on the planet. That worked fine to transmit information back to the Goo for three billion years—everything that could be known was in the sea. Then something happened."

"Animals left the water?"

"Exactly. Until then, everything there was to know—every piece of information that could be known—was transmitted through DNA, replicators, in creatures that lived in the seas. The Goo knew everything. Mind you, it might take a million years to learn how to make an arthropod's segmented shell. It might take two million years to learn to make a gill or, say, twenty million to make an eye, but it had its safe niche, so it had the time—it didn't have anywhere it needed to be. Evolution doesn't really have a destination. It's just dicking around with possibilities. The Goo is the same way. But when life left the water, the Goo got a blind spot."

"I'm having a little trouble seeing the immediacy of your story, Colonel. I mean, why, beyond the obvious that I'm sitting inside this thing, is this supposed to be urgent?"

"Because four hundred million years later, the land creatures came back into the water—sophisticated land animals."

"Early whales?"

"Yes, when mammals came back to the sea, they brought something that even the dinosaurs—the reptiles and amphibians that had come back to the water—didn't have. Something the Goo didn't know. Knowledge that didn't replicate itself through DNA. It replicated through imitation, learned knowledge, not passed on. Memes."

Nate knew about memes, the information equivalent of a gene. A gene existed to replicate itself and required a vehicle, an organism, in which to do it. It was the same with memes, except a meme could replicate itself across vehicles, across brains. A tune you couldn't get out of your head, a recipe, a bad joke, the Mona Lisa—all were memes of sort. They were a fun model to think about, and computers had made the idea of a self-replicating piece of information more manifest with computer viruses, but what did that have to do with— But then it hit him. Why he'd learned about memes in the first place.

"The song," Nate said. "Humpback song is a meme."

"Of course. The first culture, the first exposure the Goo had to something it didn't understand. What, maybe fifteen million years ago it found out it wasn't the only game in town. Three billion years is a long time to get used to living in what you think is your private house only to suddenly find out that someone moved into an apartment above you while you were sleeping.

"For a long time the Goo didn't perceive that genes and memes were at odds. Whales were the first carriers. Big brains because they need to imitate complex behaviors, remember complex tasks, and because they could get the high-protein food to build the brains the memes needed. But the Goo came to terms with the whales. They're an elegant mix of genes and memes, absolute kings of their realm. Huge, efficient feeders, immune from any predation except from each other.

"But then something started killing whales. Killing them in alarming numbers. And it was something from the surface world. It wasn't something the Goo could find out about from its ocean-borne nervous system, so that's when I think it created the whale ships, or a version of them. Late seventeen or early eighteen hundreds, I'd guess. Then, I think when it had somehow gotten back enough samples of human DNA, it made the whaley boys. To stay camouflaged but to watch, to bring people back here so it could learn, watch us. I may have been the final link that started the war."

"What war? There's a war?" Nate had a quick vision of the paranoid megalomaniacs that the Colonel said he'd considered for pseudonyms, Captain Nemo and Colonel Kurtz, both complete bedbugs.

"The war between memes and genes. Between an organism that specializes in the replication of gene machines—the Goo—and one that specializes in the replication of meme machines—us, human beings. I brought electrical and computer technology here. I brought the Goo the theoretical knowledge of memes and genes and how they work. Where the Goo is now and where it was before I came is the difference between being able to drive one and being able to build a car from lumps of raw steel. It's realizing the threat. It's going to figure it out."

Ryder looked at Nate expectantly. Nate looked at him as if he wasn't getting the point. When he'd studied under Ryder, the man had been so cogent, so clear. Grumpy, but clear. "Okay," Nate said slowly, hoping Ryder would jump in, "so you need me to . . . uh . . . ?"

"Help me figure out a way to kill it."

"Didn't see that coming."

"We're at war with the Goo, and we have to find a way to kill it before it knows what's happening."

"Then don't you think you should keep your voice down?"

"No, it doesn't communicate that way." The Colonel looked perturbed at Nate's comment.

"So you want me to figure out how to kill your god?

"Yes, before it wipes out the human race in one fell swoop."

"Which would be bad."

"And we have to kill it without killing everyone in Gooville."

"Oh, we can do that," Nate said, completely confident, the way he'd seen hostage negotiators in cop movies tell the bank robbers that their demands were being met and the helicopter was on the way. "But I'm going to need some time."

The strangest thing was, as Nate left the Colonel's chamber after being in direct contact with the Goo for only a few minutes, his hangover was completely gone.

CHAPTER THIRTY-THREE

Could Be Worse,
Could Be Dog Years

Evidently," said Nate, "where we screwed up was killing the whales."

"No way," said Amy.

"We tipped our hand."

"About being meme machines, right?"

"Yeah. Are you sure you're not spying for him?"

"Nope. Know how you can tell? When I was spying, did I ever touch you here?"

"No. No, you did not."

"And did I ever let you touch me here?" She moved his hand for him.

"No, you did not. Especially not in public."

"Yeah, we should probably go back to your place."

She had called him on his buzzy, bug-winged speaky thing, about which he made a mental note to ask what the name of it was at his first convenience. They'd met for coffee at a Gooville café that catered to whaley boys. She'd assured him that no one would notice them, and, strangely enough, the whaley boys had completely ignored them. Maybe he was no longer news.

"If they say anything, I'll just tell them that we're having sex," Amy said.

"But you said you didn't think I should tell the Colonel I'd seen you."

"Yeah, but that was before he let you in on his secret plan."

"Right."

"Although I'm a little ashamed of how old you are. We should talk about that."

"So should I move my hand?"

"Yeah, down and a little to the right."

"Let's head back to my place."

～❧⮑

BACK AT HIS APARTMENT, STANDING IN THE KITCHEN, HE SAID, "HEY, what do you call this thing?" He pointed to that thing.

"The phone."

"No kidding?" He nodded as if he'd known that all along. "So where were we?"

"Killing whales was where we went wrong?"

"Yes."

"Or how old you are?"

"So," he continued, "killing whales was a big mistake."

"Which you knew, because that's what made you want to become a nerd in the first place."

"No, that's not right."

" 'Scuse me, *action* nerd."

"You want to know how I got into this field, really?"

"No. I mean, sure. You can tell me about the destruction of the human race later."

"You have to promise you won't laugh."

"Of course." She looked incredibly sincere.

"My sophomore year at the University of Sasketchewan in the Sticks—"

"You're kidding."

"It's a good school. You promised you wouldn't laugh."

"Oh, you meant even this early in the story I'm not supposed to laugh? Sorry."

"I mean, I'm sure it doesn't measure up to Gooville Community College—"

"Not fair."

"Home of the Gooville Fighting Loogies—"

"Okay, you made your point."

"Thank you. So a friend and I decided that we're going to go to break out of our boring small-college lives, we were going to take some risks, we were going to—"

"Talk to a girl?"

"No. We decided to drive all the way to Florida for spring break, just like American kids, where we would then drink beer, get sunburned, and *then* talk to a girl—girls."

"So you went."

"Took almost a week to get there, but yes, we drove in his dad's Vista Cruiser station wagon. And I did indeed meet a girl. In Fort Lauderdale. A girl *from* Fort Lauderdale. And I talked to her."

"You dirty little tramp. Like, 'How's it going, eh?' "

"Among other things. We conversed. And so she invited me to go see a manatee."

"He shoots! He scores!"

"But I thought it was an American way of saying matinee. I thought we were going to a movie. You know, you don't think about those things as being real."

"But it was."

"She did volunteer work for a rescue hospital for injured marine mammals, mostly manatees that had been hit by boats. They had a bottlenose dolphin, too. We stayed there for hours, caring for the animals, her teaching me about them. I was hooked. I hadn't even picked my undergrad major, but as soon as I got back to school, I went for biology, and I've been studying marine mammals ever since."

"Oh, my God, you didn't get laid, did you?"

"I found a passion for life. I found something that drives me."

"I can't believe I fell for such a pathetic loser."

"Hey, I'm pretty good at this whale stuff. I'm respected in my field."

"But you're dead."

"Yeah, before then, I mean. Hey, did you say that you fell for me?"

"I said I fell for a pathetic loser, if the shoe fits . . ."

He kissed her. She kissed him back. That went on for a while. They both found it excellent. Then they stopped.

"You said you wanted to talk about our age difference," Nate said, because he always picked women who broke his heart, and, figuring that his heart was now into this whole thing far enough to be broken, he wanted to get on with it.

"Yeah, we probably should. Maybe we should sit down."

"Couch?"

"No, at the table. You might want a drink."

"No, I'm okay." *Yep, heartbreak,* he thought. They sat.

"So," she said, curling her legs up under her, sitting like a little kid, making him feel ever more the creepy old guy leching on the young girl, "you know that the whaley boys have been pulling people in here from shipwrecks and plane crashes for years, right?"

"That's what Cielle said."

"She wants you, I can tell, but that's beside the point. Do you know that they pulled whole crews off sunken submarines, plus they've yanked sonar guys out of port for years?"

"I didn't know that."

"Doesn't matter, has nothing to do with what I'm telling you. So you realize that some people who have been lost at sea, like the crew of the American sub *Scorpion* that sank back in '67, actually ended up here?"

"Okay. That makes sense. More of the Goo looking out for itself. Gaining knowledge."

"Yeah, but that's not the point. I mean, those guys helped put together a lot of the technology you saw on the whale ship, the human technology, but that doesn't matter. The important part is that the world thinks that the crew of the *Scorpion* is at the bottom of the Atlantic Ocean, even though they're not. Got it?"

"Okay," Nate said, really slowly, the way he had spoken to the

Colonel when he was losing the point—much the way he was waving in the conversational wind right now.

"And you realize that when I applied with you and Clay, that I gave my real name, which is Amy Earhart, and that Amy is short for Amelia?"

"Oh, my God," Nate said.

"Ha!" Amy said.

⌖

THE SHIP BROKER FOUND CLAY'S SHIP IN THE PHILIPPINES, IN MANILA Harbor. Clay bought it based on faxed photographs, a spec sheet, and a recent hull certification for just under $2 million of the Old Broad's money. It was a 180-foot-long U.S. Coast Guard fisheries patrol vessel built in the late fifties. It had been refitted several times since then, once in the seventies for fishing, once in the eighties for ocean survey, and finally in the nineties as a live-aboard dive boat for the adventure tourist. It had plenty of comfortable cabins as well as compressors, dive platforms, and cranes to raise and lower support vessels onto the rear deck, although, except for the lifeboats, it came with no support craft. Clay thought they could use the rear deck as a helicopter-landing pad, even if there wasn't a budget for a helicopter, but—you know—someone with a helicopter might want to land there, and it helped no end to have a big H painted on the deck. There *was* a budget for painting a big H. The ship had efficient, if not quite state-of-the-art, navigation equipment, radar, autopilot, and some old but functioning sonar arrays left over from its days as a fishing ship. It had twin twelve-hundred-horsepower diesel engines and could distill up to twenty tons of freshwater a day for the crew and passengers. There were cabins and support for forty. It was also rated a class-three icebreaker, which was a feature that Clay hoped they wouldn't have to test. He really didn't like cold water.

Through another broker Clay hired the crew of ten men, sight unseen, right off the docks of Manila: a group of brothers, cousins, and uncles with the last name of Mangabay, among whom the broker guaranteed that there were no murderers, or at least no convicted murderers, and only petty thieves. The eldest uncle, Ray Mangabay, who would be Clay's first mate, would sail the ship to Honolulu, where Clay would meet them.

"He's going to be driving my ship," Clay said to Clair after he'd gotten the news that he had a crew and a first mate.

"You have to let your ship go, Clay," Clair said. "If he sinks it, it wasn't really yours."

"But it's my ship."

"What are you going to call it?"

He was thinking about the *Intrepid* or the *Merciless* or some other big-dick, blow-shit-up kind of name. He was thinking about *Loyal* or *Relentless* or the *Never Surrender,* because he was determined now to find his friend, and he didn't mind putting that right on the bow. "Well, I was thinking about—"

"You were thinking deeply about it, weren't you?" Clair interrupted.

"Yes, I thought I'd call her the *Beautiful Clair.*"

"Just the *Clair* will be fine, baby. You don't want the bow to look busy."

"Right. The *Clair.*" Strangely enough, on second thought, that pretty much encompassed *Intrepid, Merciless, Relentless,* and *Loyal. Plus, it had the underlying meaning of keeper of the booty, which was sort of a bonus in a ship name,* he thought. "Yeah, that's a good name for her."

"How long before she gets here?"

"Two weeks. She's not fast. Twelve knots cruising. If we have somewhere to go, I'll send the ship directly there and meet it at a port along the way."

"Well, now that she's called the *Clair,* I hope they bring her in safe."

"My ship," Clay said anxiously.

⋙◦◦⋘

"SO," NATE SAID, "YOU'RE WHAT, IN YOUR NINETIES? A HUNDRED?"

"Don't look it, do I?" Amy posed: a coquettish half curtsy with a Betty Boop bump at the end. Indeed, it would have been a spry move for a woman in her nineties.

Nate was really glad he was sitting down, but he missed the sensation he would have had of needing to sit down.

"Your whole attraction was based on my age, wasn't it?" She sat across from him. "You were working out your male menopause on the fantasy of my young body. Somehow you were going to try to recapture your youth. Once again you'd feel like more than a footnote to humanity. You'd be virile and vital and relevant and all alpha male, just because a younger—and decidedly luscious, I might add—woman had chosen you, right?"

"Nuh-uh," Nate said. She was wrong, right?

"Wow, Nate, were you on the debate team at Moose Dirt U? I mean, your talent—"

"Sasketchewan in the Sticks," he corrected.

"So the age thing? It's a problem?"

"You're like a hundred. My grandma isn't even a hundred, and she's dead."

"No, I'm not really that old." She grinned and reached across the table, took his hand. "It's okay, Nate. I'm not Amelia Earhart."

"You're not?" Nate felt his lungs expand, as if a steel band around his chest had broken. He'd been taking tiny yip breaths, but now oxygen was returning to his brain. Funny, he was pretty sure that none of the other women he'd been with had been Amelia Earhart either, but he didn't remember feeling quite so relieved about it before. "Well, I should have known. I mean, you don't look anything like the pictures. No goggles."

"I was just messin' with you. I'm her daughter. Ha!"

"Stop it! This isn't funny, Amy. If you're trying to make a point, you've made it. Yes, you're an attractive young woman, and maybe your youth's a part of why I'm attracted to you, but that's just biology. You can't blame me for that. I didn't make a move on you, I didn't harass you when we were working together. I treated you exactly as I would have treated any research assistant, except maybe you got away with more because I liked you. You can't ridicule me for responding to you sexually down here when you came on to me. The rules had changed."

"I'm not ridiculing you. Amelia Earhart really is my mother."

"Stop it."

"You want to meet her?"

Nate searched her face for signs of a grin or a tremble in her throat that might indicate the rise of an Amy *Ha!* Nothing there, just that little bit of sweetness that she usually tried to hide.

"So somehow, living down here, you haven't aged. Your mother?"

"We age, but not like on the surface. I was born in 1940. I'm about the same number of years older than you than you were older than me a half hour ago—kinda sorta. You going to dump me?"

"It's so hard to believe."

"Why, after you've seen all this? You've seen what the Goo can do. Why is it so hard to believe that I'm sixty-four?"

"Well, for one, you're so immature."

"Shut up. I'm young at heart."

"But for a second there I was so sure we were doomed." Nate rubbed his temples—trying to stretch them, maybe—to make his head bigger to hold the whole concept of Amy's being sixty-four.

"No, it's okay, we just haven't gotten to that yet. We're still doomed."

"Oh, thank goodness," Nate said. "I was worried."

~∞~

LATER, AFTER THEY HAD PUSHED THE WORLD AWAY FOR A WHILE, made love and napped in each other's arms, Amy made a move to start another round, and Nate awoke to an immediate and uncertain anxiety.

"Are we really doomed?" he asked.

"Oh, goddamn it Nate!" She was straddling him, so she was able to get a good windup before thumping him hard in the chest with her fist. "That's just un-fucking-professional!"

Nate thought about how the praying mantis female will sometimes bite off the male's head during copulation and how the male's body continues to mate until the act is finished.

"Sorry," he said.

She rolled off him and stared up at dim strips of green luminescence on the ceiling. "It's okay. I didn't mean to bite your head off."

"Pardon?"

"Yes, we're probably doomed. We're doomed for the same reason that I look the way I do, that most of the Goos look much younger than we really are. Turn a gene on, you age; turn it off, you don't. I've even seen some people down here who seem to get younger. Flip a switch, pancreatic cancer at age twenty-two; flip another, you can smoke four packs a day and live to be a hundred. If the Goo thinks that the human race is a danger to it, it just has to flip a switch, pick a gene, make a virus, and the human race would blink out. I hadn't really thought about it as a threat before. My whole life I've worked for the Goo. Service, you know? It takes care of us. It's the source."

He didn't know what to say. Did he need to actually take the Colonel's request for help seriously? Did he need to help find a way to kill this amazing creature in order to save his own species? "Amy, I don't know what to do. Two days ago I just wanted to get out of here. Now? The Colonel and you both said I was lucky to be alive. Has the Goo killed people who were close to finding out about it?"

"Honestly, I don't know. I've never seen it or heard of it happening, but I—we—each just do our own part down here. We don't ask a lot of questions. Not because we're told not to or anything—it's just that you can live a long time without asking yourself big questions when your needs are looked after." For the first time Nate could see the experience of years in Amy's face, marked not by wrinkles but by a shadow in her eyes.

"I'm asking," he said.

"Do I think the Goo is *ethically* capable of killing the human race?"

"I guess."

"I don't even know if the Goo *has* ethics, Nate. According to the Colonel, it's just a vehicle for genes and we're just vehicles for memes and nature says that a head-on collision is inevitable. What if it's not? This battle has supposedly gone on for millions of years, and now the Colonel wants to force an endgame? What I do know is that you've got to talk him out of trying to kill it."

"But he's your leader."

"Yeah, but he didn't tell any of us about this. I think he's doubting his own judgment. So am I."

"But you said that it could kill everyone on the planet at the flick of a switch."

"Yeah." She rolled over and propped herself up on her elbow. "You hungry? I'm hungry."

"I could eat."

CHAPTER THIRTY-FOUR

Necrophiliacs Anonymous, Gooville Chapter

Amy was carrying two stoppered porcelain bottles of beer when she entered the Colonel's chambers. The ruler of Gooville came sliding out of the pink wall as if it had given birth to him. He extended his arms to hug her, but instead of returning his embrace, Amy held up a beer.

"I brought you a beer."

"Amy, you know I don't really eat anymore."

"I thought you might like a beer, for old times' sake."

"Why are you here?"

"I hadn't seen you since I got back from Maui. I thought you'd want to debrief me or something."

"I've talked to Nathan Quinn."

"You have?"

"Don't be cute, Amy. I know what's going on between you two."

"I really don't have any choice, Colonel, I *am* cute. It's the burden I have to bear."

"He doesn't know what you are, does he?"

"Drink your beer, it's getting warm. Why do you keep it so steamy in here anyway?"

The Colonel accepted the beer from her and took a long pull. When he came up for air, he stared at the beer bottle with a look of surprise, as if it had just spoken to him.

"My, that's good. That's really good. I'd forgotten."

Amy toasted him with her own bottle and took a drink. "Colonel, we've known each other a long time. You've been like a father to me, but you are out of touch. I'm worried about you. I think you need to come out of here occasionally, like you used to. Walk around. Have some interaction with the people in town."

"Don't try to get in the way of what I'm doing, Amy."

"What are you talking about? I'm just worried about you."

The Colonel looked at the beer bottle in his hand again, as if it had just been teleported there, then he looked back to Amy with a little panic in his eyes. "Nate didn't tell you, then?"

"Tell me what? Nate doesn't have anything to do with this. You *have* lost touch."

The Colonel nodded, then leaned back into the wall of Goo behind him. It cradled him and formed a chaise longue, which he sat down on as he rubbed his temples. "Amy, did you ever do anything for a purpose greater than your own ambition? Did you ever feel a duty to something beyond yourself?"

"You mean, like persuading people that I'm something that I'm not to gain their trust so they could be kidnapped or killed in order to preserve my community? Yes, I have some concept of the idea of serving the greater good."

"I guess you do. I guess you do. Forgive me. Perhaps I do spend too much time alone."

"You think?"

"Could you leave me now? I do have to think."

"So you want to be alone now? That's what you're saying? This is how you're going to address the problem of spending too much time alone?"

"Go, Amy, and please don't interfere with Nate."

"Not yet."

"What do you mean, 'not yet'?"

"There's a deposit on that bottle. I'm not leaving without it."

"Then, Nate, he's not a problem? You're sure?" Here the Colonel forced a smile that looked much more like something menacing than an actual smile. "Because I will tell him about you if I must."

"The greater good," Amy said, returning the forced smile with a real one.

"Good," said the Colonel, draining the last of his beer. "Come back. And bring me another of these."

"You got it," Amy said. Then she took the bottle from him and left the chamber. *Thin line between genius and full-blown batshit,* she thought. *Very thin line.*

❧

FOR TWO WEEKS THE COLONEL DIDN'T SEND FOR NATE. CIELLE NUÑEZ had stopped by the third morning that Amy was at Nate's apartment. "Well, you don't need me anymore," Cielle had said. "I'd just as soon get back to my ship anyway, although it doesn't look like we're going anywhere soon." Nate was disappointed that she hadn't been jealous.

"He's afraid of the cupboards, the fridge, and the garbage disposal," Cielle told Amy, as if she were talking to the dog sitter. "And you'll need to take him to get his clothes cleaned. You know he's going to be terrified of the washing machines."

"I'm right here," Nate said. "And I'm not afraid of the appliances. I'm just cautious."

"Your mother will be thrilled for you two, Amy. Her ship should be back at base soon."

"No, she's not due in for another six weeks," Amy said.

"Not anymore. The Colonel's called all the ships back to base."

"All of them? Why?"

Cielle shrugged. "He's the Colonel. Ours is not to question why. Well, Nate, it's been a pleasure, really. I'll probably see you around. You're in good hands."

She hugged Nate quickly and started out the door.

"Cielle, wait. I want to ask you something. If you don't mind."

She turned. "Ask away."

"When did your husband's yacht sink?"

Cielle raised an inquisitive eyebrow at Amy. "It's okay," Amy said. "He knows."

"Nineteen twenty-seven, Nate. In retrospect it was a blessing of sorts. He died doing what he liked doing, and two years later he would have been wiped out when the stock market crashed. I'm not sure he would have survived that."

"Thanks. I'm sorry."

"Don't be. Cal and I have a really good life."

"Cal? Cal from the ship? You didn't tell me that—"

"He's my husband? The Colonel thought you might be more comfortable with a single woman to orient you. Women down here have never taken their husband's surname, Nate."

"Females run the show in a whale society," Amy explained. "You know, as it should be."

Cielle Nuñez looked from Amy to Nate and smiled. "Oh, Nate, what have you gotten yourself into?" And then she snickered like a whaley boy and left.

"She wanted you," Amy said. "She hides it really well, but I could tell."

From then on they went out together every morning. Nate insisted that Amy take him far into the catacombs during the day. There they found Gooville's underground farms: tunnels where grains of wheat grew right on the walls—no stalks—others where you could pick tomatoes from two-inch stems that seemed to grow directly out of rock.

"How does any of this ripen without photosynthesis?" Nate asked, handling an apricot that was growing not on a tree but on a broad stem like a mushroom.

"Don't know," Amy shrugged. "Geothermal heat. The Colonel says the Goo extends deep under the continent, where it draws heat from the earth. I'll show you the kitchens where they prepare most of the food—it's all geothermal. The old-timers say that at first there was only seafood to eat, but over the years the Goo has provided more and different foods."

"What are these? Chicken nuggets?" He plucked one from the ceiling. A whaley boy working nearby whistled and clicked harshly.

"He says not to pick them, they're not ripe."

Nate tossed the nugget to the floor of the cave, where a softball-size multilegged thing scurried out of a hatch, retrieved it, and scurried back into its trapdoor.

"I've seen enough here," Nate said.

～◆◇◆～

IN THE AFTERNOON THEY DID ERRANDS AND SHOPPING, BUT STILL NO one asked Nate for any form of payment, and he'd stopped offering. In the evening they usually had dinner in his apartment. After they had shared two meals out at Gooville cafés, Amy had insisted that they eat in.

"You're studying them," she said, meaning the whaley boys.

"No I'm not. I'm just looking at them."

"Who are you kidding? You have that look, that researcher look, that lost-in-your-theories look. You think I don't know that look? I worked with you, remember?"

Nate shrugged. "It's what I do. I study whales." He'd been trying to learn the whaley boys' whistle-and-click language. Emily 7 had come by his apartment a couple of afternoons when Amy was away, and while he thought she might have come for amorous reasons, he managed to channel her energies into lessons on whaleyspeak. They'd become friends of sorts. He hadn't mentioned the lessons to Amy, afraid that she might tease him about Emily the way the whale-ship crew had. "I observe. I collect data and try to find meaning in it."

Amy nodded, thinking about it, then said, "So if rescuing manatees and dolphins got you into the field, why didn't you do something more active to help the animals? Veterinary medicine or something."

"I always wonder. I've thought about the people at Greenpeace and Sea Shepherd, putting themselves in harm's way, ramming whaling ships, running Zodiacs in front of harpoon guns to try to protect the animals. I've wondered if that was the way to go."

"And you thought you could do more as a scientist, studying them?"

"No, I thought that being a scientist was something that I *could* do. There's a path to becoming a biologist—an educational process. There isn't for being a pirate."

"No, you're wrong, there *is* a school for that. I saw it on a matchbook when I was in Maui. I'm sure it said you could learn to be a pirate if you passed a simple test."

"That's learn to *draw* a pirate."

"Whatever. So you compromised?"

"Did I? I think what we—what I do has value."

"So do I. I'm not saying that. I'm just wondering, you know, now that you're dead, do you feel your life was wasted?"

"I'm not dead, Amy. Jeez, that's an awful thing to say."

"You know, effectively dead, I mean. Your life being over. Jeepers, does that make me a necrophiliac? When we get out of here, maybe I'll have to go to a meeting or something. Do they have those?"

"Amy, I'm wondering if maybe I don't want to get out of here." He'd been thinking about it a lot. Life here really wasn't bad, and since he'd been looking for a way out on their daily excursions (only to be reminded that he'd have to go through the miles of pressure locks only to emerge six hundred feet below the sea), maybe he and Amy could make a future together. The whole Gooville ecosystem would certainly keep him interested.

"Hi, my name's Amy, and I hump the dead."

"Maybe, if I can talk the Colonel out of his plan, I can stay here with you. You know, adapt."

"I can't imagine that they'd get up at a meeting and say, 'Hi, my name's so-and-so, and I like to bone the dead.' It's sort of crude. Although strangely appropriate."

"You're not listening to me, Amy."

"Yes I am. We're not staying here. I'll find a way out, but we can't stay. You have to convince the Colonel not to try to hurt the Goo, but then we're leaving. As soon as possible."

Nate was a little shocked at how adamant she was. She seemed to be staring at nothing, concentrating, thinking about something she didn't want to share, and she didn't seem happy about. But then she brightened. "Hey, you're going to get to meet my mother."

A WEEK LATER IT HAPPENED.

"Well, you always said that the jazz of what you do was knowing something that no one else in the world knows," Amy said. "You jazzed?" She took his arm and draped it around her neck as they walked.

They had just left the Gooville apartment of Amelia Earhart.

"She looks good, doesn't she?" Amy asked.

Amelia was a beautiful, gracious woman, and after sixty-seven years in Gooville, the aviatrix didn't look a day over fifty. She'd been just under forty when she disappeared in 1937. In her presence Nate had felt as if he were fifteen again, out on his first date, stuttering and stumbling and blushing—blushing, for Christ's sake—when Amy mentioned that she'd been spending nights at his place. Amelia made Nate sit next to her on the couch and took his hand as she spoke to him.

"Nathan, I hope what I'm about to say to you doesn't sound racist, because it's not, but I want to put your mind at ease. I have had a very long time to get used to the idea of my daughter's being a sexually active adult, and, frankly, if after all these years you are the one that she has chosen to fall in love with, which appears to be the case, I can only tell you how relieved I am that you are of the human species. So please relax."

Nate had shot a look to Amy.

She shrugged. "Every girl has her adventurous period."

"Thank you," Nate said to Amelia Earhart.

Now, out on the street, to Amy he said, "I shouldn't have asked how the flight was."

"She's still a little sensitive about that. Even after all these years. My dad was her navigator. He didn't survive the crash."

"But you said you were born in 1940. How could that be if your father died in 1937?"

"Robust sperms?"

"Three years? That's really robust."

She punched his arm. "I was rounding up. Give me a break, Nate, I'm old. You never grilled the Old Broad for accuracy like this."

"I wasn't sleeping with the Old Broad."

"But you wanted to, didn't you? Admit it? You were hot to get into her muumuu."

"Stop." Nate glanced at some whaley-boy males who were hanging out in front of the bakery (they always seemed to be there) doing a synchronized display wave with their willies, and he was about to defend himself with a comment about Amy's past, but then he decided that there was just no need to watch that little brain movie, let alone use it as some kind of weapon against what was essentially just Amy-style teasing—one of the things he found he adored about her as soon as he'd allowed himself to admit that he *could* adore someone again.

The whaley boys snickered at him as they passed.

"You guys are all just big, squeaky bath toys," Nate said under his breath, knowing they could hear him anyway. Nate had been insulting them every time he and Amy went by for a week or so, just to irritate them. Maybe Amy was rubbing off on him.

The whaley boys blew a collective sputtering raspberry.

"Sentient? You guys can't even spell sentient," Nate whispered.

And then the reward. He loved watching creatures with four digits try to flip him the middle finger.

"Yeah, I'm the immature one," Amy said.

Life is good, Nate thought. For the first time in as long as he could remember, he was happy. Kinda.

In the morning a brace of whaley boys came to take him to the Colonel. Amy wasn't even there to kiss him good-bye.

CHAPTER THIRTY-FIVE

Yeah, but You
Can't Dance to It

The Colonel was standing in the middle of the mother-of-pearl amphitheater when the whaley boys led Nate in.

"You two go on now," the Colonel said to the whaley boys. "Nate can find his way back."

"You came out of your lair," Nate said.

The Colonel looked older, more drawn than when Nate had seen him before.

"I don't want to be in contact with the Goo for what I'm going to tell you."

"I thought it didn't get information that way," Nate said.

The Colonel ignored him. "I was hoping you would have had a brainstorm to solve my problem, Nate, but you haven't, have you?"

"I'm working on it. It's more complex—"

"You've been distracted. I'm disappointed, but I understand. She's a piece of work, isn't she? And I mean that in the best sense of the word. Never forget that I chose to send her to you."

Nate wondered how much the Colonel knew about them and how he knew it. Reports from the whaley boys? From the Goo itself, through osmosis or some extended nervous system? "Distraction has nothing to do with it. I've thought a lot about your problem, and I'm not sure I agree with you. What makes you think the Goo is going to destroy humanity?"

"It's a matter of time. That's all. I need you to carry a message for me, Nate. You'll be responsible for saving the human race. That should go some measure toward consoling you."

"Colonel, is there any chance you can be more direct, less cryptic, and tell me for once what the hell you're talking about?"

"I want you to go to the U.S. Navy. They need to know about the threat of the Goo. One well-placed nuclear torpedo should do it. It's deep enough that they shouldn't have any problem justifying it to other countries. There won't be any fallout. They're just going to need someone credible to convince them of the threat. You."

"What about the people down here? I thought you wanted to save them."

"I'm afraid they're going to be a necessary sacrifice, Nate. What are five thousand or so people, most of whom have lived longer than they would have on the surface, compared with the whole human race, six billion?"

"You crazy bastard! I'm not going to try to convince the navy to nuke five thousand people and all the whaley boys as well. And you're more deluded than I thought if you think they'd do it on my word."

"Oh, I don't expect that. I expect they'll send down their own research team to confirm what you tell them, but when they get here, I'll see to it that they get the message that the Goo is a threat. In any case you'll survive."

"I think you're wrong about the Goo finding us dangerous. And even if you were right, what if it just decides to wait us out? On the Goo's time scale, it can just take a nap until we're extinct. I'm not doing it."

"I'm sorry you feel that way, Nate. I guess I'll have to find another way."

Nate suddenly realized that he'd blown it—his chance to escape. Once he was outside Gooville, there would have been nothing to force him to do what the Colonel wanted. Or maybe there would be. Right then he wanted very badly to see Amy.

"Look, Colonel, maybe I can do something. Couldn't you just evacuate Gooville? Drop all the people on an island. Let the whaley boys find somewhere else to live. I mean, if I reveal the Goo to the world, it's all sort of going to be out of the bag anyway. I mean—"

"I'm sorry, Nate, I don't believe you. I'll take care of it. Evacuation wouldn't make any difference to the people here anyway. And the whaley boys shouldn't exist in the first place. They're an abomination."

"An abomination? That's not the scientist I knew talking."

"Oh, I admit that they are fabulous creatures, but they would have never evolved naturally. They are a product of this war, and their purpose has been served. As has mine, as has yours. I'm sorry we didn't see eye to eye on this. Go now."

Just like that, this crazy bastard was going to plan B, and Nate had no idea how to stop him. Maybe that was what he was really brought here for. Maybe the Colonel was like someone who makes a suicide attempt as a cry for help, rather than an earnest attempt to end his life. And Nate had missed it.

He started to back away from the Colonel, desperately trying to think of something he could say to change the situation, but nothing was coming to him. When he reached the passageway, the Colonel called out to him from the steps by the giant iris.

"Nate. I promised you, and you deserve to know."

Nate turned and came a few steps back into the room.

The Colonel smiled, a sad smile, resolved. "It's a prayer, Nate. The humpback song is a prayer to the source, to their god. The song is in praise *of* and in thanks *to* the Goo."

Nate considered it. A life's work contemplating a question, and this was the answer? No way. "Why only male singers, then?"

"Well, they're males. They're praying for sex, too, aren't they? The females choose the mates—they don't need to ask."

"There's no way to prove that," Nate said.

"And no one to prove it to, Nate, not down here, but it's the truth. Whale song was the first culture, the first art on this planet, and, like most of human art, it celebrates that which is greater than the artist. And the Goo likes it, Nate, it likes it."

"I don't believe it. There's no evolutionary pressure for it to be prayer."

"It's a meme, Nate, not a gene. The song is learned behavior, not passed by birth. It has its own agenda: to be replicated, imitated. And it *was* reinforced. Have you ever seen a starved humpback, Nate?"

Nate thought about it. He'd seen sick animals, and injured animals, but he'd never seen a starved humpback. Nor had he ever heard of one.

The Colonel must have seen something in Nate's reaction. "There's your reinforcement. The Goo looks after them, Nate. It likes the song. I wouldn't be surprised if all of whale evolution—size, for instance—was accelerated by the Goo. We should have never started killing them. We wouldn't be at this juncture if we hadn't killed them."

"But we've stopped" was all that Nate could think to say.

"Too late," the Colonel said with a sigh. "Our mistake was getting the Goo's attention. Now it has to end. The gene has had its three and a half billion years as the driving force of life. I suppose now the meme will have its turn. You and I will never know. Good-bye, Nate."

The iris opened, and the Colonel walked into the Goo.

~❧~

NATE RAN ALL THE WAY HOME, NOT SURE HOW HE HAD NAVIGATED through the labyrinth of tunnels, but found his way without having to backtrack. Amy wasn't at his apartment.

His pulse was throbbing in his temples as he approached the buzzy, bug-winged speaky thing to try to call her, but he decided instead to go directly to her on foot. He checked at her place, and then at her mother's, then at every place they'd ever been together. Not only was Amy gone, but no one had seen her mother either. Nate slept fitfully, tortured by the notion of what the Colonel might have done to Amy because of his own stubbornness. In the morning he went searching for her again, asking everyone he encountered, including the whaley boys by the bakery, but no one had seen her. On the second day he went back through the corridors to the Colonel's mother-of-pearl amphitheater and pounded on the giant black iris until his fists were bruised. There was no response but a dull thud that echoed in the huge empty chamber.

"I'll do what you want, Ryder!" Nate screamed. "Don't hurt her, you crazy fuck! I'll do what you want. I'll bring the navy down on this place and sterilize it, if that's what you want—just give her back."

When at last he gave up, he turned and slid down the iris facing the amphitheater. There were six killer-whale-colored whaley boys standing in the passageway opposite him, watching. They weren't grinning or snickering for once, just watching him. The largest of them, a female, let loose a quick whistle, and they crossed the amphitheater, walking in a crescent-shaped hunting formation toward him.

❧◦❧

SHORT OF BEING A PROFESSIONAL SURFER OR A BONG TEST PILOT FOR the Rastafarian air force, Kona thought he had found the perfect job. He sat in a comfortable chair watching sound spectrograms scroll across one computer monitor, while on another a program picked out the digital sequence in the subsonic signal and broke it into text. All Kona had to do was watch for something meaningful to come across the screen. Strange thing was, he really had started to learn about spectrographs and waveforms and all manner of whale behavior, and he was meeting the day feeling as if he was really doing something.

He ran his hand over his scalp and shuddered as he read the nonsense text that was scrolling across the window. Auntie Clair had bought him four forties of Old English 800 malt liquor, then waited until he'd drunk them, before persuading him to let her cut his dreads down so they matched on both sides (because his true natural state should be one of balance, she said. She was tricky, Auntie Clair). The problem was, in jail his dreads had been almost completely torn off on one side, so by the time she finished evening things out, he was pretty much bald. Out of deference to his religious beliefs (to allow him a reservoir for his abundant strength in Jah, mon), Clair had left him a single dread anchored low on the back of his head, which made it look as if a fat worm was exiting his skull after a hearty meal of brain cells in ganja sauce.

And speaking of the sacred herb, Kona was just on the verge of sparking up a bubbling smoky scuba snack of the dankest and skunkingish nugs when the text scrolling across the screen ceased being nonsense and started being important. He took a quick sip of bong water to steady his nerves, placed the sacred vessel on the floor at his feet, then hit the key that sent the streaming text to the printer.

He stood and waited, bouncing on the balls of his feet for the printer to expectorate three sheets of text, then snatched the pages and dashed out the door to Clay's cabin.

~∽◇∽~

"I MUST BE OUT OF MY MIND," CLAY SAID. HIS SUITCASE WAS ON THE bed, and he was taking clothes out of the drawers and putting them into the case, while Clair was taking clothes out of the case, grouping them by a precise system he would never understand, and replacing them in the suitcase so that he would never find anything until he returned home and she helped him unpack. They had done this a lot.

"I must be nuts," Clay said. "I can't just go wandering around the oceans randomly looking for a lost friend. I'll look like that little bird in the book, the one that walks around asking everyone, 'Are you my mother?' "

"Sartre's *Being and Nothingness*?" Clair offered.

"Right. That's the one. It's ridiculous to even leave port until we have something to go on—steaming around, burning up fifty gallons of fuel an hour. The Old Broad may have money stashed, but she doesn't have that kind of money."

"Well, maybe something will turn up in the whale calls."

"I hope. Libby and Margaret have a lot of sonic data streaming in from Newport, but it's still like looking for a needle in a haystack. Clair, she saw guys climbing into a whale—"

"So, baby, what's the worst that happens? You go to sea and do your best to find Nate and you fail? How many people ever did their best at anything? You can always sell the ship later. Where is it now anyway?"

Just then the screen door fired back on its hinges and smacked against the outside wall with the report of a rifle shot. Kona came tumbling through the door waving pages of copy paper as if they were white flags and he was surrendering to everyone in the general Maui area.

"Bwana Clay!" Kona threw the pages down on Clay's suitcase. "It's the Snowy Biscuit!"

Clay picked up the pages, looked at them quickly, and handed one to Clair. Over and over the message was repeated:

41.93625s__76.17328W__-623__ CLAY U R NOT NUTS__AMY

Clay looked at Kona. "This was imbedded in the whale song."

"Yah, mon. Blue whale, I think. Just came in."

"Go back and see if there's more. And find the big world map. It's in the storeroom somewhere."

"Aye, aye," said Kona, who had begun to speak much more nautically since Clay had purchased the ship, making his bid to go along on the voyage to search for Nate. He ran back to the office.

"You think it's from Amy?" Clair said.

"I think it's either from Amy or from someone who knows everything about what we're doing, which means it would have to be someone Amy talked to."

"What are the numbers?"

"A longitude and a latitude. I'll have to look at the map, but it's somewhere in the South Pacific."

"I know it's a longitude and a latitude, Clay, but what's the minus six hundred and some?"

"It's where pilots usually express altitude."

"But it's a minus."

"Yep." Clay snatched the phone off of his night table and dialed the Old Broad as Clair looked quizzically at him. "Equipment change," he whispered to Clair, covering the receiver with his hand.

"Hello, Elizabeth, yes, things are going really well. Yes, they've picked up considerably. Yes. Look, I hate to ask this—I know you've done so much—but I may need one other little thing before we go to look for Nate and your James."

Clair shook her head at Clay's blatant playing of the missing-husband-shoved-up-a-whale's-bum card.

"Yes, well, it may be a little expensive," Clay continued. "But I'm going to need a submarine. No, a small submarine will be fine. If you want it to be yellow, Elizabeth, we'll paint it yellow."

After fifteen minutes of cajoling and consoling the Old Broad, making calls to Libby Quinn and the ship broker in Singapore (who offered him a quantity discount if he bought more than three ships in one month), Clay stood over a world map that was roughly the size of a Ping-Pong table, which Kona had spread out over the office floor, pinning the corners down with coffee cups.

"It's right there, off the coast of Chile," Clair said. She taught fourth-graders, and therefore basic world geography, so she could read a map like nobody's business. Kona placed a bottle cap on the spot where Clair was pointing.

"We'll need nautical charts and the ship's GPS to be exact, but, basically, yep, that's where it is." He looked at Kona. "Nothing else since that message?"

"Same thing for five minutes, then just normal whale gibberish. You think the Snowy Biscuit is with Nate?"

"I think she knew me well enough to know that I'd be thinking I was crazy to be looking. I also think that even if I believe the Old Broad's story about her husband, that doesn't explain how Amy was able to stay down for an hour on fifteen minutes' worth of air, so there was something going on with her that could be connected to this weirdness. She obviously knows more than we know, but—most important—we have nowhere else to look."

Kona looked at Clair, as if maybe she would answer his question. She nodded, and he resumed drinking his beer.

Clay got down on his hands and knees on the map. "The ship broker says there's a deepwater three-man sub here, in Chuuk, Micronesia, that's about to finish up with some filming they're doing of deep shipwrecks."

Kona put a bottle cap on the atoll of Chuuk, Micronesia.

"The owners will let me lease it for up to two months, but then a research team has it reserved for a deepwater survey in the Indian Ocean. The *Clair* is here, just north of Samoa." Clay pointed.

Kona put a third bottle cap just north of Samoa and did his best to drink off that beer while balancing the other two that he'd opened to get the caps.

"So the *Clair* can probably be in Chuuk in three days. I'll fly in and meet them, pick up the sub, and then we can probably steam to these coordinates in four or five days if we cruise at top speed," Clay said. "Now we're here—"

"We can't be, we can't be there," said Kona.

"Why not?"

"Out of beers."

"So you get to that spot. Then what?" Clair asked.

"Then I get in a submarine and see what there is to see six hundred and twenty-three feet down."

"So we're sure it's feet, not meters?"

"No. I'm not sure."

"Well, I just want you to know that I am not comfortable with you doing this sort of thing, Clay."

"But I've always done this sort of thing. I sort of do this sort of thing for a living."

"So what's your point?" Clair asked.

CHAPTER THIRTY-SIX

Black and White
and Red All Over

Once, off the coast of California, Nate had followed a pod of killer whales as they attacked a mother gray whale and her calf. They first approached in formation to separate the calf from the mother, and then, as one group broke from the pod to keep the mother busy, the others took turns leaping upon the calf's back to drown it—even as the mother thrashed her great tail and circled back, trying to protect her calf. The whole hunt had taken more than six hours, and when it ended, finally, the killer whales took turns hitting the exhausted calf, keeping in a perfect formation even as they ripped great chunks of flesh from its still-living body. Now, in the amphitheater, as the killer whaley boys approached—their teeth flashing, the breath from their blowholes puffing like steam engines—the biologist thought that he was probably experiencing exactly what that gray-whale calf had during that gruesome hunt. Except, of course, that Nate was wearing sneakers, and gray whales almost never did.

It was a big room. He had space to move. He just had to get around them. His sneakers squeaked on the floor as he came down the steps, faked right, then went left at a full sprint. The whaley boys, while amazingly agile in the water, were somewhat clumsy on land. Half of them fell for the fake so badly that they'd need a postcard to tell them how it all came out. They stooged into a whaley pile near the steps.

The remaining three pursuers tried to fan out into a new formation, the alpha female coming the closest to getting between Nate and the exit. Nate was running in a wide arc around the amphitheater now, and by virtue of sheer speed he could tell he'd beat at least two of the remaining killers, but the alpha female was going to intersect with him before he got clear. She probably weighed three times what he did, so there was no going though her with a vicious body check. Maybe if he'd been on skates, he'd have tried it: pit his pure, innate Canadian skating force against her paltry cetacean hunting instinct and drive that bitch to the mother of pearl. But there were no skates, no ice, so at the very last second, as the female was about to slam him in a bone-breaking crunch against one of the benches that lined the walls, Nate pulled a spin fake, a move that was much more Boitano than Gretzky but nevertheless sent the big female tumbling over a bench in a tangle of black-and-white and ivory—like a flaccid piano botching the vaulting horse. Nate high-stepped the last twenty yards to the door, thinking, *Yeah, three million years of walking upright not for nothing. Rookie. Meat.*

About the third step into his jubilation, Nate heard the sound of a great expulsion of air from his right, then a wet splat. Suddenly he saw his sneakers waving before his face. He felt the freedom of weightlessness, the exhilaration of flight, and then it was all gone as he slammed to the floor, knocking the wind out of himself. He slid to a stop in the huge loogie of whale spit that one of the trailing males had expectorated at his feet. Had he been able to breathe, he might have called a foul, but instead he struggled to get to his feet as the two males closed on him, showing dagger-toothed grins as they approached. *Oh, my God, they're going to eat me!* he thought, but then he saw that they both had unsheathed their long pink penises and were leading with a sort of a pelvic thrust. *Oh, my God, they're going to fuck me!* he thought. But when they got to him, one picked him up by the arms and bent him over forward, and he felt the great teeth scraping his scalp as his head slipped into the whaley boy's mouth. *No, they're definitely going to eat me,* Nate thought.

And in that suspension of time, right before the final crunch, amid the slow motion of an infinite last moment, clarity came to him, even as he screamed, and he thought, *This is probably not going to go as well as the last time I was eaten. There's probably not going to be a girl at the end of this one.*

And then the female whistled shrilly, and the male stopped biting down just as his teeth were starting to cut into Nate's cheeks. The biting male pulled back and apologetically wiped saliva and blood from Nate's face, then propped him up and fluffed him a little, as if to show that he was good as new. Nate was still being held fast by the other male, but the biter was grinning sheepishly at the alpha female and making a squeaking noise that Nate, even with his limited understanding of whaleyspeak, understood as meaning "oops."

A half hour later they threw him into his apartment, and the alpha female grinned at him as she tore the stainless-steel doorknob out of the wall. The wall bled for a while after she left, then clotted over and rapidly began to heal.

Nate stumbled into his bathroom and looked at himself in the mirror. There were bloody gashes down his forehead and cheeks. In another place and time, he realized, he would have gone to the emergency room to get stitched up. His hair was matted with blood, and he could feel at least four deep dents in his scalp where the whaley boy's teeth had broken the skin. There was a large knot at the back of his head where he'd hit the floor when he fell, and evidently he'd hit an elbow, too, because every time he bent his right arm, a sharp, biting pain shot all the way down to his fingertips.

He pulled off his bloodstained clothes and climbed into the shower. Then, ignoring the strange fixtures that usually gave him pause, he leaned against the shower walls and let the water run over him until the bloody crust was gone from his hair and his fingers had shriveled with the moisture. He dried himself, then collapsed into his bed, wishing for a last time before he fell asleep that Amy was there, safe, next to him.

He slept deeply and dreamed of a time when all the oceans were filled with a single living organism, wrapped like a cocoon around a single huge land mass. And in his dream he could feel the texture of every shore as if it were pressed against his skin.

NATE AWOKE IN THE EARLY HOURS BEFORE LIGHT CAME UP IN THE grotto. He went into his living room and sat in the dark by the big oval picture window that looked out over the street and, ultimately, the Gooville harbor. There were shapes out there moving in the dark. Every now and then he'd catch the reflection of some dim light on a whaley boy's skin, but mostly he could tell they were out there by the sonar clicks that echoed around the grotto and by the low, trilling whistles of whaley-boy conversation.

After an hour sitting there in the dark, he padded to the door and tried to open it. There was nothing but a smooth scar where the doorknob had been. The seal around the door was so tight it might have been part of the walls that framed it. In trying to work his fingers into the doorjamb, he realized that his elbow wasn't grating as it had been when he went to bed. He reached up to touch the gashes across his forehead and felt the scab flake away as easily and painlessly as dry skin. He immediately went to the bathroom and looked at himself in the mirror under the bright yellow bioluminescence. The gashes were healed. Completely healed. He brushed away the dried blood that had seeped after his shower to find new, healthy skin. It was the same with the dents in his scalp and the great goose egg at the base of his skull. He didn't even have a sore spot.

He returned to the living room, fell into the chair by the window, and watched the light come up in the grotto. Outside, there was a lot of movement in the street and the harbor, and, watching it, Nate started to feel sick to his stomach, despite his miraculous healing. All the movement outside was that of whaley boys. There wasn't a single human out there anywhere.

FOR TWO DAYS HE DIDN'T SEE ANY OTHER HUMANS IN GOOVILLE, AND even when he had screwed up his courage to use the buzzy, bug-winged speaky thing on the wall, he realized that he had no idea how to make it connect. By noon on the third day, he decided that he had to get out of the apartment. Not only couldn't he find Amy or do anything else while in here, but he was rapidly running out of food.

He reasoned that the best time to make a break for it was in the middle of the day, when it seemed that the number of whaley boys out on the street was sparsest, because so many of them went down to the water at that time to swim. He dressed in long pants and sleeves for protection, then made the first attempt at the window. He tore one of the bone chairs from the floor in the kitchen, wiggling it first, as if loosening a baby tooth. He cast the chair at the center of the window with all his strength, preparing as he did to make the ten-foot leap to the street when it went though. But it didn't. It bounced back into the room.

Next he looked for something sharp to try to puncture the window, but the only thing he could come up with were shards of the mirror in the bathroom, and although the mirror spider-webbed when he struck it, his fist wrapped in a towel, the shards stayed adhered to the bathroom wall, so all he'd really done was create a shiny mosaic. Finally, frustrated after three hours of ineffective attacks on the big window, he decided to hit it with the heaviest thing in the apartment: his body. He backed into the bedroom, sped through the living room, leaped into the air about halfway across, curled into a ball, and braced for impact. The window bulged out about three feet, until it appeared to the whaley boys outside that someone inside was trying to blow a giant bubble, and then it sprang back, trampolining Nate across the room into the far wall. At the bottom of the wall someone had installed a couch for just such an emergency, and Nate slid neatly into it with his newly flattened side down.

"Well, that was just stupid," he said aloud.

"Boy, that was stupid," Cielle Nuñez said. She came into the living room and sat in a chair across from where Nate was piled onto the couch. "You want to tell me what in the hell you started?"

"How did you get in? The knob is gone."

"Not on the outside. Come on, Nate, what did you do? Every human in Gooville has been locked down for the last three days. If I weren't the captain of a whale ship, I wouldn't have been able to come here either."

"I didn't do anything, Cielle, honestly. Where's Amy?"

"No one knows. Believe me, that was the first place they went."

"Who?"

"Who do you think? The whaley boys. They've taken over everything. Humans aren't even allowed near the ships. Ever since some of them heard you yelling about bringing the navy down here."

"I was. He has Amy, Cielle. I was just trying to get her back."

"Him? The Colonel? Why would he take Amy? She's one of the few who've ever even seen him. She's a favorite."

"Yeah, well no one is his favorite now." Right then Nate made a decision. He wasn't going to get out of this place on his own, and the only person he could even consider an ally was sitting right there in front of him. "Cielle, the reason the Colonel called your ships back, the reason no one is allowed to leave the harbor, is that he wants you all here when the place comes down. He's got some plan to get the U.S. Navy, or somebody's navy, to attack Gooville with a nuclear torpedo. He thinks that the Goo is going to destroy the human race if he doesn't destroy it first. He wanted me to go to the navy. He thought I could convince them of the threat because of my scientific credibility, but I said no. That's when he took Amy."

"So all that yelling I heard you doing in the amphitheater—that wasn't you talking about bringing the navy here, that was just you trying to get Amy back?"

"Yes. He's a loon, Cielle. I don't have any interest in bringing this place down. He thinks that there's some grand war going on between memes and genes, and that humans and the Goo are on opposite sides of it."

The whale-ship captain stood and nodded as if confirming something to herself. "Okay, then. That's what I needed to know. That's why he sent me here. I'll try to get them to send you some food."

"What? Help me get out of here." Nate suddenly had a very bad feeling about this whole exchange.

"I'm sorry, Nate. They have Cal. The whaley boys have him. You know how that feels. They told me I had to find out if you were plotting against the Colonel. Thank you for telling me. I think they'll let him go now."

She walked to the door, and Nate followed her. "Get me out of here, Cielle, at least—"

"Nate, there's nowhere to go. The only way out of here is a whale ship, and whaley-boy pilots are the only ones who can run them. They've been on notice not to let you on since we got here. Right now I couldn't leave if I wanted to." She pounded on the door. "Open!"

The door clicked open, and two all-black whaley boys stood outside waiting. They caught Nate by the shoulders and threw him back into the apartment as he tried to rush by them.

"My own crew, Nate," Cielle said. "See what you've done."

"He's going to kill you all, Cielle. Don't you see that? He's crazy."

"I don't believe you, Nate. I think you're the crazy one."

The door slammed shut.

BACK AT PAPA LANI, CLAY WAS DOING A FINAL CHECK ON THE EQUIP-ment he was taking with him to meet his new ship. Diving and camera equipment lay spread out across the office floor. Kona was going through the checklist on the clipboard with a felt-tip pen.

"So you tink the Snowy Biscuit going to be there?"

"I'm going. I just wish that we could answer her. Tell her I'm on my way."

"You mean, like, put the digital in the whale sound and send it?"

"Yeah, I know, we can't do it. Did you find a canister of soda lime for the rebreather's CO_2 scrubbers?"

"I can do that." Kona held up the canister Clay was looking for and checked it off the list.

"You can?"

"I been looking at it long time. She not that hard to put that message back in the call. But how you going to send it? You need some gi-grandious big speakers under the water, mon. We don't have nothing like dat."

Clay stopped his inventory and pulled Kona's clipboard down so he could see his eyes. "You can put a message into the waveform so it would come out the same way we've been taking it out?"

Kona nodded.

"Show me," Clay said. He went to the computer. Kona took the chair and pulled up a low-frequency waveform that looked like a jagged comb, and then he hit a button that took a small section and expanded it, which smoothed out the jags.

"See, this part here. We know this a letter B, right? We just cut it and paste with other letters, make a goofy whale call. I got all the letters but a Q and a Z figured."

"Don't explain, just do it. Here." Clay scribbled a short message in the margin of Kona's checklist. "Then play it for me."

"I can play, but you won't hear it. It's subsonic, brah. Like I say, you going need some thumpin' speakers to send it. You know where we can steal some?"

"We might not have to steal them."

While Kona pieced together the message, Clay grabbed the phone off his desk and dialed Cliff Hyland. The biologist answered on the second ring. "Cliff, Clay Demodocus. I need a favor from you. That big sonar rig of yours, will it broadcast subsonic frequencies? . . . Good, I need you to take us out on your boat tonight, with your rig."

Kona looked at Clay. Clay grinned and raised his eyebrows.

"No, it has to be tonight. I'm flying out for Chuuk in the morning. If I need to send out a signal, what can I plug in to it? Tape, disk recorder, what? Anything with a pre-amp?" Clay covered the receiver with his hand. "Can you put it on an audio disk?"

"No problems," Kona said.

"No problem," Clay said into the phone. "We'll meet you at the harbor at ten, okay?"

Clay waited. He was listening, pacing in a little circle behind the surfer. "Yeah, well, we were just talking about that, Cliff, and we figured that if you said no, we'd just have to steal your boat and your rig. I could probably figure out how the rig works, right?"

There was another pause and Clay held the phone away from his ear. Kona could hear an irritated voice coming out of the earpiece.

"Because we're friends, Cliff, that's why I'd tell you in advance that I was going to steal your boat. Jeez, you think I'd just steal it like some stranger? All right, then, we'll see you at ten o'clock." He hung up the phone.

"Okay, kid, get this right. We have to have it ready and to the harbor by ten."

"But what you gonna do the bad guys get it?"

"Even if they do, only Amy will know what it means," Clay said.

"Cool runnings, brah." Kona was concentrating on putting the message together, his tongue curled out the corner of his mouth as an antenna for focus.

Clay leaned over his shoulder and watched the waveform come together on the screen. "How did you figure this out, kid? I mean, it doesn't seem like you."

"How's a man supposed to work his science dub wid you yammerin' like a rummed-up monkey?"

"Sorry," Clay said, making a mental note to give the kid a raise if any of this actually worked.

CHAPTER THIRTY-SEVEN

A Whaley Death

Nate was five more days alone in the apartment before they came for him. It started at dawn on the sixth day, when he noticed a group of whaley boys gathering around below his window. There had been humans out on the streets since the day he'd told Cielle about the Colonel's plan, but Gooville hadn't quite returned to normal (given that normal in Gooville was still extraordinarily weird to begin with). He could tell that the humans and whaley boys alike were on edge. Today there were no humans in the streets, and all the whaley boys were emitting a shrill call that he was sure he'd heard before, but strangely enough it hadn't been in the city under the sea. Hearing the hunting call in these circumstances made him shudder.

He watch them gather, rubbing up against one another as if to strengthen the bond among them, milling around in small walking pods as if working off nervous energy, each of them raising his head occasionally and letting go the hunting call—flashing teeth, jaws snapping like bear traps. He knew they were coming.

Nate was dressed and waiting for them when they came through the door. Four of them took him, lifted him in the air by his legs and shoulders, and carried him over their heads down the stairs to the street, then on into the passageways. The whole crowd moved into the passageways, their calls becoming more frequent and deafeningly shrill in the smaller confines.

Even as his captors' long fingers dug into his flesh, a calm resolve came over Nate—an almost trancelike state, the acceptance that it was all going to be over soon. He looked to either side, only to have mouthfuls of teeth snarl at him, and even among the frenzy, here and there he heard the characteristic hissing snicker of a whaley-boy laugh. *Well, they do know how to have a good time,* he thought.

He soon recognized the path they were taking him down. He could hear the calls of hundreds of them echoing through the caverns from the mother-of-pearl amphitheater. Maybe the entire whaley-boy population was waiting there.

As they entered the amphitheater and the calls reached a crescendo, Nate stretched his neck and saw two big killer-whale-colored females holding the Colonel in the middle of the floor. The whaley boys holding Nate lowered him to his feet, and then two of them pulled him back against the benches to watch with the others.

One of the big females holding the Colonel shrieked a long, high call, and the crowd calmed down, not quite silent, but the hunting calls stopped. The Colonel's eyes were wide, and Nate wouldn't have been surprised if the old man had started to bark and foam at the mouth. When things quieted down enough for him to be heard, he started shouting. The big female who was holding him clamped a hand over his mouth. Nate could see the Colonel fighting for breath, and he struggled against his own captors in empathy. Then the female started to speak— in their whistling, clicking language—and the crowd stopped even snickering. Their eyes bulged, and they turned their heads to the side to better hear her.

Nate couldn't understand much of what she was saying, but you didn't have to know the language to understand what she was doing. She was listing the Colonel's crimes and pronouncing a sentence. It was no small irony, Nate thought, that the whaley boys who saw to justice were colored like the killer whales, the most intelligent, most organized, most glorious and horrible of all the marine mammals. The only animal other than man that had exhibited both cruelty and mercy, for one was not possible without potential for the other. Maybe memes were triumphing over genes after all.

When she finished speaking, she handed the Colonel's arm to the other female, so that he was bent over forward, his hands held together high behind him. Then the female let out another extended shrill call, and the whole ceiling of the amphitheater dimmed until it was completely dark. When she finished her call, the light came back up again. The Colonel was screaming at the top of his lungs, random curses and mad pronouncements—calling the whaley boys abominations, monsters, freaks, railing like some mad prophet, his brain fried by God's fingerprint. But when the light was full again, he caught Nate's eye, just for a second, and he was quiet. There was something there, the depth and wisdom that Nate had once known the man to possess, or maybe it was just sadness, but before Nate could decide, the big female bent over and bit off the Colonel's head.

Nate felt himself start to pass out. His vision tunneled down to a pinpoint and he fought to stay conscious, to concentrate on his breathing, which he realized had stopped momentarily. His vision came back, as did his breath, harsh and panicked through his gritted teeth as he watched.

The killer spit the head across the amphitheater to a group of whaley kids, who picked it up and tore at it with their teeth. Then the female started tearing great chunks of meat out of the Colonel's body with her teeth, even as it twitched in the hands of her cohort—throwing the chunks to the crowd, who shrilled the hunting calls even more frantically than before.

Nate couldn't tell how long it went on, but when it was finally done, and the Colonel was gone, there was a large red circle in the middle of the amphitheater floor, and all around him he saw bloody teeth flashing in whaley grins. Even the two whaley boys who held Nate's arms had partaken in the communion, grabbing chunks of meat and eating them with their free hands. One had hissed and sprayed blood in Nate's face. Then they dragged Nate to the middle of the amphitheater.

He felt faint, the pulse banging away in his ears, drowning out all other sound. Everywhere he looked, he saw bloody teeth and bulging eyes, but he felt strangely detached. As the big female began another oration, he remembered a thought he'd had right after the humpback whale had eaten him. It came through to him like a malicious déjà vu: *What an incredibly stupid way to die.*

Then there was another long, whistling call and Nate closed his eyes, waiting for the death blow, but it didn't come. The crowd had gone quiet again. He squinted through one eyelid, almost regretful that the moment had been delayed, and he saw teeth before him, but not the bloody teeth of the killers.

The shrill whistle went on and on, made by the mottled blue whaley-boy female that had come out of the passageway and was striding across the amphitheater toward Nate. At her side was a very determined, petite brunette with unnatural maroon highlights, wearing hiking shorts and a tank top. The whaley boys holding Nate seemed confused. The female who had killed the Colonel was looking for some sort of guidance from the one holding Nate when Amy pulled the stun gun from her pocket and blasted her in the chest, knocking her back five feet to convulse on the bloody floor.

"Let him go," Amy commanded the one who was holding Nate, and for some reason, maybe just because it sounded so definitive, she let go of Nate's arms, and he fell, at which time Amy pulled up a second stun gun and pressed it to the big killer's chest, knocking her to the floor to twitch with her companion. Through it all, Emily 7 had continued to whistle.

"You okay?" Amy asked Nate. He looked around at the situation, not sure at all if he was okay, but he nodded.

"Okay, Em," Amy said, and Emily stopped whistling.

Before the crowd could react or a murmur of whaleyspeak start, Amy shouted, "Hey, shut up!"

And they did.

"Nate didn't do anything," she continued. "The whole thing was the Colonel's idea, and none of us knew anything about it. He brought Nate here to help him destroy our city, and Nate said no. That's all you need to know. You all know me. This is my home, too. You know me. I wouldn't lie to you."

Just then the first big female started to recover, and Amy leaped in front of Nate to stand over the killer. "You get up, bitch, I'll knock you on your ass again. Your choice." The female froze. "Oh, fuck it," Amy said, and she zapped the big female on the nose with both stun guns at once, then wheeled on the other one, who was getting up but quickly dropped and played dead under Amy's gaze. "Good," Amy said.

"So we clear?" Amy shouted to the crowd.

There was whaleyspeak murmuring, and Amy screamed, "Are we fucking clear, people?"

"Yeah, clear," came a dozen little mashed-elf voices in English.

"Sure, sure, sure, you know it," said one little voice.

"Clear as a window," came another.

"Just kidding," said an elf-on-helium voice.

"Good," Amy said. "Let's go, Nate."

Nate was still trying to find his feet. His knees had gone a little rubbery when he thought his head was going to be bitten off. Emily 7 caught him by the arm and steadied him. Amy started to lead them out of the amphitheater, then stopped. "Just a second."

She went back to where the lead killer female was just climbing to her feet and zapped her in the chest with the stun gun, which knocked her flat on her back again.

As Amy strutted past Nate and Emily 7, she said, "Okay, now we can go."

"Where are we going?" Nate asked.

"Em says you slept with her."

Nate looked at Emily 7, who grinned, big and toothy, and snickered.

"Yeah, slept. Just slept. That's all. Tell her, Emily."

Emily whistled, actually a tune this time, and rolled her eyes.

"Really," Nate said.

"I know," Amy said.

"Oh." Nate heard squeaks coming from behind them in the corridor. "Wasn't that a little risky, taking on a thousand whaley boys with a couple of stun guns?"

"I love these things," Amy said, clicking the buttons to make miniature blue lightning arc across the contacts. "No, I didn't take on a thousand whaley boys, I took on one—an alpha female. Know what that makes me?" She smiled and then, without even breaking stride, threw her arms around his neck and kissed him. "And never forget it."

"I won't." Then that last week's anxiety about losing her came tumbling back over him. "Hey, where did you go? I thought the Colonel had taken you."

"I went out on my mother's ship to send a message."

"What message?"

"I was calling our ride. All the whaley boys had been put on notice: No pilot was going to take his ship out of here with you on board, still won't. But I could go, so I went out with my mother to pick up some supplies. And I called a ride."

"What, Emily 7 can't pilot a ship?"

"Uh-uh," squeaked Emily 7.

"Only pilots can pilot a ship, duh. Anyway"—Amy checked her watch—"your ride should be in the harbor soon. I have to go by my place and grab something I want to take."

━━◦◦━━

AN HOUR LATER THEY STOOD AT THE WATER'S EDGE IN THE HARBOR, and Amy was checking her watch again. "I am so pissed," she said, tapping her foot frantically.

It seemed as if every thirty seconds they had been cornered by some human resident of Gooville, and Amy had to tell the story again. Emily 7 was the only one of the whaley boys, other than the crew of Amy's mother's ship, that was still in the grotto.

"You think they'll revolt, hurt humans?" Nate asked.

"No, they'll be fine. That was a first. It's not every day you find out that your messiah is plotting to kill you. Give 'em a day or two to get over the embarrassment—everything will be back to normal."

"I guess it's just as well that we're getting out of here. You don't want to face those two females you zapped."

"Bring it on," Amy said, patting the pockets of her shorts. "Besides, I'm sort of special here, Nate. I don't want to sound egotistical, but they really all do know me, know who I am, what I am. No one will bother me."

Just then Nate spotted a light coming from deep in the mirror-calm water.

"That's him," Amy said.

"Him?"

"Clay, coming to take you home."

"Me? You mean us."

"Em, can I get a minute?" Amy said.

" 'Kay," said Emily 7, skulking away from the shore toward town.

When Emily was out of hearing range, Amy put her arms around Nate and leaned back to look at him. "I can't go with you, Nate. I'm staying."

"What do you mean? Why?"

"I can't go. There's something about me you don't know. Something I should have told you before, but I thought you wouldn't . . . well, you know—I thought you wouldn't love me."

"Please, Amy, please don't tell me you're a lesbian. Because I've been through that once, and I don't think I could survive it again. Please."

"No, nothing like that. It's about my parents . . . well, my father really."

"The navigator?"

"Uh, no, not really. Actually, Nate, this is my father. She pulled a small specimen jar out of her pocket and held it up. There was a pink, jellylike substance in it.

"That looks like—"

"It is, Nate. It's the Goo. My mother was never intimate with her navigator, or with anyone in the first three years she was here, but one morning she woke up pregnant."

"And you're sure it was the Goo, not just that she had way too many mai-tais at the Gooville cabana club?"

"She knows it, and I know it, Nate. I'm sort of not normal."

"You feel normal." He pulled her closer.

"I'm not. For one thing, I don't just look a lot younger than I really am, but I'm also a lot stronger than I look, especially as a swimmer. Remember that day I found the humpback ship by sound? I really can hear directional sound underwater. And my muscle tissue is different. It stores oxygen the way a whale's tissue does, I can stay underwater without breathing for over an hour, longer if I don't exert myself. I'm the only one like me, Nate. I'm not really, you know . . . human."

Nate listened, trying to weigh what it really meant in the bigger picture, but he couldn't think of anything except that he wanted her to go with him, wanted her to be with him, no matter what she said she was. "I don't care, Amy. It doesn't matter. Look, I got over all this"—he gestured to all that—"and the fact that you're sixty-four years old and your mother is a famous dead aviatrix. As long as you don't start liking girls, I'll be fine."

"That's not the point, Nate. I can't leave here, not for long anyway. None of us can. Even the ones who weren't born here. The Goo becomes part of you. It takes care of you, but you become attached to it, almost literally. Like an addiction. It gets in your tissues by contact. That's how my mother had me. I've been gone a lot already this year. If I left now, or if I left for longer that a few months at a time, I'd get sick. I'd probably die."

At that moment a yellow research submersible bubbled up to the surface of the lagoon, a dozen headlights blazing into the grotto around a great Plexiglas bubble in the front.

"That's it, then. I'll stay. I don't mind, Amy. I'll stay here. We can live here. I could spend a lifetime learning about this place, the Goo."

"You can't do that either. It will become part of you, too. If you stay too long, you won't be able to leave either. You had to have noticed that first night we got drunk together, how fast you recovered from the hangover."

Nate thought about how quickly his wounds had healed, too—weeks, maybe months of healing overnight. There was no other explanation. He thought about spending his life with only fleeting glimpses of sunlight, and he said, "I don't care. I'll stay."

"No you won't. I won't let you. You have things to do." She shoved the specimen jar in his pocket, then kissed him hard. He kissed her back, for a long time.

The hatch at the top of the dry exit tower on the sub opened, and Clay popped up to see Nate and Amy for the first time since they'd both disappeared.

"Well, that's unprofessional," Clay said.

Amy broke the kiss and whispered, "You go. Take that with you." She patted his pocket. Then she turned to Clay as she checked her watch again. "You're late!"

"Hey, missy, I set a time when I'd be at the coordinates you sent—six hundred and twenty-three feet below sea level—and I was there. You didn't mention that I had another mile of submarine cave with some of the scariest-looking rock formations I've ever seen." He glanced at Nate. "They looked alive."

"They are alive," Amy said.

"Are we close to the surface? The pressure is—"

"I'll explain on the way," Nate said. "We'd better go." Nate stepped onto the sub as Clay slipped down inside the hatch to allow him to pass. Nate crawled into the hatch and looked back to Amy before he closed it.

"I'll stay, Amy. I don't care. For you I'll stay. I love you. You know that, right?"

She nodded and brushed tears out of her eyes. "Yeah," she said, Then she spun around quickly and started walking away. "You take care of yourself, Nathan Quinn," she shouted over her shoulder, and Nate heard her voice break when she said his name.

He climbed down into the sub and secured the hatch above him.

Clay had watched Amy walk away from the big, half-submerged Plexiglas bubble in the front of the sub.

"Where's Amy going?"

"She can't come home, Clay."

"She's okay, though?"

"She's okay."

"You okay?"

"I've been better."

They were quiet for the long ride through the pressure locks to the outside ocean, just the sound of the electric motors and the low hum of instruments all around them. The lights of the sub barely reached out to the walls of the cave, but every hundred yards or so they would come to a large, pink disk of living tissue, like a giant sea anemone, which would fold back to let them pass, then expand to fill the passageway once they had gone through. Nate watched the pressure gauge rise one atmosphere every time they passed through one of the gates, and it was then that he realized he wasn't escaping at all. The Goo knew exactly where and what they were, and it was letting him go.

"You're going to explain what all this is, right?" Clay said, not even looking away from the controls.

Nate was startled out of his reverie. "Clay, I can't believe—I mean, I believe it, but— Thanks for coming to get me."

"I never told you, you know—it's not really appropriate or anything—but I have pretty strong feelings about loyalty."

"Well, I respect that, Clay, and I appreciate it."

"Yeah, well, don't mention it."

Then they were both a bit embarrassed and both pretended that something was irritating their throats and they had to cough and pay attention to their breathing for a while, even though the air in the little submarine was filtered and humidified and perfectly clean.

CHAPTER THIRTY-EIGHT

Pirates

Nate was standing with Clay on the flying bridge of the *Clair* as she steamed into the Au'au Channel.

"You'd better put on some sunscreen, Nate."

Nate looked down at his forearms. He'd lost most of his color while in Gooville, and he could feel the sun cooking him, even through his T-shirt.

"Yeah." He looked off toward Lahaina, the harbor he'd piloted into a thousand times. They'd have to anchor far outside the breakwater with a ship this size, but it still had the feeling of coming home. The wind was warm and sweet, the water the heartbreak blue of a newborn's eyes. A humpback fluked about eight hundred yards to the north of them, its tail glistening in the sun as if it were covered with sequins.

"There's still a month left of the season," Clay said. "We can still get some work done."

"Clay, I've been thinking. Maybe we can be a little more purposeful in what we're doing. Maybe a little more active, conservation-wise."

"I could go for that. I like whales."

"I mean, we have the resources now, and even if I could prove the meaning of the song—somehow decipher the vocabulary of it—I could never prove the purpose. You know, without compromising Gooville."

"Not a good idea." During the trip home Nate had explained it all.

"I mean, there's no reason we can't do good science and still, you know—"

"Kick some ass."

"Well, yeah."

Clay affected an exaggerated Greek accent. "Sometimes, boss, you just got to unbuckle your pants and go looking for trouble."

"Zorba?"

"Yeah." Clay grinned.

"Great book," Nate said. "Is that the *Always Confused*?"

Clay pulled up a pair of binoculars and focused on a speedboat that was rounding the Lahaina breakwater, showing more wake than she should in the harbor. Kona was driving the *Always Confused*.

"My boat," Clay said, somewhat distressed.

"You need to get over that, Clay."

The speedboat came around to a parallel course with the *Clair* as the ship cut her engines in preparation to drop anchor. Kona was waving and screaming like a madman. "Irie, Bwana Nate! Irie! The lion come home! Praise Jah's mercy. Irie!"

Nate came down the steps from the flying bridge to the deck. Whatever resentment he might have had for the surfer at one time was gone. Whatever threat he might have felt from the boy had melted away. Whatever irrelevancy Kona's youth and strength might have underscored in his own character was irrelevant. Maybe it was time to be an example instead of a competitor. Besides, he was genuinely glad to see the kid. "Hey, kid, how you doing?"

"Jammin' now, don't you know."

"That's good. How'd you like to go be a pirate?"

———⌇———

BECAUSE THE NAVY DIDN'T MAINTAIN PERMANENT OFFICES ON MAUI, Captain L. J. Tarwater had been given a small office that the navy sublet for him in the Coast Guard building, which meant that, unlike on a naval base, here the public could pretty much come and go as they wished. So Tarwater wasn't that surprised to see someone come strolling through his office door. What he was surprised by was that it was Nathan Quinn, whom he thought quite drowned, and who was carrying a four-gallon glass jar full of some clear liquid.

"Quinn, I thought you were lost at sea."

"I was. I'm found now. We need to have a chat." He set the jar on Tarwater's desk, leaving a wet ring on some papers there, then went back and shut the door to the outer offices.

"Look, Quinn, if this is some kind of stunt, like spray-painting fur, you're wasting your time. You guys act like the military is the great Satan. I'm here to study these animals. I grew up in the same generation you did, and so did most of the people in the navy who do what I do. We don't want to hurt these animals."

"Okay," Nate said. "We only have two things to talk about here. Then I'll show you something."

"What's in the jar? That better not be kerosene or anything."

"It's seawater. I got it at the beach about ten minutes ago. Don't worry about it. Look, first you're going to finish your study and you're going to strongly recommend that the navy's torpedo range not be moved into the sanctuary. You will not let that happen. The animals do dive to depths where they can be hurt by the explosions, and they *will* be hurt by the explosions, which you'll be setting off not to defend the country but just so you guys can practice."

"There's no evidence that they ever dive deeper than two hundred feet."

"There will be. I've got data tags coming in from the mainland, I'll have data in a month."

"Still . . ."

"Shut up," Nate said, then thought better of it and added, "Please." Then he continued. "Second, you need to do everything in your power to back off of testing low-frequency active sonar. We know that it kills deepwater hunters like beaked whales, and there's probably some chance that it also injures the humpbacks, and under no circumstances do you want to do that."

"And why would that be?"

"You know what my work has been for the last twenty-five years, right?"

"You've been studying the humpback song. What, trying to figure its purpose?"

"I found it, Tarwater. It's a prayer. The singers are praying."

"That's preposterous. There's no way you could know that."

"I'm positive of it. Absolutely positive. I know it's a prayer, and that the torpedo base and LFA will harm a God-fearing animal." Nate paused to let it sink in, but Tarwater just looked at him like he was an annoying rodent that had crawled in from the cane fields.

"How could you possibly know that, Quinn?"

"Because their prayers are answered." Nate took a portable tape recorder out of his shirt pocket and set it on the desk next to the seawater, into which he'd already mixed part of the Goo that Amy had given him. He pushed the "play" button, and the sound of humpback-whale song filled the office.

"This is ridiculous," Tarwater said.

"Watch," Nate said, pointing to the water, which began to swirl, a tiny pink vortex forming in the middle.

"Get out of here. I'm not impressed with your Mr. Wizard tricks, Quinn."

"Watch," Nate said again. As they watched, the pink vortex expanded while the whale song played, until half the jar was filled with a moving pink stain. Then Nate turned off the tape.

"So what?" Tarwater said.

"Look more closely." Nate opened the jar, reached in, strained out some of the pink, and threw it on Tarwater's desk. Tiny shrimp—each only an inch long—flipped about on the blotter. "Krill," Nate said.

Tarwater didn't say anything. He just looked at the krill, then scraped a couple into his hand and examined them more closely. "They are krill."

"Uh-huh."

"What, it's like Sea Monkees, right? You had brine-shrimp eggs in there."

"No, Captain Tarwater, I did not. The humpbacks are praying, and God is answering them, giving them food. We could run this little experiment a hundred times, and that water would be clear when we started and full of krill when we ended. Trust me, I've done it." And he had. The little bit of Goo in the water created the krill out of the other life in there, the ubiquitous SAR-11 bacteria that existed in every liter of seawater on the planet.

Tarwater held up the krill. "But I thought they didn't eat when they were here."

"You're thinking on too small a scale. They don't feed for four months, and then they do nothing but feed. They're thinking in advance—the way you might think about breakfast before you go to bed at night. Doesn't matter, really. What you need to do, Captain, is everything in your power and influence to stop the range and the LFA testing."

Tarwater looked stunned now. "I'm just a captain."

"But you're an ambitious captain. I can have a jar of seawater on the secretary of the navy's desk in ten hours. Do you really want to be the one to explain to this administration that you're hurting an animal that prays to God? Particularly *this* administration?"

"No, sir, I do not," said Tarwater, looking decidedly more frightened than he had been just a second before.

"I thought you were an intelligent man. I trust you'll handle this, and this will be the last anyone will hear of my jar."

"Yes, sir," Tarwater said, more out of habit than respect.

Nate took his tape recorder and his jar and walked out, grinning to himself, thinking about the praying humpbacks. *Of course, it's not your particular God,* he thought, *but they do pray, and their god does feed them.*

He headed back to Papa Lani to make the calls and write the paper that would torpedo any hope of Jon Thomas Fuller's ever building a captive dolphin petting zoo on Maui.

A pirate's work is never done.

❧◉❧

THREE MONTHS LATER THE *CLAIR* CRUISED INTO THE COLD COASTAL waters off Chile on her way to Antarctica to intercept, stop, harass, and generally make business difficult for the Japanese whaling ship *Kyo Maru.* Clay was at the helm, and when the ship reached a precise point on the GPS receiver, he ordered the engines cut. It was a sunny day, unusually calm for this part of the Pacific. The water was so dark blue it almost appeared black.

Clair was below in their cabin. She'd been seasick for most of the voyage, but she had insisted on coming along despite the nausea, using her saber-edged persuasive skills on the captain. ("Who's got the pirate booty? All right, then, help me pack.")

Nate stood on the deck at the bow, his arm around Elizabeth Robinson. Above them swung an eighteen-foot rigid-hull Zodiac on a crane, ready to drop into the water whenever it was needed. There was another one on the stern, where once the submarine had been stowed. Up on the flying bridge, Kona scanned the sea around them with a pair of "big-eye" binoculars on a heavy iron mount that was welded to the railing.

"There's one, a thousand yards."

Clay came out onto the walkway beside Kona. They all looked to starboard, where the residual cloud of a whale blow was hanging over the calm water.

"Another one!" Clay shouted, pointing to a second blow closer to the ship off the port bow.

Then they started firing into the air as if triggered by a chained fuse: whale blows of different shapes, heights, and angles—great explosions of spray erupting so close to the ship now that the decks started to glisten with the moisture. Then the backs of the great whales rolled in the water around them, gray and black and blue, hills of slick flesh on all sides, moving slowly, then lying in the water. Nate and Elizabeth moved up to the bow railing and watched a group of sperm whales lolling in the water like logs just a few feet off the bow. Next to them a wide right whale floated, bobbing gently in the swell, only a slow wave of the tail revealing that the creature was alive. It rolled to one side, and its eye bulged as it looked at them.

"You okay?" Nate asked Elizabeth, squeezing her shoulder. This was the first time she'd been out on the water in over forty years. In her hands she clutched a brown paper lunch bag.

"They're still amazing up close. I'd forgotten."

"Just wait."

There were probably a hundred animals of different species around the ship now, most rolled on their side, one eye bulged out to focus in the air. Their blows settled into a syncopated rhythm, like cylinders of some great engine firing in succession.

Kona jumped up and down next to Clay, praising Jah and laughing as each animal breathed or flicked a tail. "Irie, my whaley friends!" he shouted, waving to the animals close to the boat. Clay desperately resisted the urge to grab up cameras and start blasting film or digital video. It felt like he had to pee, really badly, from his eyes.

"Nate," Clay called, and he pointed to a bubble net forming just outside the ring of floating whales. They'd seen them dozens of times in Alaska and Canada, one humpback circling and releasing a stream of bubbles to corral a school of fish while others plunged up through the middle to catch them. The circle of bubbles became more pronounced on the surface, as if the water were boiling, and then a single humpback breached through the ring, cleared the water completely, and landed on its side in white crater of splash and spray.

"Oh, my goodness!" Elizabeth said. Flustered, she pressed her face into Nate's jacket, then looked back quickly, lest she miss something.

"They're showing off," Clay said.

The lolling whales lazily paddled out of the way, opening a corridor to the ship. The humpback motorboated toward the bow, its knobby face riding on top of the water. When it was only ten yards from the bow, the animal rose up in the water and opened its mouth. Amy stood up, and next to her stood James Poynter Robinson.

"Hey, can we get a ladder down here?" Amy shouted.

"Praise Jah's mercy," Kona said, "the Snowy Biscuit has come home."

Nate threw a cargo net over the side, then climbed halfway down and pulled Amy up onto the net. He held her there as the ship moved in the swell, and she tried to kiss him and nearly chipped a tooth.

"Help me with Elizabeth," Nate said.

Together they got the Old Broad down the cargo net and handed her to her husband, who stood on the tongue of a whale and hugged his bride after not seeing her for four decades.

"You look so young," Elizabeth said.

"We can fix that," he said.

"You'll get old?"

"Nope." He looked back to Nate and saluted. Nate could hear whaley-boy pilots snickering inside the whale.

"I brought you a pastrami on rye," she said.

Poynter took the paper bag from her as if he were accepting the Holy Grail.

Nate and Amy scrambled up the cargo net and stood at the bow as the whale drifted away from the bow.

"Thank you, Nate," the Old Broad said, waving. "Thank you, Clay."

Nate smiled. "We'll see you soon, Elizabeth."

"We will, you know," Amy said as the whale ship closed and sank back into the waves.

"I know."

"I have to come back here every few months, you know."

"I know."

"Forever."

"Yeah, I know."

"I'm the new colonel now. I'm sort of in charge down there, you know, since I'm sort of the daughter of their god. So we'll have to spend time down there."

"Do I have to call you 'Colonel'?"

"What, you have a problem with that?"

"No, I'm okay with that."

"You realize that the Goo really could decide to wipe out the human species at any minute."

"Yep. Same as it's always been."

"And you know if I live out here, I'm not always going to, you know, look like this?"

"I know."

"But I will always be luscious, and you—you will always be a hopeless nerd."

"Action nerd," Nate corrected.

"Ha!" Amy said.

Science and Magic

"THE SCIENCE YOU DON'T KNOW LOOKS LIKE MAGIC," KONA SAYS IN Chapter 30. I have generally come down on the side of magic, simply because it involves less math, but with *Fluke* it was necessary to learn a little science. Because so much of *Fluke* does fall into the realm of magic, though, I thought it only fair to give you, gentle reader, some idea of what's fact and what's not.

The body of knowledge on cetacean biology, especially as it relates to behavior, is growing at such a staggering rate that it's hard to be sure of what you know from one day to the next. (This happens to be exactly the way I live my life, so that worked out nicely.) Scientists have been studying humpback song for fewer than forty years, and it's only in the last decade that studies have been undertaken to try to relate the song to social behavior and interaction. (And a challenging question there: *What constitutes interaction in an animal whose voice can carry a thousand miles?*) As I write this, September 2002, much about the humpback song is still unknown. (Although scientists do know that it tends to be found in the New Age music section, as well as in tropical waters. There is no reasonable explanation for this, but as of yet no tagged humpbacks have been tracked to the New Age section at Sam Goody's.)

At this point no one has ever seen or filmed the mating of humpbacks, so while it would appear that the song has something to do with mating, because it is performed only by males and because it is sung only during the mating season, no one has drawn a direct correlation between the song and mating. Theories abound: The males are marking territory sonically, they are showing their fitness and size by singing, they are calling mates, they are just saying "howdy"—all of the above, none of the above. The fact remains that, regardless of its purpose, the humpback-whale song is the most complex piece of nonhuman composition on earth. Whether it's art, prayer, or a booty call, the humpback song is an amazing thing to experience firsthand, and I suspect that even once the science of it is put to bed, it will remain, as long as they sing, magic.

Beyond the song, much of the whale behavior and biology described in *Fluke* is accurate, or as accurate as I could keep it and not overburden the story. (Excepting the whale ships, the whaley boys, and every killer whale's being named Kevin, all of which I made up. Killer whales are actually all named Sam. Duh.) The acoustic data, and the analysis thereof, is generally balderdash. While scientists do indeed collect data in the manner described, much of the analysis process came from my imagination. For the record, though, low-frequency whale calls can and do travel thousands of miles under the sea.

While the Lahaina Harbor is indeed inundated with whale researchers every winter, and while there are indeed lectures given periodically at the Whale Sanctuary visitor center, the acrimony, competition, and tension described among the researchers is completely of my own creation, as are the individual descriptions and personalities of the characters. Tension among a bunch of neurotics is just more interesting for a story than is a description of dedicated professionals doing their work and getting along, which is the case in reality. When in doubt, assume I made it up.

The reason we shouldn't kill whales
is because they fire the imagination.
—JAMES DARLING, PH.D.

HEY, I THOUGHT THEY WERE SAVED ALREADY! NO ONE LIKES THE
"We're glad you enjoyed this story about the rain forest with all its cute lit-
tle animals and charming native people, BECAUSE IT WILL ALL BE
A CHARRED DESERT NEXT WEEK!" approach, and I hate to do it
to you, but you should know that much of the conservation information
in *Fluke* is accurate. They aren't quite saved.

The Japanese and the Norwegians continue to practice whaling,
each taking up to five hundred minke whales a year under "scientific research" permits (the meat ends up in markets in Europe and Asia). Despite "free market" arguments to the contrary, whaling is not a profitable
business in Japan. It is subsidized by the government, and, to bolster
consumer demand, they have introduced whale meat into the school
lunch program so children will develop a taste for it. (Good thinking
there. Don't we all crave the cafeteria cuisine of our youth? Mmmm,
mashed peas.) Biologists working undercover in Japanese markets (spy
nerds), by running DNA tests, have found endangered whale species
(including blue whale) in cans of whale meat labeled as "minke whale
meat." (So someone is still killing them.)

Except for scientific whaling, the International Whaling Commission's moratorium on hunting great whales is still in effect, but several
whaling nations are rallying hard to have the moratorium lifted and finance survey studies to prove that great-whale populations, including
humpbacks and grays, have recovered enough for them to resume hunting. The U.S. antiwhaling position in the IWC is severely compromised
by the fact that they support aboriginal whaling—that is, subsistence
hunting by indigenous people. The argument for aboriginal whaling by

the actual indigenous people is seldom made on a basis of subsistence, but more often because hunting whales is a "cultural tradition of their people that must be preserved." This, of course, is utter bullshit. It's a tradition of Americans of European descent to commit genocide on indigenous people, but that doesn't mean we ought to start doing it again. Even some old ideas are still bad ideas.

While it is true that many whale species seem to be recovering, like the gray and the humpback, other populations still struggle, and some, like the North Atlantic right whale, may yet disappear from the planet. (Not due to hunting, but as one researcher, whom I won't name, said, "because they're stupid as shit and won't get out of the way when they hear a ship coming." Hell, I almost wreck when a squirrel runs in front of my car, and there're millions of them. I can't imagine trying to keep a supertanker from going in the ditch while swerving to avoid one of the last remaining right whales.) Recent surveys estimate (and they can only estimate, because scientists can't find enough of the animals to actually count—I guess when you find one, you just have to count the bejeezus out of him, then extrapolate with algorithms and computer projections) that there may be fewer than three hundred North Atlantic right whales left in the world.

But on a happier note, some of the populations are recovering, and although the Japanese government appears to be a bunch of nimrods (and who are we to talk?), the Japanese people seem more interested in watching whales than eating them, so the pressure to extend the hunt may relent.

The kicker to all this is probably that habitat loss and pollution, not hunting, present the greatest threat to marine mammals. (Wha . . . ? Habitat loss, don't they have the whole ocean?) For the most part our oceans are great, wet deserts, with millions of square miles in which life is very sparse. Predictably, human populations have started to compete with marine mammals for the food sources, and, under increased demand and improved fishing methods, many once rich fishing grounds are becoming as barren as a clear-cut forest. Hydroelectric dams that restrict the migration of salmon and other species to their freshwater breeding grounds are already having an impact on the populations of marine mammals that feed on the adult salmon.

As industrial pollution and agricultural runoff take toxic chemicals to the ocean, it would seem that the enormous volume of seawater would dilute these chemicals to harmless levels, and that's what happens until the chemicals are gathered up by a mechanism called the food chain. Recent studies of tissue samples of some toothed whales (killer whales and dolphins, who feed fairly high up on the food chain) show levels of man-made toxins so high that the animal's blubber actually qualifies as toxic waste. Studies are now going on to determine if declining marine mammal populations on the west coast of North America may not be caused by the lower birth rates and the compromised immune systems of animals who feed on toxic fish. (Oh yeah, guess who else is at the top of the seafood chain?)

You want to help? Pay attention. Caring about the condition of our oceans does not make you a psycho, tree-hugging, bleeding-heart liberal, it just makes you smart. The health of all life on this planet depends on the health of the oceans. It's just good business. (Even a supply-sider has to admit that if you fish a population to extinction, there will be no supply, so there will be no demand. It's bad economics from the right or the left.) So watch what you eat, and don't eat fish that are being overfished (like Chilean sea bass, for instance). And don't pour the used oil from your oil change down the storm drain unless you want your next shrimp platter to taste like Quaker State and you sort of like the idea of having your own children born with flippers.

And go look at some whales. Not captive ones, wild ones. It all comes down to economics, and as long as it's more profitable to have whales around to look at, we'll have them around to look at. If you don't live near water and can't get to any, rent a whale video. It all comes around.

Barring that, just yell at people randomly to stop killing whales. It could catch on. Really.

("Would you like fries with that?"

"Shut up and stop killing whales!"

"Thank you. Drive through, please.")

· A C K N O W L E D G M E N T S ·

FIRST, MY THANKS TO THE HOME TEAM: TO CHARLEE RODGERS, AS usual, for thoughtful reads and cogent comments; to my editor, Jennifer Brehl; and to my agent, Nicholas Ellison, who a couple of years ago said, "Hey, how about a book about whale song? I don't know—like there's meaning in it or something. You figure it out." Blame or credit goes to Nick for that. As always, thanks to Dee Dee Leichtfuss for being my "reader without an agenda." Thanks, too, to Galen and Lynn Rathbun, for taking time away from studying the hose-nose shrew to fill me in on the home life of the field biologist and for putting me in touch with the people at NOAA.

My thanks also to Kurt Preston for geological information, to Dr. David Kirkpatrick for information on genetics, to Mark Joseph for my "Introduction to Sonar" phone lecture, and to Bret Huffman for Rasta-Pidgin tutoring.

Much of the background on genes, evolution, and memes came from the work of Richard Dawkins: *The Selfish Gene, The Blind Watchmaker, The Extended Phenotype,* and others; also from Daniel Dennett's *Darwin's Dangerous Idea* and from Susan Blakemore's excellent book *The Meme Machine.* I recommend them all for further reading, but when you're finished, you may have to read several of my books and watch a lot of TV just to get stupid enough to function in the modern world again. Fortunately I am gifted in this respect and have recovered nicely, thank you.

The laser-measurement algorithm described in Chapter 1 was formulated by Dr. John Calambokidis of the Cascadia Research Collective. He should get credit for that as well as for many other contributions to the field.

Many of the research anecdotes I used in *Fluke* were fashioned out of stories told to me by the researchers themselves. The story of the Japanese whalers being affected by seeing a mother sperm whale and her calf (Chapter 30) was told to me by Bob Pittman of the Southwest Fisheries Science Center. The story of the Pacific Biological Research Project, where the military funded a feasibility study to use seabirds as a biological-warfare vector, was told to me by Lisa Ballance, Bob's wife, who also works at NOAA's Southwest Fisheries Science Center.

Thanks, too, to Dr. Wayne Perryman, also from NOAA, who shared many hours of stories, providing me with information about the lifestyles of researchers. My thanks to Dr. Perryman as well for inviting me to observe the California gray whale survey in person and not insisting that I always bring the pizza.

Thanks to Jay Barlow from NOAA's Southwest Fisheries Science Center for information on navy research projects and the relationship between researchers and the navy. Much of which I blew off so I could put Captain Tarwater in Maui, but still, thanks, Jay.

My thanks, too, to Carol DeLancey of Oregon State University's Marine Mammal Program, who told me the great story of the female right whale using a researcher's Zodiac as a diaphragm while the researchers were assaulted by a pair of prehensile whale willies (Chapter 8)—something that happened directly to Dr. Bruce Mate, but which I embellished in that I don't believe that the whales ejaculated in the boat, and Dr. Mate did not become a lesbian.

For information on underwater acoustics and the nature and range of blue-whale calls, much of which I totally ignored, many thanks to Dr. Christopher G. Fox of the Hatfield Marine Science Center in Newport, Oregon. It was Chris's description of an unidentified, persistent throbbing noise coming from deep under the Pacific Ocean, somewhere off the coast of Chile, that first inspired the undersea city of Gooville.

For the inside story on harbor life in Lahaina and the dating life of the female researcher, my thanks to Rachel Cartwright and Captain Amy Miller, who study humpback cow/calf behavior and biology in Maui in the winter and Alaska in the summer.

My thanks, too, to Kevin Keyes for whale and dolphin stories, as well as for his infinite patience in teaching me ocean kayaking and providing the "cold-water discipline" safety training that probably kept me from drowning while trying to get out among the animals.

Finally, my deepest thanks to Dr. Jim Darling, Flip Nicklin, and Meagan Jones, who for two seasons allowed me to ride along and observe their research in Maui, as well as for giving generously of their time to answer my questions both in person and by e-mail. While most of the information about humpbacks and humpback song in *Fluke* came out of these trips, the inaccuracies and liberties taken with the information are my own. The anecdotes and science I learned from these folks, all of whom have spent their lives working in the field, were enough to fill two books, and were certainly too voluminous to list here. Simply put, this book would not have been possible without their help. Kinder, more intelligent, more dedicated people than these do not the face of this earth walk.

To support their ongoing research on humpback song and behavior, send your tax-deductible donations to:

Whale Trust
300 Paani Place
Paia, HI 96779

STRAP YOURSELVES IN, LADIES AND GENTLEMEN,

IT'S CHRISTOPHER MOORE TIME!

FOOL: A Novel
ISBN 978-0-06-059031-4 (new in hardcover) • ISBN 978-0-06-171987-5 (large print) • ISBN 978-0-06-171259-3 (unabridged CD)

"This is a bawdy tale. Herein you will find gratuitous shagging, murder, spanking, maiming, treason, and heretofore unexplored heights of vulgarity and profanity, as well as non-traditional grammar, split infinitives, and the odd wank. If that sort of thing bothers you, then gentle reader pass by, for we endeavor only to entertain, not to offend. That said, if that's the sort of thing you think you might enjoy, then you have happened upon the perfect story!"

YOU SUCK: A Love Story
ISBN 978-0-06-059030-7 (paperback) • ISBN 978-0-06-122718-9 (unabridged CD)

C. Thomas Flood (better known as Tommy) has awakened. He and the girl of his dreams, Jody, have just shared a physical intimacy unlike any Tommy has known before. He opens his eyes, sees Jody smiling down at him, opens his mouth, and says, "You bitch, you killed me. You suck!" For Jody is a vampire. And now Tommy's one, too.

A DIRTY JOB: A Novel
ISBN 978-0-06-059028-4 (paperback) • ISBN 978-0-06-087259-5 (unabridged CD)

Charlie Asher's safe life is about to take a really weird detour when his daughter, Sophie, is born—minutes before his wife dies of a freak medical condition. As if being a widower and single parent aren't enough, soon people begin to drop dead around Charlie, and he discovers that his worst fears were molehills compared to the mountain of poo he's now in.

THE STUPIDEST ANGEL: A Heartwarming Tale of Christmas Terror
ISBN 978-0-06-084235-2 (hardcover) • ISBN 978-0-06-073874-7 (unabridged CD)

Ah, Christmas—the hap-hap-happiest season of all! Except for Pine Cove constable Theo Crowe, who's looking for the evil local developer who disappeared after playing Santa at the Caribou Lodge Christmas party. Meanwhile the town braces for the annual onslaught of holiday tourists and the storm of the century. Oh, and did we mention the tall blonde stranger—a clueless angel sent to Earth on a mysterious mission—who arrives looking for "a child"? Yikes! Pass the eggnog.

FLUKE: Or, I Know Why the Winged Whale Sings
ISBN 978-0-06-056668-5 (paperback) • ISBN 978-0-06-123879-6 (unabridged CD)

Every winter, whale researchers Nate Quinn and Clay Demodocus ply the warm Pacific waters off Maui, trying to solve an age-old mystery: Just why do humpback whales sing? Then one day a whale moons Nate, lifting its tail to display a cryptic scrawled message: *Bite Me.* And the weirdness only gets weirder when Nate gets a call telling him a whale has made contact—by phone.

LAMB: The Gospel According to Biff, Christ's Childhood Pal
ISBN 978-0-380-81381-0 (paperback) • ISBN 978-0-06-123878-9 (unabridged CD)

The birth of Jesus has been well-chronicled, as have the years after his thirtieth birthday. But no one knows about the early life of the Son of God—"the missing years"—except Biff. Ever since the day he met six-year-old Joshua of Nazareth resurrecting lizards in the village square, Levi bar Alphaeus, a.k.a. "Biff," was the Messiah's best bud. That's why the angel Raziel has resurrected Biff to write a new gospel, one that tells the real, untold story.

THE LUST LIZARD OF MELANCHOLY COVE
ISBN 978-0-06-073545-6 (paperback)

The town psychiatrist has decided to switch everybody in Pine Cove, California from their normal antidepressants to placebos, and soon business is booming at the local blues bar. Trouble is, those lonely slide-guitar notes have also attracted a colossal sea-beast with a thing for explosive oil tanker trucks. Suddenly, morose Pine Cove turns libidinous and is hit by a mysterious crime wave, and a beleaguered constable has to figure out what's wrong and what, if anything, to do about it.

ISLAND OF THE SEQUINED LOVE NUN
ISBN 978-0-06-073544-9 (paperback)

Tucker Case is a hopeless geek trapped in a cool guy's body who works as a pilot for the Mary Jean Cosmetics Corporation. But when he demolishes his boss's pink plane, Tuck must make a run for his life – straight into the demented heart of a tropical paradise of cannibals, mad scientists, ninjas, and talking fruit bats.

PRACTICAL DEMONKEEPING
ISBN 978-0-06-073542-5 (paperback)

Moore's ingenious debut novel introduces one of the most memorably mismatched pairs in the annals of literature. The good-looking one is one-hundred-year-old ex-seminarian and "roads" scholar Travis O'Hearn. The green one is Catch, a demon with a nasty habit of eating most of the people he meets. Behind the fake Tudor façade of Pine Cove, California, Catch sees a four-star buffet. Travis, on the other hand, thinks he sees a way of ridding himself of his toothy traveling companion.

www.ChrisMoore.com